MAE

DEATH'S YOUNGEST DAUGHTER

Mae - Death's Youngest Daughter by Axel Martens

This is a work of fiction. Any names or characters, businesses or places, events or incidents, are fictitious. Any resemblance to actual persons, living or dead, or actual events is purely coincidental.

Copyright © 2024, ProjectWitchcraft LLC.

ISBN: 979-8-9901842-0-6 (Hardcover)
      979-8-9901842-1-3 (Paperback)

Visit us at project-witchcraft.com

Be Careful What You Witch For!

AXEL MARTENS

MAE

DEATH'S YOUNGEST DAUGHTER

IF EVIL IS YOUR ONLY CHOICE, HOW CAN YOU BE GOOD?

"Besides, the world isn't split into good people and Death Eaters. We've all got both light and dark inside of us. What matters is the part we choose to act on."

– Sirius Black[1]

---

[1] J. K. Rowling (2003): Harry Potter and the Order of the Phoenix

FOR MY MOM

Table of Contents

Back Cover Blurb

Mae is a dark witch, and she hates it. Her world shattered when the duke's men slaughtered her family, and a vile curse transformed Mae into a monster who must kill humans to stay alive.

On the island of Heilladur, where witchcraft is outlawed after a brutal Viking invasion, Mae pursues her vendetta from the shadows, driven by a relentless thirst for vengeance.

When her ambush fails and the duke escapes, Mae meets Jarne, a teenage boy determined to liberate their homeland. Mae spares his life, and hope ignites.

The witch vows to use her cursed magic to achieve Jarne's dream. Yet every violent act pushes her closer to becoming the very evil she'd set out to destroy. If Mae can't break her curse, will the curse consume her soul?

The Stag

THE DEER WHIPPED its head to the right, nostrils flaring. Mae froze, crouching behind a blueberry thicket. Her foot had snapped a dry branch, hidden under the carpet of leaves, and the sharp sound alerted the animal. All afternoon, she'd followed the game trails—tracking prints, examining droppings, and searching for fur caught on brambles. Finally, she spotted the majestic stag pawing the ground near the river with its hooves.

Approaching from downwind as her father had taught her, Mae had crept closer, her patched cloak of grays and greens providing excellent camouflage. She'd come within twenty paces before one careless step threatened to spoil everything.

For several tense heartbeats, neither moved. Ears pricked, the deer remained a hair's breadth from flight, eyes scanning every shadow. Mae felt its anxiety emanating in waves, fueled by the accelerated pumping in the animal's chest. Her heart raced, too, beating so loud she feared the sound might give her away.

Lengthening shadows stretched like fingers across the forest floor. In the distance, wolves howled, gathering for the nightly hunt. While Mae was sure the stag could neither smell nor see her, the deer crouched low, ready to vanish into the undergrowth.

Don't be afraid, Mae thought, *I won't harm you.*

Hiding her hunting knife under her cloak, she extended her left hand, palms up, in a gesture of peace. To her utter surprise, the stag reacted. Tail swishing, it took two hesitant steps toward Mae, wading into the river.

Large brown eyes looked in her direction. The ears kept twitching, yet some tension left its body. Slowly, Mae rose and left the cover of the underbrush.

Mae's body trembled from excitement. She'd been laughed at when declaring to pet the twelve-point stag their father had spotted roaming the area. Nobody believed she could—not her father, not her mother, and especially not her annoying little brother Eilif. With an air of defiance, she'd set out after breakfast. Mae wanted to prove her skills. She wanted to show her family. But most of all, she wanted to know: *Could she?*

Days before, the adolescent girl had calmed a frantic squirrel, luring it into her lap with sunflower seeds. Excited, she'd run home to their isolated cottage in the Deepwoods in time for dinner. Yet her tale was met with laughter. Her brother sprayed his porridge across the wooden table, and her father ruffled her short, spiky hair with a disbelieving smile. Only her mother had remained quiet, a curious expression on her face.

"But, I did calm the squirrel," Mae insisted. "I felt its hunger, and I told it to trust me."

"Maybe it thought you were a tree," her brother guffawed. "Mind you, you're so often covered in dirt and leaves, it's an easy mistake to make."

"Shut up, snotface," Mae snapped, flicking a spoonful of porridge at Eilif.

"Enough!" Mae's father commanded in his no-nonsense voice. "Winter is almost upon us, and we don't have food to waste." In a milder tone, he continued. "Mae, I'm sure that's how you felt. But I think the food was a stronger argument than your words."

"May I go?" Mae retorted. She leaped to her feet, sending her chair clattering to the floor. "I don't want to waste more food by eating, and I need to brush my hair. I'm a girl, and I must not look as filthy as the rest of you." She turned and stalked toward the ladder leading to the loft.

"Mae!" her father scolded, but her mother placed her hand on his.

"Let her go," she soothed, "she's thirteen. A lot is going on."

"Yeah," her brother taunted, "she's realizing no prince wants to marry a beanstalk," earning him a smack on the back of his head.

* * *

NOW, WITH THE sun touching the horizon, she'd proven them wrong. Mae stood in the open, looking the stag in the eyes. The animal looked back at her, and a jumble of emotions flooded Mae's mind. Some felt strange. Could she read the deer's mind? Could she influence it?

Come here, she projected, *I'm your friend. I have an apple.*

The proud animal wavered, shaking its antlered head. Mae sensed a fierce inner turmoil: fear, curiosity, mistrust, and compulsion. Then, to her astonishment, the deer approached, leaving the river and climbing the bank. Triumph surged through Mae. She'd done it. She made the stag trust her. She...

The sharp twang of a bowstring shattered the spell. Pain pierced her side even before she heard the thud of an arrowhead finding its mark. The stag reared, eyes wide. Yet the shot was true, killing the animal immediately. With a loud splash, the deer toppled into the river. Red streaks spilled from its wound, racing away with the current and taking all life with them.

Mae whirled, anger blazing in her eyes. Eilif lowered his longbow, a sheepish grin on his face, while her father patted his back. Fury, like she'd never felt before, boiled in her veins. Clenching her fists, Mae shook with rage. Her disgust and burning hatred of these murderers pulsed outward, threatening to set the forest on fire. Mae screamed. The piercing cry reverberated through the trees, startling the birds into flight. With tears blurring her vision, she ran home, vowing to never look at either of them again.

* * *

"How could they?" Mae sobbed against her mother's chest.

"I've had a word with both of them. They're the size of dormice."

"But how could they?"

"Your father is a hunter. He's killed many deer." Stroking her daughter's hair, the mother stated, "You've never objected before."

"Today was different," Mae sobbed. "The stag trusted me. I betrayed it. I'm a murderer."

"No, Mae," the mother soothed, "hunting for food isn't murder."

"So, *they* did nothing wrong, and I'm the evil one?" Mae pulled back, eyes flashing.

"Eilif followed your father's lead. And he loves teasing you—that's what siblings do," the mother smiled, wiping the moisture from Mae's cheek. "He'll make it up to you. He loves you. But your father..." The mother's face hardened. "He made a mistake, and I've made that clear. Without your consent, he used your gift like bait on a hook. He didn't fully grasp what's happening." She paused. "But he does now, and he regrets it deeply. You're his forest fairy, his warrior princess."

"What didn't he know?" Mae wailed. "What *is* going on?" She felt caught in a vicious whirlpool, her emotions churning and changing with the ferocity of rapids during snowmelt.

"Two things," her mother replied. With the same curious glint in her eyes, she took Mae's hands. "For one, you're becoming a woman. Your body is changing, yet your mind requires time to accept the fact." A hint of mischief played on the older woman's lips. "Every girl experiences this change. I remember giving my mother the same exasperated stare when she talked to me."

"Father doesn't know about that?" Mae asked, furrowing her brow. She'd always believed her father knew everything. Of her family, only he went regularly to the markets. He spoke to outside people. He must have seen the whole world since he'd traveled to Thorshofn and even Makevinger.

"He knows … some," the mother smiled. "But remember, I'm a healer. And there's more," her mother continued in a lowered voice. "What you felt with the animals of the forest—the squirrel, the stag, and maybe others—something is awaking in you. Yet, not every girl will encounter this sensation. I'd say very few girls will ever share your experiences. Your connection with nature, the ability to touch the world around you…" The mother took a deep breath. "Behind closed doors, people call it *magic*."

PART ONE

Earning Trust

"You still have some things to learn about friendship, Vin.
I hope someday you realize what they are."

– Kelsier[1]

---

[1] Brandon Sanderson (2006): *Mistborn*: The Final Empire

CHAPTER ONE

The Ambush

THE FULL MOON crept slowly over the treetops, bathing the world in a pale pattern of light and shadows. Three figures crouched on the bluff, overlooking the old mine road. Wrapped in long hooded cloaks, they huddled motionless, almost indistinguishable from the numerous outcrops of volcanic rock dominating the landscape. Only their eyes gave them away, sparkling in the reflected moonlight—one pair of pale gray, one pair of amber, and one pair of piercing green.

The sun had set several hours ago, and the land fell asleep, soothed by the gentle rustling of leaves. An owl hooted in the distance. Awaiting their quarry with a semblance of patience, the three figures watched the winding road as it squeezed its way between the jagged cliffs and the dark forest marking the island's eastern tip. Yet the calm was an illusion. Tension bristled like the surging charge in a thundercloud, yearning for a lightning bolt to strike.

"I'm cold!" Renya's hiss broke the silence. All evening, her petty complaints had marked the passage of time with predictable frequency. Turning to her left, she glared at the figure beside her. "How much longer do we have to wait?"

Mae took a deep breath, clenching her fists so tight her nails bit into her palms. It wouldn't do to snap back at Renya; it never did. Still, Mae struggled to ignore her companion's constant whining, especially tonight. The three women had waited too long to execute their plan. Mae's energy was running low, weakening her tenuous control over the anger that always boiled below the surface like molten lava, threatening to erupt. Thankfully, Sigri stepped in.

"The plan hasn't changed since last you asked. We'll wait until he arrives."

"We might freeze to death before then," Renya retorted, snapping her head to the right and sending her flaming-red hair flying.

"Perhaps," Sigri replied, her voice even. "Then I should have said: until he arrives or we've died from exposure—whichever happens first."

Mae could have kissed Sigri. Her dry tone was the perfect response to Renya's mercurial temper. But then, Sigri was Renya's older sister and had dealt with her moods for almost two decades. Sitting up straight, the tall woman reminded Mae of an elegant birch tree ignoring the impertinent yapping of a wolf pup. If Mae was honest, she felt cold, too. A capricious breeze stirred the night air, which still had a bite despite midsummer not being far off. But spring came late this year, adding to Mae's general feeling of misery. She missed the warmth. Being the smallest of the three women, her slender body was almost boyish in appearance. Deep shadows ringed her green eyes, and her furrowed brow wrinkled an otherwise youthful face, leaving no doubt about her mood.

"Is he coming at all?" Renya challenged.

"Yes, Renya," Mae sighed. "We know he dined with the mayor of Thorshofn, but the duke never stays overnight."

Duke Erik Gunner Finsgúr, the lord of the southern province, was well known for his fondness for lavish evening entertainment. As the province's largest settlement, the port town of Thorshofn provided the duke with income and amusement in equal measure. Returning to his fortified estate, his carriage had to travel along the lonely road upon which the three women spied.

"Forgive me for asking," Renya taunted, not hiding her scorn. "Only, this wouldn't be the first time one of your brilliant plans failed. I don't get your obsession with the duke."

"My plans fail?" Mae retorted, resenting the injustice. "When have you ever made any? Or Sigri, for that matter? Everything falls to me! Yet do I hear a word of appreciation?" Forcing herself to take deep, calming breaths, Mae squeezed her eyes shut before declaring, "He'll come, and he'll get what he deserves."

Renya was about to argue further when Sigri raised her hand. The faint jingling of horses' tack reached their ears, accompanied by the rattle of coach wheels on the dirt-packed road. Without another word, Mae crept along the cliff's edge toward a ravine, where rugged basalt columns formed a natural staircase leading to the road. Reaching the bottom, she adjusted her hood to cover her short, silver-blond hair and crouched behind a rock where she could see without being seen.

Mae had plenty of very personal reasons for choosing tonight's target. Still, even among aristocrats, Duke Finsgúr stood out as a deplorable human being. Not satisfied with squeezing every last krona out of his impoverished peasants, the lord of the province exulted in handing out harsh punishments for little or no reason. Moreover, any young woman lived in fear of catching the duke's lustful eye. If someone needed killing, Duke Finsgúr topped the list. *And a killing there must be.* Too long had Mae gone without the rejuvenating life force her existence required.

The carriage approached. Sigri and Renya got into position, loosened their shoulders, and flexed their fingers. As soon as the duke had passed, Renya would block the road behind the carriage with a rockslide while Mae raised a hidden chain in front and spooked the horses. Hemmed in between the dense forest and the sheer cliffs, the frightened animals could only rush forward. They'd trip over the chain, and the three witches would swoop in to collect their prize.

Mae's nerves stretched to a breaking point, and Renya's persistent nagging didn't help. Wiping her sweaty hands on her trousers, she centered her energy. The magic that witches like Mae and her sisters wielded wasn't as all-powerful as ordinary people believed. Tonight's success depended on preparation, synchronization, and surprise. Any small mistake could ruin everything.

To soothe her racing heartbeat, Mae let her senses wander, absorbing all the minute details—the gravelly road, the fickle breeze, the rustling trees, the hidden chain. The moon had risen higher. Its cold light illuminated the road while deep shadows transformed the opposite forest into a solid wall of darkness, uniform and impenetrable. Still, Mae could sense life and movement among the trees. The forest was never fully asleep.

Only a handful of seconds had ticked by in agonizing sluggishness when the groan of tortured wood grabbed Mae's attention. A mighty tree not far down the road started to tilt, and it toppled with loud grinding and snapping. There it lay, twenty paces shy of the prepared ambush, creating a formidable barrier that blocked Mae's plans in the truest meaning of the word.

The rustling of leaves continued until three figures on horseback exited the thickets opposite the witch's hiding place. Taking position in the middle of the road, they faced the fallen tree and the approaching carriage of Duke

Finsgúr. Two hulking riders on either side carried torches, the one in the middle a loaded crossbow.

Highwaymen? Here? Mae thought. *By all the Norns' wicked sense of humor!*

* * *

MAE'S THOUGHTS RAN wild. Should she abandon the ambush? Should she attack the highwaymen? Could they work together? Before she reached a conclusion, Duke Finsgúr's entourage had closed the distance to the makeshift barrier. Four mounted soldiers surrounded the carriage. Moonlight glimmered on breastplates, helmets, bridles, and plenty of weapons. Whatever the highwaymen had planned, to Mae, it didn't seem well thought out. Still, the robbers stood their ground.

"Stand where you are!" the central figure shouted in a strangely high-pitched voice. "Surrender your wealth or forfeit your life."

What a quaint demand, Mae thought, *and that voice?*

Without waiting for orders, the two additional soldiers riding atop the carriage raised crossbows and fired. One bolt struck the left highwayman, and he toppled off his horse like a flour sack. Astonished, Mae watched how true the metaphor rang; the hulking figure turned out to be some kind of scarecrow propped up to hold a torch. The central robber returned fire, yet his shot went wide. No longer threatened, the mounted guards drew their swords and prepared to jump the barrier. Facing inevitable defeat, the failed marksman turned and fled in the opposite direction.

"After him!" the lead soldier yelled. The guards spurred their horses, cleared the obstacle without much effort, and reached the third robber. A swift sword stroke exposed another scarecrow. Still hiding behind the stone, Mae watched in disbelief. *What a disgrace of a robbery.*

Suddenly, the fallen tree erupted in flames. Renya must have adjusted the plan, seeing the duke separated from his guards. Roused from bewilderment, Mae cast her spells. A shout and a clap caused a ball of blinding light to explode in midair. Her second incantation faltered, and she needed three attempts to raise the hidden chain. The failed robber had already disappeared down the road. The soldiers giving chase didn't fare as well. Disoriented, three horses in full tilt collided with the chain, sending men and beasts tumbling onto the bed of sharp stones beyond. The fourth horse reared up, nearly throwing off the rider. Hanging on with all his might, the man lost his helmet, and the firelight illuminated his face.

"It can't be him." Mae gasped, rooted to the spot. "How can he be here?"

But it had to be him. The distinctive scar over one eye left no doubt. His hair had gone gray, yet Mae would never forget that face. Bile rose in her throat. And something else, raw and powerful, clawed its way up from deep inside her, blocking out all other thoughts. Finally, she would have her revenge.

Mae started toward him. However, the guard regained control before she could get near. Spurring his beast on, he followed the robber into the night.

"The coach is gone!" Sigri yelled, running toward Mae. "They turned in haste and fled like the devil chased them."

"Where are the soldiers?" Renya wheezed, following behind her sister.

"Three have fallen over there. One got away," Mae replied, her eyes fixed on the retreating rider. Her face had gone pale as curdled milk. "I'm going after him," she declared.

"Is it worth it?" Sigri asked. "When the duke reaches the next village, he'll raise the alarm. He must have recognized our use of magic. The hunters will be after us like wolfhounds."

"Actually, they might *use* wolfhounds," Renya added.

"*I don't care!*" Mae's temper flared, her eyes glowing red. "You harvest what you can and get away. Take one horse and go home. I'll follow later."

"Why? What's going on?" Renya asked.

Mae ignored her and rushed to one of the robbers' spooked horses. Close up, the beast looked more like a draft horse than a swift ride. But even a dull blade was better than bare hands in a knife fight. Touching the horse's mind, she soothed the frightened animal.

"Why go after him?" Renya insisted, her voice rising. "Who is *that* soldier?"

"No time to explain. Get to the soldiers before it's too late, or everything was for nothing."

"What about you?" Sigri sounded confused. "Don't you want any?"

In place of an answer, Mae jumped on the horse's back and urged the beast forward. The one-eyed soldier had quite a head start. Still, Mae was an excellent tracker. Without a backward glance, she left her sisters and the bounty behind.

* * *

"Idiot," Jarne scolded himself. "You are such an utter fool."

The failed robber had galloped away as fast as his stolen mount could carry him. Entering the dark forest, he dismounted to avoid low-hanging branches cracking his skull. He led the animal along a deer trail through the dense brush. Only sparse moonlight filtered through the canopy, leaving wide swaths of darkness on the treacherous path.

Jarne pondered if he should leave the horse behind. Farmer Holgrim would skin him alive for abandoning the mare in the forest as a feast for the wolves. However, that might not make a difference, since Jarne had stolen all three of the farmer's prized animals and already left two behind at the ambush site.

"Ambush" was a grand word for this night's fiasco. How could he be so foolish as to believe he would succeed? In the stories, the daring highwayman always got the bounty and sometimes even won the girl.

Stories—am I a child? He was almost a man grown and still as stupid as a bairn in swaddling clothes. But he had no choice; he needed the money. His mother was sick. *Now what?*

Jarne heard noises. At least one of the duke's guards must have followed. It was no good; he wasn't fast enough with the horse in tow. With a sad glance back, Jarne let go of the reins and took off alone. He knew the forest well, having grown up in its shadow. If he crossed the ridge, he would come to a clearing where a majestic oak stood. Jarne loved climbing trees and could take cover high up in its branches. No soldier would be able to find him there.

* * *

HERLEIF UNGRIN, CAPTAIN of the duke's personal guards, pursued the fleeing robber with haste. He had made a snap decision. The vile attack on the duke's life came from at least two different directions. Suspecting witchcraft was involved, the captain left his injured men behind and followed the lone rider. He would bring his lord the head of that foolish criminal.

Nobody can be in two places at the same time, Herleif thought, finding it prudent to follow the more promising line of investigation. Who would dare to accuse him of alternative motives?

Among the trees, the path was almost pitch black. Still, Herleif had little difficulty tracking the robber's trail. Long years of service had brought him some unusual benefits. After losing his left eye during a raid several years ago, the king's black sorceress had enhanced his remaining one as a reward. Herleif was grateful for the gift.

Of course, he hadn't dared to question the king's right to retain a sorceress, even though witchcraft was outlawed in Heilladur. Still, when she'd touched him, he'd felt like a mouse in the claws of a malicious cat, or worse, like a beetle she could crush with no more effort than taking a breath. Thus, Herleif was even more grateful to be far away from any woman of her kind.

These days, prey could seldom escape him, especially in this forest. Thorn thickets lurked everywhere, capable of tearing the clothes of even the most careful sneak thief. Herleif almost chuckled. It reminded him of the child's game, where one player hid, yet left clues along the way.

Hawking up phlegm, he spat on the floor. He'd never played that game. Herleif hadn't been popular as a child. That's why he'd become a soldier. And being a captain, he didn't need popularity; he had obedience.

Climbing a steep slope, Herleif came upon the robber's abandoned horse. The fugitive must have realized that someone was chasing him. The captain quickened his stride. He had to catch the would-be robber before the night was out. The duke would expect swift results, and Herleif did not dare to disappoint the duke—long years of service or not.

* * *

REACHING THE SPOT where the robber and the guard had disturbed the forest's slumber, Mae jumped off the animal's back and entered on foot. Nimble as a cat, she wove through the foliage, her feet barely touching the ground. Several minutes later, Mae reached a clearing where a giant oak stood and crouched behind a fallen log. She had spotted the guard gathering dry wood as if to build a bonfire. Where was the robber? The hooded figure hid high up among the branches. *So, the hound has treed his prey but can't follow him up. Does he want to smoke him out or burn the tree down?* Regardless, the soldier's actions gave Mae an excellent opportunity to finish them both.

Mae was a black witch. She needed to kill humans in order to stay alive. Yearning to retain her humanity amidst the darkness of her powers, the witch targeted only people who "deserved" to die, like Duke Finsgúr. This was her obsession, as Renya had called it. Still, there were always casualties. Mae had few reservations about harming the duke's men-at-arms in tonight's ambush. She didn't know whether those men were evil. But then, "evil" was such a vague word. The soldiers undoubtedly worked for a despicable person, and Mae needed their life force.

However, the moment she recognized the one-eyed guard, that man had eclipsed all other thoughts. *What irony caused our paths to cross years after I stopped looking for him?* Mae thought with sinister satisfaction. *It's been ten long years since he killed my family and destroyed my life.* At the time, she'd only been able to take his eye. Tonight, she would take his life—and for once, she would enjoy it.

And the robber? Should I kill him as well? Renya wouldn't hesitate. His ill-timed disruption had destroyed tonight's plan. Mae's fiery haired sister would make him pay for all the wasted effort.

Why do I even care? Mae thought. *Does the wolf care whether the stag is evil?* But she did. A small voice in her head, planted there by her dying mother's wish, urged her to try to be *good*, regardless of what she had become.

Observing the movement of the two men, Mae prepared her attack. This time, she wouldn't allow anything to get in her way. As soon as the soldier returned with another armload of wood, Mae muttered her spell.

A loud crack reverberated through the night air. The enormous branch on which the robber hid broke, knocking the unsuspecting guard captain to the ground. Judging by the high-pitched yell and dull thud, the robber had fallen, too. Yet the heavy limb hadn't been completely severed. Mae's low energy weakened her magic.

With a snarl of frustration, she exploded the last stubborn strands tethering the branch to the trunk. Before the wood hit the ground, Mae was sprinting. Her target didn't deserve a single extra breath.

Scratched and bruised, the one-eyed guard scrambled back to his feet. Stepping free from the tangle of twigs and leaves, he planted his feet and drew his sword. He seemed to have little difficulty spotting the approaching witch. Not breaking her stride, Mae pulled a throwing knife from her belt and propelled it toward him. He ducked. Still, the distraction gave Mae enough time to close the distance. She slid on the dewy grass and kicked his legs out from under him. Toppling over, the soldier buried his sword almost to the hilt in the soft ground.

Mae pushed herself to all fours. She scrambled onto him, clawing her way to his face. He was ready. His elbow struck her temple, snapping the witch's head sideways. Mae's vision blurred. Then, he was on her. Large hands grabbed her throat and squeezed. Dazed, Mae tried to pry his hands away. She needed to burn him or drain his life. But he wore thick leather gloves, blocking her from skin-to-skin contact.

"What's this!" the soldier snarled. "Don't I know you? Ah, yes... I remember," Herleif lifted one hand to rub his eyepatch. "Missing Mommy and Daddy?" He backhanded Mae. "I'll send you their way. Maybe you'll meet your useless brother, too," he spat. Squeezing her throat harder, he loomed over her, his face inches from Mae's.

Mae had been on the brink of passing out when his cruel taunts cleared the haze, replacing it with undiluted rage. Letting go of his hands, she grabbed his ears. Her nails bit deep, drawing blood.

"Bitch!" he cursed, seizing one of her hands before his graying hair erupted in flames. Shrieking, her tormentor tried to get away. Mae held on, rejoicing in his suffering. The awful smell of burning hair filled her nostrils. The witch forced a sneer onto her face. Then, she rammed a mental spike into the vessel holding the soldier's life force. In the blink of an eye, Mae yanked his rotten soul out of his charred body.

The soldier's energy gushed into the furious witch, accompanied by a soft glow. Warmth flooded her being, and her body shuddered in delight. Strength returned, hardship and pain were forgotten, and joyful satisfaction filled her mind. All her angst and anger vanished. This moment of pure bliss was the true perversion of her existence—the most pleasurable reward for the most heinous act.

As always, it took Mae a few heartbeats to return to her surroundings. She had done it; she had avenged her parents. Rolling the soldier's lifeless body into the dirt, Mae got to her feet. The night felt warmer, the moonlight brighter, and the wind played a soft melody with the rustling leaves. Mae breathed deep, basking in her satisfaction.

* * *

A nearby whimper pulled Mae from her reverie. She'd almost forgotten about the robber. Mae spotted him near the trunk, struggling to free his trapped arm from under the fallen branch.

He's scared. He saw what I did to the soldier. Mae couldn't muster any empathy. The memories of her dying parents fouled her mood. Striding toward him, the witch decided to end him quickly. Then she saw his face. For the second time that night, Mae stood rooted to the spot in shock.

He's a boy, still a child! Pale-blue eyes stared out of a dirt-smeared face. He couldn't be much older than twelve, fourteen at most. The full moon overhead revealed the unmistakable signs of panic—his clenched jaw, his quivering lips. But there was more: a determination not to show weakness, a desire to meet whatever may come like a true Northman. Mae had learned the hard way how fear and greed caused the actions of men far more often than bravery and honor. *Perhaps this boy still believes in these fabled virtues.*

"What are you doing here, boy?" she blurted, her agitation subdued by surprise.

"Get away from me, witch!"

So, he also exhibits the stupidity of most men.

"Don't you think it wiser to guard your tongue now that you have deduced my nature?" Mae opted for a softer, more frightening tone. "I won't ask again. What are you doing here?"

"Lying on the forest floor, trapped by a giant branch."

Feisty—Mae had to give him that. Still, several seconds of the witch's icy stare broke the façade, and a floodgate of information opened.

"I need money. My mother is sick, and nobody will help." He swallowed and continued in a deflated voice. "My brothers are dead, and my father left. The neighbors close their doors. The medicine is expensive, and the duke has money. More than he can ever spend." Raising his voice, he challenged her. "I needed to do something. She has only me. I am the man in the house."

"You thought *you* could rob the duke alone? How old are you, boy?"

"I'm not a boy," he spat. "I'm almost fourteen, and I had a plan."

"Your scarecrows? Clever idea, but utterly pointless. The guards fear the duke more than any foe."

"What is it to you, witch? What do you care for the plans of humans?"

"I am human," Mae replied, trying that same soft and silky voice. But his comment stung worse than this child could imagine. Mae yearned for nothing more than to be an ordinary human, a woman without a curse. By then, she might have had children of her own, a good husband, a small house by the sea, and friendly neighbors. Ice crept back into her voice. "But if you insist," she hissed, "I can give you another—a final demonstration of my witchiness."

In a heartbeat, the panic was back, painted all over his face. All the bold bravery disappeared. A small and frightened child lay there, helpless, facing his worst nightmare in the flesh. Mae might have done many evil things in her life, in her cursed existence. But she could not—*would not*—harm this boy.

"Listen carefully!" Mae loomed over him. "I'll put a hex on you. Then I'll let you go. Your horse is where you left it. Get away from here as fast as you can." Returning to the menacing whisper, Mae added, "If you tell anyone what happened tonight or what you think happened tonight—anything at all—you will *die*."

Mae stepped back, widened her stance, and traced intricate patterns in the air. With a clap, another bright light appeared. The heavy branch flew away like a leaf in a breeze.

The boy squeezed his eyes shut; his whole body shook. Mae knew that his skin would feel like he was bathed in ice, and his world would spin for a time, inducing vertigo. When his eyes eventually adjusted to the darkness again, the witch would be long gone.

CHAPTER TWO

About Witches

Mae had tricked the boy's senses with a useful little spell, confusing his mind for a few minutes. She hadn't hexed him. Contrary to his scarecrows, the witch's threat was believable. His fear of her wrath alone should compel him to act as intended. Inching her way back toward the horses, she recalled his dirty face. His eyes had exuded that curious mixture of determined bravery and childish fear. He'd risked it all. To save his mother, he attacked the duke and confronted a witch—all for nothing.

It is the world's fault, not mine.

Still, Mae felt like she should have done more. He was a desperate child, and she was a black witch. What good were her powers? She could break trees, shatter bones, and kill soldiers. But was a single person better off because of her cursed existence? Triggered by renewed self-doubt, the painful memories of another lost boy stabbed their way into her mind.

Ten years ago, Mae hadn't been able to protect her little brother Eilif either. She had watched, powerless and frozen, as soldiers abducted him. Despite years of feverish searching, she never saw Eilif again. Yet her mind recalled with brutal clarity the fear in his eyes. Mae stumbled, grabbing a tree for support. She couldn't breathe; iron bands constricted her chest. Fighting to stay upright, she braced herself against the crushing mountain of her failures.

It was not my fault. I tried. With all my heart, I tried.

Unrelenting, the guilt forced Mae to her knees. The regrets of the countless lives she had ruined—all her vile deeds hidden away under her grand plans—they took cruel revenge. Mae's heart pounded. She gasped for air. Her vision blurred, and nausea rose in her stomach. Never before had the witch suffered such a severe spasm of dismay. She had to get up, get away from here.

Heartbeat by heartbeat, Mae reasserted control over her trembling body, shoving her trauma back into the locked box at the hindmost corner of her mind. Nothing was gained if the duke's men caught and executed her; neither boy was better off. Mae had to get to safety. And the failed robber needed to take care of himself. At least she had let him live.

Wiping the dirt off her shaking knees, the witch dragged herself toward the soldier's horse. The sky already grew lighter—dawn couldn't be far off. Renya and Sigri should have an ample head start. Mae, on the other hand, didn't dare to risk a daylight escape across the open country. Too great was the danger of running into a mob of townsfolk wielding torches and pitchforks driven by the insane desire to see her burn. Instead, the black witch would lay low for a few days, waiting for the storm to blow over.

Witches hadn't always been feared, hated, and hunted on Heilladur. There was a time when the inhabitants of the remote island admired women with knowledge and skill, employed their services when needed, and worked hand in hand to avert disaster. Everything changed with the conquest over thirty years ago. Viking raiders from the south overran the land, replacing the belief in nature and magic with a pantheon of angry gods. With their ships came hordes of axe-wielding brutes who thought women were powerless—only suited for domestic duties. The idea of women *with* power frightened them to the core. Hence, they spun tales of devil worship, child sacrifices, and evil curses, instilling a hatred of witchcraft in the general population.

Mae thought that therein lay a certain irony. She would have loved nothing better than to meet one of these witch-haters alone to prove how evil witches could be. In doing so, the man could experience firsthand that some of his prejudices were warranted—right before he died. But that was Mae; she was a black witch.

Very few witches still lived in these lands after decades of brutal purging. Fearing detection and denunciation, the women explored their powers in secret. The old, forbidden tales spoke of the first settlers coming in contact with the *huldufólk*—the hidden folk or elves, as some call them. The elves taught humans to sense nature's energy and harness its power.

Women proved more adept, forming several distinct groups with a broad spectrum of strengths and hereditary abilities. Green witches like Sigri excelled at interacting with living creatures, brewing potions, and healing the sick. Sigri could also see glimpses of the future. Gray witches like Renya possessed more external powers like conjuring fire, moving inanimate objects, and hexing people.

Black witches were different. They weren't born; they were *made*. When the dark curse touched a woman, a demonic essence entered the victim like a parasite, overshadowing her soul and driving the bearer to despicable deeds. Whispers spoke of terrible powers, insatiable hunger, and never-ending life—earning these witches the title of *Death's Daughters*.

Mae was once an ordinary young woman of seventeen when the black curse took her. Time itself froze around her, her youthful bloom forever trapped in amber. But with immortality came a terrible price: a ravenous hunger dominated her existence ever since. Each breath became a desperate struggle against the encroaching darkness. The choice of good or evil was no longer hers, as Mae must kill humans—kill and kill again—or she must die.

Right then, Mae wasn't willing to ponder whether the world was justified in eradicating her. She preferred to be alive and, hence, needed a place to hide. Searching through the saddlebags on the soldier's horse, she found a bedroll, food, a waterskin, and a change of clothes.

But where to hide? Renya's assertion about the witch hunters using wolf-hounds might well come true, in which case, Mae couldn't stay out in the open. Any imbecile would search this forest first, given its proximity to the scene of the crime. Luckily, Mae had wandered through these woods often and knew a waterfall behind which a small crevice led to a sizable cave. If she hurried, she could reach it in one hour and conceal the entrance with a spell. The horse, sadly, wouldn't fit. Mae jolted its rump with a sharp sting, and off it went.

Hoisting her pack, Mae started toward the hiding place, her mind still buzzing with all the night's calamities. Nothing had gone as planned. She hadn't killed the duke. Instead, she settled an old score with the one-eyed soldier. And the boy? She almost scared him to death, but then, she let him go. Her sisters wouldn't be happy. No use worrying now. After tonight's excitement, Mae looked forward to a few days of bitterly needed rest.

* * *

Renya stood for a while, staring in the direction Mae had left. She wondered, not for the first time, why she was still putting up with that witch's antics. Tonight's ambush had been Mae's idea, including all the weeks of preparations. Now, the black witch had left the bounty behind, meager as it was, to put herself and everyone in danger.

Sigri, always more pragmatic, had already rushed over to the first fallen soldier and relieved him of his soul. Grimacing, Renya went to the man nearest her and knelt. This wasn't how she liked doing it; she preferred to play with her food.

Renya was a woman who made men's heads turn when she walked by. Two inches shorter and six years younger than her sister, she had a narrow waist, long legs, and gentle curves. Her fiery red hair framed an angelic face with the perfect measure of mischief promised by her full lips and a handful of freckles on her cream-colored skin. And Renya knew how to take full advantage of her allure to men. She was always flirtatious and didn't see the need for unpleasantness in the whole business. First, enjoy a man's attention, then enjoy the man's soul.

Looking down at her victim-to-be, Renya realized that no amount of flirtation would make any difference. He was in pain, his body broken. So, she bent down and lifted his head in her hands.

The soldier's gaze found her gleaming amber eyes. For a few heartbeats, the witch wondered who he was. Why had he joined the duke's service? Was he a cruel man, or did he need the money to feed his family? It was so easy to hate all soldiers from a distance. Holding his head in her hands, he became a person who may or may not deserve to die on a lonely road in the middle of the night.

He coughed blood, reminding Renya that it was too late to change her mind. Steeling herself, she forced a smile onto her face, blew him a kiss, and took his life. The question of who would get the third soldier resolved itself. The poor lad had expired before either sister could get to him.

"That settles it," Renya exclaimed, letting her easy anger overwrite her unwanted confusion. "Mae's plans aren't worth crows' droppings. I won't be part of them anymore." She brushed off her dirt-coated knees with more force than needed. "Weeks of planning, stalking in the dark of night. Weeks of freezing my butt off and almost more magic expended than we got in return. And on top of it, a mindless mob will be hunting us soon."

"You are right, sister. A hunting party will be after us soon. We should go."

"Let them come," Renya challenged. "I could still use some more."

"That sounds like way too much effort for your taste," Sigri smirked.

"Not this time! One soul each, can you believe it?" Renya raised her arms to the heavens, wallowing in her unfulfilled expectations.

"Well, I can't say I am happy myself. There were too many surprises."

"But how could that happen? Aren't you supposed to see the future?"

"You know full well the limitation of my skills, as I know the bluster in your anger."

Silence followed these stinging but accurate remarks.

"Still, the prudent thing is to move on," Sigri amended. She looked at the horse, and the animal trotted over. "We can talk about tonight when Mae comes back."

"*If* she comes back, you mean," Renya corrected.

"Oh, she will," Sigri said. "Why don't you mount first? The wind on your face might cool your temper." Renya scowled as she jabbed her foot into the stirrup and swung onto the horse.

"You take her side, I presume? The whole 'do not harm good people' nonsense?"

Sigri sighed, hoisting herself onto the horse behind her sister. A few years ago, when their paths first crossed, the sisters hadn't known what to make of Mae. She was a black witch—there was no doubt. But she didn't like killing. For the sisters, it felt like meeting a vegetarian wolf or a fish afraid of water. Sigri and Renya didn't need to take the lives of humans to replenish their magic. Like most witches, the sisters could channel the energy from nature itself. Yet, the effects were pitiful compared to the ecstasy of absorbing someone else's soul. Mae, on the other hand, had to kill to keep existing.

"It's her choice," Sigri replied with a shrug. "Who am I to judge someone else for their morals?"

"That is my point," Renya scoffed. "Black witches don't have morals—or, at least, they shouldn't."

"Why not?" Sigri asked. "You have morals, too."

"I do not. How often have you seen me be evil?"

"I've seen you *pretend* to be evil. You envy Mae. For you, being a black witch is a great prestige. But I've seen you help that widow..."

"I don't like hurting women."

"...and you let that woodsman go..."

"He wasn't... He didn't... He had a family—a wife and children at home."

"...and you seemed excited to get to Duke Finsgúr."

"Because of the promise of a large bounty, which we didn't get, if you haven't realized," Renya stated, glad to regain the argument's high ground.

"All I am saying is things aren't always black or white—more... gray."

"Oh, haha, very funny."

Renya still fumed, but the realization sank in that Sigri was right, as she so often was. Yes, Renya killed men for pleasure, but did she kill indiscriminately? Or did she let the good guys go and only make the bad guys pay?

"Bad guys are more fun," Renya declared, concluding her inner discussion. Then, both sisters fell quiet. It was a long ride home, and both women were exhausted. As the horse trotted along, Renya wondered about morals. *How bad might things have gotten?* she asked herself. *How evil might Sigri and I have become if we hadn't met Mae?*

* * *

MAE FOUND THE waterfall with the cave and cast her protective spells. The place was beautiful. Gnarled trees clung to the rocks surrounding a circular pool into which the bubbling stream tumbled. The area reminded Mae of her youth, deep in another forest where she had lived a sheltered life far from civilization. She imagined staying there forever. Hidden behind a curtain of water, the cave's entrance was easy to conceal, and the surrounding woods provided ample game and firewood. But it was lonely. While Mae liked animals, she also craved the company of humans, preferably those who didn't yearn to kill her. That's why she had stayed with the Guðmundsdóttir sisters after stumbling upon their home four years ago.

By necessity, witches' dwellings needed to be off the beaten path. Renya and Sigri had taken over the ruin of a long-forgotten castle high up in the mountains. At first sight, the dwelling didn't look inviting, perched upon a cliff with ragged spires rising upward. Still, the sisters had covered a few walls with thatch and created a cozy two-room home.

Mae had been wandering through the mountains when a spring snowstorm surprised her. Spotting the desolate fortress, she hiked up the mountain path seeking shelter, and her appearance startled Renya. The gray witch attacked. In the ensuing skirmish, the exchange of magic spells revealed both sides as witches. Mae still remembered Sigri's timely intervention. As logical as always, the green witch had pointed out that a prolonged battle might result in serious injuries or drive off one party. Both outcomes sounded quite unpleasant in the current weather. Smarting from minor bruises, the women agreed to a truce, wary of each other.

Mae stayed. Over the following months, the women learned to trust and like each other. *I was little more than a feral beast back then,* Mae remembered, *full of uncontrollable anger and clueless about how to harness my powers.* Mae was excited to see that witches could live a happy and relatively normal life. Sigri taught Mae about the nuances of magic and mind control, while Renya enjoyed experimenting with Mae on how to blow things up. In turn, the black witch impressed her hosts with displays of raw power. *They gave me a new purpose,* Mae acknowledged with grim satisfaction. *Finally, I had comrades to pursue my vendetta.*

Nestled in her cave, Mae realized how much she would hate losing Sigri and Renya's companionship, having wandered these lands alone for too long. Thus, Mae started the journey home as twilight fell on the third day since the ambush. It would take her at least three days, four if she stayed off the King's Road.

Stepping out of the forest's canopy, Mae reached the spot where their plan had failed. She didn't see any lingering signs of the ambush. Neither tree nor chain blocked the road. No dead horses or fallen soldiers decorated the landscape. Instead, a new gruesome structure marked the sight. Three women hung from crude wooden gallows. With their feet bare and their hands bound behind their backs, their swollen tongues stuck out from deep-purple faces. Mae retched at the horrific scene. But there was relief, too.

Thank the devils, Renya and Sigri got away. After Duke Finsgúr's unsuccessful witch hunt, the deplorable man must have ordered his soldiers to grab three random women to set an example. Mae trembled with rage. More than ever, she needed to kill him. This duke was a curse upon the land, more terrible than any black witch could be. It took all her willpower to restrain herself from storming his estate and laying her vengeance upon this monster.

Now is not the time. Despite her fury, Mae didn't stand a chance by herself. She needed Sigri and Renya's help, which she might not get after the latest disaster.

Still, Mae's blood boiled. She wouldn't leave these innocent women as a feast for the crows. Harnessing her outrage, Mae channeled her newly acquired life force. The energy crackled in her fingertips, causing her hair to stand on end. With a grunt and a clap, the hateful contraption erupted in flames. The searing heat bathed Mae from fifteen paces away. In moments, the bodies had been consumed, sending the poor women's souls with the smoke toward the heavens. Nothing remained other than a heap of ashes with a few smoldering timbers. Mae felt good and righteous until her anger waned, and an unwanted thought entered her mind.

The duke will hear about it and renew the hunt. Mae was still far from safety. She needed to move off the road and into the highlands. Had anybody seen the flames? Darkness had fallen, and the nearest settlement lay over an hour away. Regardless, Mae rushed onward, trying to gain as much distance as possible, her mind occupied by thoughts of the duke's cruelty. She didn't stop for food or rest until the sun had risen.

Climbing a gentle hill, Mae looked around. She couldn't spot any signs of pursuit. Relieved, the exhausted witch lay down on the moss covering the gray rocks. Mae intended to sleep for a few hours before searching for food and water. Hiding under her cloak, she vanished from sight, becoming one more gray boulder adorning the vast, barren landscape.

The King's Road

THE HORSE CAME out of nowhere. One moment, Mae was wandering alone through a picturesque wildflower meadow, her thoughts occupied with the failed ambush and its aftermath. Next, a twelve-hundred-pound animal came barreling toward her with froth around his muzzle and mad panic in his eyes.

Mae screamed. Throwing herself sideways, she stretched her arms toward the approaching beast as if she could arrest its momentum with her bare hands. Her hip smacked into a hidden rock, causing a jolt of pain to shoot through her body. *Fire!* The sudden thought came to her aid. Mae projected the image with brute force into the animal's mind. The beast reared up, its forehooves clawing the air inches from Mae's face. She willed the horse to retreat. Neighing and snorting, the animal shook its head while its hooves tore the ground.

"Easy there," Mae soothed with a shaking voice. She scrambled back to her feet, strengthening her control over the animal's mind. The beast blew and grunted yet didn't shy away. Mae sensed a burning pain spreading from its nostrils. Extending her arm with her palm raised, she approached, spotting two puncture marks on the horse's nose. "Something bit you there, huh? Surprised a snake in the high grass? Let me help you with that. Hold very still!"

Mae grabbed the beast's head with both hands. Willing the animal to stay calm, she pressed her lips around the wound and sucked, spitting the venom out. Thrice more, she repeated the process before she felt the pain receding. "There," she said, wiping her mouth, "isn't that better? Where did you come from anyhow?" As if in answer to her question, Mae heard running footsteps.

Since leaving the failed robber under the tree, Mae had wandered through the wilderness to avoid capture and hadn't met a soul. That morning, however, she needed to approach the King's Road in order to cross the Villtur, a fast-running, rocky river swollen by snowmelt at this time of the year. With midsummer two weeks away, the nights were too short, making it impractical to only travel under the cover of darkness. Instead, Mae relied on the distance already accomplished and her inconspicuous attire—dark men's clothes under a gray hood—to pass as an innocent traveler enjoying a stroll through the hinterland. As two men approached in a hurry, Mae started to doubt her decision.

The figure in front looked younger, a wiry youth with flax-blond hair whipping in the wind. An older man lagged behind, holding his side as if he was suffering from a stitch. Mae wound one hand tight into the horse's mane while the other slid toward her belt knife. Fight or flight? She hadn't decided by the time the lead runner was almost upon her.

"You caught Gullfax, wonderful!" he shouted, sinking to his knees ten paces away. "I feared," he wheezed, "we had to chase the beast ... all the way back to Erikssund." Sweat glistened on his skin, and his lungs heaved from the exertion.

The older man had stopped two stone throws away and rested with his hands on his knees. Mae looked in bewilderment from the man in the distance to the youth nearby and finally back to the horse. The animal's coat was a dirty brown, and its mane looked more gray than golden, but who was she to judge its name?

"I'm Tjorben," the younger man said after catching his breath. Hoisting himself back to his feet, he continued, "And over there, that's my father, Morton Svenssen."

"Helga," Mae said, using her mother's name. "Helga Magnúsdóttir."

"Well met, Helga," Tjorben replied, following the greeting with a formal bow. "We truly are in your debt."

His speech and manners surprised Mae. Tjorben seemed not much older than the boy who'd masqueraded as a highwayman. Yet he exuded refinement and poise, marking him as a scion of a wealthy family. Was Tjorben in league with the duke? Perhaps a witch hunter? Mae's fingers squeezed the hilt of her knife. In the meantime, the father had approached.

"Father," the youth shouted, "this is Helga. She has calmed our Gullfax and saved our journey." Turning back to Mae, he'd asked. "How did you do it? It was like magic."

"It was nothing of that sort," Mae snapped but then regretted her outburst. "I am good with horses, that's all," she grumbled. "I grew up among animals."

"I wasn't implying," he stammered, turning red. "I was only..."

"Forgive his loose tongue," the father interjected. "He has been beside himself since winning the leikmót tournament. Tjorben will represent our fylki in Hagndal."

"I'll compete before the king," the youth explained with pride. "And if I fight with honor, I might be taken on as a king's guard."

"Congratulations," Mae offered, eager to gloss over her earlier unwise reaction. "And good luck." She half turned to leave, but the father stood between Mae and her pack.

"Thank you," Tjorben replied with a smile. "I was sure my dream was over when our horse ran off. What might have gotten into it?"

"A snake bite," Mae answered absentmindedly. Should she make a run for it or not? Deciding against flight, she added, "Happens sometimes when a horse surprises a snake in the high grass. I was able to suck the venom out."

"Amazing!" The young man beamed. He was quite handsome. A head taller than Mae, he had broad shoulders, wavy hair, and sky-blue eyes.

"Indeed," the father agreed. "Can we offer you a ride as a small token of our appreciation? Where are you heading?"

"I'm on my way home. My father built a cabin in the Deepwood forest, south of Hestavik." Mae always found that nothing made lies more convincing than a dash of truth.

"We can take you for a good part of the way. The Western Road branches off the King's Road near Hestavik. It'll save you at least two days of walking."

"Oh please, it is the least we can do," Tjorben insisted. "You can ride with me in the back. The cart is full of cloth and soft blankets."

Mae gave him a look that could freeze a bonfire. He blanched. Then, color flooded his cheeks, and he stammered an explanation. "I didn't mean... I wasn't implying... My mother gathered those wares to sell in Hagndal. She's waiting by the cart."

"Sometimes, my son," the father scolded, "it behooves you to think more and talk less." Yet Mae saw a twinkle in the older man's eyes. "Take the horse and lead on." With that, the father hoisted Mae's pack, leaving her no choice but to follow along.

MAE HAD TRAVELED with Tjorben and his parents for a few hours when she spotted a cloud of dust rising over the road about a mile behind them. The four-wheeled cart moved no faster than she could walk, despite Gullfax's best efforts. Still, the bundles of clothes provided comfortable cushions. Mae had even nodded off for a while after the first round of conversation had run its course. Tjorben sat across from her and remained silent. Perhaps he still felt embarrassed by his earlier blunders. When he saw Mae's expression change, he turned, curious to see what she had seen.

"Father," he called, "riders are coming up. Looks like a patrol of soldiers in great haste, judging by the dust cloud and the rate of their approach."

"Keep your wits and a civil tongue. Best let me do the talking. If they are in a rush, their mood might be prickly."

"But we have nothing to hide," Tjorben stated with indignation. "I'm on my way to Hagndal to join the king's guard. If I'm accepted, the local soldiers must show me respect."

"Please do tell them," his father mocked, "but let me get away first such that I don't have to hear your whimpers when they beat you. The duke's soldiers are proud men," he continued in a serious tone. "They don't take kindly to being reprimanded by a village boy."

Ten minutes later, seven soldiers caught up with the cart. The lead rider ordered them to halt, and the mounted men surrounded the wagon.

"State your names and your destination," the commander barked.

"May I ask the reason for questioning us?" the father replied.

"I'm asking the questions," the soldier shouted, "and you answer, or we tear your wagon apart." Placing his hand on his sword hilt, the sergeant moved his horse closer. "Who are you?" he snarled in a low growl. "Who is with you? And where are you heading?"

"I am Morton Svenssen, a merchant from Erikssund. This is my family. My wife Fridda." He pointed with an open hand to the woman beside him. "In the back are Tjorben and Helga. We're heading to Hagndal to offer our wares while my son competes in the midsummer tournament."

"A merchant's son," the soldier jeered. "Will you fight with turnips or bales of clothes?"

Tjorben was about to rise to the provocation when Mae placed her hand on his knee, restraining him with a slight shake of her head. She didn't know what made her do it. This wasn't her affair. Still, Mae knew exactly what would happen if the young man challenged the duke's sergeant.

"Better listen to your sister," the rider laughed. "She has more brains. And judging by her fierce gaze, she also has bigger balls than you, boy." Mae hadn't realized she was glaring at the soldier, so she averted her eyes. "Svenssen, you say." The soldier returned his focus to the father. "Not Svensson? Are you claiming Viking blood?"

"I'm not claiming anything. I was born on Heillaður, but my father came from the south."

"And he took a native wench," the sergeant nodded, a knowing smirk on his lips. "Well, Morton Svenssen, we're hunting witches. Have you seen any travelers along the road? Women in particular?" he whispered.

Silence.

Mae tensed, wild ideas running through her mind. She could rile up the soldier's horses, set their clothes on fire, or use her throwing knives. She could deal with one or two. Yet nothing in her arsenal seemed powerful enough against seven. And what would her hosts do?

"I heard the witches had already been caught and executed," Fridda spoke for the first time, letting fear color her voice.

"Some have, but there were more. Someone used dark magic to destroy the warning we left. The duke is furious. He sent us to rouse the garrison in Kralsvik with orders to sweep south, while the soldiers from Makevinger comb the land toward the north. We'll find these fiends. And this time, there won't be a quick hanging—I promise you that."

"We haven't seen anyone on the road for days," Morton declared. "Not since we passed Thorshofn."

Tjorben looked from his father to the soldier and finally to Mae. Her narrowed green eyes bore into his, and he lowered his gaze.

"Then pray it remains that way until you reach Hagndal," the sergeant goaded. "Most of these so-called witches are old crones who strangle cats to cure warts. But if you encounter a black witch, she'll freeze your blood and steal your soul. I've fought many, and I killed a few," he boasted. "But you... She'll leech you dry and make a necklace from your fingerbones." He leaned closer and continued in a conspiratorial tone. "They aren't humans, them Death's Daughters. They're pure evil. You'd feel your blood run cold when they came near. Safe travels."

He offered a final leer before commanding his men to press on.

* * *

MORTON WAITED SEVERAL more minutes for the dust to settle. With a whistle and a snap of the reins, he steered the wagon back onto the road, letting

Gullfax pull at a gentle pace. The sun shone from a clear blue sky with only a scattering of puffy white clouds. Still, a somber mood had replaced the earlier relaxed atmosphere. Nobody spoke. Mae sat stiff as a board, her hands balled into fists and her jaw clenched. She should get off the wagon while she had the chance and cut through the countryside.

What about this family?

Mae needed to take care of them first. She couldn't leave any witnesses behind. Tjorben's bare ankle lay inches from her left hand. He wouldn't feel a thing. Could she kill the father before the influx of life energy stunned her? And Fridda, would she fight? Mae's stomach churned at the thought of murdering these innocent people.

"Are you all right, Helga?" Tjorben asked, looking concerned. He sat upright. Pulling his legs back, he leaned his upper body toward her. She must do it. *Now!*

Mae couldn't. She wouldn't give the sneering sergeant the satisfaction of being right about her kind. These people had done her no harm. After her recent energy harvest, the black witch was strong enough to suppress her dark urges. She mustn't stoop that low as long as she could help it.

"I should go," Mae muttered, pushing herself to her feet, ready to jump off.

"Why?" Tjorben asked.

Before Mae could answer, Fridda spoke.

"I don't think that's a good idea. You've heard the soldier. Any woman traveling in these parts is a suspect. You're much safer sticking with us."

"But you're not. Better if I was gone," she said. Tjorben placed his hand on her wrist to hold her back. "Let go!" she hissed, red anger burning in her eyes. He recoiled like he touched glowing lava.

"You're too easy to spot in this open landscape," the father explained in a calm tone after stopping the horse. "Stay with us at least until we reach the woodlands. We should be there by midday tomorrow."

"Why? You lied for me back there," Mae challenged. "What is it to you how I fare?"

"Let's say I don't like how... women are treated in these lands. My mother was a 'native,' as the soldier pointed out. She raised me to respect all people." He looked Mae in the eyes, and she believed his gaze conveyed a deeper meaning than his words. Mae stood undecided. What choice did she have? She wouldn't harm these kind people, and she was in danger walking alone. Reluctantly, Mae accepted the wisdom and sat back down.

"I'm sorry," Tjorben said in a small voice.

"I'm sorry, too," Mae snapped. Then she took a deep breath and added, "You folks are very kind to me. Thank you." Tjorben gave her a hesitant smile. Mae tried to remember how to smile without mocking, leering, or scaring him to death. In the end, she lowered her gaze, awkwardly patted his hand, and muttered, "Sorry for snapping at you."

"Don't mention it," he laughed, returning to his earlier jovial mood.

"He's right," the father chuckled, urging Gullfax forward. "We all would have to walk if you hadn't used your 'skills' to calm our horse."

* * *

Tired, dirty, and hungry but unharmed, Mae arrived at the Witches' Castle, as she called it, two days later. The last leg up the steep mountain was taxing. Not for the first time, she wished the old stories of witches flying on brooms were true. Pleasant wood smoke rose from the chimney, and one of the robbers' horses stood tethered in the courtyard.

"You took your sweet time," Renya greeted in her usual disapproving tone.

"Missed you too," Mae replied. "And besides, I needed to hunt down the soldier. And then I had to tread carefully to avoid becoming a gruesome roadside decoration."

"What do you mean?" Sigri asked, carrying a tray of tea and biscuits.

"Three women were hanged at the spot of our ambush," Mae explained. "The duke's doing, I'm sure, to frighten people away from witchcraft. The roads are crawling with soldiers on patrol. Once the frenzy has calmed down, we must find a different way to get to him."

"No! We absolutely must not." Renya's temper, ever so close to boiling, flared up. "We're not doing another crazy attack with high risks and almost no rewards. Besides," she challenged, "if you think about it, it's our fault these three women died. We could have snatched them ourselves and wouldn't be worse off."

"That wasn't our fault." Mae shook her head in frustration. "We aren't the evil ones; Duke Finsgúr is. Well, he's the eviler."

"Mae," Sigri started in her consoling voice, "Renya is right. We haven't gained much except for the ire of a powerful nobleman and renewed anti-witch sentiment. I've told you many times before—we should stick to the lone traveler here and there."

"But we're not doing this for our amusement!" Mae balled her hands into fists as anger flushed her cheeks. "We're doing evil; it must also do good."

"That's your reasoning, not mine," Renya shot back. "Get over your good-and-evil obsession. We are what we are, and we do what we do, and that's all there is to it."

"I'm not hiding behind my curse to justify hurting innocent people," Mae snarled, glaring at Renya. "I won't lose my soul to this curse. Even if you don't care, I can fight my fate and use my powers to change the world for the better."

"But Mae..." Sigri laid a calming hand on her friend's shoulder. "Does your vengeance make the world better? As long as you kill, even evil men like the duke, you'll hurt innocent people. Parents, children, lovers, or sometimes bystanders—they'll suffer whether your goal is doing good or not. Either accept that fact or stop killing." Sigri paused, giving Mae a sad smile. "Since you don't have that choice, why torture yourself?"

Mae looked into Sigri's face, lost for words. Was that how the green witch saw it? Should Mae simply accept what she was? Didn't she have a choice?

"Anyhow," Sigri continued, forcing a cheerful voice. "You know how much Renya hates putting in the effort. We only got one each. At least you got two."

"One," Mae replied, her mind still reeling.

"So one got away from the famous black witch?"

"Shush, Renya!" Sigri admonished. "Why only one? What happened? Let's have some tea and hear the whole story."

Sigri ushered the women to sit in the courtyard and share their adventures. Her tea was excellent—hot and sweet, with the tiniest trace of spice. Mae could feel her fatigue disappearing. This cup held true magic. Her muscles relaxed, her agitation quieted, and her mood lifted. The biscuits, sadly, had more in common with the pebbles dotting the mountainside.

Sigri talked at length about the sister's uneventful journey home in an apparent attempt to give everyone's temper time to cool down. As the sun dipped behind the surrounding peaks, the witches headed inside, where Sigri helped Mae prepare dinner.

Mae had returned with three rabbits she caught on the way. Sigri stoked the fire and chopped vegetables while Mae skinned the animals. The green witch didn't enjoy harming any living creature. Still, she appreciated Mae's cooking and looked forward to a hearty meal. Soon, the kitchen was filled with the delicious aroma of rabbit stew.

After dinner, the women moved closer to the hearth. At Renya's insistence, Mae explained her curious behavior after the failed ambush. The black witch recounted the story of her family's death, detailing the role of the one-eyed soldier in this horrible affair.

"So, you got him in the end. Serves him right!" Renya applauded. "But you could have told us. I wouldn't have objected. You know me." She grinned. "I love sweet revenge."

"I had no time. It was hard enough to follow his trail," Mae replied, glad for Renya's approval. Still, the black witch didn't join in her sister's celebration. "I felt good and righteous in the moment," Mae explained. "But since then, I realized he had been an underling—a henchman acting on the duke's orders. And the duke got away from me—again!" Anger flickered across Mae's face. Renya, too, narrowed her eyes at the renewed mention of the duke. To diffuse the rising tension, Sigri tried to change the subject.

"What I don't understand is..." the green witch ventured. "If the tree branch trapped the robber, how did he escape?"

"I let him go," Mae mumbled.

"You *what?*" Renya shrieked.

"I let him go. He was a child, a young boy."

"He saw you, and he recognized you as a witch. He probably lives a stone's throw from the duke's estate, and you let him go?" Renya had risen from her chair, pointing an accusing finger.

"Yes, I let him go. I scared him to death." Mae, too, had jumped up. "He will not tell on us. He is nothing more than a boy who needed money for his sick mother."

"You can't be sure he won't tell on us. Tell on *you*, that is," Sigri interjected. "Especially if he still needs money. There is a large bounty on any witch caught. He might risk your wrath to save his mother's life."

Mae faltered. "I hadn't thought of that."

"You haven't thought at all, you mean," Renya spat, her voice venomous. "Not what the boy will do, not what the duke will do if he finds the boy. And worst of all, not of *us*! We took you in, and you put us in danger—over and over again."

"So what should I have done, oh wise woman, pray tell?"

"*Kill him!*" Renya shouted. "Get it done. Be quick and gentle, but eliminate the threat for good."

"Well, it is too late for that."

"I don't think so," Sigri said. Her even voice got under Mae's skin in moments like this. "The boy may need time to make up his mind. The duke may need time to find the boy. I hate it as much as the next witch, but the boy has to die—the sooner, the better."

"*She* wouldn't hate it." Mae pointed at Renya.

"Be that as it may, I must agree with my sister. We took you in, and we accepted your ideas and your restrictions." Sigri's lips thinned, her face almost displaying anger. "In return, we require you to respect our need for safety. I am going to bed."

"You better fix this, or you are no longer welcome here." Renya, too, left for their bedroom.

Mae stared into the glowing embers, at a loss for what to do. Oh, Renya could go to hell! Mae wasn't that weak. She didn't need to appease the other witch to have a roof over her head. Mae had managed before, and there was the cave by the waterfall. But Sigri's logic was impeccable, as always. The duke would insist on a thorough investigation. They would find the robber's horse and his things, and then they would find his village and him. Who knew what he would say under torture? *What a mess!*

Mae needed to do something. While she could use some rest, she gathered her things and left, having no intention of sharing the bedroom with those... witches. Instead, Mae climbed the crumpled tower and lay under the stars, hoping to see answers in the vast night sky. But she already had the answer; she just didn't like it. She would lie there until daybreak and then be off again, hunting a boy.

CHAPTER FOUR

Eliminating a Threat

After traveling for six days, Mae arrived in the presumed area where the would-be robber must live. On her way, she evaded multiple armed patrols and overheard the word "witchcraft" whispered in many conversations.

Sigri was right again, she thought. *We've caused a mighty witch hunt.* Mae needed to be careful. A woman traveling alone and looking as young as Mae did couldn't enter a tavern and ask questions without arousing suspicions or being accosted. While she could defend herself in most situations, repelling an attacker with magic in front of witnesses wasn't advisable.

Given that a young boy had arrived at the ambush site with three stolen horses and two scarecrow-like contraptions, Mae was sure his village was close to that spot, most likely on the forest's other side. Two settlements fit that description. Mae went first to Erikssund, the larger hamlet. She decided to mingle where the local women gathered: the well, the bathhouse, and, in this case, the market. Donning her only dress with the more inconspicuous green cape, Mae made her way to the town square. Luckily, today was market day, although she had arrived late. Many vendors were already packing up their wares. Mae looked around and approached a matronly woman behind a vegetable stall.

"Good afternoon, ma'am." Mae bobbed a curtsy as a young woman should. "Would you be from around here?"

The woman was preoccupied with arranging her turnips, exhibiting the care and loving touch of a jeweler presenting his most valuable creations. Startled, she raised her gaze.

"I am indeed. And who would you be?"

"I'm on my way south. I was wondering... Could you recommend a place for the night? Is there a safe place for a young woman?"

"I didn't ask where you're going." The woman looked Mae up and down, creases showing on her forehead. "Who are you? You ain't from around here."

"No, ma'am, I'm not."

"Then what are you doing? A young girl by herself—out with it." Putting her hands on her ample hips, she glared at Mae. "Are you up to any mischief?"

"Oh—no."

"You can't fool me. I've raised five daughters. I know the ways of misguided children. You plan to run away with a boy you took a fancy to, isn't that so?" The woman shook her head in seeming disapproval of all young people. "Tell me who you are, and we can return you to your parents. That'll be the end of it."

"No, ma'am, it's nothing like that. There isn't a boy. Well, there is a man, but I'm not running away with him—I'm running away *from* him. I'm never going home, ever."

"Don't be foolish. Your parents must be worried sick. They want you back, safe and sound. Your father may use his belt, but that is only for your best."

"I don't fear a beating, but my parents... They want to marry me to an old man. He is over thirty and a soldier in the duke's guard. I'd rather slit my wrist than spend my life with this horrid man."

A moment of silence followed. Mae was delighted to see the woman's expression change from stern disapproval to sympathy and concern.

"A daughter should obey her father in all matters. But a duke's soldier, that's a cruel choice. Those men have a nasty reputation. Many claim to be of Viking blood, looking down on us natives." The woman's chest rose and fell in agitation. "Even if this man were gentle, most villagers would shun you. We don't have no love for the duke or his soldiers." She stopped and looked around, probably wondering if she said too much.

"Can you help me? Oh, please."

"Why do you want to go south?"

"My brother lives there with his good wife. He'll take me in. And he'll find me a good husband," Mae added after another stern look.

"Hmm, good thing you're heading south. Some unsavory things happened here lately."

"What do you mean? I haven't heard anything. I was hiding near the forest."

"The *forest*? You must avoid it! Rumors have it that evil witches killed travelers there. They attacked the duke's soldiers with fire. And in Kristiansund..."

"What happened in Kristiansund?" Too eager, Mae could have bitten her tongue. The woman's mistrusting stare was back. "Forgive me for interrupting, ma'am. I'm a simple girl; I don't know nothing of the world. Your talk of witches had me quivering."

The woman continued to eye her, likely remembering that Mae still hadn't given her name. Mae held her breath, not needing to act to appear anxious. Finally, the woman relented.

"In Kristiansund, six miles up the coast, someone stole Farmer Holgrim's horses on the night of the witches' attack. They say they caught the fiends, but you never know. There might be more around, in disguise." The woman lowered her voice to a stage whisper as if the witches were listening in, and at least one was.

"You think there are still witches in Kristiansund? That is up north?" Mae put as much fear as was believable into these questions. "I'm definitely going south and sticking to the road. I never liked that forest. There are wolves and such."

"Aye, there are wolves and other dangers for young women. You'd better find somebody you could travel with. Only journey in daylight. Where exactly are you going, and where do your parents live?"

Time to go, Mae thought.

"I will, ma'am. Thank you so much." Mae pulled away from the woman. "I have to get my things. That is, I left my bundle at the forest's edge. I didn't bring it along in case someone stole it. But now, I fear for all my linens. Those would be my dowry items if my brother was to find me a good husband."

"You *left them* by the forest? By all the gods, silly girl, go and fetch them!"

"Yes, ma'am, I'll collect them."

Mae rushed up the meadow. True to her words, she headed toward the forest's edge, but there would be no dowry items. For a brief moment, the realization stung, like the sharp pain from twisting one's back. Mae had no time to waste on fanciful dreams and what-ifs. This afternoon's activity had been a complete success. She was sure the boy lived in Kristiansund, where he had stolen the horses.

Mae made her way north toward the village of Farmer Holgrim, fighting her way through the underbrush. She wondered why the soldiers hadn't followed the same gossip to exact the duke's "justice." Did they consider women an unreliable source of information? Or did the women withhold the news because they disliked the duke? Regardless, it seemed like nobody had caught and questioned the boy yet.

MAE REACHED THE outskirts of Kristiansund well after nightfall on a moonless night. This village was small. About fifteen or twenty houses clustered around the fishing harbor, with a handful of farms beyond. Regardless of Mae's acting abilities, there was no chance to engage any village woman in a conversation about boys and rumors this late. Since she wasn't aware of any spell to reveal the unknown boy's location with magic, she would rest until daybreak.

Despite being a black witch for a decade, Mae knew little about magic and her abilities. Witchcraft was taboo. Hence, there was no place to learn except by trial and error or the companionship of other witches.

Instinctively, Mae could manipulate the elements: light, wind, water, and fire. She had experimented with spells to move and destroy nearby objects. And even before being cursed, Mae could touch the minds of people and animals. The more life force she held, the more powerful her spells became. But she needed to be calm and focused for her magic to work. A good night's sleep was the best preparation for the things to come. Mae spotted a sheep barn. With the animals staying outside in the summer, she could enter undetected and climb into the hayloft.

The following morning, Mae rose rejuvenated. Brushing off the hay and stepping outside, she surveyed the village below. The world looked enchanted in the soft glow of the rising sun. Most of the boats were long gone since fishermen rose early. The rest of the village looked to be fast asleep. *How to find the boy?* Mae wished for Sigri's logical mind to solve this riddle. On her own, she had to rummage around and hope for a lucky break.

Her luck changed as a dozen soldiers marched up the road. *This complicates things,* Mae thought. *It seems the duke's soldiers have caught up with the news after all.* Staying well off the road, Mae crept closer, intending to observe the proceedings.

The soldiers reached the village square and blew their horns. All around, the windows and doors opened as the villagers wanted to find out what was happening. One middle-aged man stepped out of the smithy.

The man addressed the lead soldier. "What is going on, Captain?"

"Are you the village's steward?"

"We don't have a steward, but I am the smith. Everyone here knows and respects me."

"Well, smith, there has been a heinous crime—an attack on the duke's life. It happened a fortnight ago. We followed a lead to this village. What can you say?"

"What can I say? I know nothing about such things."

"And would you tell me if you knew? Or are you sympathizing with the criminals? Or are you one of them?" The captain moved his horse closer, and the other soldiers put their hands on their swords.

"Oh, no. I don't know anything, sir. I am an obedient subject to his lordship. I work hard, and I pay my taxes." The smith rushed his words. "I have two sons who served in the king's army when the duke demanded men. We live in a small village. We know each other well, sir. There are no criminals among us."

"The robbers used horses from this village. After sharp questioning, the owner told us what he knew. Someone stole his horses, but he didn't know who. I am willing to believe him. In my experience, a dying man's lies aren't that convincing."

The smith looked shocked. "He is dead? You *killed* him?"

"Guard your tongue, smith, or lose it. I'm acting on the duke's orders and his authority. I'm telling you what we did to ensure your full cooperation. Now tell me: Who are the bandits? Where are the bandits? Speak, or I will put every man, woman, and child to the sword, starting with your sons."

"I don't know anything, I swear. Most here are fishermen and farmers, with some crafters. We are honest people."

"You are dirty, lying peasants, and I grow tired of your evasions." The captain jumped off his horse and looked around at the villagers stepping out of their simple wooden houses, a look of utmost contempt on his face. "My men and I have worked hard chasing the criminals. We will rest here for an hour or two, ensuring nobody leaves. You, smith, will find us our bandits. If you haven't presented the guilty individuals to us by midday, all of you are guilty. And my men will burn this miserable excuse for a village with you inside your homes. Have I made myself clear?"

"Yes, sir. I will... We *all* will find whoever has disgraced our village."

"I am sure you will. In the meantime, my men will round up all women and children and put them over there, into that nice, flammable-looking shed, with their hands and feet tied. It's for their safety, you understand, and as an additional motivation."

* * *

MAE HEARD THE entire conversation from behind two rain barrels. These soldiers were as bad as they came. They would kill and torture to get their answers. Mae's time was running short. Some villagers may indeed have seen the boy doing something strange. Or they would deliver him as a scapegoat.

Mae needed to ensure that he wasn't captured alive. Unwanted thoughts came to Mae: *If the soldiers butcher the entire village, I don't have to kill the boy myself.* Then she scolded herself. *Despicable, hoping for mass murder to achieve my goal.* Instead, she should attack the soldiers to protect the innocent.

On the captain's command, his men went from door to door, dragging out women and children, some still in their nightshirts. Only a handful of village men weren't out to fish. They huddled in front of the smithy, discussing what to do. The soldiers searched each house from the loft to the root cellar. One guard exited an especially miserable-looking shed empty handed and complained to his comrades.

"You got all the good-looking whores. Here is only a half-dead crone. I'm not going near her—don't want to catch anything. She can burn where she lies."

That must be the boy's mother. Mae cast a spell to weave a glamour, making it harder for anybody to spot her as she crept toward that house. If someone had looked at her, they would only have noticed a distortion, like in the air over an open flame. But everybody was too occupied with rounding up the women or searching for a way to protect them.

Mae peeked into the sick woman's house through a back-facing window. She had seen many dismal dwellings, but this single-room cabin was barely large enough to hold a small bed and a wobbly table. An unconscious woman lay on the thin mattress. Sweat glistened on every square inch of her exposed skin and drenched the sheets. The woman was burning up. Her face sunken, her skin stretched tight over the cheekbones. She looked like a corpse. Still, her chest was rising and falling with a sick rattling.

Not seeing anybody else, Mae climbed in and crept closer. Kneeling beside the bed, she touched the woman. Immediately, a feeling of disease and corruption reached her mind. Mae was no healer. Yet even Sigri, with all her prodigious skills, might not have been able to save this woman. Mae couldn't do anything except to ease her passing. Taking her head in both hands, she was about to drain the woman's life when the papery eyelids opened. The woman looked at Mae, glassy eyes straining to focus, and her parched lips struggled to form words.

"It is you. You're here to free me," the woman said in a rasping whisper. "I am ready, dark sister. I am ready." Then, she grabbed Mae's hand with surprising strength and demanded, "Jarne, my son, you must help him. Protect him! He needs you, and you... you will need him, too." Hacking coughs and wheezing followed. Her emaciated body spasmed, and her arms fell limp. "I am ready," she whispered almost inaudibly.

Mae's mind reeled, her hands shaking. She took that poor woman's last ounce of life almost without conscious decision. Instead of feeling euphoria, Mae sank to the floor, dejected. There she sat, her back against the central pillar, her arms around her knees, and her head bent. A lump formed in her throat, and Mae blinked tears away.

This woman must have been a witch, too, living in disguise among ordinary people. And she had recognized Mae's power, welcoming her as an angel of death, bringing her relief and oblivion. But then the woman burdened Mae, charging her to look after her son. *Isn't my life doomed enough? Another dying woman's wish? How could she do this?* The cruel Norns had sent the curse, turning Mae into a living nightmare. But then they tortured her—no, they made Mae torture herself, to fight what she was, to deny herself what she needed to do.

* * *

As the sun rose higher, so did the tensions in the village square. The soldiers took defensive positions with their hands on sword hilts, awaiting further commands. Eventually, the captain raised his voice.

"Time's almost up. Such an old wooden structure can easily catch fire with the sun so bright." To the villagers' dismay, three soldiers took torches from their mounts and muscled their way into the smithy to light them.

"Please, sir," the smith begged, "we don't know who attacked the duke."

"Too bad. His lordship will be disappointed, especially when, on top of everything, he hears about the horrible misfortune that has befallen this village."

"Have mercy, sir. We are loyal subjects to his lordship, but…"

"But?"

"But there have been things happening."

"Go on," the captain said, his voice becoming sweet as honey.

"Olaf Jonsson used to live in the house down the road. He was a drunkard and a no-good."

"You think he was the bandit?"

"No, I don't think so. He left years ago."

"Then why waste my time?" The captain jumped up from his comfortable perch on a stack of crates and drew his sword, advancing on the smith.

"His son, Jarne, still lives with his mother. There were rumors the boy wasn't Olaf's, and Olaf left, beating his wife green and blue." The captain pointed his sword at the smith's neck, and the frightened man rushed on.

"The boy is always up to something. The mother is sick and has been for a while. There is no money—we don't have money to spare. But they still live here. I am sure the boy steals, but nobody can prove anything."

"So, your brave attempt to save your women and yourself is to accuse a boy? A fatherless child has mounted an armed attack on the duke?"

With a quick jab, the captain's sword entered the smith's throat, and he withdrew it, six inches coated bright red. Gasping, the smith fell to his knees. In vain, he tried to staunch the wound, utter shock and disbelief painted on his face. The captain bent over as if to whisper in the smith's ear. But he only wanted to wipe his blade on the shirtsleeves of the dying man. Standing back up, he kicked his victim into the dirt and turned to the foremost of the stunned villagers.

"You, tell me! Where is this boy?"

"I don't know. Haven't seen him today, sir. But," the man added as the captain moved his sword toward him, "the mother is in that house. If we were to take her hostage?"

"Burn the house!" the captain barked. "Let the fire be a signal to call the boy home to Mommy."

The soldiers with the torches rushed forward. Two more carried crates and used them to block the hut's door. Then they set fire to the house. The warped wooden boards were bone dry from the sun, the wind, and the salty air. The greedy fire licked at the wood, dancing across the entire front. Once the flames reached the thatched roof, the fire became an inferno. Sparks carried by the wind ignited neighboring buildings. The few village men started to rush forward, wanting to fight the destruction of their home, but the remaining soldiers blocked their path.

"See how good my foresight was, bringing all your beloved wives and children to safety," sneered the captain. "Let's hope the wind doesn't turn."

* * *

MAE HAD STILL been kneeling next to the dead woman when the soldiers approached the house. She jumped up, her eyes wet, yet her mind switched to survival mode. Moving back through the house, she climbed out the window. Once the flames had grown into a bonfire worthy of burning a fellow witch, she had no problem moving undetected.

Where to?

The mother was dead. The boy could be anywhere. What if Mae ignored this woman? She hadn't known her at all. In fact, she had killed her. So, how binding could her last wish be? Again, Mae knew the answer. The woman had been a sister. And even if she hadn't, she had been a mother asking Mae to save her only child.

With these thoughts still painting a dark picture of the path ahead, at least the problem of locating the boy resolved itself. A twang sounded. *A crossbow shot?* A head and upper body poked from one of the rain barrels behind which Mae had crouched earlier. The boy stood there with a crossbow in his hand. Mae followed the presumed line of fire and saw that he had hit his target this time. The captain lay in the dirt, a crossbow bolt protruding from his back, a dark stain expanding around him. *A perfect shot. Was it luck? Or was it bad luck last time?* Mae had no time to wonder. Two soldiers bent down, trying to rescue their commander, while the others rushed toward the boy with swords drawn.

The distance measured only a few strides. Still, between the assassin and his victim lay the stack of crates on which the latter had perched only moments before. Mae exploded the boxes, nails and splinters flying everywhere. The leading soldiers got the full blast and died on the spot. The men following tripped over their comrades. The boy climbed out of the barrel and advanced toward the soldiers, trying to rewind his crossbow. There was bravery, and then there was stupidity.

Still flushed with power, Mae summoned a whirlwind, pulling burning planks from the surrounding buildings and sending the debris into the fallen soldiers as they tried to get back up. Smoke, ash, and cries of pain filled the air.

When the dust settled, Mae saw, to her astonishment, the villagers attacking the injured soldiers. Two men hurried to the shed to free the women. But the others charged, led by the man whom the captain had threatened last with his sword and who was now holding the same. They rushed to repay the soldier's "kindness."

Mae staggered. She had put all her power into the spells. The exertion had her muscles shaking and her head pounding. In the midst of all the confusion, the boy had managed to reload the crossbow and was looking for a new target. Then he spotted her. *How wonderful.* Mae had no time to think. She exploded his weapon. Surprise, fury, hurt, and hatred crossed the boy's face before he sank to the ground, pierced by multiple splinters of what had once been a crossbow.

CHAPTER FIVE

The Banishment

So much for saving the boy, but Mae had no time. And even if she had, what could she have said to stop the boy from wanting to kill her? *Hi, I'm the witch who threatened and almost killed you last time. But I have spoken to your dying mother, and she asked me to protect you. Oh, and then I killed her before the soldiers burned her to ashes.* Yeah, that would have made a difference.

For all he knew, she was in league with the soldiers. That's why she had hunted him last time, and that's why she was here now. *Too bad he'll never know the truth.* She'd come here to kill him for her *own* reasons. And then, for a short moment, she changed her mind before actually killing him. Boy dead, threat eliminated, sisters happy—she could go home and continue her life like before.

And you… you will need him, too. Those were the dying mother's last words. What did she mean? What *could* she mean? Did she possess the sight, like Sigri? Or were these words the delirious ramblings of a dying woman? Or even a blatant lie to entice Mae to fulfill the first part of the wish?

Protect him! He needs you. Mae would never know. Yet, as sure as sunrise followed sunset, it would always bother her.

Her mind occupied, she approached the boy. Behind her, the battle had turned ugly, at least for the soldiers. Mae thought most of them were already dead or dying; her spells and the villagers' initial charge had seen to that. But this morning's fear and frustration had broken down all restraints. The villagers kept bashing the fallen invaders with anything that came to hand, breaking bones, shattering teeth, and cracking skulls. Nobody advanced toward her.

The boy lay on his face, although there couldn't be much left of it. Mae didn't know how she felt. She experienced no relief about finishing her "job," but she felt no remorse about defending herself either. She was sad. A boy had died who had risked everything for his mother. He had fought the odds and had tried to be the man in the house. In the end, he died because of a misunderstanding—a gap between expectations and reality that Mae couldn't breach in the short time it took to erase him forever.

Tears streaked down her cheeks again, but she didn't stop them. She didn't hide them. He deserved it all: her pain, her tears, her sadness. She wanted to say *goodbye*. She wanted to say *sorry* for a world that didn't care about witches and orphan boys. So damn bad she wanted to hold him, and take his anguish away, and be there for him like she had done for the brother she once had. She knew his name, Jarne, so she knelt next to his body, touched the back of his head, and whispered.

"I'm sorry, Jarne. I'm so very sorry." Mae started in surprise; she could sense his heart beating. *How can that be?* Turning him over, the witch saw angry red scratches. Fragments of the crossbow must have grazed his cheeks and forearms but left no severe injuries.

However, the bow's shaft had embedded itself deep into his right shoulder. The large piece of wood plugged the wound, preventing heavy bleeding. Jarne breathed shallowly, but Mae couldn't hear any rasping or gurgling. The attack hadn't harmed his lungs. She needed to do something: help him. But first, they needed to get away. *Where to?*

Still on her hands and knees, Mae ordered two horses over. She didn't bother with the gentle soothing she had used last time, nor did she mirror Sigri's polite request. Instead, she forced the command into the animals' minds—direct, urgent, and unambiguous. One of the villagers looked at her, his arms bright red up to the elbows. She sent a cloud of dust into his eyes, and he cursed and sputtered.

Mae lifted Jarne onto the first horse. He was almost the same height and weight as her, but she had magic to spare. Once he slumped against the horse's neck, she ensured no pressure rested on the wooden spike in his shoulder. Mounting up, she took the lead of his horse into her hand and moved toward the forest.

Mae considered traveling to the cave behind the waterfall. But that seemed too far, too hard to reach, and unnecessary. This time, no witch hunt would follow. The duke would enact dire retributions if he learned what happened here. But if the soldiers' bodies disappeared into the sea, the soldiers' horses into the cookpots, and the soldiers' weapons into the hay barns and attics, how would he ever know? Anyhow, that was none of Mae's concern.

Riding along the forest's edge, she looked for a convenient spot to enter the woods and find a soft hollow where they could spend the night. A deer trail looked promising, and Mae thought she could hear the faint gurgling of a brook. Guiding the horses toward the stream at a snail's pace, the witch delved for Jarne's vital signs. He was still alive but getting weaker. After twenty agonizing minutes, the travelers came across a small meadow on the elevated bank of the stream. *This will have to do.* Mae tied the horses to a tree and took the bedroll off her saddle. Then she lowered Jarne onto the improvised bed. He was ashen faced, with pain painted across his features.

What now? What does he need? Bandages. Mae rummaged through the saddlebags and gathered all the soldiers' spare clothes, intending to rip them into strips.

Where the hell is my bloody knife? She must have lost it somewhere while running, hiding, fighting, and killing today. Without wasting time looking for another sharp instrument, she ripped the cloth with her teeth and nails. Once the bandages were ready, she knelt beside Jarne. Blood had drenched his shirt, and dark specks covered his neck and cheeks. She needed to remove the wooden shaft. *But how?* Mae had never done this before. What would she give to have Sigri's skills? Even better: to have Sigri here to help. *But would she?*

The question was moot. Sigri wasn't here, and Mae had to act despite her limited experience, or the boy would die. Brushing the hair off his forehead, she steeled herself. First, she took a small twig and put it between his teeth. Even unconscious, the jolt of pain could cause his teeth to bite off his tongue. Gripping the broken shaft hard with one hand and holding a wad of bandages in the other, she put one knee over his chest. Mae closed her eyes, focused her energy, and forced his skin and flesh away from the wooden spike with magic. Immediately, the bleeding intensified.

"Sorry, Jarne. This will hurt a little." She yanked with all her might. The shaft came free, and an animal-like squeal escaped Jarne's mouth. Mae toppled over backward, hitting her shoulder hard on a tree root. Ignoring her pain, she rushed back and pressed the cloth onto the wound. Alarming amounts of deep red spread through the fabric. Jarne spasmed in pain. Mae threw the material away and pushed a new wad onto his shoulder. That time, the bleeding slowed somewhat.

Mae wrapped the shoulder as well as she could, her hands shaking. Then, she sat back, relieved to see his chest rising and falling. Not knowing what else to do, she held his left hand between hers, tethering him to this life. Or was it Mae who needed to hold on to something? She stayed motionless, unknowingly channeling her energy into the boy, synchronizing her breathing and heartbeat with Jarne.

Hours passed, and the sun began to sink before the boy stirred and opened his eyes. Fresh tears ran down his cheeks, leaving light streaks on his oh-so-dirty face. He wasn't fully awake. Still, his eyes found hers.

"You?" he croaked. "Get away from me, witch." Then he fell back into unconsciousness.

I won't, she thought. *I won't until you are healed and safe.* A small part in the back of her head amended, *And maybe not even then.*

* * *

The following morning dawned cold and wet. Fog and low clouds had moved in overnight, and Mae regretted not finding or building a shelter. She hadn't slept much. After the "operation," she let the boy rest and went searching for healing herbs.

A common misconception claimed that all witches were skillful healers. Sadly, Mae wasn't good at brewing potions and mixing poultices. *I'm much better at inflicting wounds than healing them.* But she remembered a few things her mother had told her. Mae returned with hands full of wormwood against fevers and willow bark against pain. She prepared the medicine by chewing the ingredients and spitting them back out.

Then, she redressed Jarne's shoulder. The wound looked bad. The flesh and skin had turned red, hot, and swollen. Dark blood oozed out of the jagged hole. After changing the bandages, Mae tried coaxing some water down his throat. The water also gave her the idea to wash his face, neck, and shoulders, cleaning the minor scrapes. She washed his hands, forearms, and, for whatever reason, also his feet. The rest could wait until he was able to bathe on his own.

Mae piled dry moss under his head after exhausting her pitiful healing abilities. Draping him in her green cape, she realized, bewildered, that she was still wearing the dress. Her proper clothes and knife must still be in the barn where she had slept the night before. She hadn't lost her things in the heat of the action. She had been so overwhelmed by the morning's beauty that she had forgotten to take her belongings.

Should I go back and fetch them? Too risky. The villagers would be on alert after the soldiers' invasion. Mae would need to get new things later in exchange for the horses. Then she could get Jarne some new clothes, too. They must be almost the same size.

Jarne continued to moan and cry out during the night. Mae rushed over each time but was unable to do anything. The wet and chill hadn't helped either. He looked paler in the morning. She knew she must look frightening, too, but she at least still had plenty of life energy left.

Food was the next concern. Mae had found some blueberries—still tart, yet better than nothing. She used a large leaf in which to mash the berries into a pulp and finger-fed them to Jarne. Despite her best efforts, only a minuscule amount of berry mash had gone into his mouth. His face and shirt, as well as her dress and hands, looked like they had received the bulk.

Mae feared her inept care alone wouldn't keep the boy alive for long. His injury required the treatment of a proper healer. Lacking another option, she decided to return with the boy to the Witches' Castle, seeking help from Sigri. Renya would be furious, and her powerful hexes could undo all the progress. But Mae had no choice. She wouldn't let him die.

Heaving Jarne back on the horse, Mae led the animals through the woods toward the bluff. From there, they traveled into the highlands, along a trail that was quite familiar by now. The wind had picked up. Mae wondered about her riding in a dress yesterday without realizing it. Was her mind going? She had been under a lot of stress. First, she wanted to kill the boy, and then she tried to save him. Later, he wanted to kill her, and then she tried to kill him. And finally, she had done her best to keep him alive. That would confuse anyone. With the adrenaline waning, she felt the cold wind biting into her exposed skin, which proved how stupid dresses were.

By late afternoon, they'd progressed less than a third of a day's march. Mae hated their crawling speed but didn't dare to move any faster. She had secured Jarne in the saddle with ropes and laid his upper body onto a pile of blankets tied to the horse's neck. Still, she feared him falling off. The boy moaned at every other of the horse's steps, and her neck complained about the frequent turning. She couldn't do anything but press on, hoping everything would turn out fine.

When they finally stopped for the night, a fever had a firm hold of Jarne's body. His skin was clammy, but his forehead burned. Mae tried to coax some more water down his throat to keep him hydrated. She didn't know if she had succeeded. Her hands trembled. Why was she so emotional? Why was this boy's fate so important to her? It couldn't be because of the woman's dying wish, could it? No, it was more than that.

I've killed so many since the curse took me, Mae realized, *but I've never saved a life. Even when trying to rescue my brother, all I did was sink ships and burn villages.* Her eyes stung, tears welling up.

"I don't want to be a monster!" the witch bellowed into the wind, clenching her fists. *And this boy...* Mae looked at his face. *He reminds me so much of my brother. I need to save him!*

"Is that too much to ask?" she sobbed, pinning all her hopes for redemption onto this scrawny boy whom the Norns had placed in her path.

Mae wiped her face, disgusted by her moment of weakness. With renewed determination, the witch focused on the things in her control. She changed the bandages, applied her crude medicine, and laid a wet cloth on the boy's forehead. And Mae prayed—not to any specific gods, and definitely not to the invader's deities of war and thunder. She reached out to the world, asking her parents for guidance, offering bargains to the wind—good deeds in exchange for this boy's life. There was no answer, no comfort given, no beam of light shining down through the broken clouds. The world seemed not to care. A witch and an orphan boy didn't matter in the grand scheme of things. But there was also no lightning strike, no wolf pack attack, and no patrol of hostile soldiers. The two survived another night, weak and weary but still able to move on toward the faint hope of salvation.

The following days went by in a blur. Mae became mechanical in her actions. In the morning, she wiped Jarne's face and gave him something to drink. Every single day, she was expecting to find a corpse. Yet, the boy clung to life with the same stubbornness he had shown when attacking the duke and confronting an angry witch. After breakfast, she secured Jarne on his mount, and they started their slow procession. They stopped at midday to rest. Mae went off to scour the surroundings for water and anything edible. Jarne was rarely awake. Sometimes, he looked at her with bloodshot eyes. Mae didn't believe he saw her. *Does he see his mother?* She hoped so, as that would provide him more comfort.

Finally, they reached the foothills of the Smoking Mountains, and it started to rain. Dark clouds clung to the craggy peaks, drenching the travelers in icy downpours. Mae wasn't surprised. Why wouldn't the wicked Norns punish her further for all her evil past? And instead of attacking her, they made her suffer by harming someone else—a boy, for example—someone she had started to care about. Anger rose, and with defiance, she screamed her curses into the wind. No more begging, no more bargaining. The world would do better to watch out who it antagonized. If the boy died, she would become a menace the likes of which hadn't been seen in centuries. Fueled by her fury, the travelers managed the torturous climb up the mountain path.

Mae reached the castle drenched, miserable, angry, relieved, and tired to the bone.

"Have you lost your mind?" Renya's shouts greeted Mae as soon as her horse stepped into the courtyard. "By all the devils, you were supposed to kill him. Why bring him here?"

"Where is Sigri?" Mae had no energy left to respond to Renya's accusations.

"Sigri went searching for healing herbs. She foresaw your foolishness. I was sure she was mistaken. Even *you* couldn't be that stupid."

This time, Mae didn't acknowledge Renya's insult at all. Weary, she got off her horse and went over to Jarne. He was still alive, *Álfheimr blessings be thanked*, he was still hanging on.

"Give me a hand," Mae requested in a tired voice. "We have to get him inside, out of the rain."

"I will not! And you won't bring him into our house."

"Get over here," Mae demanded, her voice turning to ice, "and give me a hand!"

Turning toward her fellow witch, Mae's eyes burned with red fury. She was done accepting rejections. Her whole body trembled with rage. A gust of air rose from her feet, whipping the gray witch's cloak and hair. Behind Renya, several stones of the crumbling castle walls exploded. Something inside Mae had broken open. An essence, primordial and powerful, rose to the surface, ready to strike out at anyone or anything that stood in her way. She emanated pulses of undisguised menace.

Renya took several steps backward. In the middle of the courtyard, Mae stood tall—for all the world to see, a black witch in all her terrible might. Despite her morals, noble intentions, and desire to be good, nothing could erase nor contain the raw and undeniable *evil* at the core of her existence.

"Where to?" Renya asked, voice quavering.

"Into the bedroom," Mae ordered. "I need to get him out of his wet clothes. Set water to boil, and fetch Sigri!"

Renya helped carry Jarne inside, not daring to look at the black witch. Mae didn't spare any thought for Renya's trepidations. Her only concerns were for the boy. *Hold on, Jarne*, she thought. *Oh please, by the mother of all, hold on!*

* * *

IT DIDN'T TAKE Sigri long to return to the castle. Her kitchen already contained an extensive collection of herbs and plants. She only needed some fresh Calendula flowers to offset the blood poisoning. The green witch hadn't decided whether to help the boy. But she wanted to prepare—the mark of a proficient healer.

"Mae waits for you in the bedroom," Renya shouted as soon as her sister entered. The gray witch stood beside the boiling cauldron, scooping the hot water into bowls. This behavior confused Sigri. She had expected to find Renya in high agitation: yelling, screaming, and throwing things.

"Are you all right? What happened?"

"She came back with the boy," Renya explained. "He is injured. She sent me to fetch you immediately. She was quite demanding."

"Since when do you accept demands from Mae?"

"You don't understand." Renya's voice rose. "She is angry, really angry. The red glint in her eyes chilled me to the bone. Her power... You must go to her at once."

Sigri stared at Renya for one more moment, wondering what kind of terror had caused her blustering and sometimes condescending sister to cower in fright. Depositing her harvest on the table, the green witch stepped into the bedroom.

Mae was still in her wet clothes, making puddles as she bent over the boy. He looked thin and gangly, like a youth on the verge of manhood who had grown too quickly. Mae had removed his clothes and thrown them into the corner, using the blankets to rub his body dry. Getting closer, Sigri saw a fever-ravaged face.

"The infection is bad. He might not make it." Sigri's cold, analytical voice pulled Mae out of her trance.

"Sigri, finally!" Mae exclaimed. "Help him!"

"Why?"

"I need your help. He needs your help. I'm no healer."

"That much is obvious. So, let him die."

* * *

Mae turned around. Sigri had always been cool, dispassionate, and logical. But there was more this time. Her voice dripped venom. Mae stood up and faced her sister. The green witch was taller, and Mae didn't like looking up at her stony face.

"You brought him here after we asked you to eliminate this threat," Sigri continued, shaking her head in apparent disgust. "You brought him here, and you threatened my sister. Why?"

"He is weak. I needed to get him inside. Renya was obstinate, as always."

Sigri didn't respond, nor did she move. Her body and facial expression seemed carved from ice. The boy tossed and moaned, caught in a fever spike. Still, the healer didn't so much as glance his way. Her eyes rested on Mae with all the warmth of an arctic snow blizzard.

Usually, the green witch couldn't watch any living creature hurting. She needed to help or end the agony. This time, however, it seemed like she wanted Mae to suffer—payback for grievances accumulated over a long time. This wasn't about the boy; this was personal.

"Let's hear it then." Mae broke the frosty silence. "You knew I was coming. You knew I would be bringing this boy along. You went through all the trouble to collect herbs for a healing you don't intend to perform. There must have been lots of thoughts going through your brilliant mind. I won't stop you from sharing your 'wisdom.'"

Sigri didn't rise to the bait. Whether she recited her favorite recipe for blueberry pie or plunged a verbal dagger into her sister's back, her tone didn't change.

"The infection is bad," she repeated.

"You don't care about the boy."

"I'm not talking about the boy," Sigri clarified. Mae looked surprised, but Sigri continued in the same, even voice. "You are the infection. Your refusal to accept what you are—what we are. It corrupts and destroys all around you. You think you are better than us."

"I don't think that I'm better."

"Yes, you do, but you aren't. You look down on us for accepting the world as it is. *'We don't need to be evil,'* you keep saying. Did you ever consider that we wanted to be evil—at least according to your skewed definition of that word? We have been born with a gift and can harvest more power, but you want to keep that power all to yourself."

"When did I ever...?"

"*ALL THE TIME!*" Sigri's voice rose for the first time in Mae's recollection. "All the time, you keep preaching about good and evil. All the time, you have us starving ourselves until we find a 'deserving' victim. Every time we follow your stupid plans and personal vendettas, you put us in danger.

"We aren't monsters. We're like any other predator. We only hunt when we need to. We take the weak and the careless, keeping the balance of nature. But you, you are unnatural! You kill for your own reasons—playing God. This one deserves it, and this one doesn't. You accept no other point of view."

Sigri took deep, calming breaths and continued in her usual voice. "We have taken you in because you are a black witch."

"What is that supposed to mean?" Mae asked.

"That we were afraid of you, but also that you could protect us. All the world is afraid of you, Death's Daughter. But now, you have brought this boy."

"You are afraid of this boy, too?" Despite the intense confrontation, Mae couldn't help but let her scorn and sarcasm show.

"You aren't? Then you aren't only reckless but shortsighted, too." Sigri replied without any hint of insincerity.

"He is a boy."

"But he won't stay a boy forever. He will grow up. How will he react when he learns you wanted to kill him? How do you think he will take to our way of life? Do you think he will help us hunt and kill people?" Sigri shook her head, showing her disbelief at Mae's naïveté. "How will he react to the promise of riches for turning us in or cutting off our heads? And how will it end for us all when none of that happens? What if he grows into a strong and handsome man, and then Renya seduces him before taking his life?"

"You don't know if any of that will happen."

"I do know, not because of my sight, but because I have a brain. I know a stone comes back down after you have tossed it in the air. And I know that disaster will come down at us if the boy stays."

The two women locked stares, trying to read the bluff in each other's eyes. There was none. Instead, there was almost a slight undertone of sadness when Sigri continued.

"The infection needs to be cut out. The boy or us—you choose."

Mae hadn't known all the hurt she had inflicted on her hosts. She hadn't even considered the possibility of her causing damage. Sigri was right; Mae was rooted too deep in her inner struggles, forcing them onto her sisters and overshadowing any opposition. She was sorry for her arrogance, her blindness, and for her bullying. But most of all, for the sadness hidden under Sigri's calm facade.

Mae knew that Sigri didn't want her to leave. Sigri didn't want to go back to a life without hope of betterment. But Sigri also didn't understand Mae. Mae couldn't choose what was easy if she knew it wasn't right.

"Heal the boy," Mae said, fighting with tears, her voice sounding defeated. "Heal the boy, and we will leave in the morning."

CHAPTER SIX

———

Not Easy to Trust

THE MOMENT MAE proclaimed her decision, Sigri started to tend to the boy with calm efficiency. Throughout the night, the green witch brewed tinctures and administered remedies. She cleaned and drained the festering wound, cooled his face and body with wet towels, and infused him with the energy to fight the infection.

Whether her heart was in it or not, the healer's work was immaculate as always—dedication to a fault. But the effort had taken a lot out of her, out of all of them. Renya knelt beside her sister most of the night, lending her strength and assisting in any possible way. She exhibited care and tenderness like Mae had never seen before. Observing the sisters, Mae felt utterly alone. Whatever camaraderie she had experienced living with the two witches for the last four years, she'd never been that close to either of them.

Mae needed to get out. Her nerves were too raw, her emotions too wild, and her mind too strained with confusion about what had been and what would be. Instead, she sought refuge atop the crumpled tower, searching the endless starry sky. Mae begged for guidance from the countless constellations. None was given. The witch felt small and insignificant, and despite her exhaustion, sleep was slow in coming.

As soon as the rising sun peeked over the mountaintops, Mae woke, stiff and sore. She headed to the living quarters yet hesitated to enter, unsure what to expect. Hearing noises, Mae stepped in. Renya rummaged among the shelves, preparing tea. The gray witch's face looked drawn and pale; deep shadows ringed her eyes. In a toneless voice, she addressed Mae.

"Sigri is with the boy. She is sleeping now. You cannot move him today, or all will have been for nothing. I must go back in. Your stuff is over there." Renya jerked her head toward a chest in the opposite corner, where Mae's clothes and personal possessions lay dumped into a heap. Mae grunted her assent, but Renya had already left for the bedroom, closing the curtain with inexorable finality. Standing there, dazed, Mae looked at the ripples in the fabric. Her brain refused to accept the new reality.

With enormous effort, the witch willed herself to move to change into her usual attire of a dark shirt and pants. It took Mae mere moments to sort through the few possessions, deciding what to take and what to leave behind. But in these moments, the realization sank in that when she left this time, she would never return.

As soon as the sun rose for the second time after her confrontation with Sigri, Mae was on her way. Leaving her predictable life behind, she moved toward an uncertain destination with the boy in tow. Mae wondered if she could have acted differently. What if she killed him now, claiming a rockslide had struck? Could she return? Would the witches be able to overcome their differences? What if Mae accepted who she was and didn't fight it? *Who would be worse off?* She would. And her inner conflict would poison their relationship as her ideas had. There was no way back; there never had been.

* * *

"Where are you taking me, witch?" Jarne's voice sounded hoarse from the lack of use. These were the first words spoken since leaving the Witches' Castle behind the previous morning. Sigri's efforts had made a big difference. He was able to sit up by himself, get on his horse with Mae's help, and eat berries, mushrooms, and even some rabbit grilled on a stick over an open fire. But he hadn't spoken—neither curses nor thanks. During the night, Jarne kept moaning. But when awake, he remained mute and watched her. Mae worried that the fever and blood loss had made him simple, but his eyes looked alert and intelligent. He had pale-blue eyes, the color of a winter sky.

"My name is Mae. Actually, it is Mette—Mette Annegret Einarsdóttir, but everybody calls me Mae." Mae didn't know why she had said that. He would only call her witch or worse things, but she craved some friendly conversation. She, too, hadn't spoken since leaving the sisters. Mae had wanted him to talk first. He wouldn't believe anything she said unprompted, but there was a chance he would if he asked.

"Where are you taking me?" Jarne repeated with a note of irritation, not offering his name.

"South," she replied. "There is an empty house, well hidden in the woods, about two days of travel from here. We can rest there for a while."

"Why there?"

"It will take time for you to heal." Mae evaded his question. "My sister tended your wounds and helped you fight the infection with her art, but you are still very weak."

"But why there?" he insisted.

"Where else is there?"

Jarne looked back the way they'd come, asking an unspoken question. Following his gaze, Mae clenched her teeth, and her mood darkened. *So much for conversation.* She decided she was better off without it.

After the mountain descent, Mae and Jarne traveled over empty, moss-covered highlands. No signs of animals or habitation marred the landscape. It felt like they were the last two people in the entire world. A light breeze pushed puffy white clouds across an otherwise clear blue sky. Beyond, in the distance, shimmered the blue sea. *So much blue*, Mae thought.

"Why do you care, wit—" Jarne stopped himself at the last second. Mae glared; she was good at that. He faltered. "Why did you heal me? Why drag me to the end of the world?" His eyes roamed over the emptiness. "Is boiling me in a cauldron more fun when I'm healthy?"

"Boil you in a cauldron?" Mae chuckled in surprise. "Honestly, who do you think I am? All right, don't answer that. But rest assured, I'm not spending that much effort for a meal. I have seen squirrels with more meat on them."

"Then why?" His question was more forceful this time, earning him a coughing fit.

"I promised your mother." That wasn't strictly true, as she hadn't promised anything. *No—his mother burdened me without my consent.* Still, it sounded friendlier this way.

"You knew my mother? How? Why?" More intense coughing followed, and Jarne grabbed his shoulder, pain painted all over his face.

"We can talk later." Mae softened her tone. "I'll answer your questions. For now, save your strength. It wouldn't do if you died after all the trouble we went through to keep you alive."

Jarne looked mulish but kept quiet. His pain seemed intense. Mae pulled her horse closer and handed him a flask.

"Drink. It will help with the pain." When he didn't move, she added, "It isn't poison. If I wanted you dead, things would be so much easier, believe me. I would be back up there." Mae nodded toward the mountains they had come from. "And you wouldn't have suffered. All the pain you feel now is trivial compared to mine, because it can be dulled with a pull from this flask."

They moved on, and Mae watched Jarne out of the corners of her eyes. She was sure he did the same, but neither spoke. Mae was dying to know what went on in his head. Did he think that witches ate people? Or was he overplaying the whole witch thing to get information out of her? Well, he would have to ask again; she wasn't volunteering.

* * *

THE FINE WEATHER held, and the unlikely couple reached the forest's edge late on the fourth day of their journey. Jarne used to feel at home among the trees. He had spent the happiest days of his childhood climbing up their branches, stalking deer, and collecting berries. Most of all, he enjoyed the solitude while wandering on shaded paths. This forest, however, felt very different—old, secretive, and forbidding. Gnarled trees and stunted underbrush formed an almost insurmountable barrier, dissuading the outside world from entering.

Through a small and almost invisible gap in the trees, the witch penetrated the woods and urged her beast forward. Jarne struggled to keep up. As they rode deeper into the strange forest, the light faded, and his horse stumbled. Night sounds soon filled the air. Jarne feared they would fall to their doom if they came upon a cliff or sinkhole in the darkness. In the distance, he heard water splashing and churning. Would they tumble down a waterfall? Without a word, the witch adjusted their path to steer clear of the presumed river's course. Desperate to see ahead, he stood up in his stirrups, and a branch knocked his head.

Jarne had lost all sense of direction when, without warning, the witch slowed her horse and jumped off. Leaving the animal where it stood, she bounded forward. Jarne thought the faint starlight revealed a structure ahead. *Is that the day's destination?* Within seconds, the witch had disappeared from view without tripping or stumbling. He looked around bewildered. *It's so dark, I can barely see my hand in front of my eyes. Do witches have better eyesight?*

Jarne remained on his horse, uneasy about unseen dangers lurking in the darkness. He'd been glancing left and right when a light appeared. A lantern or a candle outlined the window and door of an eerie-looking hut ahead. There was no invitation, but Jarne decided he wasn't spending the night outside, alone in this creepy forest. His heart pounding, he felt his way to a nearby tree, tied the animals to a branch, and inched toward the door.

The cabin comprised a single room with some crudely made furniture. Two candles on a rickety table provided the only illumination. Cobwebs coated the walls and draped the windows. Half-rotten herbs, rusted pots, and all sorts of weird contraptions hung from the low ceiling beams. In one corner, Jarne spotted the dried remains of a dead mouse. He found himself in a quintessential witch's hut. That shouldn't have been a surprise, given the current company. But then, he had always expected forest-dwelling witches to be old and ugly.

Mae lit a fire in the hearth. She straightened up as he entered, brushed her hands on her trousers, and turned around. Old or young, the witch's glare could have curdled milk. Her body language stopped all questions before they had time to form in Jarne's brain. With a jerk of her head, Mae directed Jarne toward the back of the room, where two low cots stood. He followed her gaze and raised his eyebrows, questioning the soundness of the ancient-looking beds with their moldy blankets. The witch's narrowing eyes were all the encouragement he needed. *Was there a glint of red?* Jarne didn't dare to object. He slept on the ground often enough, so he always had that option if the fragile furniture broke under his weight. Without a word, the witch slipped back out, leaving him alone in the creepy hut.

Not knowing what else to do, Jarne went to his assigned cot and sat down, disregarding his earlier trepidations about its stability. The long days of travel had exhausted him, especially since he felt the aftereffects of a severe illness. His memories were fuzzy, lacking most details. But scattered bits and pieces hinted at how the puzzle fit together. He had fought soldiers in Kristiansund when he got injured, and then the witches—more than one, he thought—had done stuff to him. Now he felt better, and she had brought him here. The only problem was that he had no clue where "here" was.

He would only rest for a minute, stretching out his aching body. And then, he needed to plan his escape. He was in a witch's hut, accompanied by a witch, deep inside a bewitched forest. Who wouldn't run away if they had a chance? If he fell asleep, he'd never wake. The witch would do more things to him now that she had lured him to her lair, and this time, it wouldn't be to his benefit. He had to fend her off until sunrise. If only the bed wasn't so comfortable and his eyelids so heavy.

Dappled sunlight shining through a dirty window woke Jarne the following day. He'd had the weirdest dreams of witches, crossbows, fires, mountains, and blueberries. Looking around, Jarne needed a moment to orient himself. The light took away some of the frightening impressions of last night. The house looked more ordinary, if old and abandoned. Mae sat on a stool across from him, skinning a small deer with her sleeves rolled up. Her arms and hands were bloody, and a stern expression showed on her face.

"You came to my village with the soldiers. Why?" Jarne asked without preamble, realizing some aspects of his dreams were his memories.

"I didn't come *with* the soldiers."

"Then why did you come? You were looking for me, weren't you? Did you want to kill me after all?"

"Yes," Mae replied without hesitation, ripping the skin off the deer carcass. Jarne was shocked. He had never expected her to be so blunt. Nothing made sense.

"Why?" he asked, in a much smaller voice.

"You were a threat. You could identify me." Mae looked up from her gruesome task, brandishing the bloody knife. "You could have told the soldiers about me for money or under torture."

"Why didn't you kill me? Why drag me here? Why heal me?"

Mae stood, blood glistening red on her pale skin. "Do you want to be dead?"

"No, please!"

"Then stop asking stupid questions," she snapped before stepping outside.

Jarne shivered. This witch was dangerous. He had to get away. Could he get to the horses? Would he be able to outrun her? He was fast—that is, he used to be fast. He still felt weak, and she looked nimble, too. Panic welled up in his chest.

* * *

Washing off the blood in a rain barrel, Mae closed her eyes and took deep, calming breaths. She had returned home, and the word tasted like acid in her mouth. Her parents chose this spot to escape the troubles and unrest following the Viking invasion. Being a hunter and fur trader, her father always loved the forest. It wasn't until many years later that Mae learned finding better hunting grounds wasn't the predominant reason for this remote location. Regardless, the troubles had found them. This cabin was the place where all of Mae's dreams came to a violent end—where the duke's soldiers killed her family and the dark curse took her.

Mae's body trembled, echoing the bitterness of her memories in a visceral reaction. Left with no place to go after her banishment from the Witches' Castle, she'd decided to return here without considering the toll it would take. Ramming her knife into the scabbard on her belt, the witch forced herself to return inside. One look told her all she needed to know. While she hated being back here and missed her sisters, and while her life was a mess and the wicked Norns had screwed her over, none of this was the boy's fault. Well, he hadn't caused any of that intentionally. So, she made an effort to soften her voice.

"Listen, you aren't dead yet. Does that tell you anything?"

"What do you mean?"

"I don't want to kill you. I spent the last ten days keeping you alive. My sisters banished me for protecting you. So, stop…" Mae squeezed her eyes shut and swallowed, needing to calm her emotions. "Please, believe me. I'm no danger to you."

"Can I go then?"

"You are too weak," Mae replied. "You need to get stronger, and then you can go if you want." What a mess all this was.

"I want to go now." He was stubborn.

"Fine!" Mae hissed. "Go!" What had she expected, eternal gratitude? Why would he care about her life being difficult? He didn't owe her anything. "I'm making game stew," she added in a meek voice. "Do you want to stay for supper?"

"Are you a good cook?"

"Does it matter?" Mae laughed at the childish question, her emotions all over the place. "There isn't a better cook around for leagues and leagues."

"My mother was a great cook," Jarne said, volunteering the first personal information.

"All mothers are. I'm not as good as my mother, probably not as good as yours."

"Where is your mother?"

"Dead! Now, remember what I said about asking stupid questions." The boy fell quiet at once. *You are such a great conversationalist*, Mae thought. *That silver tongue of yours will win him over.*

"Mine too," Jarne said in a small and frightened voice.

"I know, Jarne. I know."

* * *

MAE CONCENTRATED ON preparing the meal. Keeping busy helped her silence all other thoughts. Jarne got up and asked permission to go out.

"I'm not your mother," Mae said, trying to smile. "It's not up to me to tell you what you can and can't do." He looked surprised, mischief twinkling in his eyes. Torn between laughing and telling him off, regardless of her prior declaration, the witch warned, "Don't fall into the river; the current is swift and dangerous. Dinner will be ready in about two hours."

Jarne went to the door, stopped, and turned around. With her head as heavy as a millstone, Mae gave him a curt nod, and the boy stepped out. *There, he's gone, and I'll never see him again,* Mae thought. *And after all the trouble he caused, that would be too soon.*

But the boy came back not long after. The smell of bubbling stew filled the hut. He looked expectantly at the simmering cauldron. *Such an innocent expression.* This time, Mae couldn't help it—she smiled. The two sat at the rickety table, each with a wooden bowl of stew, and ate in silence. Mae knew this wasn't the best meal she had ever eaten, not even close. The kitchen in the Witches' Castle had been much better stocked with herbs and spices. But it was hot and satisfying. Jarne's appetite was back—a good sign. As he put down his bowl, after eating second and third helpings, Mae knew the questions would come again. She would answer this time, and then he would run away, cursing her name. Best to get it over with.

"What do you want to know?" she asked, putting her bowl down.

"Are you a witch, a real witch?"

"Yes."

"An evil witch?" The words tumbled out before he could stop them. He was still a child—naïve and direct to a fault. But then, this was the most important question. Mae took a deep breath and answered.

"I have done things others would call *evil*, and I have done things I would call *good*." Seeing he was more confused, she amended: "I don't enjoy hurting or harming people. I don't want to be evil."

"Why did you try to kill me then?"

"I didn't. You aimed a crossbow at me. I can die as easily as you can. I had no time to explain."

"Explain what?"

"Your mother asked me to protect you."

"You lie!" There was fire in Jarne's tone. "You didn't know my mother. You came to kill me, and when you failed, you made some other plans."

"It's true." Mae tried to calm him. "I didn't know your mother well. I only met her for a few moments. I... She died in my arms. With her last breath, she asked me to protect you, Jarne. That is how I know your name."

"Protect me from what? Protect me from *you*, you mean? You wanted to kill me. And now..."

"Now what?"

"Now you'll put some hex on me to enslave me as your servant or worse."

"Jarne…"

"I want to go now. I ate your food. You said I could go if I wanted. I want to." His voice rose. Mae looked into his eyes and saw upheaval, uncertainty, and loss. For a brief moment, he wavered. Mae held her breath. But then he looked down and repeated, "I want to go now."

There, Mae hated to be right. But hadn't she fulfilled the mother's wish? The boy was safe—safe-ish. Safe from her, at least. The witch stood, and with an immense effort, she steeled her heart and leveled her voice.

"You can stay, or you can go. It's your choice. When you leave, you can take a horse and whatever else you need." She wanted to say *if you leave*, but she had no doubt. Walking toward the door, she added, "I will gather firewood. That way, I won't be able to stop you."

Mae stepped out, leaving the door wide open. Once there, she halted. The sunbeams danced on the leaves, and the warm summer air caressed her cheeks. This clearing could be a lovely place to live under different circumstances. Then, her cruel mind called her back to reality, and she walked away from the cottage, away from the boy.

Farewell, Jarne, she thought, *and be good.*

CHAPTER SEVEN

Evil Deeds

For many hours, Mae meandered through the woods, giving the boy enough time to get away. She knew she couldn't do or say anything to stop him. Still, the witch feared she might have tried regardless. The sun was sinking when she finally returned, laden with dry branches. Jarne was gone. A faint echo of the warmth from happier moments lingered—as it had a decade ago. But too soon, the cold hollowness took over. Mae was the only living being in this accursed dwelling.

Her father had built this house with his own hands. There wasn't a straight angle in the entire construction. The wind blew through the gaps between the logs, and the roof often leaked in a heavy downpour. Still, it had been home, the haven of her childhood—a safe shelter from where to explore the world, pursue adventures, and return to her mother's fabulous meals with dirty hands and scraped knees.

Far away from any settlement, Mae's parents had chosen this spot to raise a family in balance with nature. They never needed much. Her father had been loving, hard working, and always quick with a smile. During the years of unrest and the bitter winters, he never complained, never showed weakness, and they never went hungry. But he also had never told the family he needed to borrow money. Mae's world shattered when the debt collectors came. Soldiers with weapons and steel helmets entered the house uninvited, ransacking it for anything valuable. Her father didn't stop them. Like a bear, he stood in front of his family, protecting what was most valuable to him.

The intruders tore open chests, scattering the content across the floor. A young sergeant was in command. Leaning against the doorframe, he cleaned his nails with a dagger while appraising the women with lewd glances. When it became clear that deerskins and wood carvings didn't suffice to pay off the debt, the sergeant demanded that Eilif, Mae's fourteen-year-old brother, join the king's army in lieu of payment. Her parents refused, and a scuffle broke out, turning into a full-on fight. Chaos enveloped the tiny space as furniture toppled and wood splintered. Pots and pans clattered to the floor. Both children joined the melee to drive off the intruders.

One soldier cracked his head on the hearth. Another broke his neck, crashing into the table. The young sergeant lost an eye before her father lay dead on the floor, his throat slit by a sword stroke. Mae's mother threw herself onto her husband. Uttering an ear-piercing scream of denial, she drove the remaining soldiers from the hut with blood running from their ears and noses, shouting witchcraft as they went.

Mae stood there, the knife in her hand still bloody from slicing into the sergeant's eye. Her entire body felt bruised. Her clothes were torn, but all her attention focused on the lake of crimson spreading on the floor. Her father was dead. Time froze. Seconds passed, or hours—Mae wouldn't know. She hadn't moved. Noises reaching her from the outside didn't make sense; there was yelling, banging, and scraping.

Suddenly, the door burst open again with crossbow bolts zipping through the air. Three bolts hit Mae's mother, where she crouched over her dead husband. Half a dozen soldiers barged in, taking a defensive position with shields up and swords drawn. Then, a woman appeared in the doorway, wearing a long black cloak over an elaborate, floor-length dress of poisonous green. Runes tattooed on her forehead and around her eyes stood out in stark contrast to her pale, ageless skin. Her long, raven-black hair spilled from her hood over her shoulders and bosom. Taking slow and measured steps, she surveyed the gruesome scene in the manner of a proud parent appraising her children's excellent work. Mae attacked. She didn't care about the consequences. She had to make this woman pay, and the soldiers, and everybody else involved.

"None of that," the woman said, stopping Mae midstride with a lazy flick of her hand. "You stay where you are." Her voice was calm, displaying only the slightest disapproval, like a governess scolding her charge. Mae couldn't move a muscle. "And you, boy," the black witch continued, curling her finger, "come with me."

Her magic forced Eilif to step forward against his will. Mae fought with all her might. Her parents lay dead or dying on the floor. Soldiers abducted her brother. Still, Mae could only watch as her world imploded. The black witch turned her head and smiled.

"You are a fierce little girl, aren't you? I should bring you as well." Looking from Mae, to her dead mother, to Eilif, and back to Mae, she added, "What an interesting family. I'm so glad I came on this little excursion. There was power in your mother, rest her soul. And there is power in you, too. A few coins given, and in return, we get two recruits: one for the king and one for myself."

Mae didn't care for the woman's ramblings. She wasn't a little girl. She was seventeen, and she would show her. She would kill her. She would…

"You can't fight me." The sorceress chuckled. "You have neither the strength nor the skill to challenge one of Death's Daughters. But I can teach you." Her voice was as sweet as the smell of meat gone bad. "Wouldn't you like to learn?"

Eilif had reached the door. Two soldiers rushed to bind his hands and pulled a sack over his head. The sergeant had covered his bleeding eye with a hasty patch. His remaining eye stared unblinking at Mae as his men dragged her brother away. As long as she lived, the witch would never forget that look of fear and betrayal on Eilif's face before they pulled the cloth down.

With her little brother gone and her parents dead, Mae's fury focused on the black witch. The evil woman followed the proceedings with contemptuous amusement. Mae would have given everything she had, everything she was, to wipe that self-satisfied smile off the witch's face. Torturing her muscles to the point of breaking, Mae fought her entrapment. The knife was still in her hand. It had been a name-day present for her brother Eilif. Delicate runes decorated the blade. Mae's finger pressed onto the edge, causing the metal to bite into her flesh. As her blood flowed across the engravings, something in Mae broke free. With a roar of defiance, she overcame the binding spell, rushed forward, and plunged her weapon to the hilt into the witch's chest.

The two women went down, rolling on the floor like feral dogs. Mae wanted to pull the knife out and ram it back in. She wasn't sure the blade had been long enough to inflict mortal harm. But the vile woman held Mae's hand in place. Their eyes met, and the black witch's stare bore into Mae with pure and undiluted venom. The witch hissed a curse, spraying Mae with blood and spittle. The words didn't make sense, sounding like a foreign language. Still, Mae's ears rang with an unnatural echo. For a few heartbeats, nothing happened. Then, Mae gagged as her body convulsed in agony. An iron fist squeezed her intestines. Her entire skin burned like she had plunged into ice. She couldn't scream, couldn't move, couldn't breathe.

Cold, invisible hands squeezed Mae's throat. Her head threatened to explode. She fought to get free, to stay conscious. Yet inexorably, her strength failed, and all went black.

When Mae regained consciousness, the black sorceress was gone, but her terrible touch lingered. Nauseated, Mae pushed herself onto all fours and crawled to her parents. Her mother lay on her dead husband, blood running from her mouth. Mae lifted her head with shaking hands.

"Mae? I can't see you." The whisper was barely louder than a falling leaf.

"Shhh, I'm here." Tears poured down Mae's cheeks as she cradled her mother in her arms.

"I'm so sorry."

"It's not your fault," Mae replied without knowing what her mother apologized for.

"You must be... strong!" Her mother coughed more blood. "Don't let... cruelty destroy you. Find... happiness."

"But how?" Mae howled in agony.

"Trust yourself, believe... Be *good*." The injured woman tried to smile before a gurgling cough rocked her torso. Dark blood spilled from her mouth. Mae's whole body shook as her mother's breathing got fainter and fainter until, too soon, it stopped.

Mae wept throughout the night, holding on to her mother—to the last remnant of her family, her happiness, her life. When the sun rose, Mae's throat was raw, and her eyes swollen. Numbing emptiness filled her. There had been so many deaths that day. She wished she'd died then, too.

And I have. The naïve girl with dreams, hopes, and happiness died that day.

In her stead, a black witch wandered the earth, evil and bitter, carrying those long-forgotten echoes of her prior existence. And now she was back, at the cursed place where it had all happened, alone and without any purpose.

Mae didn't want to remember. All that had happened so long ago—over a decade. Yet every day, as long as Mae lived, she would feel the evil curse. Shivering, she curled on the cot, hugging her knees to her chest and wishing she could fade away. *I'm long overdue; no one would mourn me—neither my sisters nor the boy.*

The boy, Jarne—at least he was better off. He would have died the night of the ambush or that day in the village when he charged the soldiers. She had rescued him, seen to his health, fed him, and brought him to safety. Thanks to her, he could live his life and make his own choices. Thus, Mae had fulfilled his mother's dying wish. This tiny light of hope, a flickering candle in a raging storm, filled her heart and eased her mind into a bitterly needed sleep.

All the stress and emotional upheaval of the last weeks fell off, and oblivion took her.

* * *

There was no rest for the wicked. Only seconds later, or at least it felt that way, rough hands around her throat woke Mae.

"What have we here?"

Jarne? No, the voice was deeper, the hands were bigger, and the breath smelled foul of rancid meat and stale ale. Instinctively, Mae cast a defensive spell. The man jumped back, his hands burning like he touched glowing coals.

"We'll be having none of that!" a second man shouted, kicking her hard in the stomach. Mae gasped in pain. Another kick followed. The man knelt on her chest, pressing a blade to her throat. "This knife is silver. I'll open your throat from ear to ear if you move so much as a finger."

Mae swallowed her groans of pain. Confused and disoriented, she couldn't help but wonder about the reference to silver. Did they believe she was a werewolf?

"Get over here and bind her hands," her assailant barked to his comrade.

"I'm not going near her," complained the man who had touched her first. "She burned me."

"And I'll spill your guts if you don't. So, what will it be?" Pressing the knife tip harder against her throat, the man pricked her skin, and blood rolled down her neck. "Now, you will be very quiet." He ripped a piece of cloth from her sleeve and yelled, "Open your filthy mouth, witch!"

Mae obeyed, and he rammed the gag deep. The second man had found some twine and started to bind her hands. The rope was rough, and he pulled it very tight, cutting off her circulation. Then, he tied her legs as well.

"We caught ourselves a witch," the man with the knife exclaimed. "A real witch! There's good money in that. And she is young, a bit scrawny, but we could still have some fun before she burns."

"You can't be serious! She's a witch. Your prick will fall off if you force her."

"Pity, but you are probably right. But we could look." He rolled Mae onto her back with a shove of his boots. "Cut her a little"—his grin widened—"and put some hot coals in her pants."

"Yeah, she burned me."

"And what about her toes? Should we cut them off?"

"Her toes? Why?"

"Can't hurt."

"Will hurt *her*."

"That's kind of the point, idiot. Oh look, her eyes are full of fire." The man knelt and put his filthy hand on her inner thigh. "She likes the idea of coals in her pants... or something else in her pants." His hand moved higher, and Mae shuttered in disgust. "Later, my darling. I'll let you pine for my attention a little bit longer. I'm thirsty and hungry; I'll see to these needs first. Please don't go anywhere. I'll come back to you."

Then he dragged her by her hair off the mattress and onto the floor. Another kick to her abdomen sent spasms of pain through her body. He must have cracked a rib or two this time.

The other man stoked the embers in the hearth and added new firewood. Flickering light flooded the hut, and the shadows painted her assailants' faces even more diabolical.

"There is a stack of firewood, and she cleaned up." Mae's assailant nodded. "This house was a mess the last time we came through here. She is good at this household stuff. Wouldn't it be nice to have a servant?"

"She is a witch! We must bring her to the duke and collect the bounty before she turns us into toads."

"Stop being such a craven. And we aren't taking her to the duke. We'll take her to the king. His Majesty's black sorceress is always welcoming to any of her sisters."

"That hag is evil. I'm not going near her."

"Do you think she will see you? She doesn't deal with the likes of us. That doesn't mean her people won't pay us."

Still suffering the agonizing pain from the beating and fighting to breathe, a cold chill ran down Mae's spine. Not only would her death be a prolonged and excruciating affair, but it would also include *her*—the witch who had cursed her. How poetic that her maker would unmake her.

* * *

THE TWO MEN sat at the table, eating their travel rations and smoking foul-smelling pipes, their dirty boots only inches away from her face. One was tall and broad with arms like tree trunks and an uneven stubble of red hair. The other was shorter and lean. Wavy black hair framed a pointed face. From time to time, he looked at Mae, giving her a wink and a cruel smile. Mae recoiled, racking her brain for any magic that could save her. But with her hands bound, her mouth gagged, and her entire body hurting, she couldn't cast any spell to overpower both men before they slit her throat.

The hut's door creaked open. Both men jumped up, facing the entrance. Nobody came in. Only predawn's faint glow shone through the open door. *It must have been the wind.*

"What are you waiting for? Close the door," the presumed leader with the cruel fantasy barked.

"Why me?"

"Because I said so. Is there anybody else?"

"You. Close the door yourself."

"You don't have the wits to piss straight. Without me, you would have been hanged a dozen times over. But even with your limited faculties, you should have realized by now: I'm the brain, and you are the muscle."

"What's that supposed to mean?"

"It means I tell you what to do, and you do it."

"Or what?"

"Or I will cut you open when you sleep and strangle you with your own stinking guts. Now, close the door!"

The red-haired man shuffled to the entrance, sending dirty looks toward his companion. Instead of closing the door, he opened it wide to look outside. A small river rock flew through the air, hitting him straight on the forehead. Dazed, he stumbled back two steps before a second stone smashed into his face, breaking his nose. Seeking shelter, the man retreated further and tripped over his stool. He landed in front of Mae, his head slamming the packed dirt floor with a dull sound. Mae clambered onto him. Pressing her bound hands onto his bleeding face, she yanked his life force in a single heartbeat.

Despite all his lofty words, the black-haired man wasn't much brighter. He crouched under the window, trying to spot their attacker. He didn't spare a single thought for his comrade, dismissing what a bound witch could do. Mae took advantage of his diverted attention. She pulled her gag free and untied her feet. Whispering a spell, she set the ropes that bound her hands on fire, ripped them apart, and extinguished the flames. The smell of burned rope got the first man's attention.

He started toward her, his silver knife flashing. Mae dodged, sending the firewood flying. Yet, the wood couldn't gather enough momentum in the tight confines to incapacitate him. He grunted, pushing through the maelstrom.

Then he was on her again, kicking the legs out under her.

Mae fell sideways, slamming her head onto a wooden beam.

His knife jabbed toward her torso, and she deflected the weapon with her left forearm. The blade sliced to the bone. Pain exploded.

Desperate, Mae slapped his face, burning his cheeks with the same hex she'd used earlier. He backhanded her, sending Mae to the floor, her vision blurring.

The attacker loomed over the defenseless witch, preparing for the kill.

In the meantime, and unbeknownst to either combatant, the hut's door had opened again. A slender figure entered, arm raised, and threw a rock. The projectile glanced off the back of Mae's attacker with enough impact to make him stumble.

Instead of finishing Mae with a well-placed stab to the heart, the man turned toward his new opponent. That was all the opening Mae needed. She kicked hard at the back of his legs, forcing him to his knees. A second kick to his head sent his face smacking into the dirt.

Screaming in pain, Mae crawled over and grabbed his hair. She lifted his head and slammed it down with fury.

Dazed, he struggled to get up, but Mae had her knee between his shoulder blades. Over and over again, she bashed his face into the ground. Blood spurted from his broken nose and split lips, and a nauseating, wet thumping filled the hut.

When his cries became muffled moans, she let go of his head. Her whole body shook. With a herculean effort, Mae rolled him on his back. Straddling his chest, she pushed her thumbs deep into his eye sockets. Inhuman sounds escaped his bloody mouth.

Savoring his agony, the witch ripped his soul out, howling in delight like the mad werewolf they had thought her to be.

An Accommodation

JARNE STOOD IN the door, rooted to the spot, not believing what his eyes had witnessed. In his beloved childhood stories, brave men fought men with axes and shields on the field of battle. Never was there any mention of cowards attacking women with fists and knives in a dark hut in the woods. And he definitely knew no stories about what he had seen Mae—the witch—do. When she looked at him, a sinister fire glowing red-hot in her eyes, she exuded the undisguised joy of pure evil. He was staring into hell's deepest pits from whence this demon had sprung. Jarne dropped his remaining stones, turned, and ran.

* * *

SEVERAL MINUTES PASSED before Mae surfaced from her state of vindictive rage. Her entire body hurt. Blood covered her face and torso; not all was hers. Still, she bled from at least three wounds. A crimson stream ran down Mae's forearm, dripping from her fingertips. A couple of her ribs were bruised, some probably cracked, and her face felt like a battering ram had kissed her. Shaking her head slowly to clear the fog, Mae needed a few moments to recollect what had happened. She'd killed two men of the vilest sort in self-defense. But she'd also given herself up to her base instincts, relishing in the act. The witch had taken her cruel revenge, and he had seen her—Jarne.

Jarne had come back. No, not only that—he'd rescued her. Mae would be dead or worse if it wasn't for him. But then, he'd witnessed firsthand her evil deeds. She wasn't a tame witch with a slight good-and-evil problem. Jarne had seen a fiend from hell, a nightmare of the ugliest kind. As the boy stared in shock at the gory scene, Mae saw disbelief and betrayal etched into his face—reminding her of the last time she saw her brother. Mae needed to go after him. *And then what? Shall I lure him back with cookies?*

Jarne was long gone.

The witch slumped, pain and despair threatening to overwhelm her when a thought swam into focus. *His mother's last words.* She had been right. Mae had needed Jarne; he'd saved her. So now, they were even, and both could go their separate ways.

Careful to avoid further aggravating her many injuries, Mae got to her feet. She cleaned and bandaged her forearm. The cut was deep but hadn't severed any tendons. With her ribs aching, Mae changed her clothes. She missed Sigri. What would she give for a skilled healer caring for her wounds—a good friend, a true sister? And she missed Renya too. Although, that sister would have bitten Mae's head off for being caught unaware by two unwashed brutes. The gray witch always surrounded herself with magic wards and concealed hexes. But Mae was in the middle of a remote forest. And anyhow, those hexes would have hurt Jarne when he returned.

Jarne was gone for good, and so were Sigri and Renya. *What's the point of torturing my mind with all these thoughts?* Focusing on more practical issues, Mae tossed the corpses into the river after dragging them with the horse's help. She'd planned to hunt for food next, but discarding the bodies had intensified her pain. Dizzy and short of breath, Mae limped back to her hut, crawled onto the cot, and let exhaustion take her.

* * *

THE SUN WAS already sinking when the witch woke again. Her stomach rumbled; she hadn't eaten since the previous day's game stew. Weary and slow, Mae shuffled toward the entrance, intending to forage for food in the fading light. Opening the door, she stopped in surprise and rubbed her eyes in confusion. Food lay on her doorstep: berries, mushrooms, nuts, and apples. Unsure about trusting her sight, she bent down to touch the unexpected treasure. It was real, and the berries tasted sweet. *Since when do witches get baited with sweets?* Looking around, she spotted a pair of eyes high up in a nearby tree.

"Thank you!" Mae shouted and picked up the gifts. Ensuring the door remained wide open, she stepped back inside, lit the candles, and started a fire. With deliberate care, the witch rearranged the furniture. The better of the two beds went between the hearth and the still-open door. She put all the best blankets on it, leaving her cot bare in the back corner. After hauling water from the river, Mae chopped the apples, mushrooms, and nuts to make a forest soup. She also sorted the herbs and found a few to brew tea. Then, she waited. Darkness had fallen in earnest, owls hooted in the distance, the hut smelled of herbs and apples, and a shy boy stepped through the door. Mae's heart leaped. Still, she tried to be very calm and nonthreatening.

"I've put your bed over here. You'll be warm, but there is nothing between you and the door. I'll stay back there." Mae gestured toward the far corner without taking her eyes off him, fearing the boy would disappear if she did. "And there is tea. Do you like tea? We don't have cups, but we can drink from the bowls."

"Why?" The single word hung in the air, challenging the world to reveal all its secrets.

"Why don't we have cups? Don't know. Misplaced them, I guess," she answered. He looked irritated. Apparently, this wasn't the right time for wisecracks yet.

"Why did you do all this?" he clarified.

"I don't want you to be frightened."

"That might be a bit too late," he said, his voice stern but with the tiniest hint of sarcasm.

"The forest is big and very dark at night. You might not feel safe out there."

"And I should feel safe in here?" This time, there was no trace of humor.

"I wish you would. No, wait!" Mae's words tumbled out rushed, tripping over her tongue. Taking a deep breath, she continued in a slow and even voice. "I wish you could. I know you won't, not yet, maybe not ever. But I wish you could."

"Why?"

"I once had a brother. He was taken from me when he was about your age." Mae now gestured to the table and chairs, inviting Jarne to sit, indicating this might be a longer story. Jarne didn't move, so she continued. "I couldn't protect him back then. You reminded me of him when I first saw you, trapped by the branch. That's why I let you go. I didn't want to hurt you."

"But you came after me. You changed your mind. You realized I wasn't him?"

"It's complicated. *I'm* complicated. Can we eat first?" Mae pleaded. "To answer all your questions, that will take some time."

"But to kill me, that would be quick?"

"I'm not going to kill you."

"Because you 'promised' my mother?" he asked.

"In your village, yes, because of that. But now, because I don't want to. I'm sorry for what you have seen me do."

"You killed those men. You murdered them, and you enjoyed it. Isn't that true?" His voice rose under stress, and his eyes reflected fear and revulsion.

"They attacked me because I'm a witch. I'm still alive because I'm a witch." Then, Mae corrected herself. "No, I'm still alive because you came to rescue me. Thank you, Jarne."

A long silence followed. Mae held her breath. Jarne's face gave nothing away.

Finally, the boy stepped in and closed the door. They sat at either end of the table, drank tea, and ate the soup. Neither of them spoke much. Mae sensed apprehension and uncertainty in Jarne. But there seemed to be curiosity, too. *Even longing?* In the end, he stayed for the night. Mae wasn't sure what changed his mind. Did he trust her enough, or was staying in the wicked witch's hut the lesser evil compared to sleeping in a creepy forest? Was he simply too tired to care? Regardless, Jarne went to bed shortly after dinner and fell asleep.

The witch also went to bed on her side of the cottage. Yet, her sleep was slow in coming. She wondered about Jarne, her unlikely savior. He'd come back knowing Mae was a witch. She'd told him she had intended to kill him at one point, and he questioned the entire story about the promise to his mother. Still, he'd come back and attacked two very violent grown men. *What a strange boy.* And with this thought, Mae, too, sank into sleep.

The next couple of days went by with minimal conversation. Instead, the two established a pattern of sharing the chores and giving each other space. Mae went hunting and prepared the food. Jarne fetched water and firewood and started repairs on the hut. In the evenings, they patched their clothes and kept their thoughts to themselves. Both had recent horrors from which to recover.

Day by day, the ghost of that terrible night faded away, and the mood lightened. Jarne opened up, talking about his life in the fishing village. In return, Mae spoke about her childhood in the forest with her little brother. He had been a brat and a constant pain in the behind. There were some laughs. Yet, too soon, all stories reached the point where levity disappeared, and tragedy followed. They tried sailing around these unpleasant topics, shifting the conversation. But neither of them was fooled. One afternoon, after they had eaten a slightly burned mess that Mae called "blueberry pie," another of these awkward moments arose. Jarne attacked the topic head on.

"What is it like to be a witch?"

"Simply magical," Mae replied, her voice laden with sarcasm.

"No, tell me." He looked at her without blinking.

"I don't want to talk about it," she snapped.

"I know, but I think you should."

"Oh, thank you, wise one," Mae jeered. "What would I do without your sage advice?" To her surprise, she saw honesty and open-mindedness on his face, not hatred or disgust. So, she relented. "Why do you want to know?"

"Because you *are* a witch."

"Thank you again. I hadn't noticed."

Now, he looked annoyed. Mae took a deep breath and continued.

"It is different for everyone. My mother was a witch, too. She knew herbs and healing. She might have been a green witch."

"Green witch?"

"Like Sigri, my sister in the mountains who healed you."

"I don't remember that."

"I wouldn't think so," Mae said. "And anyhow, it doesn't make any difference. All I'm saying is that my mother seemed perfectly normal to me. For a long time, I didn't even know that her abilities were special. We lived far away from civilization, from anyone else. Still, there was nothing 'witchy' about her." Mae's eyes lost focus as she remembered a warm and caring woman who loved to sing and make silly faces. "I might have been the same," she whispered. "I'd felt something as I grew older, a connection with the forest, a link to the creatures within."

Mae remained silent for a long minute, looking past Jarne to the hearth, where the pots and herbs hung from the ceiling beam. Then, a dark shadow forced its way into her memories, and bitterness dripped into her voice.

"I could have learned so much from my mother," Mae snarled, "if she hadn't... if I hadn't..." Squeezing her eyes shut, she turned around, wishing he would go away.

"What happened?" Jarne asked, insisting that she spell it out.

Mae clenched her fists; she didn't want to go there again—not there, not then, not to satisfy the inappropriate curiosity of this child. Why was he torturing her? She needed to go outside—to escape it all. But the wind had picked up, swirling sinister clouds overhead and shaking the trees. Heavy droplets pelted the window. Mae pulled the door wide, staring into the downpour. Rivers gushed from leaf to leaf, forming a miniature ocean in front of the house.

Behind her, Jarne didn't speak. He didn't move. He sat, waiting. This situation balanced on a knife's edge; any false move could tip it. Wrenching herself away, Mae turned around.

"Most witches are regular women with knowledge and different skills," she hissed. "They are as good or bad as everyone else. My mother never hurt a living soul. But not me." Mae whispered so loudly that the echo bounced from the wooden beams. "I'm the wicked witch. I was cursed to kill, here, in this house—cursed to be a black witch. Happy? Is that what you wanted to know?" Her eyes blazed with anger Jarne didn't deserve. Still, she let it out on him.

"A demonic essence resides inside me, driving me to despicable acts!" she bellowed. "It roils my anger, controls my thoughts, urges me to hurt people, and makes me scream at silly boys."

Jarne blanched, fear flickering across his face. Still, he didn't shy away. With apparent effort, he reasserted his composure. Only the tiniest tremor colored his voice as he continued.

"You aren't evil, not entirely evil," he stated. "You can't be. You saved me."

"I've saved one boy!" Mae cackled. "And that makes me a *good* person?" She stepped closer. "Saving one life is my salvation after I've killed dozens?" Another step closer. "One boy who's too stupid to run away from the most dangerous creature in the forest?" Reaching the table, she loomed over him. "I don't know if saving such an imbecile even counts as *good*."

Now, he looked frightened. Now, he tried to push back from the table, but it was too late. The witch bore down on him.

"Old folks call my kind Death's Daughters. Do you know why?" The witch placed her hands on the uneven surface, leaning in closer. "I suck the souls out of living humans to stay alive. Is that evil enough for you?" she whispered, venom dripping from every syllable. Her eyes burned red. Her grin showed too many teeth. "The longer I go without killing, the darker my thoughts become—until I stop seeing people, and they simply become prey."

Jarne gaped, unable to move.

"I hate killing!" the witch shrieked, her whole body trembling. "Yet still, I do it. Innocent men, women, or children." She leered at him. "I killed them all! Villages burned, ships sank, and families disappeared because of me. I do everything I need to keep existing!"

Her breathing quickened. Her skin burned. Mae felt the overpowering urge to attack him, to show this gullible boy what kind of witch she was. With a loud crack, the wooden table split under her hands. Squeezing her eyes shut, Mae stepped backward, struggling to calm her rage. Raising the palms of her outstretched hands, she needed all her strength to fight the dark impulse.

"You don't know me!" the witch shouted. "I'm the villain of your stories, the demon of your nightmares. Remember what you've seen me do!" She grabbed the door frame for support. "When I lose control... I'm not safe."

The wind whipped her shirt, raindrops pelting her back.

"I can't defeat the evil inside me," Mae muttered, barely audible over nature's fury. "And you... You should get away from me... while you still can."

With that, she stepped out into the deluge, leaving the stunned boy behind.

* * *

MAE DIDN'T GO far, only a few strides away from the hut. Rain splattered her face, sending icy torrents running past her neck, into her shirt, and down her body. She hated it all: this place, these memories, and most of all herself. Two horses stood tied to a tree not far from her. The witch envied them—dumb beasts that only cared for food and water and one more thing when it was the right season. She was neither beast nor human. Her curse drove her to despicable acts, demanding violent satisfaction. But her conscience, her soul, made her pay for it.

She didn't know how long she stood there; it felt like hours. Mae had nowhere to be. Standing here was as reasonable as anything else she could do.

Should I go a bit further? The boy wouldn't leave in this weather. But if the rain stopped and she wasn't nearby, he might finally take the hint and run away.

Contemplating where to go, the witch felt a hand on her shoulder—a light touch, not a threat. Looking around, bewildered, she saw Jarne. Standing beside her, he held a blanket over his head. Their eyes met at almost the same height. Still, Mae couldn't read his expression. Rivers of water flooded her eyes, not all from the rain.

"Come back in," Jarne said. Not a command nor a plea, but more of an encouragement. "You'll catch your death out here."

Mae blinked, like she had surfaced after a dive, but didn't move. They looked at each other, two lost souls in the middle of a remote forest, slowly being drowned by heavy rain. Then, to her utter astonishment, Jarne took her hand and pulled her back inside. Mae followed without remembering her decision to do so.

Jarne closed the door. He piled dry blankets onto the table and turned around. Apparently, she was to get out of her wet clothes, and he was affording her the necessary privacy.

Mae marveled at his chivalrous behavior.

After all the horrible things that had happened, the vile acts he'd witnessed, and the nasty truths I've thrown at him? The beginning of a smile tugged at her lips as she undressed and wrapped herself in the blankets. Sitting down, she waited, eager to see what would happen next.

The noise of her dragging the chair signaled Jarne that it was safe to turn around. He looked into her eyes. Then he glanced down at her blanket-wrapped body and blushed deep red. Hurrying to her discarded clothes, he hung them up to dry. Next, he added more logs to the fire.

Mae watched his every move, not saying a word. When he'd run out of things to straighten, clear away, or tend to, Jarne handed her a bowl of what looked like tea. Since her hands held the blankets, he put the bowl onto the table and stepped back, looking at his feet. Mae ignored the tea, her eyes never leaving his face. A long silence followed, accompanied by the crackling of the fire. Water dripped from her clothes.

"I don't know if I used the right herbs," Jarne admitted. "I didn't pay attention last time when you made the tea. I don't know if there is enough or too little in the bowl." He rambled on. Mae remained silent, tilting her head, while he fidgeted with the hem of his shirt.

"Men can be evil, too," Jarne blurted out. "My father, he was evil. He was a drunkard, and he beat my mother. He would have beaten me, too. Only, he couldn't catch me," he added with pride. "I don't know if my brothers were evil. Soldiers took them when I was little and pressed them into the king's army. They might have died; I don't know. They never came back." He spoke in a rush, not seeming to breathe between words. "But my neighbors were evil. My mom fell sick, and nobody helped. They closed their doors. They wanted my mother to die. Me, too, I guess. There were foul rumors. I hate the lot of them... They are evil!" Jarne shouted the last words.

Abashed by his outburst, he looked down. Averting her gaze for the first time, Mae blew on her tea, allowing the boy to compose himself.

"You're right... I don't know *you*," he continued. "I only know what you have done. You have cared for me."

Now, it was her time to speak. She tried to push the emotions away.

"I needed to heal you because *I* injured you."

"But it was in self-defense. Your instincts were true. I would have shot you."

"I could have diverted the bolt or ripped the crossbow from your arms."

"But there was no time," he protested. "The what-ifs only come to your mind afterward. You were afraid for your life, weren't you?"

Was he seeking confirmation? Was he giving her a way out? Was he implying she could be afraid, like a human?

"You could have walked away," Jarne ventured. "And your sisters, they didn't like what you did. I can't remember much, but you hinted afterward. They wouldn't have saved me."

It felt so good to be praised, like the summer's sunshine on bare skin. And because of that, she needed to stop this boy before he forgot who she was.

"Your father, your neighbors," Mae challenged. "Did you ever see them do anything like what you saw me do?"

He shuttered; there was still some sense in his muddled brain.

"I have never seen anything like that, and I pray to the gods that I will never see something like that again." His voice became a whisper, like speaking it aloud would bring down the doom on him. "But they attacked you. I didn't see it all. I only heard your screams and their laughter." Color had flooded his face again, but his eyes burned even fiercer. "They were vile people, and they were planning vile things. They deserved what they got."

"Nobody deserves that," the witch responded with disgust. "I could have ended them quicker. I didn't because something inside me enjoyed their pain. Deep down, I am evil."

She lowered her gaze, ashamed and sickened by her admission. This time, Jarne's eyes rested on Mae's face, reading her distress.

"Maybe," he started, "you did evil that night because their foul words and actions had made you do evil upon them." Jarne leaned forward, putting his hands on the table, palms up. "But that's not who *you* are. An evil person wouldn't try so hard to be good."

Mae couldn't take it any longer. His encouragement, well meant, cut her like a torturer's glowing knives. How she yearned for his words to be true. From the day the curse took her, she had fought to remain human. She'd always wanted to regain her former life, to be good—to be the person he thought her to be. She wasn't. She was a danger to him—to everyone. The pile of corpses she'd left along her way was irrefutable evidence. *Only one way to make him understand.*

"Look at me!" The witch stood, toppling the chair. "I'm a black witch; I've killed more people than live in your village!" With a powerful gust of air, she threw open the door and the window. The candles went out, the blankets fell off, and the firelight painted her body in flames of hell. No more masks, no more hiding. Her body trembled, yet her eyes burned with enough fire to scorch a hole in reality. "I came to kill you, remember?" The rain had drenched her bandages, sending blood down her forearm. Pointing her crimson finger at Jarne's shoulder, Mae snarled, "I may have spared your life, but I killed your mother."

Jarne recoiled, toppling over backward. Getting back up, he grabbed a knife from the table, holding it with outstretched arms. Mae saw his face, frozen in disbelief, thaw as the weight of the revelation settled. A flicker of molten fury ignited in his eyes, sending shockwaves to his shaking hands. Finally, she had gotten through to him.

"But, you said..." he shouted. "You said she asked you to save me? You said she died in your arms?" His entire body trembled in rage. The knife gleamed in the firelight. It was that same knife with the runes that had started it all.

"I went searching for you," Mae admitted in a toneless voice, her menace replaced by dejection. "I found her lying on the filthy bed. I listened to her last words. And then, I took her life. That is all I'm good at. I am cursed, I am a curse, I am *evil*."

Stepping closer, she let her hands fall to the side, offering her bare chest as an inviting target for his knife thrust. Jarne stared in disbelief, gripping the blade's handle so tight that his knuckles shone white. His lips quivered, and Mae saw tears welling in his eyes.

"She was so sick, in so much pain," Jarne wailed, dropping the knife. "She would have died soon." Violent tremors rocked his body, making him stutter. "I didn't have the money. We couldn't afford the medicine. It is all my fault!" he screamed. Sinking to the floor, the boy buried his face in his hands. "She is dead because of me. It is all my fault."

Heaving sobs rattled his chest, rendering him incoherent—a child in utter despair. Jarne was alone, guilt ridden, and frightened. And finally, Mae realized the truth. It wasn't that he didn't care whether she was evil. He didn't *want* her to be evil. Because she was the only person in the world that he had left. She'd cared for him, and he wanted to be cared for, because he was still a child who had lost his mother. That's why he hadn't run away, that's why he had come back, that's why he had saved her. He needed her.

And her? To keep fighting and break her curse—to remain human—she needed him, too.

Mae picked up the blankets and closed the door. Very carefully, she approached Jarne. Kneeling beside him, she threw one blanket over them and embraced him. He flinched, his body convulsing from the pain.

"Listen to me, Jarne. It was *not* your fault," Mae whispered. "You did all you could. You were so brave." Her free hand stroked his damp, unruly hair, trying to brush away all the hurt. "I have you now. Your mother asked me to protect you, and I will."

She squeezed his shoulders. Holding on to a fellow human, the witch gathered her strength before challenging the world with a solemn vow.

"Jarne Ólafsson, hear me well. As long as my heart keeps beating and blood runs through my veins, I swear I'll protect you! As long as my lungs draw breath and my chest rises and falls, I swear I'll keep you safe! By all my powers and all my being—by my unbending soul—I swear I'll never abandon you!"

Emotions overcame Mae, and she started crying in earnest, too. Jarne melted into her. There, they sat together, holding each other and sharing their grief, yet lending each other strength and soothing their pain.

Is this my chance for redemption? Mae thought. *A witch caring for an orphan boy? We're quite a pair—two lost souls the world has chewed up and spit out—daring fate together.*

OF LIVING AND KILLING

"A choice between killing and dying is no choice at all.
You have to be realistic about these things."

– *Logen Ninefingers*[1]

---

[1] Joe Abercrombie (2007), Before They Are Hanged

CHAPTER NINE

For the Greater Good

MAE PEEKED OVER the crater rim, peering down to the circular lake and the small meadow beyond, a sigh of relief escaping her mouth. Her quarry had arrived, finally.

She'd waited three days, camping in the open, before the welcoming creak of poorly greased axles signaled her target's imminent arrival. *Two carts and at least four guards,* she pondered. *A larger group than expected.* Mae needed to be careful. With over an hour until sunset, that meant more waiting. Mae was never patient, even in the best of times. Yet, having delayed her foray as long as possible, these times were far from the best, and she started to regret her decision.

Nestled in a bend of the Western Road, the flat patch below had become a popular way-stop for eastbound traffic. The lake offered crystal-clear water, and the stunted trees across the road provided firewood for a comfortable night's rest before the arduous climb over the mountain passes. Lucky hunters might even catch the occasional game bird or rabbit.

Hiding behind the crater walls, Mae watched the sun sinking behind the horizon, and she let her mind wander. Three years had passed since she confronted Jarne with the truth about his mother's death. That night, a fierce battle had raged inside her chest, almost tearing her apart between her loneliness and her disgust of her cursed existence. The witch had screamed, trying to make him see her for what she was, doing her best to frighten him away.

To Mae's surprise and relief, Jarne hadn't left.

In the beginning, Mae thought of him as her little brother. Soon, however, he grew taller than her, changing the dynamic not entirely to her liking.

Sometimes, they jested and bantered as if the last thirteen cursed years hadn't happened to Mae. Jarne talked about his hopes and dreams for a better world. Mae didn't share his optimism. Still, she wanted to give him as normal a life as possible, which included concealing most of her dark nature from him.

She didn't fool Jarne; he knew exactly why she had to leave for a few days on a handful of occasions. Still, he played along, not asking her for details. To minimize the risk, Mae changed her approach, putting her vendetta against the duke on hold. Instead, she targeted criminals like those in the prisoner carts below.

As the sun disappeared behind the Smoking Mountains, the soldiers started a fire, settling in for the night. The dancing flames pulled Mae from her reverie. She crept along the crater walls, descending with care over the treacherous gravel field.

This convoy came from the nearby town of Kralsvik—the northernmost settlement of the southern province. Once a month, a magistrate from Makevinger traveled north to hear petitions, pronounce judgments, and sentence prisoners. Serious crimes like rape or murder used to carry the death penalty. However, the Viking invaders had brought the concept of enthrallment from their lands. Men and women could lose their freedom and become thralls—slaves for life—as punishment. And the duke's mills and copper mines always needed laborers.

Mae despised the practice. In killing a convicted criminal before he reached the mines, she accomplished three goals in one stroke. She upheld the old law, rejecting the foreign concept of slavery. She deprived the duke of a worker to boost his riches. And, of course, she satisfied her inner demons—her craving for life force to sustain her existence—with minimal evil.

Reaching level ground about fifty paces from the prisoner carts, Mae saw their silhouettes backlit by the campfire. The wheeled cages seemed much larger than usual; two horses had pulled each. Unharnessed, the animals stood tethered near the lake, feeding on hay and oats while noises of merriment drifted over from the soldiers. *Only the prisoners must go hungry tonight.*

Mae crept closer yet stayed hidden until the soldiers went to sleep, and the quiet covered the night like a blanket. One guard remained on watch, his back toward her. It was time; Mae's fingers had grown numb from squeezing the hilt of her belt knife in anticipation. *What if there is more than one in each cage?* The thought entered Mae's mind unbidden. She had to risk it—her life energy was running out. Approaching the nearest wagon, Mae took a chunk of bread from her bag, intending to offer it to a prisoner. Once she made skin-to-skin contact, she would harvest what she came for and be on her way before anyone was the wiser.

The carts stank of sweat and excrement. *Have these prisoners been confined for multiple days? Why?* Kralsvik lay only twelve miles to the west, and travelers usually reached this rest stop after one day. Ten paces from the first wagon, Mae stopped cold in her tracks. *By the devils!* The wooden cage held at least a dozen people. Crammed together, the figures stood like sheep for the slaughter. Some looked small, like women or children. *Those can't be murderers or rapists.* One woman spotted Mae.

"Help us," she begged in a carrying whisper.

"Who are you?" Mae asked.

"Oh, please... Help us! We've been made slaves. My daughter, too. Can you free us?"

"For what crime?" Mae asked, baffled.

"The taxes!" The woman wept. "The new magistrate... He demands full payment despite two years of bad harvest. Many couldn't pay. He condemned us to slavery. What'll happen to my daughter?" the woman wailed.

"Keep your voice down," Mae urged, fearing they drew too much attention.

"Quiet back there!" the guard barked from the campfire. "Don't make me use the rod again."

"I'm hungry." A tiny figure clung to the woman. The girl's weak and frightened voice tugged on Mae's heart. Without thought, Mae handed over the bread, realizing her mistake too late. The mother cried out, thanking Mae, while more prisoners started begging. The combined noise drew the soldier away from the fire.

"I told you to be quiet," he barked, approaching. "Who made that noise? All on this side, put your hands forward. I'll teach you to obey your masters." A stocky soldier stomped toward the wagons, carrying a wooden rod. "Once you're in your new home, you'll have worse," he boasted. "You'll thank me then for my mercy."

Mae's blood boiled. With a snarl, she pulled a knife from her belt and threw it, propelled with magic. But her spell faltered. Missing the required force, the blade stuck in his leg instead of sinking into his throat. Toppling over backward, the soldier cried out in alarm.

Mae took a running leap. Landing on his torso, she buried her second knife into his forehead. He wouldn't hit any more women and children. Still, his yells had woken the remaining soldiers.

Scrambling to their feet, three men rushed Mae with their swords drawn. The witch scarpered. Unable to pull the knife from the dead guard's head, she grabbed the one in his leg and rolled under the first wagon.

The pursuing soldiers fanned out, one going left, one right, and the third remaining in front of the wagon. Coming to a halt between the two carts, Mae jumped to her feet, intending to dash toward the horses, but the first soldier blocked her way. Tall and broad, the man had slept in his mail shirt and held his double-edged sword in a confident grip.

She couldn't win a one-on-one battle. Instead, the witch forced her thoughts into the horses' minds, instilling fear. The tethered animals snorted, whinnied, and reared up. Expecting an attack from behind, the soldier turned.

Mae barreled past him, almost getting away when his hand grabbed her cloak and pulled her to the ground.

She landed on her back, the impact knocking the wind from her lungs.

Using the momentum from the fall, Mae rolled onto her shoulders and pulled her knees over her head. She uncoiled, kicking her feet into his face.

Cursing, the soldier stumbled backward. He dropped his sword and gripped his broken nose, blood seeping through his fingers.

By then, the second soldier had arrived. Running past his dazed companion, he lunged, stabbing his sword toward Mae's heart. Still lying on the ground, she tried to push herself out of the way.

She didn't manage.

Pain shot through Mae's body, blood spilling from her wound. The soldier had put all his weight into the thrust. Luckily, the noise of a heavy object hitting the prisoner cart diverted his attention at the last second.

Missing her torso, the soldier's blade pierced her lower left arm, running clean between the bones, and sank almost a foot into the hard ground. The motion bent him over, and Mae swiped her knife across his face, cutting him deep. Stunned, the soldier let go of his weapon, lost his balance, and fell onto her chest.

The strain on Mae's arm caused renewed spasms of mind-numbing pain. Screaming like a banshee, the witch brought her arm back, ramming her knife hilt-deep into his jugular. Hot red blood gushed like a geyser, spewing his life into the dirt.

Mae couldn't lift his lifeless body. She had no energy left, neither physical nor magical. Searing pain emanated from her pierced arm, and a throbbing lump formed at the back of her head. With despair, she saw the broken-nosed soldier regaining his composure. He picked up his sword and advanced, weary at first. But he grew more confident since a third armed figure sprinted toward the fight.

This is the end, Mae thought.

She'd tried to harvest the soul of the man lying on top of her, but she couldn't establish steady skin-to-skin contact. When her shaking hand slipped off the knife hilt, she let her tortured body fall limp.

The first soldier wiped the blood from his face. He turned toward his presumed companion to see the approaching figure running him through with a sword. The impact carried both men to the ground. Mae's vision blurred. She tried to raise her head, needing to make sense of it. Yet all went black.

* * *

"How are you feeling?"

Mae hadn't opened her eyes when she heard a voice that didn't belong there. Willing herself to wake, she commanded her eyelids to open. The bright light hurt. Blinking, Mae tried to shield her eyes with her left arm. The limb wouldn't move; it felt restrained. She raised her right hand instead, but the speaker had already moved, shading her with his silhouette. Mae couldn't see his face, but the unruly hair and his protruding ears confirmed her suspicion.

"Jarne?" she croaked. "Where am I? What's going on?" Blinking a few more times and shaking her head, she finally found the tone she was aiming for. "What are *you* doing here?"

"I rescued you—again!" He smiled, his pride and satisfaction evident in his voice. "You should drink something. Let me help you up."

Mae would have liked nothing more than to jump up and berate him for his foolishness. But she'd needed rescuing, and he'd done that. So, she let him pull her into a sitting position, grimacing from the pain in her left arm.

Mae looked around. *No prisoner carts, no dead soldiers.* Instead, she found herself in a hollow behind a clump of trees. A horse stood nearby, and Jarne knelt beside her. Grinning from ear to ear, he moved a waterskin toward her mouth, intending to help her drink. Mae snatched the container with her right hand and pulled the cork with her teeth.

"Explain!" she commanded before taking deep gulps of the cool water.

"I went looking for you. You've been away for too long," Jarne said, no hint of guilt in his voice. She narrowed her eyes but didn't interrupt. "I had a pretty good idea where you went."

"When?"

"Two days ago. I arrived yesterday, following the carts."

Mae couldn't believe it. "With the carts? Where were you?"

"Among the trees across the road." He pointed in the direction they had come from. "I was sure you would attack the camp. I waited for your move."

"You waited for my attack?"

"Of course," he replied, his tone full of confidence in the virtue of his actions. "After you came back last time all bruised and beaten up, I figured you need looking after."

Jarne had pushed her too far. Mae would whack him behind his ears for his impudence. She didn't care that he was five inches taller, at least forty pounds heavier, and technically the same age as her. She didn't need looking after. Sadly, Mae had no magic left to teach this whelp.

"Last time," she growled, giving him the evil eye, "I tripped on the way back and tumbled down a mountain slope. A few scratches—I was *not* beaten up!"

"Of course not." He smiled, toning down his protective bravado. "But I was worried," he said in a serious tone. "You try so hard—only killing one prisoner, not harming the soldiers or lone wanderers. And you waited so long." He squared his shoulders and declared with a stern expression, "You take too many risks!"

"You think I shouldn't be so picky?" she asked, her sarcasm unharmed by last night's fight. "You think I should swoop down on whoever comes my way? There was once a foolish young boy. I let him go. Maybe I shouldn't have?"

"I don't mean killing whoever comes your way. But you could use your powers for worthier goals than to execute prisoners." Jarne raised his hand just as Mae was about to argue. "Let's get out of here first. I didn't go far last night. I'd rather be in our hidden cabin than near the wreckage of the prisoner convoy. Are you up for riding?"

Mae glared for a few more seconds, but then she nodded, letting Jarne help her stand.

"Who taught you all this?" she asked, watching in amazement as he buried the fire with dirt and used dead branches to cover their tracks.

"The highwaymen in my mother's stories always covered their traces to escape the evil lord's henchmen."

"I'm not sure your mother gave you the right moral compass..."

"But *I* am," he grinned, offering to help her mount up. "You can be a victim, or you can fight back."

Shaking her head yet inwardly smiling, Mae accepted his help. Jarne swung onto the horse's back behind her, reaching around her to grab the reins.

"Tell me what happened," Mae asked as they trotted through the foothills of the Serpent's Spine mountain range and toward their cabin in the Deepwood forest.

"After sunset, I thought I saw a shadow clambering down the crater's slope," he explained. "Since there were two carts and four guards, I anticipated trouble. I saw the prisoners earlier. I knew you wouldn't harm them." Mae was baffled by his matter-of-fact references to her need to kill and his complete confidence in her good intentions. "But that meant you would attack the guards. So, I rushed in."

"To stop me?" she asked, irritated.

"To help you."

"You were going to help me kill people." Her tone grew icy.

"Evil people," he replied. "You have to do it, and I'd rather you didn't get hurt doing it."

"You don't think I deserve to be hurt or killed for killing others?"

"Anyhow," he continued, ignoring her last question. "I saw you take down one guard and roll under the cart when the other three chased you. I hit the soldier guarding your retreat with a rock, and he crashed into the cage. The prisoners attacked him. Grabbing his hair, they punched and pummeled him senseless. They must have strangled him in the end. I took the sword from the soldier you fought. You saw what I did."

His voice broke, and Mae felt him shudder. Jarne had killed a man. A vile deed that had become a sad constant in her existence, he was forced to do it for the first time.

"I'm sorry, Jarne," Mae said, reaching for his hand, "for what you had to do. You don't deserve that."

"But you do?" he asked with anger in his voice. "How can someone like you deserve such a bitter fate?"

Mae was silent, a lump forming in her throat. She was glad for the wind in her face, drying the moisture pooling in her eyes. The witch knew living with her couldn't be easy, even without the curse. Growing up in a remote cabin deep in the forest, she'd never felt comfortable among strangers. As a child, Mae had often roamed the woods for days on end without speaking to another person. Her isolation grew deeper after her parents died, and the curse took her. She'd often kept to herself even when staying at the Witches' Castle with Sigri and Renya.

Life with Jarne was easy, though. He loved the forest, complained little, and made her feel useful, appreciated, and happy.

The two rode on in silence for a while. Sitting behind her on the horse, his arms around her slender body, Jarne felt joy and relief to have Mae back. He hadn't been sure he would succeed. Jarne had feared being too late or unskilled to save her. After, he'd worried Mae would chase him away for following her. But most of all, there was the small yet justified fear that her injuries and low energy could cause her to lose control and attack him. He'd seen glimpses of the black witch's temper over the years, and Mae had waited very long before going on this unsuccessful raid.

Riding at a slow pace, Jarne felt the tension leaving her muscles. Mae leaned into him.

"Tell me everything that happened," she asked in a sleepy voice.

"After all soldiers were… dealt with, I rushed toward you and pulled the sword free. There was a woman in the prisoner cart. She urged me to let her out, saying that she could help. I tied my belt around your arm to stop the bleeding. Then I looked for the keys. There were none. Metal rods driven through overlapping eyelets held the cage doors shut. I couldn't get them out. In the end, I had to use one soldier's axe to break the cage open—my fear for you stoked the fury."

"Good thing you aren't a boy anymore." Mae's drowsy voice whispered near his ear, where she had nestled her head against his shoulder.

"A few men were among the women and children. The woman who'd called out stepped forward. She and two others bandaged your wounds using strips torn from the soldiers' uniforms. I stayed by your side while the men freed the remaining prisoners."

Mae made a soft noise—a moan that could have meant acknowledgment or appreciation.

"They dragged the dead bodies into the cages and pushed the carts into the lake," he continued, "hoping the deep water would swallow all evidence. The woman helped me lift you onto one horse, leaving the other three with the freed prisoners."

Jarne paused; Mae had fallen asleep. Sighing in contentment, he steered the horse in a gentle walk, acutely aware of her warm body in his arms, her spiky hair tickling his cheeks, and the smell of sunbaked skin filling his nose.

The riders reached their cabin well after sunset, yet twilight still lingered that time of the year. Jarne dismounted and led the horse for the last steps.

"Did you sleep well?" he asked when Mae stirred.

"Like a babe being rocked in the cradle," she replied, rolling her neck, and Jarne couldn't detect any sarcasm.

"Ready to hear my ideas, then?" he ventured, encouraged.

"Do I have a choice?"

"No," he told her, offering her help with dismounting. "You could only ask for a stay of execution until morning."

"That might be wiser," she said. "I only got a tiny bit of life force. I might be more receptive after a good night's sleep."

She let him help her off the horse. Then, she hugged him.

"Thank you, Jarne."

* * *

THE NEXT MORNING, Jarne woke early and checked the chicken coop. He found three eggs. Together with the leftover smoked boar, this morning's feast would be rich indeed.

Good. Jarne was eager for any leverage to convince Mae about his ideas. Yesterday, she seemed amenable to at least hearing him out. *Still, better to have a good breakfast before broaching that subject.*

By an unlucky coincidence, Jarne had stopped Mae and her sisters from killing Duke Finsgúr three years ago. Since then, she'd cared for Jarne, denying her own needs and ambition for the sake of an orphan boy. He was a boy no longer. The daring rescue must have shown her what a capable ally he could be. Together, they could use her powers for the greater good—if she agreed to target the oppressors of the foreign regime.

As often as he dared, Jarne had questioned Mae about her curse. She'd responded only reluctantly, partly because she didn't know the answers and partly because she was ashamed of her past. There was no place to learn how to be a black witch.

After her parents' death, Mae had struggled with loss, survivor's guilt, confusion, and helplessness for almost a year before her growing need led her to her first kill. Her memory of those days was vague; at least, she said so.

But Mae remembered darker and darker thoughts dominating her mind. The desire—the hunger—became ever stronger until her inner demons took over, and she attacked a woman on an isolated farm. Bent over the woman's lifeless body, Mae hadn't seen the husband and three teenage boys charging her with pitchforks until it was almost too late. Fueled by rage and the freshly harvested soul, the witch had fought like a vicious beast, killing everybody and setting the farmhouse on fire.

Afterward, Mae had been so distraught that she decided to kill herself. She'd climbed the cliffs of the Deepwood peninsula, filled her pockets with rocks, and was about to jump when a warship passed. The drums beating the rhythm for the oarsmen reminded her of her brother Eilif, who might have been on such a boat, involuntarily going to war.

Back then, she'd made herself a promise. Mae would use her powers to track his whereabouts and save him. Yet, despite seven years of searching, she'd never found Eilif. Still, Mae had left a trail of dead soldiers wherever she went. Like a poppy addict, she'd fallen into a devil's spiral of disgust about her existence, rage against the people she blamed, loss of control in fits of violence, and renewed shame.

Only when Mae met Sigri and Renya—after she learned of her brother's death in one of the king's pointless wars—did she find a way to channel her curse. Ever since, Mae had fought her urges to spare the lives of innocent people. But going as long as possible between attacks took a toll on her. With every passing day, her mood soured, her temper became volatile, and her control over her magic weakened. Jarne had observed the pattern. His idea would help her to find the right balance between morals and sanity. He wanted her to pick targets that made a difference, and he wanted to come along. *Surely, she would see the benefits of working as a team, wouldn't she?*

Stoking the embers, he added fresh logs. Once the flames crackled, he hung the pan over the fire and added the sliced pork. The smell of sizzling bacon woke Mae.

"You're up early?" she asked, clambering out of bed and trying but failing to hide her grimace of pain.

Adding the eggs, Jarne reached for the jar of salt. "We're almost out of salt. We should go to the market."

"For salt?" she scoffed. "We have little to trade. You haven't cured the two deerskins yet." Flexing her left hand, she continued, "And anyhow, you have another resource in mind that needs replenishing, don't you?"

"I do?"

"Don't play coy." Mae narrowed her eyes. "You planned to soften my mood with breakfast, am I right?"

"Did you learn divination from Sigri?" he asked with an innocent grin.

"I don't need mysterious skills to read the future," Stepping closer, Mae peeked over his shoulder into the frying pan. "I can read you well enough."

"So, you are an all-seeing sorceress. Tell me what I'm thinking now."

"Right now, you fear my wrath if you let the eggs burn."

"Oh, Hella take me," he scolded himself.

Jarne took the pan off the fire and scooped the only slightly burned omelet into two bowls. Mae filled the kettle with water and placed it on the fire. Then, both sat down and began to eat. Jarne shoveled the eggs into his mouth, then huffed in pain as the blistering hot food burned his tongue. Mae gave him an exasperated look.

"How can you forget that the eggs are hot? You cooked them yourself."

Jarne tried to swallow to make a dignified response, but that made things even worse. Mae laughed, shaking her head. Then she spooned some egg and blew on it. But the piece of bacon within was unbalanced, and the egg fell back into the bowl. It was Jarne's turn to laugh. Both grinned and finished their breakfast without further mishaps.

The kettle boiled, and Mae poured the water onto the tea leaves. Returning to the table, she waited for him to talk.

"The plan with the prisoners didn't work out," Jarne started, clearing a lump from his throat.

"You don't say."

"Because you were alone against four."

"And I should take you along? Did you enjoy killing?" Ice had crept into her voice. "Are you eager to take another man's life?" she challenged, anger glowing in her eyes.

Mae's comment stung. Yet Jarne couldn't blame her. She hated killing and couldn't understand why he wanted to be part of her attacks. He took a deep breath, willing her to see his good intentions.

"No, I didn't enjoy it. I wouldn't have done it if I'd seen another way. But you can't." He looked at her, his mouth dry, his palms sweaty, and his heartbeat racing like a hummingbird's wings. "You have no choice, and still you feel guilt because you must kill to stay alive."

"Shouldn't I?" Mae asked through gritted teeth. "Why is my life more important than someone else's?"

"If you take the moral high ground and talk about a random person, it's a valid question, and there is no easy answer." Jarne leaned toward her. "But it is the wrong question."

"So, what is the right question?"

"Is there a person who should pay for his misdeeds and whose death would be justified, even welcomed by other people, and you could be the judge?"

"The executioner, you mean. And would I be doing it for selfless reasons?"

"Not entirely, but you could use an 'evil' act for the greater good."

Mae got up, poured the tea into two cups, and brought them to the table. Jarne could see her mind working, ideas battling each other. He'd planted a seed. If it took root and grew, his dreams for a better world and his desire to make Mae happy could both come true. Mae was silent for a long while.

"Should we plan another raid, then?" Jarne asked, not able to tolerate the suspense any longer.

Still, Mae didn't answer. Instead, she circled the rim of her teacup with her index finger with a faraway look in her eyes.

"A raid," he insisted. "Should we plan another one? You know, to replenish."

Mae looked at Jarne, holding his gaze. He couldn't read her expression. Neither anger nor excitement burned in her eyes. Eventually, she replied with her own question.

"Do you remember asking *why* we didn't have teacups all those years ago?"

Jarne looked perplexed, but then he remembered.

"I didn't," he chuckled. "You tried to divert the conversation."

Mae tilted her head and gave him an innocent smile.

"All right," he said, "I'll tan the two deerskins. But you'll think about it?"

"I will."

CHAPTER TEN

Makevinger

"You're sure you know how to sail?" Mae grabbed the low railing as the tiny boat swayed precariously from side to side, bobbing on the angry waves that rolled in from the south. Her stomach, which had emptied against her will over an hour ago, still believed it had more to offer to the sea.

Mae and Jarne had danced around the topic of another raid for almost a month, and Mae's mood grew darker with each day, which didn't help the conversation. The day before, the two had squabbled about trifles when Jarne pointed out Mae's ferocious temper.

"I do not have a temper," she had yelled. Jarne stood very still, looking her in the eyes, neither smugness nor fear on his face. A couple of heartbeats later, Mae capitulated.

"Sorry, Jarne. I…"

"No, Mae, I'm sorry. I cannot imagine how it must feel."

"But it isn't your fault."

"Neither is it yours. We're in this together," he continued. "I can make suggestions, but it is your decision."

"I don't want to decide. I want to push it all far, far away from me. Ignore it, if I could. But I can't. We have to go soon." Mae didn't complete the "or else" part, not even in her head.

That morning, Mae and Jarne started on their first joint mission, heading toward Makevinger, the principal settlement in the southern lowlands. After traversing the Deepwood to the peninsula's southern tip, Jarne commandeered a færing—a single-masted sailboat.

Grimacing, Mae stepped aboard, and Jarne steered the vessel in a direct line across the open water. The choppy waves fought their ship relentlessly. Jarne pulled hard on the sheets while trying to keep the rudder steady.

"I do know how to sail," he replied, sounding strained. "I grew up in a fishing village on an island in the middle of the ocean."

"And I grew up in a forest next to a river. That still doesn't give me the ability to gnaw down trees." In Mae's mind, it required no feat of genius to determine that crossing a body of water aptly named Shipwreck Bay on a windy day wasn't the best of choices. She was about to voice that sentiment when another heave threatened to spew more than words from her mouth.

"Trust me," he pleaded. "The wind is a bit stronger than expected, that's all."

Jarne had suggested paying the steward of Makevinger a visit after hearing stories about the man's nasty reputation for taking the farmers' daughters against their will. If everything went well, Mae would have enough life force for an entire year.

The plan was sound, if it wasn't for the fact that Jarne had never sailed in his life—a circumstance he conveniently forgot to mention. All his maritime knowledge stemmed from overhearing the fisherman in his home village. But those men couldn't always be regarded as trustworthy sources of information. Halfway between the two neighboring peninsulas, however, Jarne thought it wasn't a good time to be completely honest with Mae.

"We are almost there," he shouted. "Look!"

Mae lifted her head from her lap and gazed toward the land, which still looked far off. She closed her eyes again to fight the nausea, and a wave broke at the bow, splashing icy water onto her face. Jarne didn't laugh; he suppressed the urge in the nick of time. Nonetheless, a painful shock jolted his body. He looked at Mae, hurt and upset visible in his eyes. It had been quite a while since she had hexed someone without conscious thought. Yet she reasoned he deserved it for putting her through this ordeal.

After what felt like an eternity, the seafarers reached land. Mae thanked the Norns for the solid ground under her feet. She shuddered at the thought of their return journey. They needed to cross the treacherous sea again after finishing their mission. Assuming they made it home without adding a new shipwreck to the bay's collection, Mae vowed never to step into another boat thereafter.

Stomping toward the wheat field, she left Jarne behind to secure and cover their vessel. The world had finally stopped swaying. Mae took deep, steadying breaths. She needed to get her temper under control, because Jarne's plan was risky. They needed to work well together to succeed. He tried so hard to help her, and she would make it up to him. As soon as her stomach had settled, she would go hunting. With a camp for the night on firm ground, a rabbit roasting on a crackling fire, and the fireflies dancing in the darkness, they could treat the time before the attack as a summer vacation. In late August, the nights were still mild.

* * *

"Come in, come in," the balding man bellowed from behind a massive desk, reacting to a firm knock on the door.

"I was told you were busy, not to be disturbed." A young man stepped in. Despite the mild summer day, the guest wore thick furs to demonstrate his station with opulence, hiding his lanky frame. Everybody knew who his father was, and that opened doors, letting him interrupt almost anyone in the southern province. He liked it that way. The problem was that everybody also knew who his mother was, and she wasn't the duchess. He hated their snickering behind his back and finger-pointing when he wasn't looking. He would show them who they were dealing with—his outfit was the first step.

"Nonsense, my boy." Rising from his chair, the steward of Makevinger spread his arms in welcome. "For you, I always have time."

"My father sends his regards," the young man stated, closing the door behind him. "He will arrive soon. There was a matter that needed his attention. He sent me ahead."

"I hope the duke is well and the circumstances of his delay aren't too unpleasant."

"Of course he is well," the guest replied, a sharp note of irritation entering his voice. Jónveig Svartravn, favorite bastard son of Duke Finsgúr, didn't care for this bold caretaker of the arse-end of nowhere implying otherwise.

As for the circumstances delaying the duke, they were indeed unpleasant, just not for Duke Finsgúr. The duke fielded a small army to deal with an uprising among the slaves working the copper mines. Erik Gunner Finsgúr was never a lenient man, but a revolt challenging his authority in his backyard? He couldn't have that. The duke needed to bring swift and harsh punishment, and people needed to see him doing it.

"Forgive me; I was overstepping myself." The steward's voice was oily with fake diffidence, but at least he remembered his place. "Can I offer you refreshments? You picked a fortunate day to arrive."

"I did?" Jónveig asked. "Usually, my father's vassals aren't too keen to pay the tributary. Are you so far ahead in collecting the duke's taxes?"

"Well, not quite." The older man chuckled, making his ample belly bounce. "The peasants here are as bad as anywhere, I assume. They're squirming and wiggling to shun their obligations. Some tell heart-wrenching stories about sick children and wolves killing livestock. It's actually beneficial that your father will arrive in a few days."

"Then, I don't understand." Jónveig stepped forward and sat in the armchair by the fireplace without waiting for an invitation. It seemed his host had forgotten his manners, being so occupied with self-aggrandizing ramblings.

"Well, the peasants will pay, but sometimes, it isn't coin that my soldiers collect. Your father granted me the authority to force debtors into servitude and even enthrallment. Today, for example, I expect a more carnal payment. The young daughter of the tanner will arrive here soon. And she will stay the night, if you catch my meaning."

Jónveig rolled his eyes. What was there to catch? The depravities of this old man were well known throughout the entire province—perhaps the whole kingdom. And a tanner's daughter? The wench would smell worse than the sewers.

"If she pleases your eye, I would only be too glad to offer her to you."

"You spoke of refreshments?" the bastard reminded his host with the disdain worthy of a trueborn duke's son.

"Of course, forgive me." The steward hustled over to a chest on which a pitcher and ceramic cups stood. He poured two generous measures and handed one cup to the sitting man. "Some of the finest mead in all of Heilladur. To your father's health and yours."

Jónveig doubted the quality, but he was thirsty. Before he could take a sip, a knock at the door sounded.

"Hersir Persson," a strong voice called through the closed door. "The girl you asked for is here."

"Wonderful, come in."

A soldier entered, pulling a waif roughly by her arm. The guard closed the door behind him and bolted it. This time, indeed, the steward wanted to avoid disruptions.

Jónveig took a closer look at the girl and realized his low expectations weren't misplaced. She looked young but boyish, with short hair and green eyes that wished everyone in the room a slow and painful death. His father would never have tolerated such an impudent stare. The duke's soldiers would have beaten respect into her. But given her task tonight, these southern grunts might not have dared to disfigure her body.

"Bring her over here," the steward ordered. "Give our distinguished guest a good look." The soldier pulled the girl forward, and she shuffled along as fast as her shackled feet allowed.

"This is Jónveig Svartravn," the steward announced, "son of Duke Finsgúr and his envoy. You will please him in any way he desires. What is your name?"

"It doesn't matter," Jónveig cut in. "I'll call her Hilda. I always call the whores Hilda."

Stepping closer, the younger man grabbed the front of her smock, intending to rip it open. Suddenly, the girl's hands encircled his wrists. For one second, bewilderment crossed Jónveig's eyes. Before his surprise changed to anger, he twitched. His muscles jerked, and he crumpled to the ground like a ragdoll.

Everything was over in two heartbeats. Neither the steward nor his guest, who now lay on the floor, had made any sound. Only the soldier had reacted. He had drawn his sword. Holding it by the blade, he clubbed the still-dumbfounded steward over the head with the pommel.

The balding man went to the ground with a comical "oh" on his lips. And the woman, whose name wasn't Hilda, knelt to relieve the steward of his soul.

* * *

JARNE RUSHED TO the door and put his ear against it, listening for unusual noises. Nobody had raised the alarm. Many hours might pass before anyone dared to enter this room. Breathing a sigh of relief, Jarne turned back to Mae. Then his eye fell on the young man on the floor, and the anxiety returned.

"We killed the duke's son."

"I killed the duke's *bastard*, his steward in this town, and two of his soldiers." Mae removed the shackles from her ankles. They hadn't been locked, but still, her legs showed angry red marks.

"This is no matter for bragging. The duke doesn't give a rat's fart about the steward or the soldiers. But his son? We need to get away from here."

"I wasn't planning to stay the night. Calm down, Jarne," Mae soothed. "We'll be safe. Nothing points to us."

"Do you think the duke will seek the truth?" Jarne's face had turned red, and sweat glistened on his forehead. "He will be out for vengeance, and it will be terrible. No one in this town is safe. They'll grasp for any straw to deflect the guilt, and two strangers would make perfect scapegoats."

Jarne was right, of course. This morning, when Mae had dispatched the two soldiers ordered to fetch the girl, she had ensured nobody saw her. The bodies were floating down the river behind the tannery. But townsfolk had seen Mae and talked to Jarne over the last few days. And, while strangers often came to Makevinger, any unusual circumstances would warrant a thorough investigation in light of the severe crime committed today.

"Let's leave this town and go home. Keep your soldier's guise on."

"And you?" Jarne asked. "If the servants see the girl leaving early, they'll enter this room."

"I'll take the bastard's clothes. All those furs should mask my body shape. I'll pull the hood up, and you do the talking."

"What shall I say?"

"*I* don't know. This was your plan." Mae shrugged her shoulders. Then she looked at the old man who had ordered a young girl to his chambers. With disgust, she hissed, "Say the steward will be busy for a few hours."

* * *

"You can't come in here." A servant's voice carrying a note of panic sounded through the closed door, stopping Mae in her tracks. "The steward and his guest... they aren't to be disturbed." Mae had taken the bastard's furs, boots, and britches off and was about to dress up like him.

"I'm here on the duke's orders," a deeper voice replied. "Out of my way!" Seconds later, the door latch rattled, but the door remained locked. "My lord Svartravn," the voice bellowed, accompanied by banging of fists against the door. "Your father sent me on urgent business. Open the door, please, my lord." More banging followed. "Your father requires your immediate return."

"That's not good," Jarne whispered.

"Oh really?" Mae replied. "Your profound grasp of the situation astonishes me. Out the window!" She abandoned the furs and pulled the britches over her thin dress, hobbling to the back of the room while pulling the drawstrings tied. More banging followed.

"Is there another way in?" the duke's messenger barked.

"From the kitchen, there is a passage to the bedroom," the frightened voice replied. "But we must not use it. The steward forbade any interruption."

"Show the way!" The footsteps moved away from the door.

Jarne had opened the window's shutters and looked out. They were on the second floor. Below stretched a meadow down a gentle slope.

"Jump and roll," Mae commanded, and then she did just that. Jarne looked for handholds to climb down. Not spotting any, he lowered himself from the windowsill. The insistent messenger had entered the room and shouted in alarm, having spotted the bodies. Jarne let go. He landed awkwardly, pain shooting through his leg. Mae had already reached the low stone wall encircling the steward's manor. Unwilling to put weight on his leg, Jarne half stumbled and half rolled down the hill.

Mae pointed toward the stables, fifty paces away, behind the estate's flower garden.

"We won't make it," Jarne shouted. To support his statement, armed men rushed out of the manor house, cutting off their path to the horses. "Into the wheat fields," he called. "We may lose them there." Gritting his teeth, Jarne limped toward the endless sea of wheat lying beyond the town's borders.

Mae ran beside him, holding back to match his pace. Turning around, she spotted mounted guards in hot pursuit. In a forest or the mountains, Mae could outrun or outwit any hunter. But this town lay on a vast open plain with nowhere to hide. From the horses' backs, the soldiers had no problem spotting them running through the waist-high stalks, leaving a canyon of devastation in their wake. As the guards closed in, the unappealing prospect of public torture, followed by execution, loomed ever larger. The pursuers herded Mae and Jarne toward the cliff's edge, where the wind carried the salty spray from the churning sea below. Jarne turned his back to the abyss and gathered stones. Stepping between Mae and the soldiers, he readied himself for a fight.

"This is suicide!" Mae yelled. "There are too many." She raised a whirlwind, sending dust and debris into the soldiers' eyes. Then, she took Jarne by the hand, urging him onward.

"You can't be serious!" he shouted, his face pale, looking at the forty-foot drop toward the gray waves below. In response, Mae clamped her hand tight around his and jumped, pulling Jarne with her.

The water was deep, the cliff's vertical basalt columns extending far below the waterline. Yet even at the end of summer, the water felt icy as currents from the north pushed past these shores. Gasping and spluttering, Mae surfaced and paddled toward the wall, seeking handholds. She wasn't a good swimmer. Relieved, she reached Jarne and grabbed his shoulder.

He pulled her onward with powerful strokes, fearing a crossbow bolt piercing his back any second. Fifty yards to the south, an overhang provided protection. Concealed behind rocks, they clung to the wall, catching their breaths, and considered their options. Mae increased her blood flow instinctively to deal with the cold. But Jarne had no magic. His whole body shivered, and mumbled curses escaped his chattering teeth.

They kept swimming and emerged onto a rocky beach as night fell, frozen to the core. Mae needed to find warmth for Jarne but couldn't risk a fire in the open. Instead, she led the way toward the Brennand Valley, where hot springs and mud pools dotted the landscape. Her idea was dangerous. Some ponds were scalding hot. Others contained poisonous liquids. Still, if they could get near enough, the heated ground alone might provide sufficient relief from the cold.

Mae and Jarne walked for almost two hours, following the sulfurous smell and stumbling in the darkness. Jarne hadn't spoken a word since leaving the water. Even his shivering slowed. He staggered, tripped, and tumbled often. Mae lent a shoulder to keep him upright, desperate to move forward over the rough ground. She knew she couldn't carry him if he hurt himself or fell unconscious; he was too heavy.

With a last-ditch effort, they descended an uneven slope and reached a small pool fed by a gurgling brook. Blissful steam rose. Jarne plunged in immediately, not worrying about any danger. He collapsed on his back and lay motionless, rejoicing in the warmth. Mae hesitated, dipping only her toes into the clear water. The pool was shallow, and the ground was muddy but free of sharp rocks. The water felt heavenly. About body temperature, it carried only the faintest smell of sulfur and iron. They had found a freshwater spring heated by the earth's boundless energy.

Mae leaned against a smooth rock and stretched her aching limbs. A guttural moan of pleasure escaped her lips as the pins and needles subsided. *How wonderful!* She didn't want to leave; she didn't want to move ever again. It felt like time stood still. This moment—the warmth and safety—was all that counted. After soaking in the revitalizing water, Mae held her breath and submerged her head, shutting out everything except this miraculous sensation.

As she surfaced into the world again, the clouds dispersed, and stars appeared. She laughed; she couldn't help it. The unexpected joy of the wonderful bath, the daring escape from their pursuit, and the aftermath of her recent energy harvest had made her giddy. She scooped up a handful of mud and threw it in Jarne's direction. By the sound of his exclamations, she had hit her target. Splashing and grunting followed before she received her share of mud in return.

Like small children, they splashed and sputtered, pushed and wrestled, rolled in the muddied water. And then, she kissed him.

Tension had been building for a while. Jarne had grown into a young man, and he was still getting taller each day. She was frozen in eternal youth, an old soul frozen in the body of a young woman.

And if she felt awkward for one second, it quickly became apparent he was more than willing. With their clothes discarded on the rocks, they fumbled in the starlight, exploring their feelings and bodies as they tried but failed to control the rampaging butterflies in their stomachs.

What both lacked in experience, they made up for with curiosity, gentleness, and the boundless eagerness of teenagers. As the morning dawned, they emerged from their hideout, their skin wrinkled and their clothes damp. Grinning from ear to ear, they started toward their hidden boat, holding hands.

CHAPTER ELEVEN

Ducal Affairs

As soon as Duke Finsgúr had learned about the uprising in the copper mines, he canceled his trip to Makevinger, sending his illegitimate son to deal with the local steward in his stead. The boy whined, begging to lead the attack on the mines instead. Erik Finsgúr backhanded him.

"Never beg for command," the duke yelled. "Seize it or do as you're told!"

Riding at the head of a sizable force, the duke and his thirty men-at-arms charged north atop thoroughbred war horses, raising a cloud of dust that could be seen from leagues away. The wagons with provisions, servants, and camp followers wouldn't arrive until nightfall despite the short distance. Supply trains always crept at a snail's pace along the rutted roads.

Approaching the dreaded clump of wooden sheds clinging to the mountains, the absence of yells and clashing weapons disheartened the duke. *Has it truly been twenty years since I last took to the field of battle?* Life had been easier back then. All a warrior needed to feel like a man was sharpened steel, a swift horse, and the smell of blood and fear in the air.

An underling approached, taking the bridle of the duke's horse, and waved for two more to carry wooden steps. The duke pushed the man aside, dismounting unaided. Holding his head high, the aging lord kept his expression stern, masking the aches in his joints.

Erik Gunner Finsgúr was tall and lean, almost gaunt. Even in his youth, he had been wiry, never bulky. Many foes had mistaken his slim physique for weakness and paid with their lives. Nearing his fiftieth name day, the duke's posture remained regal. He kept his gray beard and hair short and well groomed. Yet the glare of his light-brown eyes never failed to instill unease in anyone at the receiving end. Daily, the duke practiced with sword and spear. He despised men of power who grew fat and soft in their middle years—like the current ruler, King Halvard, son of Harold the Conqueror.

"My lord," greeted the commander of his vanguard. Falling to one knee, the soldier delivered his report. "The uprising has been dealt with. Your soldiers killed eight slaves and wounded many more. We took twelve prisoners—the presumed ringleaders."

So, the fighting is done. The duke glared. I haven't even drawn my sword. All that was left for him was to dispense his justice. He would have liked nothing better than to exterminate the entire pack of these miserable slaves. Erik Finsgúr despised all natives of Heillaður since he'd come to these accursed lands as a young lad of ten summers, serving as the cupbearer to his uncle—the conquering Viking chieftain Harold.

"Where are the prisoners?" the duke asked, gripping his sword hilt so tight his knuckles shone white.

"We tied them to stakes driven into the ground on the assembly square."

"Lead the way," the duke barked, intending to let the scum feel his frustration about the demands of leadership, the pains of aging, and the glory of the battle lost to the whelp kneeling before him.

"Of course, my lord." The commander rose. "But you have a visitor."

"I have no time for visitors."

"Forgive me, my lord. But your visitor is, ahem…"

"Speak up, man," the duke shouted.

"An envoy from the king, my lord."

The duke narrowed his eyes. "From the king?"

"Yes, my lord. Waiting in the barracks, my lord. This way, please, my lord." Cowering before his lord, the battle-hardened soldier pointed toward the only building that didn't look like the next breeze would blow it apart. The duke's standards snapped in the wind on either side of the door—a silver spear on a green field. Yet above the door flew the king's banner—a golden deer on a field of red. Duke Finsgúr squinted against the sun. To him, the deer looked more like a donkey—a lazy ass like the king himself.

The two soldiers guarding the door snapped to attention as the duke approached. Rushing to open the door, the commander uttered another "my lord" before stepping aside to let the duke enter. The inside was dark despite a fire crackling.

A figure stood before the fireplace, the face turned toward the flames as if to seek warmth in the middle of the winter. The air felt stuffy, and the scent of burning herbs filled the duke's nose. As his eyes adjusted, he saw the figure wore a floor-length black cloak, the hood raised. Delicate silver stitching adorned the back and the hemline. He knew his visitor, and his reprimand for not being greeted with respect died at the back of his throat.

"It has been too long," the woman said, turning toward him and letting the firelight illuminate the dark runes tattooed onto her pale, ageless face. Shiny strands of raven-black hair flowed from her hood over her shoulders.

Her dark eyes bore into him. With her hands hidden in the cloak's long sleeves, she stood straight and regarded the absolute ruler of these lands without concern. Her dress sported a low neckline, and a silver disk etched with runes rested on her bosom, held there by a leather cord around her neck.

"Your Eminence," the duke said, offering her a respectful nod.

"Please," she mused, "we are alone." With a wave of her hand, the door latch closed. "Call me Bergrún, Erik. We have known each other for a long time. Why all the formality? Shall we sit? I poured some refreshments." She pointed to the chairs. "Forgive me for my transgression. It is your home, and I'm the guest."

"Of course... Bergrún. Nothing to forgive. Very thoughtful of you."

The duke approached the vacant chair and waited for her to sit. His face was calm and composed. Duke Finsgúr never showed fear. Yet his guest had a reputation.

"The king is fine, his whores and horses too," she elaborated in a cheerful tone, gauging his response to her open disrespect for her king. "He has five sons now, three dozen hunting dogs, and a belly that would barely fit through the door behind you. I'll tell him you inquired about his affairs and expressed your condolences for the sudden death of his favorite concubine."

"Is that so?"

"Yes, because I didn't come here to waste my time with pointless and insincere chin-wagging." She took the goblet of mead from the side table and raised it toward the ceiling in a mock salute. "You don't like him, I don't like him, and I don't think he likes himself either. He knows what a failure he is. Long live our king." She drank.

Erik Finsgúr took a pull himself. She had poured a pitcher of ale—warm, rich, and bitter. Still, the unease grew. The king's black sorceress couldn't be trusted, especially if she agreed with one's opinions.

"Then what brings you here? My province offers many more pleasant places for a meeting. My house is always open."

"Too kind, but I don't think your wife likes me. And anyhow, the king sent me here to remind you that the slaves belong to him. You are to restore order without killing more than necessary.”

“I do know how to rule over my lands,” the duke replied. His voice had lost all pleasantry.

“You have administered the lands of His Majesty—your liege lord—to our satisfaction,” she replied, mirroring the steel in his voice. “And you’ve proven yourself as a trustworthy and stalwart supporter of King Halvard.”

The duke was taken aback. Her rebuke of his claim to ownership of these lands was undisguised. Yet, her praise for his support must have been sarcasm. He didn’t care for innuendo.

“Speak plainly, my lady. I’m not good at verbal fencing nor very patient.”

“We shall, my good duke. But I’ve kept you too long already. You may execute six slaves. The king demands three gold coins for every slave beyond that number.” She leaned forward, showing off her cleavage. “Of course, we wouldn’t count the fourteen who died in the fighting. Show your mercy and feast with your commanders. Then, see me later. We have lots to discuss.”

* * *

With his mind still reeling from the unexpected encounter, the duke demanded the execution of all twelve captured slaves. There would be no quick and painless hanging for that scum. He ordered his soldiers to crush some slaves with rocks and nail others to wooden planks as axe-throwing targets. A few miners bled to death with their arms and legs hacked off. Soon, however, the duke grew tired of the spectacle, and his thoughts returned to his mysterious visitor. When the supply train arrived, he allowed his men to open a cask of mead. Leaving his commanders in charge, he retired to his hastily erected tent.

Duke Finsgúr hated to sleep in a bed that wasn’t his own. He had his servants bring the bed from the castle together with other furniture, rugs, furs, and wall hangings—everything to make his war camp as comfortable as possible. Entering the large pavilion, the duke found a small cup with a blueish liquid standing next to the entrance. He drained the content and shook to dispel the bitterness. Then he started to disrobe. Taking his time to arrange his sword and the three hidden knives in easy reach from the bed, he slipped out of his britches and tunic, folding the garments before placing them onto a stool. Then he climbed into bed, crawling under the furs.

A cold hand with long nails touched his bare chest and moved downward, leaving faint red marks in its wake.

"You look flushed," Bergrún mused. "Did you enjoy the killing?"

"I had to do what I had to do."

"Is that also the reason you came to me? You had to do it?"

"This is my bed. Where else would I go?"

"I think you give your desires too little credit, Eric." She squeezed. "You clearly missed me."

He grunted in response. She teased him for a while longer before throwing the furs back and straddling him. Varying the rhythm, she brought him close yet left him unfulfilled until her icy shell had melted and the long-forgotten human passions started to run wild in her veins. When he climaxed with a painful moan of pleasure, she almost smiled, holding on to the echo of a past life. Then she stood, her alabaster skin glowing in the semi-darkness, and poured two goblets of a deep red liquid.

"Wine from the Southlands," she said, returning to the bed. "Not as potent as mead, but all the rage at the king's court."

"Do we have to talk about him?"

"Of course. Why do you think I came here?"

For a heartbeat, he felt hurt, letting the emotion show on his face.

"Oh, Erik," she breathed, "I never lied to you. All those years ago, I was honest. I needed what I needed, never promising anything else." She handed him a drink, holding his gaze. "Still, I guess a man can never forget his first woman. You were so young, then."

"You still look the same." His voice sounded hoarse, and he coughed to clear his throat.

"What good is magic," she laughed, "if you have to get old?" Taking in his gray hair and weathered skin, she added. "Men are different—you call it experience. But believe me, you don't want me to look my age."

"So, what do you want?" he asked, gulping down the wine. It tasted sour.

"The king needs you, and I need something else."

The duke feared as much.

"What does my dear cousin Halvard need me for?"

"The uprising in the north. His men lack discipline and strength. Help him win his lands back, and the reward will be substantial. Send an army. Put your bastard son in charge."

"I have my own problems."

"You brought over forty soldiers to kill a handful of slaves who would have died of starvation in a few days. Set your aims higher. Save the realm, and it can be yours."

Her hand lay on his chest again, and he felt his blood rising to the touch.

"You speak of treason."

"I speak of succession," she corrected. "The king has a son; you have a daughter. They can marry."

"My daughter is too young!"

"She is twelve, isn't she? Don't fear. The king's favorite son is nine. It'll take years before he knows what goes where. In the meantime, the king's health might fail. His young heir will need a regent."

"What's in it for you?"

"Besides the obvious?" She looked at his manhood reacting to her touch. In one swift motion, she pulled her hand back. Two of her nails had drawn blood. Her facial expression turned to stone, and an eerie red glow burned in her eyes. "I want your daughter once she is queen. I want to teach her, and I want to take her to war. There is a troublesome witch on Urðr styling herself Queen of the Sister Islands. I need her killed, and I need your daughter near."

"Out of the question. I won't have you turning my daughter into a witch."

"I'm afraid it wasn't a question." Bergrún wiped her finger over the silver medallion she wore around her neck. Where the duke's blood touched the metal, the runes started to glow. "Just do as I say, and all will be well."

Cold shivers ran down his back, feeling the touch of her dark magic.

"And there is one more thing." She picked up her cloak. Pulling it over her naked body, she walked to the tent's entrance. Despite her threats, despite the hurt she had inflicted, despite the years—he didn't want her to leave.

"Witches are at large in your lands." She turned, tying her belt. "The disappeared slave transport? That was witchcraft. Deal with it!"

"I never asked," he challenged, raising himself onto his elbow. "Why do you hate your sisters so much?"

"You, of all people, should know how annoying siblings can be." She chuckled, the sound evoking the image of deadly icicles hurtling down to impale a defenseless fawn. "Didn't you have two older brothers who stood to inherit the title? Both died—how convenient. I heard some nasty rumors." With that, she left him, adding a headache to his returned bodily fatigue.

* * *

THREE DAYS LATER, the duke returned to his estate—weary and starting to feel his age in earnest. Sleeping in a tent, even as luxurious as his own, was a young man's sport. He would rest for a few days before he needed to visit Makevinger. He had sent riders ahead to order the immediate return of his bastard son after the "conversation" with the king's black sorceress.

Reaching the residence floor of his heavily guarded inner keep, the duke pushed open the doors to his suite. A young girl with flaming-red hair ran toward him and flung herself in his arms.

"Daddy! You are back. We waited for you. We haven't had dinner yet. Mommy said you would come tonight. Did you bring me something?"

The duke scooped his daughter in his arms and twirled on the spot, age and exhaustion forgotten.

"Let your father catch his breath," a beautiful woman called from the room. "He has just returned from a long journey."

"It wasn't that long," the duke said as he put his daughter down, smiling.

"Did you kill all the rebels?" asked a boy, younger than the girl and half a head shorter.

"Leifr, this is hardly the time for such inquiries," admonished the woman, mother of the two children and wife of Duke Finsgúr. The duke looked at her fondly. As much contempt as he held for the weak king, the current ruler's youngest sister had captured the duke's heart, becoming the joy of his middle years.

"Let him ask, Birgith, my dearest. He will be a man soon and needs to know these things." Getting down to one knee to be level with the boy, the duke addressed his son. "Leifr, you will be the duke one day. You need to understand. A duke must be firm, but he must also be merciful." Putting his hand on the boy's shoulder, he continued. "Men are like sheep, often following where others lead. You must find and punish the leaders but spare the misguided followers."

"And then they will love you," the girl piped in.

The duke chuckled and looked at his wife, asking without words for her to continue the lesson.

"Like children love their father, even if he has to be stern sometimes."

Getting back up, the duke crossed the room and embraced his wife.

"My dearest, I could never be stern with these wonderful children you have given me." And he kissed her on the cheek.

"Will you watch me ride tomorrow? My pony can jump two bars," his daughter asked, trying to regain his undivided attention.

"And you can watch me practice archery. I shoot from twenty paces back," his son interjected, not to be outdone by a girl.

"You miss the target by twenty paces, you mean."

"Hilda," the mother reprimanded, "that wasn't very nice."

"Let them measure their wits and their strength against each other. That is what siblings are for." The duke spread his arms wide, inviting both children to come to him. Taking them in his arms, he reassured them. "I will watch your achievements, and both of you will make me proud."

A knock sounded at the door. With a sigh, the duke asked his family to proceed to the dining room.

"I will be with you in a minute." He stood, waiting for them to leave. Watching the entrance door, all levity disappeared from the duke's face. "Enter," he barked the moment he was alone. A soldier with the rank of captain stepped into the room, went to one knee, and lowered his head.

"Forgive me for the intrusion, my lord."

"What is it? I'm about to have dinner with my family. I hope for your sake the matter is important."

"Yes, my lord. I'm afraid it is." The soldier swallowed. "Your son, my lord… Jónveig, he is dead."

"How is that possible?" The duke delivered each word like a sword stroke. "Speak up, man," he yelled. "How did this happen?"

"We don't know how, exactly, my lord. Servants found him dead in the steward's residence in Makevinger."

The duke grabbed the kneeling captain by the front of his jacket and pulled him up, their faces only separated by a few inches."

"Where is the steward? Speak!" Spittle flew from the duke's mouth.

"Also dead, my lord. Both men lay on the floor in the steward's private rooms. And your son, my lord, he was…"

"He was what?" The duke's angry voice rang, echoing through the hall.

"He was undressed, my lord."

The duke backhanded the captain hard, as if it had been he who killed and humiliated his son.

"Take twenty men and ride to Makevinger," Erik Finsgúr barked. "Find the guilty! Question everybody sharply. Put these filthy peasants in the stocks. Be wary of witchcraft!" The duke took deep breaths to no avail. The veins in his temple pulsed with boiling anger. "Beat them," he snarled, "but leave them alive. I will follow in two days, and I want them to know it is me whom they will answer to. I will dispense *justice*." Flickering candlelight painted demonic shadows onto the duke's gaunt face. "I'll send them to hell myself," he growled, squeezing his fists until his knuckles popped. "They shall feel pain beyond their imagination. My blood has been spilled. I want to bathe in theirs."

"Yes, my lord." The captain bowed his way out of the room, his lip bleeding.

Nobody challenges me and lives to tell the tale. Savoring the thought, the duke composed his face. He pulled his tunic straight, ran his hands through his thinning hair, and entered the dining room to join his beloved wife and children.

CHAPTER TWELVE

Needing Help

Mae couldn't breathe. Acrid smoke burned her eyes and stole the air from her lungs. Turning her face away from the fire's searing heat, Mae felt disoriented. A cacophony of shouts and bangs assaulted her ears.

Where is Jarne?

They had been together moments ago. Mae coughed, bending over as her lungs screamed for air. Was that the door ahead? The outline looked like the door, but the light barely penetrated the thick fumes. Mae stumbled over debris littering her path. The door was too far; she wouldn't make it.

Sinking to her knees, Mae dug deep and channeled her last breath into a scream of defiance. She pushed her hands forward, blasting the opposite wall into splinters. Smoke and rubble rushed by, leaving Mae in the center of the devastation like the calm after a hurricane.

Feeling dizzy, she got to her feet and wiped the ash from her watering eyes. A figure lay crumpled ten paces away. Blood oozed from several wounds, digging canyons through the thick layer of soot covering the entire body.

Jarne! Was he still alive? Mae limped toward him. His chest rose and fell. *Thank the Norns!*

Raising his head, Jarne's eyes bore into hers. Was that hatred and revulsion on his face? Mae didn't understand. What had happened? Then she spotted a crossbow propped up on his leg, pointing straight at her heart.

"Jarne?" Mae asked, confused, before the bolt punched into her chest.

* * *

Mae jerked upright, her heart racing. It was dark; the night's fading stars still shone through the tiny window. The forest was quiet at this hour, with all the birds holding their breath in preparation for the morning concert. Jarne lay beside her, fast asleep. A full Viking assault with horns blaring wouldn't wake him now.

Mae shivered, the iron bands that had constricted her chest loosening. Blood thumped in her ears. Extracting herself from the blankets with difficulty, she left the room. Mae grabbed the door frame for support as she inhaled the crisp air. Cold sweat glistened on her forehead. Seeking solace among the trees, Mae stepped away from the hut, savoring the feel of the wet grass under her bare feet. The world appeared so tranquil, providing a stark contrast to her inner turmoil. The sun would rise soon. Yet the first eager birds had already greeted its arrival, singing about their hopes for the dawning day.

There was magic in a forest sunrise. Mae focused on nature's beauty to overcome her anxiety. Nothing had happened. *It was only a dream,* she scolded herself. But was it? Many folks believed some dreams held significance. Even her mother had told Mae the boundaries between the worlds weaken in dreams, and one might glimpse of the future. *Nonsense!* How could it? Mae loved Jarne, and he loved her, too. This certainty calmed her panic.

Mae remained sunken in thoughts at the edge of their clearing until the hut's door opened. A monumental yawn shattered the quiet. She turned around and smiled as she spotted that tall, skinny bear who had woken prematurely from hibernation.

"What are you doing out here in the middle of the night?" Jarne rubbed his eyes. "Was I snoring again?"

"No," Mae whispered, clinging to the morning's serenity for one more heartbeat. Then, with a mischievous grin, she added, "But I should have said 'yes' to guilt you into making breakfast."

"You wouldn't; that would be wicked."

"Well, staying in character. I'm a wicked witch, after all."

He closed the distance with three strides and encircled her with his arms.

"I caught me a witch, then," Jarne mused. "Do I get three wishes?"

In response, she punched him in the stomach.

"Witches rather deal in curses. You can have two more if you like."

"No, Your Terrible Witchiness," he uttered with comical wheezing, doubling over in mock pain, "your gifts were plentiful. Instead, let me check if the chickens have pleased you this morning."

Jarne walked to the coop and poked his head in, Mae's eyes following.

It was so easy being around him. When a remnant of the earlier shadow reached her, Mae decided to ignore it and live in the moment.

What is the harm? she thought. *Even if my vile curse tears us apart. That won't happen today, and probably not tomorrow.* And with that certainty, Mae went back inside, eager for breakfast.

* * *

In the afternoon, Mae strolled through the market in Hestavik, looking for something nice to buy for Jarne. The picturesque fishing village lay at the tip of the Sandrfjord, within easy reach of their cabin. Thanks to the Western Road running through its center, the market provided a much more varied assortment of goods than the hamlet's size suggested. Approaching the stall of a gray-bearded garments vendor, Mae admired a thick woolen shirt with intricate embroidery on the collar and sleeves.

"Ah, my good woman, you have excellent taste. This is the finest wool from Makevinger."

Mae let the soft fabric run through her fingers. Jarne would like it, and he deserved a gift.

The last six weeks had been the happiest of Mae's life. After the attack on the duke's bastard son, Mae was brimming with life force, and Jarne had taken two fat purses from the steward and his guest. Their future looked bright. All of that had been Jarne's doing.

"Yes, this is a nice shirt," she said.

"It will keep your husband warm when you can't see to that." The vendor smiled and gave her a wink. "You're in luck. We haven't received any supply from Makevinger lately."

"Why is that?"

"Haven't you heard? It is a sad story." Despite his words, he seemed eager to share it. "Someone killed the duke's son in Makevinger. Not his trueborn son, mind you," he continued in a conspiratorial whisper, "but the duke's vengeance was terrible."

Mae's face fell, all joy disappearing within one heartbeat.

"What happened?"

"They say the tanner did it. They say the duke's son took a fancy to his daughter, and that's why the father killed him."

"And the duke executed the tanner?"

"Yes. But not only him—his entire family and the neighbors as well. The soldiers hanged the kids before their parents' eyes and burned the women like witches. Only then were the men put to the sword. All the houses on that street burned to the ground. That's why there is no more wool from Makevinger at the moment."

Mae couldn't believe her ears; that could not have happened. She knew about Duke Finsgúr's cruelty. But this? Innocent women and children? And innocent men, for that matter?

The vendor kept talking. Mae didn't listen. She took a few steps back in shock. Then, reality sank in. *It's my fault. All the suffering is my fault!*

She turned and ran. The vendor shouted, but Mae didn't care. She ran, weaving through the market. She needed to get home and tell Jarne—or did he already know? He went to the markets more often. *But he couldn't! He wouldn't keep that from me.* Untying her horse, Mae realized she was still holding the shirt. *No time.* She stuffed it roughly into her bag, mounted up, and galloped out of town. She needed to talk to Jarne. Mae hoped for his sake that he didn't know about it. *He better not!*

The two-hour ride home didn't cool Mae's temper. On the contrary, pictures of the gruesome executions came unbidden into her mind. She was furious, working the lathered beast hard and throwing caution to the wind.

A tree branch grazed her cheek, leaving an angry cut. She didn't feel it. All she could think of were the children swinging from the ropes.

Reaching their clearing, she rode straight through the vegetable garden before jumping off the horse and sprinting to the hut. Mae pushed the door open with ferocity, banging it against the table and sending the vase with flowers flying. Jarne wasn't here. He must be gathering wood or harvesting berries or something. She couldn't wait. Mae shouted his name—again and again. Finally, she heard splashing footsteps. Jarne came from the river, a fishing pole in his hands and concern on his face.

"Mae? What's wrong? Are you all right?"

"Did you know?" she called without strength. A lump had formed in her throat. Still, her eyes pleaded that he would deny it.

"What do you mean? What's wrong?"

"DID YOU KNOW?" Mae shouted. Her raw magic burst forth, enhancing her voice. As the echo bounced off the trees, she saw the answer in his eyes. Still, he tried to claim innocence.

"I don't know what you're talking about."

"You know exactly what I mean!" Her tone had chilled to the deepest winter's frosts. "How long have you known?"

Jarne stood petrified, not speaking. Was he searching for excuses?

"Three weeks," he finally admitted. He lowered his eyes, and his hand twisted the front of his shirt. But his naughty-boy demeanor didn't rescue him this time. In quick succession, Mae flattened the young trees to his left and right with forceful blasts of air before aiming a slightly milder punch into Jarne's stomach, throwing him to the ground.

With tears brimming in her eyes, Mae stormed inside, slamming the hut's door behind her.

* * *

Getting back to his feet, Jarne approached the hut and listened at the door. He couldn't hear any noise, neither the angry banging of things being thrown against the walls nor the usual clatter of day-to-day activities.

Jarne felt ashamed for not telling her earlier. Still, he knew Mae's real anger was not with him. She blamed herself, and Jarne had to prevent her from doing anything harmful. Pushing the door open, he spotted Mae sitting on her cot, crying. The sight twisted his heart. All the power of the black witch was gone. Jarne saw a fragile woman in deep distress, the woman he loved loathing herself. He walked over, sat beside her, and took her in his arms.

"Please, Mae, forgive me. It was wrong. It was selfish. You were so happy."

She didn't respond. She neither pushed him away nor leaned into him. Mae sat there, hugging her knees, her body shaking, her quiet tears running down her bare legs.

"What happened is so horrible," he said. "I couldn't bring myself to tell you. I knew how much it would hurt you. But Mae, it wasn't..."

"Don't you dare!" Her voice sounded thick, as if her nose was blocked. She looked at him, her face puffy but her eyes still full of anger. "Don't you dare to tell me it wasn't my fault. It *is* my fault, all of it. Those people are dead because of me."

"We tried to stop evil," Jarne argued. "We tried to stop this creepy old man from raping young women."

"She would have lived," Mae challenged, "perhaps with a bastard of the bastard in her belly, but she would have lived. I killed her; I killed them all."

"Then it was my fault," Jarne interjected, lifting her head. "I planned the attack. I convinced you to go to Makevinger."

"Because I need to kill people." Mae's fire went out. "Only because I am a curse, and you don't want to accept it."

There it was, the plain truth. Jarne didn't accept that Mae was evil. He never had, and he never would. And the reason for it was simple.

"I love you, Mae." Jarne hugged her closer, and Mae relented, accepting his comfort. It wasn't his fault. If the roles were reversed, she wouldn't have told him either. The two sat there until late into the night.

* * *

"How can you love me?" Mae asked after her tears had dried. "You should hate me. Don't your ribs hurt? The whole world hates witches for their evil deeds. Why don't you?"

"I deserved your anger for lying to you. But Mae, in Makevinger, you killed two evil men... and two of their soldiers," Jarne added when Mae was about to argue. "What happened afterward—that was the duke's doing and only his. The people hate him. He is at the root of all evil. He has ruined the lives of dozens—no, hundreds."

"I've killed dozens."

"That's not the same thing. His men killed your family, and the black sorceress who cursed you came with them." Jarne looked at Mae. Although it was dark, Mae saw an angry fire burning in his eyes. "We need to end him!" he continued.

"But how? I went after him many times before I met you. And afterward... You always said we couldn't succeed. It would be a suicide mission without hope of success."

"I've been thinking about this since I heard the terrible news. We had success with some challenging plans. But this? We can't do it alone."

"Who will help us?" Mae gave a mirthless laugh. "Do you want to raise an army from the townsfolk, the farmers, and the downtrodden peasants?"

"Yes, we'll need to do that if we want to liberate our homeland from the foreign regime."

"You can't be serious." Mae shook her head. "Who would follow a witch?"

"If that witch killed the duke and enacted the people's revenge, the masses might follow her."

"But there you have a circle. We can't kill the duke without the people, and we won't get the people's support without killing the duke."

"That is not what I said." Jarne took Mae's hand, willing her to understand. "I said we can't kill the duke alone. We need help."

"Who else is there?" Mae got angry and frustrated with these pointless discussions. Jarne was right; the duke had to die. He finally convinced her to return to her old self—the black witch on a revenge mission. But then, he immediately disagreed with himself. Regardless, he had succeeded in opening

Mae's eyes. She knew what to do. Mae would attack the duke. And if she died in the attempt, then that was a small price to pay. Believing she had won the discussion, Mae was about to inform Jarne about her irrefutable conclusion when Jarne spoke again.

"Your sisters."

Mae looked confused.

"What about my sisters?"

"Renya and especially Sigri, we need their help."

"I am not hurt," Mae stated in bewilderment. "This tiny cut is nothing. I don't need Sigri's healing."

"That's not what I mean."

"Then what do you mean?" Mae threw up her hands, suppressing the urge to lash out again.

"Your sisters can help us kill the duke," he elaborated. "With Sigri's mind and Renya's strength, we can pull off the attack and rid the world of this accursed tyrant."

Silence. Mae looked at Jarne in disbelief. She would have laughed, but it wasn't funny.

"You can't be serious."

"I am." There was clarity in his eyes and determination in his voice. He almost swept her away with his fervor. But then, the absurdity of his plan caught up with Mae.

"Jarne..." Mae took a deep breath and continued in the tone a mother adopts when explaining that the boy wouldn't get a pony as a Midwinter present, "Renya and Sigri won't help us. They hate us."

"I have a plan, trust me. We'll talk more in the morning. I will convince them to help."

Mae had no energy to argue. It was late. Why crush Jarne's hopes, then? She would have enough time the following morning.

* * *

"Sigri, come over here!" Renya called her sister from the top of the crumpled gatehouse. This was Renya's favorite spot in the depressing castle she called home. From there, she could see far across the outside world into which the sisters rarely ventured these days. For days on end, Renya tried to alleviate the endless boredom by watching eagles soar in the upward drafts. She wished she could join them in their boundless freedom, their careless joy, and the exhilarating thrill of the hunt.

Sigri's response came muffled from the kitchen where she was pickling frog livers, boiling salamander feet, or brewing the devil-knew-what concoctions. Renya couldn't be bothered to take the slightest interest in her only companion's passions.

"What is it, Renya? Another dragon-shaped cloud?" That joke, too, had gotten old a long time ago. Still, it demonstrated Sigri's reciprocal disinterest in Renya's affairs.

"Unless there is a cloud down in the valley looking like two travelers, I would hazard a guess that we are getting visitors."

"Visitors?" Sigri stepped out of the kitchen. Wiping her hands on the gray smock she wore over her blue dress, she approached Renya.

"Don't fake surprise; you knew about it. With so little happening here, there is no way your prodigious skills could miss such an event."

"You give me too much credit, dear sister." Sigri had reached the gatehouse and climbed the broken wall to the top. Huffing from the exertion, she continued. "But yes, in this case, I had foreseen the arrival of visitors."

"And you didn't tell me because?"

"Because I didn't want to get your hopes up too early. There was still a lot of uncertainty."

"You think the sunrise is uncertain until the glare blinds you. But let me tell you what I am certain about. I will not let these travelers escape." Renya turned to her sister and put her hands on her hips. Despite being shorter and younger than Sigri, the red-haired witch tried to assert dominance with her posture. "We haven't taken anybody's life force for over three years. We're stuck in this rotting ruin because you've developed a 'conscience,'" Renya continued, pointing an accusing finger. "And I went along with it. Don't ask me why. But this time, there is nothing you can say to stop me."

"I am afraid there is."

"Yeah, what? Give it your best shot, sis."

"It is Mae."

"What is?"

"The travelers. You are right; these two riders are coming to visit us. Mae and the boy, Jarne—that is who the travelers are."

Renya looked dumbfounded, her facial expression resembling someone who had been hit on the head with a butter churn.

"Why?"

"I dare say we will learn soon. Mae didn't visit me in my dreams, nor has she sent me a talking raven."

"But...?" Renya was trying and failing to regain her swagger. "What about the traps?" she finally asked. "Shall we leave them in place?"

"I'd say we leave the lower two. We don't want to appear too desperate for visitors, especially those two. But you'd better disarm the rockslide. I hate not knowing why Mae is coming back, and dead bodies are so stingy with information." Sigri turned. She would have liked to glide away as if all this wasn't rattling her. But the cumbersome climb over the broken rocks ruined her elegant departure.

"She isn't coming back, is she? I mean, coming back to live here?" Renya asked the retreating figure of her sister. "We won't allow that, right?"

Sigri didn't reply; she didn't know.

"She betrayed us," Renya shouted, finally finding herself again. "I'll never forgive Mae for that."

Yet Sigri knew this to be a lie Renya liked to tell herself, and Renya knew it, too.

* * *

Mae tore her eyes away from the treacherous path to look at their destination. The castle ruin hadn't changed. Angry and foreboding, the edifice loomed on the sheer rocky outcrop, promising all the coziness of a thorn thicket. Yet Mae knew that the hostile exterior was only a light summer rain compared to the furious thunderstorm the welcome of her sisters would be.

Still, there was no point in turning back now. They'd made it this far, and Sigri at least would stop Renya from doing anything crazy until both travelers reached the castle. Sigri knew they were coming; she must be dying to know why.

"That's the castle? The path looks steep." These were the first words Jarne had spoken that day. It seemed he had used all his ammunition to convince Mae to go on this fool's errand. The two had argued for days. In the end, Mae gave in just to shut him up.

Jarne was overjoyed, almost giddy, when Mae finally agreed. Immediately, he started packing their things. It was late in the year. The wind would be icy, and there might be snow already. When they finally set out toward the mountains, Jarne chatted nonstop, bubbling like a forest stream, reassuring Mae of the success of his plan. Yet, the closer they got, the more subdued his mood became.

Mae didn't blame him. He had not been conscious the last time Mae had seen her sisters. In the intervening years, Mae hadn't spoken much about

Renya and Sigri. Jarne didn't know about the silly pranks the sisters had played on each other, like the time Sigri and Mae had put nettles in Renya's nightshirt or when Mae and Renya had replaced Sigri's chamomile syrup with homemade whiskey. He only knew about the hurt and bitterness that the separation had brought.

"Yes, that is the home of the Guðmundsdóttir sisters. The path isn't as bad as it looks. Steer your horse slowly, and the animal will find sound footing. Once we reach the switchback..."

"What was that?" Jarne interrupted. "Did you hear that?"

"Yes," Mae said. "It sounded like..."

"Wolves," Jarne shouted, a slight edge of panic in his voice.

"There are no wolves in these mountains," she stated. But reality contradicted her within seconds as three wolves stepped into their path.

* * *

Mae and Jarne often heard wolves in their forest, though they rarely saw them. There, Jarne was confident. He could drive off a single wolf with his knife and climb a tree if he came across a pack. However, he wasn't looking forward to meeting angry canines on this narrow path. Mae seemed to be less concerned.

The lead wolf was an enormous black beast with fiery green eyes, flanked on either side by a smaller wolf—one rusty brown with amber eyes and one snow-white animal with eyes of a pale gray. Fletching their yellow teeth, the animals blocked the road. Their furs stood on end, and their growls frightened the horses and Jarne. What could he do? The wolves would attack the open flank if he turned his horse to flee. Should he urge his horse forward to ride them down? There wasn't enough room to gather momentum.

"Mae, can you do something?" This time, Jarne's voice carried the undisguised tone of panic.

Mae reacted, yet differently than Jarne had expected. Instead of sending bolts of lightning down on the threatening beasts, Mae laughed. Loud bursts of high-pitched squeals escaped her mouth. Jarne looked around. Alarmed, he saw Mae doubled over, her body rocking with hearty laughs and snot bubbling from her nose. *Has she gone mad?*

"Mae?"

"Oh, this is brilliant," Mae wheezed in between chuckles.

The wolves seemed unperturbed and maintained their menacing stance. Yet, they hadn't attacked either, despite Jarne bringing his horse around.

He had stopped worrying about the wolves. Instead, Jarne was frightened by Mae's peculiar behavior. For a long moment, everything remained as it was: the wolves growling, Mae laughing, and Jarne staring in bafflement from one to the other. Finally, Mae regained control, wiped her face, and urged her horse forward.

"Let's go, Jarne. I must compliment Renya on this excellent idea." And with that, she moved through the wolves—literally through them, as if they were made of smoke. Jarne's jaw dropped. The wolves still growled, but Mae rode up the mountain pass on the other side. A few strides ahead, she stopped, turned around, and shouted.

"Let me help with your horse—it doesn't know Renya's sense of humor yet."

Seemingly of its own accord, Jarne's horse moved forward, reached the wolves, and rode through.

"Magic!" Jarne exclaimed, annoyed but also very relieved.

CHAPTER THIRTEEN

Angry Sisters

"Look what the cat dragged in." Renya stood in the courtyard as Mae and Jarne rode in, her amber eyes narrowed, her red hair whipping in the wind, and her gray cloak fluttered like a banner. The castle's broken walls provided little protection from the icy gusts. Still, her unwavering stare was at least as cold as the air. Mae took comfort from the notion that some things never changed. That wasn't entirely true, as she saw lines on Renya's face which hadn't been there three years ago.

"You don't have a cat," Mae replied. "Although, it might be good for you, living with a creature who shares your sense of aloofness and superiority."

"How do you know I don't have a cat? You've been gone for three years."

"Because she knows you," Sigri clarified, approaching from the kitchen. "And anyhow, I don't think you came here to talk about cats, Mae? Why don't you come in? It must be uncomfortable in those wet clothes."

"Thank you, Sigri, indeed. I was about to congratulate Renya on the marvelous wolf illusion, but the diverted stream somewhat killed the mood."

"Then you should have taken the hint and turned around," Renya grumbled, but everyone ignored her.

Mae got off her horse and took a bag from the saddle.

"We brought you some spices and sugar from the market."

"Isn't that sweet of her?"

This time, Mae and Sigri gave Renya an identical, exasperated look. Mae almost laughed to see how easily they had fallen back into their former life. But, of course, they hadn't, and they wouldn't. A few pleasantries couldn't bridge the gulf between them.

Jarne took the lead of Mae's mount and tied the animals to a metal ring in the wall. He was about to unsaddle the horses when Mae stopped him.

"We can do this later if needed." She looked at Sigri to gauge their chance of staying the night at the castle. Yet, the green witch stood serene like a statue, tall and elegant. With her long blond hair tied into a braid, her pale-gray eyes gave nothing away. Trying to skip past this awkward exchange, Mae made the introductions.

"Sigri, Renya, this is Jarne. Jarne, meet Sigri"—Mae pointed with an open hand at the taller woman—"and her sister Renya." Mae indicated with a jerk of her head. The younger witch glared, her arms crossed in front of her chest. "Of course, you already knew who is who. But since there was no conversation the last time, I thought it proper to give the introductions."

"It is interesting to meet you, Jarne," Sigri agreed. "Please, do come in. The fire is lit, I brewed tea, and we can finally see if there's a pearl hidden in this mysterious oyster."

Sigri glided toward the kitchen, Mae ushered Jarne to follow, and Renya stomped behind.

After hanging their wet traveling cloaks on wall pegs, Mae and Jarne sat side by side at the polished wooden table. Sigri poured tea and took her place across from the guests. Only Renya stood undecided for a moment. In the end, she moved to the head of the table, placing Jarne between her and Mae.

"Now, what brings you here?" As much as Sigri was trying to hide it, this was the question she was dying to learn the answer to.

Mae took her teacup in both hands, feeling the warmth and smelling the invigorating aroma of berries, pines, and spices. She took a small sip, sighing in delight. After a pause long enough to infuriate the sisters, Mae nodded to Jarne to put their cards on the table.

"We are here to make a proposal."

"The pup speaks. Well done, boy! But now let the adults talk."

"Renya, please," Mae sighed. "Try to behave like a grown woman yourself."

Jarne continued unperturbed. He had prepared for this the entire journey and decided the best approach was to be direct.

"Mae and I are planning to kill Duke Finsgúr. And we need your help."

"That isn't a proposal," Sigri remarked, her voice even as always.

"Killing the duke is the first step of a wider uprising. We aim to overthrow the foreign regime, and in doing so, we will revoke the ban on witchcraft."

"Oh, my! I feared the infection and fever addled his mind. But dear me, this is worse than I thought," Renya commented with a mock tone of compassion.

"Please, my boy, lay down and rest your troubled head. And don't go playing with the burning logs. They look nice, but they'll hurt you."

"I wouldn't have put it that way," Sigri stated. "But, Mae, you can't be serious. The boy mentioned three impossible things which aren't even related."

Jarne was about to retort, but Mae put her hand on his.

"You can't be happy with the life you live here. Being shut away from the world, always afraid of the witch hunters—no friends, family, or lovers." Mae sat up straighter. "This land is on the brink of revolt. There have already been uprisings: the slaves in the copper mines and the Northerners in the Ever Forest. The cruelty of the duke and his underlings has reached a point where the people have nothing to lose. I've seen the villagers in Kristiansund attacking the duke's soldiers with my own eyes."

"And the duke's men killed all those people in Makevinger," Sigri added, throwing icy water on Mae's flaming words. "We still hear a thing or two from the outside world."

"Yes," Jarne said, seeing Sigri's words as additional ammunition for their proposal. "Many people have heard, and they hate the duke for his cruelty. If three witches made him pay, they'd be heroes. Don't you see?"

"No, I don't." Renya stood. Raising her voice, she glared at Mae. "You've left us to live your dream of a family life while we were stuck in this rotting ruin. You've hidden behind your morals like a snake in the high grass. Yet the venomous fangs still strike the heedless wanderer. And when the casualties of your 'good deeds' pile higher than the black death's harvest, you come crawling here to have us clean up your mess—to polish your false image of the avenging angel. I won't have any of it."

Renya's chest heaved as she dragged in noisy breaths. Mae wouldn't have been surprised to see sparks flying from Renya's nostrils. Still, the gray witch's aim was true, and the words pierced Mae's heart as they intended.

"I won't violate the guest's right," Renya hissed through gritted teeth. "There are still some misguided vestiges of propriety buried in me. You can sleep in the root cellar. But you better be gone by sunrise if you know what's good for you."

Renya stomped toward the bedroom, intending to have her accusations stand as the last word, when Jarne jumped up. Color flooded his cheeks, and he shouted at her with fists balled.

"How dare you lay the duke's despicable deeds at Mae's feet! She is out there, righting the wrongs of evil men while you sit in your stronghold, forever whining about life mistreating you."

"Keep your tongue behind your baby teeth, boy," Renya fumed, "or I'll shatter them. Mae, reign your pup in! Else you'll regret it."

"Did I hit a nerve? Is the mighty witch rattled by the truth?" Jarne's bravery sometimes bordered on foolishness. With a yelp, he flew backward, crashing into the shelves. Pots and jars rained down on him. Renya was about to send the fire poker his way when Mae, in turn, blasted her sister off her feet. Renya's head barely missed the crackling flames, hitting the bricks instead. Blood ran down her scalp, and murder was in her eyes.

"Enough!" Sigri shouted. A powerful wave ran through the room, bathing the combatants in ice and stealing the air from their lungs. "How dare you? Attacking a guest, attacking your sister—both of you, you are a disgrace! Petty, squabbling children who can't control their emotions. You stop this foolishness, now!" Sigri commanded with a hitherto unseen authority.

"Renya, press a dishcloth onto your skull, or you'll ruin your dress. I'll be with you shortly, bandaging your wound. Thank the devils for your thick head. Mae, help Jarne up and get your stuff from the horses. You can stay here in the kitchen. You better clean the mess first, mind you. I'll take a look at his injuries as well." Sigri was almost back to her usual calm efficiency. Yet, when nobody moved, she bellowed, "Get going!"

That went well, Mae thought as she stepped outside to gather their saddlebags. *So much for Jarne's plan. I couldn't have made it backfire more, even if I tried.* Mae should have known better how to deal with Renya's temper. Given more time, she might have won Sigri over. But all hope died when Renya's head hit the fireplace.

* * *

An hour later, Mae clambered up the jagged rocks to the top of the broken tower, her refuge for troublesome times. Watching Sigri tend to Jarne had made her feel useless. Mae needed fresh air, and she left the kitchen. When spending her last night up here, Mae had been sure she would never return. Now she had, and she wished she hadn't.

Low clouds obscured the stars, and the air smelled of snow—nature mirroring Mae's wintery relationship with the sisters. Shivering, Mae wondered if the healer had retired to the bedroom so Mae could return inside. Then, she saw a light approaching the tower.

"Sigri? What are you doing out here? Is Jarne all right?"

"Yes, your Jarne is fine. He is sleeping. They both are. I gave them a draft to ease the pain."

"What is it then? I wasn't hurt; I'm fine."

"No, you are not. That's why I'm here. I wonder… Is it worth risking my neck to climb up? It is pretty cold. Why don't you come into the kitchen? We can talk there."

"Yes, of course," Mae replied, dreading the scolding she knew she deserved. "But won't we disturb Jarne?"

"I've put him on your cot in the bedroom. His ribs are bruised. He wouldn't thank me for a night on the hard kitchen floor."

"In the bedroom? With Renya? And you left the two alone?" Mae started to climb down the treacherous wall in haste.

"Easy, Mae, don't break any more bones! I'm done with healing for tonight. They're fine. I told you, they are both asleep."

Mae jumped the last yard but landed awkwardly. Pain shot up her leg. She tried to hide it. Still, Sigri had seen, shook her head, and walked toward the kitchen. Mae followed, limping and embarrassed. Entering the house, Mae surveyed the devastation the earlier fight had caused.

"I'm so sorry, Sigri."

"As you should be, but not for this." Before Mae could say anything more, Sigri ordered her to sit and put a fresh cup of tea in front of her.

"Here, you hardly touched your tea earlier."

"Thank you. This smells different. Whiskey?"

"I thought we both could use some fortification."

There was the tiniest moment of hesitation as Mae wondered if the liquor hid other, more nefarious ingredients. But then she rebuked herself. This was Sigri. If Mae couldn't trust the green witch, her world had bigger problems. Taking a sip, Mae felt the wonderful warmth spreading inside her. For a few heartbeats, she almost forgot her sorrows.

"You do care for the boy, don't you?" Sigri asked, breaking the silence.

"Yes, and Jarne would object to being called 'boy.' He is a man now."

"So I have seen."

Mae shot Sigri a quizzical look.

"His chest and arms. I left his pants on," Sigri replied, miffed. Then, with a little more cheek, she added, "Honestly, Mae, what would I do with him? He's way too young. I'm not Renya."

Mae blushed at the thought of what Renya might have done under different circumstances.

"You're in love with him, then?" Sigri asked with the detachment of a healer questioning patients about their symptoms.

"Yes, and he to like me too. We are a couple, if that was your next question."

"And back then?"

"Of course not. He was a child back then. I cared because he reminded me of my brother Eilif. I failed Eilif; I didn't want to fail Jarne, too. But he isn't my brother. I mean…" Mae blushed even deeper.

"I really don't care at what age you coaxed him into your bed. I wanted to understand what about him made you choose like you did." Sigri's tone had lost all frivolity, and the sadness underneath showed through.

"I'm sorry, Sigri." Mae looked in her sister eyes. "I didn't want to choose," she said without adding, *You made me.*

"The last years were hard, Mae. That's why Renya attacked. She has been suffering; I have been suffering. We lost our way when we lost you." Sigri got up and walked to the kettle. "More tea?"

"Yes, please." Mae would have said yes to pickled toenails if it allowed Sigri to finally speak out loud what had tortured her for all these years.

Sigri returned with the tea and a dusty bottle. Pouring generous measures of both liquids, Sigri looked Mae straight in the eyes and spoke the most unexpected words of the evening.

"I'm sorry, Mae, for chasing you away. I feared the boy would harm us when he grew up, so I did it myself. I didn't mean to, but I couldn't see beyond my fear and my past. Have I ever told you about my father?"

* * *

Mae and Sigri settled in for a long night. The green witch's story was as sad as the black's, more so even since the betrayal came from her own father.

"My father was a vain man," Sigri started, her bitterness undisguised. "He only cared about status and prestige. That's why he married my mother. She was of Viking blood, the daughter of a warrior in the invading army. As far as I can remember, he never showed her affection."

"Is she still alive?" Mae asked.

"My mother died in childbed after Renya was born. I was six." Sigri took another sip from her tea, blinking away the moisture in her eyes. "My father approached the situation like his logistics problems. He hired a wet nurse for Renya and an old crone as a minder for me. *He* had no time for us; he had *important* work." Sigri emphasized the words in a pompous tone. "We lived in Thorshofn, and he was the assistant to the quarter steward.

"When I first showed signs of magic, a year or two later, he was beyond himself with fear and anger. 'What would the neighbors think?' He never cared for anything else. He beat me, and he threatened me. I was to conceal what I was if I wanted to keep the roof over my head. Whenever I could get away, I snuck into the forest, trying to understand what was happening. The people told horrible stories about evil witches. I couldn't be one, could I?"

Mae took Sigri's hand, the tea forgotten. For once, Mae didn't see the reserved and logical woman with a rational answer for everything. Instead, she glimpsed a frightened young girl—scared, confused, and lonely.

"Still, sometimes I visited him at work." Sigri sighed. "Learning letters and numbers, watching him solve problems. I wanted to please him. I hoped he would like me better then." A long pause followed. Taking a deep breath, Sigri continued.

"Renya was different; she was wild and willful. Our father was unable or unwilling to rein her in. From a young age, she fought with other children, even boys. I didn't have the means to influence her. I still don't." Sigri gave a sad little laugh. "She got into so much trouble. And then, I was twenty..." Sigri's voice cracked. Taking several deep breaths, Sigri forced herself to go on. "I never cared for the men in town. The few who courted me were dull and self-absorbed, thinking the sun shone out of their rear ends. I kept to myself. But Renya was popular. She had many friends. She'd probably played kissing games since she was eleven."

Sigri's eyes shone with admiring incredulity for one more heartbeat. Then, her face fell, and she clenched her fists so tight her knuckles shone white.

"When she was fourteen," Sigri swallowed, "something terrible happened. Renya killed a soldier with magic. She came home, distraught, not making sense. I tried to calm her, and she started telling my father and me about the horrible affair. And *what* did my father do?" Sigri had jumped to her feet, shouting the question, challenging the world to join in her condemnation. "He called her a filthy witch, devil's whore, and other foul names. He disowned her, declaring he would report her to the authorities—to save his job, his life, and his reputation. I couldn't believe my ears."

Sigri's eyes glowed with a hatred so hot Mae had never seen anything like it.

"He moved to grab Renya," Sigri snarled, "and I blasted him off his feet. There was a moment when I wanted to do much worse to him. But instead, I took Renya by the hand and stormed into his room to find my mother's jewelry. I sent Renya to bring our cloaks and everything else she could carry." Sigri placed her hands on the table and leaned forward as if the weight of the world was bending her down.

"He tried to get back up," she continued in a whisper full of menace, "and

I looked at him. All the hurt and hate I had collected over the years must have burned in my eyes. He sat back down and pissed himself. I took his horse and left my home with my little sister in tow. I never saw him again. He died a few years ago."

Sigri sat back down, and Mae took her hands. Mae hadn't known. She'd never asked about the sisters' past when she lived here. Torn between her thirst for vengeance and her struggle to retain her humanity amidst the darkness of her powers, Mae had imposed her moral restrictions onto her sisters, not even considering the harm it could do.

"Here," Sigri said after a long silence, pulling a necklace from below her dress. "This was my mother's. The only piece I ever cared for. It had been her grandmother's, from the Southlands, before the invasion." The necklace was made of blue coral and white pearls, shimmering like a rainbow in the candlelight. "It's the only piece of jewelry I remember my mother ever wearing; it's the only piece I wear. I wish I had a daughter to pass it on to."

Sigri trailed off, and many moments passed before she resumed her tale.

"When you came to us, I was so eager to learn from your adventures. You'd roamed the land, using your raw powers openly," Sigri stated with admiration. Then she shook her head. "You never had to disown what you are. I couldn't understand why you hated your existence or why you imposed your rules on our use of magic."

Mae gulped, unable to provide a defense.

"But, instead of making you understand, I drove you away," Sigri said. "I'm not better than my father. I, too, was unable to accept someone different."

"That's not true," Mae whispered. "It was my fault, and I'm so sorry."

"It wasn't your fault, Mae. You can't help it. Your inner fire drives you forward, regardless of what the world thinks. I admire you for that. And I won't let my sister's hot head get in the way of a better future for us all. But Mae," Sigri asked, her longing written all over her face, "do you believe there is any chance of this crazy idea succeeding?"

"I don't know," Mae replied. "Right now, the people hate the duke. In overthrowing him, we may become heroes like Jarne believes. Even if the chances are slim." Mae continued with more passion. "Think of the reward, Sigri. You could have a family and children and pass on your necklace."

"You paint an enticing picture. But Mae, you only talk of the duke. What about the king?"

"The duke is the key. The king is weak. The north is in open rebellion. Once we seize the south, his strength will melt like frost before the hearthfire."

"The king might be a feeble reed, but his black sorceress isn't. She'll be a much greater challenge."

"Leave her to me," Mae growled, her eyes narrowing. "I've unfinished business with her. I've ignored her for too long."

The two women finished the last tea, sunken in dreams of a glorious future and thoughts of long-overdue revenge. The fire had died, leaving only smoldering embers, and most of the whiskey had vanished.

When the oil lamps burned low, Sigri was the more sensible of the two.

"It's late. We should catch a few hours of sleep before our companions need our attention."

"How about it, Sigri? Will you help?"

"I don't know, Mae. I need to think it through. And even if I was willing, convincing Renya is a different matter altogether."

"But you'll think of it?"

"I will. I promise. Bring your pack into the bedroom. I've placed Jarne onto your cot, but there is room on the floor. The least I can offer you is a place in there." Sigri pointed with her head, giving Mae a wink. "Like in the old days."

"Thank you, Sigri."

CHAPTER FOURTEEN

A Fighting Chance

THE SUN SHONE brightly behind the curtains when Mae woke up. Feeling groggy, she needed a moment to orient herself. Mae lay on a bedroll in her old room in the Witches' Castle. Getting up with a throbbing head, she cursed Sigri for last night's whiskey.

Noises reached Mae's ears from the outside—grunts and shouts. She thought she discerned Renya's taunting voice. *Renya? And where is Jarne?* Grabbing her boots, Mae hopped into the kitchen, where she could see a section of the courtyard. What she saw stopped her heart. Jarne lay in the dirt, and Renya advanced toward him.

"No!" Mae rushed outside, one boot still in her hand.

Jarne had gotten back up. He brandished his knife. His clothes were dirty, his hands scraped, yet a fierce determination showed on his face. Renya wore black pants, also bearing signs of having made contact with the ground. As Mae took in the horrific scene, Renya sent a fireball after Jarne. He dodged and threw a rock straight for the gray witch's head in return. She deflected the projectile with a shield of compressed air.

"Stop that foolishness! Renya! Jarne! Please stop!" Mae shouted. Her head throbbed worse than ever. Still, she had to do something.

"They won't listen. I've tried." Sigri's voice came from behind Mae, where she sat on a wooden stool and regarded the deadly fight with mild annoyance. "After all my efforts in healing them yesterday—wasted. I thought they would listen to me, but no. Ungrateful brats!"

"Sigri, is that all you worry about? They're killing each other." To underscore her point, Jarne stabbed his knife toward Renya, and the witch punched his hand away with a targeted blast of air. The knife flew out of Jarne's grip, landing in the dirt mere inches from Sigri's feet.

"Much better!" Jarne shouted. "This time, you punched it clean out of my hand." He flexed the limb to shake off the sting.

"*What?*" Mae gasped, not comprehending the world.

"They're sparring. A stupid idea, given they'd already practiced the real thing yesterday, and I had to put them back together. But as I said, ungrateful brats." Sigri got up, took her stool, and returned to the kitchen, leaving a flummoxed Mae standing open mouthed in the courtyard.

Jarne picked up his knife, blew Mae a kiss, and approached Renya, clapping her on the shoulder.

"I told you, you can throw harder punches when you aim for a smaller area. If you had focused your attack yesterday, you'd have broken my ribs."

"I take it you are not sorry?" Renya smirked, dusting her hands off.

"Oh, no. I got plenty." He chuckled, rubbing a lump on the back of his head. "Those jars were heavy. What was the slimy stuff inside?"

"Some of Sigri's tinctures. I'm surprised you didn't turn into a weasel or something. Mind you, you moved like one this morning."

"No, that is just practice."

"From dodging things Mae throws at you?"

Jarne grinned and left it at that. Instead, he ran over to Mae and took her in his arms.

"Are you well?" he asked. "You look like someone walked over your grave."

"My grave? MY GRAVE?" she shrieked. "I imagined *your* grave! What were you thinking?" Pushing him away from her, Mae punched him on the shoulder. Jarne looked perplexed and stammered in response.

"But... You were sleeping, and I..."

"And you had nothing better to do than to engage in mortal combat with a skilled and ruthless witch?"

"Thanks, Mae," Renya shouted from the courtyard's other side. "At least for the 'skilled' part."

"I wasn't. We were practicing. There was no danger; I was in control."

"Sure thing," Renya sniggered, sending another blast to slap Jarne hard on his behind. He wheeled around, his eyes narrowed, and Renya blew him a kiss before disappearing into the kitchen.

Looking bewildered, Jarne turned back to Mae and met a stony-faced witch. He sighed, took her by the hand, and dragged her over to a couple of broken rocks, where they could sit and talk.

"Honestly, Mae, it was nothing. I woke up, and you were still asleep. When I went into the kitchen to find some food, Renya was there. But she was different; she wanted to talk. Renya seemed impressed by how I stood up for you yesterday."

Jarne sat up straighter and puffed his chest out. Mae's icy stare didn't waver, and he continued, somewhat deflated.

"We talked about our lives, hers in the castle and mine in the forest. She isn't happy here, that much is clear. I think, there's a good chance we can win her over. She was talkative and friendly, even a bit flirtatious." Jarne admitted, blushing.

Mae's hand jabbed forward, grabbed Jarne's ear, and pulled hard.

"Renya flirts with men she wants to kill," the black witch declared, emphasizing every single word with a painful tug on Jarne's ear.

"Ouch! Mae! Stop it!" Jarne howled.

"If I rip off your ear, will you finally realize that witches are dangerous?" Yet despite her threat, she let go of Jarne.

"I'm sorry I scared you." He took her hand and looked into Mae's eyes. "I am, but I don't think there was any danger."

"Because you know Renya better than I do?"

"No, but I could feel how Renya missed you. She wouldn't do anything to drive you away again."

Mae raised her eyebrows. "Like yesterday evening, you mean?"

"Well, if she had time to think before acting, I mean."

"Which Renya is famous for—the 'thinking before acting.'"

Jarne searched for words, but Mae relieved him by throwing her arms around him and hugging him tight.

"You scared me, Jarne. Don't do it ever again." With that, they transitioned to nonverbal communication.

* * *

The two visitors stayed at the castle. Mae was astounded that a fight—of all things—dissolved Renya's open hostility, even if it had only been a practice bout. Surely, not everything was forgiven and forgotten. Yet, on the surface, Renya was her old self: taunting, teasing, and playfully threatening—a dog that barks but is unlikely to bite. Mae was relieved she hadn't done irreparable harm last night. Still, she ensured Jarne was never alone with Renya. There were too many potential dangers her partner could encounter.

Instead, Mae sent Jarne out hunting. Bringing back a mountain goat would go a long way toward winning over the sisters. Even some rodents or birds would be well appreciated.

Sigri was busy in the kitchen, sorting through the debris from her storage shelf and trying to salvage anything still usable. She sent Mae and Renya to fetch old and dusty urns from the root cellar. The two witches cleaned them of filth and spiders in the courtyard so Sigri's rescued ingredients could find a new home. Mae didn't complain, yet Renya, whose spell had actually destroyed Sigri's prized possessions, didn't hold back. All afternoon, a constant stream of grumblings accompanied her every move. Although these utterings often became inaudible mumblings when Sigri walked by within earshot.

Mae loved both women, and hope grew in her chest. Could they overcome their differences? Could the sisters go—well, not back to how it had been before, but forward to a new understanding? *Only time will tell.*

Jarne returned in the late afternoon with a plump groundhog over his shoulder, exuding the pride of a valiant knight having slain a vicious dragon. Mae grabbed him and volunteered to prepare dinner, giving the sisters a chance to talk things over. But the evening grew cold, and both witches came inside. They sat at the table, content to watch Mae skinning the animal. Jarne chopped onions and turnips. When Mae had added all the ingredients to the cauldron and the stew simmered over the open fire, Sigri asked her and Jarne to take a seat.

"Tell us more about your crazy plan. How do you envision killing the duke?" Sigri asked.

"We don't have everything worked out yet," Jarne admitted. "We were hoping for your clever ideas. The key is to cut off the snake's head. Once the duke is eliminated, the people will lose their fear and join us in over-throwing the foreign oppressors." Jarne surveyed his audience for signs of contradiction or ridicule. When none followed, he continued. "We need to catch him off guard. In the past, Mae and I had success with disguises. I was thinking of dressing like a duke's soldier and bringing Mae as a captive."

"That wouldn't work," Sigri said as fragments of ideas zipped through her mind. "The duke takes his personal safety seriously. He'd never let an unknown guard approach him alone with a prisoner. He's afraid of assassins lurking everywhere."

"For good reasons," Renya stated, "which rules out another nightly ambush on his carriage."

"We all would like to avoid that," Mae smirked, looking at Jarne.

He blushed, and Renya immediately taunted him.

"Oh, he is so cute when the color floods his face. Does he blush at night, too?" she asked Mae. Before either could rise to the bait, Sigri spoke, continuing her train of thought as if nobody had said anything.

"We need to get closer, observe him, and find the weak points in his armor. We won't be able to devise any viable plan from here."

"What do you suggest?" Jarne asked, in an obvious effort to ignore his glowing, bright-red cheeks.

"My aunt, my father's younger sister, still lives in Thorshofn. She inherited the house after my *dear* father's death." Sigri's visage darkened at his mention, and she needed a few heartbeats to compose herself. "She lives there alone."

"Wasn't she married?" Renya asked.

"Twice, but both husbands died. Poison, I assume. She hated them."

"Is she a witch?" Mae was astounded after what she had learned yesterday.

"I don't think so. Oh, she is wicked—don't doubt. But I don't believe she has any magic."

"Are you planning to move in with Aunty Dagmar?" Renya inquired, obvious disdain coloring her tone.

"We would need a cover story. Let's eat first, and then we can talk further." The stew smelled rich and gamey, the meat was tender, and a thin layer of fat on top reflected the candlelight in rainbow colors.

"See, Sigri, this is food humans eat," Renya exclaimed between mouthfuls. "Sometimes, my dear sister confuses us with rabbits who live off dandelions and moldy carrots."

"I don't remember you ever volunteering," Sigri shot back, "to cook, hunt, or do anything for that matter."

Mae chuckled, enjoying the banter and glad of not being the target for once.

"I see you appreciate being back here," Sigri remarked. "Hence, you won't object to helping me with a small request after dinner, right? There is a full moon tonight, and I need to gather mugwort. You can come along to carry the oil lamp." That wiped the smirk off Mae's face.

"It is freezing out there," she objected with little hope of success. "And do you think it wise to leave? I mean... you and me leaving?"

"Then you better wear some warm clothes. As for those two, I'm confident we can leave them alone for a bit without them killing each other or ending up in each other's pants."

Renya grinned like a devil, and Jarne, whose color had barely returned to normal, blushed again and gathered the empty bowls to wash them.

"You behave yourself, Renya," Sigri admonished. "Better employ what is between your ears. We still need a reason to visit our aunt and stay in Thorshofn." Then, she grabbed her cloak and beckoned Mae to follow.

* * *

SIGRI AND MAE crossed the courtyard and hiked up a goat path toward a ridge behind where a lush meadow clung to the mountain's southern slope. Sigri set a brisk pace despite Mae holding the lamp. There was a full moon, but a layer of clouds allowed only a tiny amount of diffused light to illuminate the landscape. Yet, Sigri didn't waver even when a false step could result in a long and painful tumble down the mountainside.

The two women had walked for nearly ten minutes when Mae finally asked the question she had been wondering about since Sigri had invited her to join. "Why do you have to pick the herbs under the full moon? And does it even count if there are clouds?"

"What do you think?" Sigri stopped and looked back to the castle. Little of the ruin was visible from their vantage point. The green witch relaxed, spread her cloak, and sat on the cold ground.

"I don't know." Mae shrugged. "I can't imagine what clouds have to do with anything."

"Of course they don't, nor does the full moon."

"Then why are we out here, risking our necks in the darkness?"

"Because I needed to talk to you," Sigri explained, "and I didn't want your boy—sorry, your Jarne—to know about it. Renya is probably peeing her underpants, trying to hold in the laughter. Yet sometimes, playing up the witchy mystery pays off."

Mae stood dumbfounded for a couple of heartbeats, staring at her sister open mouthed.

"You better close your mouth," Sigri laughed. "Bats fly around at this hour. You don't want to swallow one."

Mae pressed her lips together, feeling her irritation growing into anger. "So what is it you needed to talk about?"

"The hole in your plan, of course."

"We don't have a plan yet, Jarne told you."

"Sorry, my mistake. I mean, the hole in your bright vision for the future," Sigri clarified.

"Which is?"

"You! Or more precisely, any witch who kills people." Sigri patted the grass beside her, inviting Mae to sit as well, since this might be a longer conversation. "Even if we rid the land of the duke, the king, and his black sorceress," Sigri continued, "even if the people hail us as heroes, that sentiment will change if they learn we kill for power."

"Oh, that." Mae sat on the dewy grass and put the flickering lamp between them, staring at the tiny dancing flame.

"Renya often acts without considering the consequences," Sigri said, "but not you. You must have thought about this problem before coming here, am I right?"

"Yes," Mae admitted.

"And I assume you haven't talked to Jarne about it?"

"No, I haven't." Mae took a deep breath. "He thinks the magic could change. The witches, too. According to old stories, witches didn't always kill."

The first fuzzy snowflakes drifted in the icy air. Mae pulled her cloak tight, wondering why they couldn't have had this uncomfortable conversation under less miserable circumstances. Blowing her warm breath like puffs of smoke onto her cold hands, she searched for any salvageable aspects in this tangle.

"There must be other ways to replenish magic," Mae explained. "Jarne's mother told him about wise women on the sister islands to the south who maintain the old rites and rituals. His mother was a witch hiding among the townsfolk," Mae amended when Sigri looked confused. "He never knew, but he suspects since living with me."

"I've heard some rumors about a witch queen on Urðr. She's supposedly as bad as they come. But anyhow... Even if Renya and I stopped killing, which we have done the last three years, you can't."

"Of course I can!" Mae retorted.

"You know what I mean," Sigri said. "If you stop, you'll die." Mae didn't respond, and after a moment of incomprehension, Sigri clapped her hand to her mouth. "Mae?" she said, her voice quavering.

"We need to rid this land of all evil," Mae declared, balling her hands into fists, "including the duke and his minions, the king and his black sorceress, and... me. My kind is the definition of evil."

Sigri looked Mae in the eyes, shock, fear, disbelief, and sadness on her face. Mae couldn't hold her gaze. Her head bent, she pulled some grass from between her feet and ripped it apart, throwing the pieces back to the ground one by one.

"There is no place for black witches in that future." Mae attempted a trembling bravado as her throat closed and tears rose in her eyes. "Too long,

I've justified my evil deeds with good intentions. It never worked. Think of Makevinger." She swallowed and forced herself to continue. "You once told me the innocent will suffer even if I target evil people. I didn't believe you then. I do now." Mae looked into Sigri's eyes; there were tears in both pairs, yet a fierce determination shone in Mae's.

"This dream is bigger than me," the black witch declared. "It has always been bigger than my own fate. All these years, I've killed people for my pitiful personal vendetta, wasting my opportunity to change the world. No longer! One last time, I'll use my powers to achieve as much as possible. I'll go after the king's black witch—she is the root of my evil deeds. And then... I'll end this cursed existence."

Sigri was at a loss for words. Instead, she took Mae's hand. "There must be another way."

"There isn't, Sigri. You know it. There isn't. I cannot ask any sister to stop killing when I do it. I cannot ask the people to help me overthrow monsters when I am one."

"And Jarne?"

"He doesn't know, and he must not know!"

"But won't he figure it out?"

"He is blind when it comes to me. I told you he loves me."

"But then, shouldn't he...?"

"He doesn't get a say. This is my decision." Mae steeled herself. "He is young; he'll find someone else, someone better. Someone like Renya."

Mae couldn't hold back the tears any longer. She curled into a ball, hugging her knees. For the first time, she had voiced her deepest fear aloud. Mae didn't have a future, but Jarne did, and it wouldn't be with her. She felt numb, tired, and powerless—as if it had already happened. As if she had already died, like a ghost lingering among the living.

Sigri moved beside her and took Mae in her arms, at a total loss for any meaningful words. She held on to Mae's shaking body and stayed at her side.

"I won't tell him, Mae," Sigri whispered, "I promise. I'll deflect all discussions if needed. I'm here for you, Mae."

It took a few minutes for Mae to regain control. She wiped her face with her sleeves and drew several deep, calming breaths. Clearing her throat, Mae asked Sigri, "Shouldn't we gather some of these herbs?"

"I don't need them; the plant grows everywhere. But we better pick some to maintain the pretense and give your face time to dry."

"What does it look like?"

"Like all the stuff you were sitting on."

"This? The entire meadow is mugwort?" Mae shook her head in disbelief. "I wish everything was that easy."

CHAPTER FIFTEEN

Jealousy

THE FOLLOWING MORNING greeted the four conspirators with that autumn's first snow, blanketing the mountains under an impeccable sheet of delicate crystals glistening in the rising sun. Jarne was the first to rise, having volunteered to sleep in the kitchen to give the three women privacy. Woken by the brilliant light, he stared in wonder at nature's magic, capable of transforming a dreary castle ruin into a fairytale landscape in mere hours. He scooped up handfuls of the powdery snow and surprised the three witches with a rather refreshing morning greeting, a mischievous grin on his face.

Luckily, all three witches got in each other's way in the struggle to extricate themselves from their blankets. Thus, none of the spells thrown at him harmed Jarne. Realizing he'd poked a hornet's nest, the foolish young man ducked out of the way, pursued by curses and insults that would have made a seasoned sea captain blush. To atone for his jest, Jarne stoked the fire and prepared breakfast. And indeed, a jovial mood filled the small kitchen after the initial irritations evaporated.

"I've been thinking," Sigri said after nibbling on the well-aged cheese, "about our reason for visiting my aunt. I think I have a decent plan."

Mae put her tea down and leaned forward, excited. Sigri calling a plan "decent" was akin to calling a hurricane a light breeze. Yet, the green witch gave Mae an ominous look, making Mae's skin prickle.

"People in Thorshofn may still remember us," the green witch explained. "Not by sight, but as my father's daughters. It's been over eight years since we left, and nobody will connect us to the unfortunate events that caused us to flee. Knowing our father, he would have spun a story that didn't leave room for the tiniest whiff of scandal." Sigri's hands balled into fists, and her lips thinned. She took two slow breaths before continuing. "That makes it possible for my sister Renya and me to return, especially in light of the tragic circumstances."

"What circumstances?" Renya and Mae asked in unison.

"My husband," Sigri said with a straight face, "died in a fire."

"Your husband?" Jarne asked, looking from Sigri to Mae, bewildered. Renya shushed him.

"Yes. My husband, Olaf Nilsen, was a renowned candlemaker and apothecary in Hestavik. He died last month when our shop burned down." Sigri bowed her head and steepled her fingers. "He was working late and fell asleep. My sister and I escaped the flames. We alerted the neighbors. But my dear husband—the smoke killed him."

"What happened to the poor children?" Renya asked with almost believable concern.

"And why was your sister living with you?" Mae cut in.

"We weren't blessed with children. As for my sister—you might not like this part, Mae."

"Why?"

"When we go to Thorshofn, we must explain who you two are. A young woman and a young man, you could be a married couple." Sigri extended her hands to Mae and Jarne to bless their union. "But why would we bring you along, and why would my aunt take you in?"

"So, what is your explanation?" Mae felt her hair rising.

"Well, my sister Renya was visiting me. She was already on her way to Thorshofn. And, of course, she brought along her husband."

Jarne snorted his tea across the table, and Renya, for once, was speechless.

"The young man"—Sigri pointed to Jarne—"is an excellent huntsman, and wants to become a man-at-arms in the duke's guard. Soldiers earn good money, and Renya craves a more exciting life. And you, Mae..." Sigri looked at the black witch, who'd gone white as the snow outside. "You are my late husband's niece. We took you in as our maid when your parents died. As I said, my husband was quite successful."

Total silence followed this unexpected development.

* * *

Mae's hands trembled, her pulse quickened, and her stomach churned.

The destructive anger, always boiling inside her like magma, started bubbling to the surface and began burning in Mae's chest.

How could Sigri do this? Jarne and Renya—especially after our conversation!

Did something happen before yesterday's sparring session? Had Sigri witnessed a different kind of tussle between those two before Mae woke?

That can't be, Mae thought in a flicker of clarity. She needed to calm down. Her logical side applauded Sigri for the elaborate story. It all made sense. Pressing her nails into her palms, the black witch took deep, steadying breaths, each one a desperate attempt to cool the infernal rage inside her. Yet, despite her understanding, the pressure built, growing in intensity with every passing moment. Mae despised the plan.

Jarne and the three witches hovered in the kitchen, unsure how to proceed. Sigri watched Mae. Her serene aloofness gone, the green witch fidgeted with the braided belt of her dress.

She must have lain awake the entire night, torturing her brain to find a better solution, Mae thought without compassion. *Serves her right!*

The black witch almost laughed with glee about her sister's sleepless night. A new wave of fury surged through her body. Suddenly, the kitchen felt too hot, too crowded, with too many eyes on Mae. Her jaw clenched tight, she turned on the spot and stepped out, leaving the first footsteps in the courtyard's untouched snow.

"Where're you going, Mae?" Jarne's voice had regained a cheerful tone.

"Out." Mae's harsh one-word answer left no doubts about the black witch's state of mind.

"Oh, great," he said, lacking the slightest misgivings about the plan. "I was thinking of having another sparring session. You know, Renya and I—what do you think? Do you want to watch?"

Renya and I? Mae clenched her fists to stop herself from blasting him to bits. With every muscle taut, the black witch fought the fiery surge, driving her toward a violent eruption.

"Ah, Jarne," Renya said in a concerned voice, "I don't think that is a good idea. With all that snow, we may lose our footing, slip, and crack our heads on one of the hidden rocks."

She's concerned, isn't she? Mae observed, grinding her teeth. *Feeling guilty? Has she already seduced that gullible boy?*

"Nonsense!" Jarne dragged out the word in a singsong voice, making both sisters cringe. "It'll be fun. We must prepare for any eventuality. You're only afraid I'll beat you again." He grinned like a fool, and then he doomed them all by adding: "And anyhow, shouldn't you listen to your husband?"

Mae wheeled around. Like a volcano splitting open, her fury burst forth, emitting pulses of menace, forcing everyone to stumble backward. Her eyes burned red, glaring at Jarne with enough ferocity to rip a hole in creation. Finally, he'd caught on. But it was too late. Mae gritted her teeth and forced a sinister smile.

"Yes, Jarne, sparring is an excellent idea," she snarled, venom dripping from every syllable. Turning to Renya, Mae asked, "How about it, Renya? Will you give me the honor?"

"Ahm, that's not what I meant," Jarne stammered.

"Nonsense!" Mae barked in a crude imitation of his earlier words. "It'll be fun." Her gaze flicked back to Jarne. "Didn't you say the other day that you'd like to see witches do battle?"

"I don't think..."

"And anyhow, Renya, my dear," Mae growled, "shouldn't you listen to your husband?"

"What do you want?" Renya asked, her voice shaking. She didn't seem eager to confront Mae in her current mood. Still, Renya never backed down from a fight.

"Oh, a friendly game of throw and dodge—snowballs and icicles," Mae smiled, barely masking her rage.

"Shouldn't we prepare for our trip to Thorshofn instead?" Sigri suggested, but Mae wasn't receptive to Sigri's ideas at that moment.

"You do that, Sigri," Mae hissed. "You've already started so brilliantly. Renya and I will be along shortly. This will be a brief fight."

Mae was done talking. She beckoned Renya to step out. The air grew thick and heavy, charged with the raw energy of the impending eruption. Jarne and Sigri watched in horror as the two witches faced off across the courtyard.

Renya attacked first, impatient as always. She punched the ground with air, sending a wall of snow gushing toward Mae. The black witch channeled the wind to divert the attack. She wove the air currents and retaliated by sending clumps of ice toward her opponent. A hailstorm of projectiles rained down on Renya and overwhelmed her defenses. The gray witch cowered, shielding her face with her arms. Mae advanced as Renya cried in pain, small rocks and icicles pelting her body.

"Stop it!" Jarne shouted. "What are you doing? Stop!"

Mae was beyond listening. Her eyes glowed red. Her skin prickled. The stones cracked under her feet as she summoned more power. The world dissolved into a haze of red and gold—the colors of burning rage. She yearned to lash out, to punish, to give her inner demons free rein. A snowball hit the side of her head hard. Enraged, she turned and spotted the boy preparing to throw another. With a powerful blast, the black witch hurled deadly shards of ice toward him, intending to rip him to pieces.

"No!" Sigri bellowed.

A shimmering sphere of air extended in the nick of time, deflecting most projectiles, pushing snow and gravel twelve feet away from her. The sounds of cracking ice filled the air as the speeding pellets smacked into the protective bubble, ricocheting in all directions.

Mae gazed in wonder. Never had she seen such a feat of magic. Sigri was amazing. She was always so unassuming, focusing on her healing, as she did at this very moment, caring for the boy—Jarne.

Jarne! Cold shivers ran down Mae's back. She stared in shock. Jarne lay sprawled on the ground, blood dripping from cuts on his cheeks and forearms, inking the snow in sickly red. To her left, Renya cowered, her cloak ripped and angry red showing through the tears.

What have I done? WHAT have I done?

Looking around, Mae hoped to spot another villain who had attacked her sister and her lover. Where was that evil fiend whom she could punish for hurting the people she cared for?

There was nobody else; only one demon stood in the courtyard. Mae turned and ran toward the goat path. She would follow it as far as she could, and then she would go on further.

* * *

MAE DIDN'T MAKE much headway. The wind had heaped the snow into drifts taller than a man. She could have used magic, but she wouldn't. *Never again will I use these accursed powers.*

She needed to get up the ridge. But was she high enough? Would she be able to hit the rock with that much snow? *Surely, I will freeze,* Mae thought. *Much more appropriate for my evil deeds.*

The wind carried a faint voice calling her name. Must be the warden of hell summoning the missing demon home. Mae turned, spotting a figure in a gray cloak following in her footsteps. So, her end would be more personal. Sitting down in the snow, exhausted, she awaited her executioner.

Is it Sigri? Will she use magic, or did she bring poison?

"Mae, it's me," Renya shouted, fighting to be heard over the wind. "Do not attack. I want to talk. Can I come closer?"

Not waiting for a response, the gray witch approached. Angry red welts marked Renya's face. Was she so weak that she needed to be closer to kill Mae?

"I won't fight you, Renya. I won't hurt you ever again. I'm sorry for everything. Please tell Sigri and Jarne." Mae's voice cracked.

"Tell them yourself!" the approaching witch huffed, her Renya-esque indignation showing through. "Although with Jarne, you might have to wait until tomorrow. Sigri gave him a strong pain remedy."

"There won't be a tomorrow for me. I won't fight you; I deserve it. Did you bring a knife?"

"*What* are you talking about? Why would I need a knife?"

"Aren't you here to take revenge?"

"No, I'm not," Renya replied. "Don't be so melodramatic!" She smiled. "I'm about to do something much more terrifying. I'm here to apologize."

Renya hunkered down next to Mae. The high snowbanks shielded the wind, and the sun shone brightly, warming the tiny hideout. Renya took two apples from inside her cloak and tossed one to Mae. Mae caught the fruit yet remained dumbfounded. *What is going on?*

"Sorry, the apples are a little old, but they still taste good."

"You came out here to apologize for the apples?"

"What? No! Oh, I see." Renya chuckled. "I guess I'm apologizing twice. The apples make it easier for me. You don't need to eat. What I'm going to tell you... I don't like to talk about it." Renya spoke all this without needing to breathe, the words tumbling out in a rush. Then, she bit into her apple and chewed. "Did Sigri tell you why we had to leave our home eight years ago?" Renya asked, her mouth still half full. "She did, am I right? But did she tell you why I killed that soldier?"

"No. Sigri said that was your story. But I don't understand. Why do you want to apologize for that?"

"I'm not. That accursed son of a bitch got what he deserved. I'd do it over again if I could. Only, I'd be slower. Make him suffer." Renya squeezed the apple, crushing the soft fruit to a pulp. Regarding her hand with disgust, she shook the mash to the ground and wiped her hands with snow. The gray witch seemed to regret the loss of her snack, and Mae offered her apple.

"Oh, thanks. And sorry for that." Renya said, looking at the remains of the first fruit, forlorn.

"Why do you want to talk about it now?" Mae asked in a whisper.

"Because you need to understand something. But this doesn't make sense to you yet. Killing that horrid man was how it ended. First, you need to know how it started."

Renya took a deep breath. She looked at the second apple, considering another bite. Thinking better of it, she put her hands in her lap.

"What I wanted to talk to you about is Katla. She was my best friend when we were kids." Renya forced out every single word, the bitter memories aggravating her face. "She was one year older, but she liked me best because I was fearless. I got us into so much trouble. My dear father couldn't control me. But her parents forbade Katla more than once to go near me. She never cared; we were the best of best friends." An air of melancholy replaced Renya's anger for a brief moment.

"What happened?" Mae whispered. Renya didn't react. Then, as sudden as the weather changes in the mountains, all softness disappeared from her face, and the ugly visage of rage returned.

"He killed her. He raped her, and when he was done, he killed her. He strangled her with his own hands. I had warned her!" Renya wailed as tears pooled in her eyes. "I told her he wasn't right for her. I'd seen him with his cruel friends, leering at every woman passing by. But she fancied him with his soldier's tunic showing off his muscled arms. And anyhow, Katla wasn't listening to me anymore; she wasn't even speaking to me..." Renya stuttered between sobs.

Mae crept closer, reaching for the other woman's hand.

"Why?" Mae asked, not knowing what else to say.

"Because I loved her and didn't want to lose her to that awful soldier. I followed him, wanting to know what he was up to. That's when I saw them. He was forcing her, and I was too late. I couldn't get there in time; I couldn't stop that monster. I was *too late*," Renya howled, squeezing Mae's hand.

Mae didn't flinch away despite the fate of the first apple. She wanted to lend Renya strength, but more than anything, she needed to understand how everything fitted together.

"Of course you looked out for your best friend," Mae whispered. "When you saw what happened... There is nothing to be ashamed of, nothing to apologize for." Her words of comfort didn't seem to have any effect. "But why didn't Katla talk to you anymore?" Mae asked.Through her bleary eyes, Renya looked at Mae as if the answer to that question was obvious.

"Because I loved her, and I told her I loved her, and she called me names."

"Because you loved your best...? Oh!" Mae hadn't expected that.

"I don't like men," Renya declared, wiping her face. "I never have." She needed to lay it out before Mae. "They like me, and I play with them. I egg them on such that their humiliation is boundless when I finally kill them. I want their desire to turn into horror when they realize they're at my mercy. And I do not have mercy!" Renya laughed bitterly. "I want them to suffer like I wish I had made this soldier suffer. For her, because he stole her from me."

Renewed sobs racked Renya's body. She needed a couple of deep breaths to calm down. Finally, she said what she came to say.

"I do this to men I want to kill. And your Jarne, he seems decent enough. I won't harm him... And I don't want to sleep with him. I like to tease; you know me. He's so cute when he blushes—your boy, your Jarne."

Astonished, relieved, and deeply ashamed, Mae hugged Renya, and Renya hugged her back. The two women laughed and cried in the middle of a snow burrow high up in the mountains.

***

THE NEXT COUPLE of days passed without further violent confrontations. Still, Mae had to endure an intense and uncomfortable conversation with Sigri. She tried apologizing for attacking Renya twice in the first forty-eight hours since returning to the castle, causing more injuries to Jarne as well. But the healer was neither interested in apologies nor excuses.

"You can't attack people left and right because they hurt your feelings," Sigri admonished. "We need to work together; we need to trust each other. Next time, try talking rather than fighting—we aren't beasts. Use your brain instead of your animal instincts!"

Mae knew she deserved Sigri's disappointment. Still, the black witch argued that her evil curse made it much harder to control emotions. Sigri wasn't having any of it.

"Do you think you are the only person with inner demons?" the green witch challenged. "Do you think your fate is the worst in all of history? Do you think being cursed relieves you of all responsibility?"

Mae had never seen Sigri that agitated. She tried to shrink away, remembering Sigri's incredible displays of magical power.

"This thing inside you," Sigri continued in a milder tone, "the curse you carry... It isn't a random foe who attacks you. You aren't a helpless victim. It is a part of you, for evil or good. Like all our fears and desires, it'll influence you and drive you toward certain actions. But remember: While the curse is a part of you, it isn't you—not all of you. You can fight it. You can control it. You can take a step back, denying it fuel for its rage. And Mae…" Sigri laid her hand on Mae's. "We can help you, but only if you let us know what goes on inside you."

Mae was amazed at how well Sigri understood her, apparently much better than Mae did herself. She wanted to apologize again, but Sigri forestalled her.

"Remember, we are on your side. Then, there is no need to dwell on it any further."

The conversations with Jarne were more fun. Renya went first, since Mae needed to recover from Sigri's sermon. As always, the gray witch was direct and told Jarne he was an idiot—a cute idiot, but still an idiot.

"You don't know how lucky you are, ending up with Mae," she said. "So, cut it with the manly bravado. Read between the lines. As for you and me, I hate to break it to you—there is no chance whatsoever. Think of me as your favorite cousin—your older, wiser, and much more beautiful favorite cousin. But if you hope for anything else, you'd better snap out of it, or it won't end well for you."

Seeing the color drain from his face under her fierce gaze, Renya started to laugh. She blew him a kiss and pranced out of the room, her hips swinging, leaving the poor boy utterly stupefied.

Mae entered the bedroom, her eyes meeting Jarne's. Neither spoke. Both had acted like foolish children and endured unsettling conversations. Jarne gestured to the cot beside him. Taking his hand, Mae lay in the muted light of the bedroom—relieved and happy to be near him.

CHAPTER SIXTEEN

Infiltration

"THIS IS THE last," Sigri declared, carrying a box with cloth-wrapped bottles out of the kitchen and looking for a place to put it. Both horses were already packed high with gear and provisions.

"Oh, thank Danu!" Renya exclaimed. "For a moment, I worried you were planning to bring the entire castle."

Yet, her comment lacked the typical sarcastic bite. While she wasn't excited by the prospect of a long journey on foot, Renya looked forward to leaving her gloomy home for the first time in years. Over the last few days, Sigri had brewed and distilled various potions while Renya sparred with Mae, friendly and voluntarily this time. Mirroring the warming feelings between the four conspirators, a change of weather had melted all the snow. Thus, the passes cleared in time for their departure.

Sigri nodded to Mae, who took the reins of her horse and walked toward the gatehouse. Jarne added Sigri's box to his horse's burden and followed Mae.

"So, we are doing this?" Renya was a little taken aback by the detached efficiency of the departure. *Shouldn't a blaring fanfare herald the heroes setting out to save the world?*

"Yes, we are," Sigri said. Seeing the forlorn look on Renya's face, she took her sister by the hand. "Isn't this what you wanted, getting away from here? Reentering the world?" Sigri smiled.

And Renya, who had missed this expression on her sister's face for so long, smiled back. "I guess so. Let's do it, then. It will be fun."

The travelers descended the mountain path, wary of loose rocks caused by the snowmelt. They reached the valley's main road in the late afternoon despite leaving shortly after sunrise. Mae suggested resting for a moment before heading east toward the King's Road. She was about to ask Jarne to check the horses when Sigri called their attention.

"Riders are approaching. Looks like a patrol."

"How many?" Renya asked.

"Only two; we can take them." Jarne took his knife from the saddlebag.

"I have a better idea." Mae stopped him. "How about sleeping maiden? Renya, Sigri, are you ready?"

"Of course," Renya replied. "I wanted to lay down for a bit, anyhow."

Jarne looked confused, but there was no time to explain. The two riders were almost upon them. Instead, Sigri turned toward the approaching soldiers and yelled.

"Help! Please, help us!"

"Who goes there?" the lead rider called.

"We're honest travelers. Help us, please. My sister, she fainted. We walked all day, and she fell to the ground without a word. I don't know what to do!" Sigri's voice was shrill, the panic undisguised.

"Calm yourself, woman. Who's with you?" Neither of the horsemen dismounted, their faces showing apprehension and distrust.

"Can't you help us?" Sigri begged. "We're three helpless women, accompanied by my young nephew. But my sister... I'm so worried."

The older soldier got off his horse, brushed the dust off his woolen pants, and approached.

"Here, boy. Hold the horse," he ordered, scrutinizing the group. "These are troubled times. In many a village, there is unrest. Guards and tax collectors have been attacked. The roads aren't safe. The word is witches are at large, stirring trouble." He continued to scan the trees, his eyes narrowed and his muscles taut like a bow string.

"Witches?" Sigri shrieked. "Here? We walked all the way from Kralsvik. We haven't seen a soul for days. We could have been attacked!"

"They won't dare come out of their hideouts," the guard declared, giving Sigri a knowing smile. "The duke's soldiers patrol the land everywhere. Some witches have already been caught. They burned at the stake!"

With a nasty grin, he nodded to his younger companion. The second soldier dismounted, took a waterskin from his saddle, and sauntered to Renya. She lay on her back, seemingly unconscious and doing it very convincingly.

"Hamar, come over here," the guard exclaimed as he got a good look at the young and attractive woman lying on the ground. "I think the tight bodice constricts her breathing. We should open it." Smirking, he knelt next to Renya.

"I don't think so." Renya opened her eyes. Smiling, she placed her hands on his as he was about to untie the lacing. "I'll be feeling much better soon." In two heartbeats, she drained his life.

The older man cried out in alarm until Mae hit him over the head with a rock. Thus, Sigri got to replenish her energy, too. The four travelers took possession of the soldier's horses, weapons, gear, and one uniform. After rolling the bodies into a ditch, they rode toward Thorshofn in much greater comfort.

* * *

JARNE AND THE witches arrived at Sigri and Renya's childhood home in Thorshofn two days later. The evening settled over the quiet street with its painted houses. Halfway up the hill, the house stood almost a mile away from the always noisy and not-always-safe neighborhoods surrounding the town's name-giving harbor.

"Who are you?" the old woman asked, looking with mistrust through a tiny porthole in the sturdy door. Few people walked the streets at this hour, and the elderly widow didn't usually welcome strangers huddling in front of her house.

"Dear Aunt Dagmar, it is I, Sigri, your niece."

"Who?"

"Sigrid Runa, you know." Sigri looked taken aback by the frosty reception. "The eldest daughter of your late brother, my beloved father, Guðmundur Erisson." Sigri had picked twilight to arrive at her aunt's doorstep in Thorshofn, fully aware of the additional scrutiny the late arrival would create. Still, she didn't want witnesses if charming the old woman failed, and they needed to resort to more aggressive means of taking possession of the house. Thankfully, Renya piped in when the old crone showed no signs of recognition.

"Oh, Aunty Dagmar, you do remember me? I'm your favorite niece, Renya Lynd. It's been too long. We're so glad to find you well after all these years."

"Renya, huh, the troublemaker? Aye, I remember you. Good riddance! I thought I saw the last of you when you ran away. You left your father alone, without a woman to care for him in the house."

"We're so sorry. It was a difficult time for all of us. Our poor father," Sigri said, battling her emotions. "We are so glad he had you."

"Aye, he had me. I cared for him after my husband died and my second husband died. In gratitude, my brother left me the house. So if you're after it, you can clear out."

"No, dear Aunty Dagmar, we don't need the house, despite all the happy memories." Renya was overdoing her sarcasm. Luckily, the old woman was hard of hearing.

"Renya has convinced me to join her and move back to our hometown, since my dear husband has recently died. I can't stand living in our old home alone. Instead, we are planning to buy a house together," Sigri explained. "Until then, we'll be staying in a hostelry. But of course, we wanted to visit you first. You could tell us so much about our father and how he died."

"Buying a house? Staying in a hostelry? So, you have money?"

"I don't know how long it might last in a fine town like Thorshofn. But my dear husband was a successful craftsman in Hestavik. And I still have my mother's jewelry."

"And who are the other two?"

"Oh, Aunty Dagmar, where are my manners?" Renya exclaimed. "This is Hamar, my husband." Renya giggled as she pulled Jarne forward to better display him to the old crone peeking through the porthole. "We 've been married for six months, and he wants to join the duke's guard. He is so strong!"

"And this is Astrið," Sigri added, "my late husband's niece. She is our maid and a fine cook. But it's getting late. We'd better make our way to the hostelry. We can come back another time, unless..." Sigri looked thoughtful for a moment.

"Unless?" the woman asked when Sigri took too long finishing her sentence.

"Well, of course, we don't want to impose ourselves. But if there was room in your home, we would be only too happy to compensate you for the trouble. And Astrið could cook and clean for us."

"It is a burden. There are four of you, and I'm an old woman. But you could stay for a day or two for your father's sake and for a coin pouch or two. Let me open the door."

Sigri was relieved her plan had worked. The four friends could stay in the house for a couple of days as their aunt's guests until the gossip spread and the neighbors accepted their presence. Everybody needed to play their roles, and the travelers had used their time on the road to practice plausible answers. Mae insisted on Jarne spending time with Renya since husband and wife knew each other intimately.

Aunt Dagmar wouldn't welcome the strangers forever, payment or not. But Sigri had planned ahead for that eventuality. Once the novelty of the visitors wore off, the poor old woman would fall sick. What lucky chance had brought back the wayward sisters to care for their feeble aunt in her time of need! As easy as that, they established a base in Thorshofn from where to observe, prepare, and finally execute the coup on Duke Finsgúr.

* * *

"There will be a great feast in a couple of days—the whole town is buzzing with the news." Mae put her basket on the table and rubbed her cold hands. Sigri had asked her to go to the market to bring back ingredients for dinner and gather gossip. "The duke ordered elaborate celebrations for his fiftieth name day, lasting an entire week."

"That could be good for us," Renya stated as she climbed down the ladder from the loft.

"How is your aunt?" Jarne asked.

"Sleeping fitfully. What did you give her, Sigri?"

"My usual sleeping potion. Her body might not agree with the ingredients."

"How is that good for us, Renya?" Mae asked after she'd sipped Sigri's delicious and invigorating tea. Winter was almost here, and the icy wind had been brutal.

"I don't know... I guess she deserves it?"

"No, not your aunt—the festivities."

"Oh," Renya chuckled, "they always need help for these events: cooks, guards, scullery maids."

"I won't work in the scullery," Mae declared. "It was bad enough to be your maid for the last week."

True to her introduction, Mae had played Astrið, Sigri's niece by marriage. She cooked and cleaned. Aunt Dagmar delighted in ordering Astrið around, handing Mae the most arduous tasks and belittled her every move. Finally, Sigri put the old hag to sleep as the black witch was about to explode the old woman.

"No, Mae. I thought I'd apply as a cook at the residence. With the ingredients I brought, I can whip up some pastries to win over even the most conceited taster. We should get Jarne into the duke's guard as planned. And Renya could work as a barmaid in a tavern frequented by the duke's soldiers."

"*Barmaid?*" Renya's eyes shot daggers at her sister.

"Yes, Renya. Those women serve meat and mead to the guests in a tavern."

"I know what a barmaid is. But I don't know why you'd force me to be one?"

"Because working as a barmaid is the best way to get secrets out of men, especially with your looks." Sigri paused in thought before adding, "Second best, I should rather say. You could also work as a…"

"Don't you dare, Sigrid Runa, don't you dare!"

"I was only saying. If you don't want to be a barmaid…"

Jarne opened his mouth to ask. But then he realized and blushed deeply.

"So what about me, then?" Mae asked to diffuse the sisters' jousting.

"With luck, we have spies on the inside. You're excellent at hiding and tracking. I thought it best if you explored the duke's estate from the outside."

"Lovely, in this weather."

"If you rather want to be a *barmaid*"—Renya put all the disdain she could muster into the word—"or whatever else Sigri thinks gets men to talk."

"No, no. I'm fine with exploring the castle's surroundings."

"Then, the three of us"—Sigri pointed to Renya, Jarne, and herself—"should head to the estate tomorrow to peddle our services."

"Who takes care of our aunty?" Renya asked.

"She has been very sick for four days; we even had the healer in the house. I fear she won't outlive the night. I'll see to her after dinner, and I'll give her a few words to carry with her to our beloved father."

Mae and Jarne looked at each other. Both had killed before, and both knew the risks of their mission. Still, Sigri's cool detachment in discussing the murder of her aunt was unsettling. Sigri saw their wordless exchange and explained.

"I'm not cruel or heartless. If I were, I would make her suffer as she had made me suffer when I was a little girl, particularly after losing my mother. She hated Renya and me—because, in her sick way of thinking, Renya had killed her brother's wife, and I was in the way of him marrying again. And when she talked about a wife for her brother, she meant a servant and a bedwarmer. Neither of them cared about anybody other than themselves."

"We didn't mean…" Mae started, but Sigri stopped her.

"No, Mae, you are right. It would be a cruel thing otherwise. I want you to know I'm not a monster because I care what you think. I care for you both." Sigri laid her hands on their shoulders and squeezed. Then she went back to business. "Come on, Renya. We should make dinner tonight. Or if you want, I can be the cook, and you can be the barmaid."

"Oh, haha, very funny." Yet Renya got up and started to clean and cut the vegetables Mae had brought from the market.

* * *

EARLY THE NEXT morning, Sigri traded the best of their horses for a dilapidated cart, and three conspirators set out toward the duke's residence.

Jarne steered the horses, and Renya sat beside him on the buckboard, putting her arm through his and leaning against his shoulder. For all the world, they represented the image of a loving couple. That was only part of Renya's intention. She was tired, as sunrise was still half an hour away and Renya hated getting up early.

Sigri, on the other hand, had been busy for hours already, baking fresh pastries. Now, she tried to sprinkle infused sugar on top of the still warm cakes—a feat hindered by the cart bouncing on the rutted road. They were on the old mine road, which wound its way toward Lake Misturvatn, where a smaller road led north to the duke's estate.

"Sigri, look. I swear I've been here before," Renya said, grinning as they approached the spot where, three years ago, two separate and desperate attempts on the duke's life had canceled each other out.

"You are right, Renya. I remember a silly boy getting in our way. Where might he be now? I'd like nothing better than to 'thank' him for the fiasco."

"Don't know what you are talking about," Jarne protested. "The stories mention a brave and handsome highwayman whose noble aim was thwarted by three wicked witches."

"Wickedly beautiful, you mean," Renya corrected.

"If you say so." Jarne had slowed the cart and looked around, trying to remember the exact spot and find some evidence. Nothing gave away the location of their fateful encounter. "They must have been amateurs," he said, "whereas we have an unstoppable plan."

It took the three travelers an hour and a half to reach the entrance to the duke's fortress. An eighteen-foot-high stone wall surrounded the estate. The sun had risen high, and a small line of horse carts and folks on foot had formed in front of the gatehouse.

"They're checking everyone," Renya remarked.

"There are guards with crossbows on the ramparts," Jarne added.

"Not to worry," Sigri said. "We have nothing to hide—nothing they would find searching the cart, I mean. Stick to the story."

The line didn't move fast. The guards admitted some folk without a second glance while inspecting others thoroughly. Finally, it was the witches' turn.

"What is your business here?"

"We're seeking employment for the festivities," Sigri said. "I'm a skilled cook and baker. I brought samples of my wares. Would you care for a taste?"

"And the others?" The guard ignored Sigri's offer and focused instead on Jarne and the sword he wore on his belt.

"I'm Hamar Anderssen. I'm a huntsman from the Smoking Mountains and wish to become a man-at-arms in the duke's guard."

"I'm sure you wish to become a man someday." The guard sneered. "But why would the duke need a hunter? For now, pull your cart over here and step down, boy. No false moves! If you draw your sword, it will be the last thing you do."

This isn't good—they are nervous and mistrusting, Jarne thought.

"Thorwald, come over here. We need to search this group."

"I'll search her," said a tall soldier with his hair in braids, ogling Renya. "She might be hiding wondrous things under her dress." He smiled, showing a missing front tooth. Stepping closer, he brought a third, wiry-looking guard along.

"I won't have my wife be spoken to thus." Jarne didn't need to fake his agitation. He'd seen enough men like this in his old village, his father foremost among them.

"Your wife, heh? What would a fine-looking woman like her want with a boy like you? Does she think of you as her babe when she lets you suck on her teats?" the first soldier mocked.

"I wouldn't mind sucking on her teats," Thorwald said, grinning. "Wouldn't you, Steinar?"

"I'd rather let her do the sucking, if you know what I mean," the third soldier jeered.

"You will apologize, you vile men!" Jarne drew his sword. The unfamiliar weapon felt wrong in his hand. He overbalanced and lunged a step forward. Seeing this as an attack, all three soldiers dropped their smirks and drew their weapons.

"Nooo," Sigri groaned, but the damage was done. Jarne was good with a knife but didn't stand a chance against three trained guards. And even if he could, they were in a castle full of soldiers. They needed to get out of there.

The first soldier tested Jarne. Parrying the jab, Jarne demonstrated his ineptitude. Bolstered, the guard attacked again with a feint. Succeeding in fooling Jarne, the follow-up stroke took deadly aim.

Renya blasted the sword off track. The soldier's hand smacked against a stone pillar. Bewildered, the attacker looked at Jarne until the young man punched the guard hard in his face.

The other two, Thorwald and Steinar, charged Jarne. Sigri tripped Steinar. He toppled into Thorwald, and both men went down.

Jarne kicked Thorwald in the face, further reducing the lewd man's number of teeth. Then, he pointed his sword at Steinar's neck.

"Apologize," Jarne growled, flushed by the victory that wasn't his. Yet, his elation lasted only seconds. More soldiers approached; this time, they had crossbows trained at him.

"Drop your sword and get down to your knees! Do it, or we'll shoot you where you stand. I won't ask a second time."

"What is going on, sergeant?" A middle-aged man with salt-and-pepper hair stepped closer. He wore a uniform of a better class, adorned with shiny rank insignias.

"This man has attacked three guards, sir. I was about to take him into custody for questioning. He must be one of the…"

"Help us, Captain," Renya shouted before the sergeant could complete his report. "We are honest people seeking employment, and these *men*"—Renya spat the last word—"have insulted me in the vilest manner. All my husband did was defend my honor by demanding an apology."

"Silence!" the sergeant barked. The captain stalled him with a raised hand.

"What is your name?" the captain asked.

"Renya Lynd Guðmundsdóttir. This is my husband, Hamar Anderssen. We recently moved back to Thorshofn, where I grew up. And this is my sister Sigrid."

"Well, Renya, I'd say I'm pleased to meet you… but your husband attacked three of my guards." The same three guards picked themselves up from the ground and dusted their uniforms while giving Jarne murderous stares.

"With all due respect, sir," Jarne spoke, "they assaulted us first, insulting my wife and attacking me with their swords."

"So you say," the captain mused, "and you laid all of them low by yourself. What kind of employment are you seeking?"

"I want to be a guard for the duke."

"Is that so, Hamar? The duke can always use skilled soldiers. It appears you have passed your entrance exam and already met three of your peers. Nevertheless, I would watch my back for a while if I were you."

Then, the captain turned to the sergeant and barked his orders.

"Sergeant, bring Hamar to the quartermaster and enlist him. Have these guards punished for insulting this poor woman and fill their posts."

"Yes, sir. Right away, sir. Björn, Ivar, and Kilían, you take these men's positions. Pétur, escort the recruit to the quartermaster. The rest, grab these miscreants and bring them to my room. Move!"

With a shrug to the sisters, Jarne sheathed his sword and followed Pétur. After the soldiers had received their orders, they dispersed, and the captain walked over to the two women.

"I do apologize for the unpleasantness. But at least your husband got his wish. What about you, Renya?"

"You will look after him, captain? These men are mean. I beg of you." Renya put her hand on the captain's arm and looked him straight in the eyes with the expression of a fawn seeking reassurance from the lead wolf.

"Soldiering is a brutal profession; your husband must fend for himself. But I'll try to separate him from the rest in the beginning," he soothed when Renya's eyes widened in fear, and she bit her lower lip. "But, what about you?"

"My sister Sigri is a masterful cook and baker. She brought some samples. Would you care for a taste?"

"Oh, I would definitely care for a taste," the captain said, his eyes fixated on Renya's quivering lips. Sigri took the tray of cakes from the wagon and offered it to the captain.

"Thank you—Sigri, is it? Oh, these are excellent," he exclaimed in delight, his mouth half full. "You," he called one of the replacement guards, "show this woman to the kitchen. Bring her directly to the head cook. The duke will be delighted."

"Yes, sir," the guard replied.

"Which still leaves you, Renya. What employment do you seek?"

"Oh, I don't have many talents." Renya looked down and played with the hem of her kirtle. "I can't fight, and I can't bake. I can sing, though. I have a fine voice." She perked up. "But, alas, there is no making a living with it. I wondered if there is a mead hall for the soldiers where I could work as a barmaid?" Her eyes were full of hope when she looked back at the captain.

"I would love to hear you sing, Renya. Sadly, there is no mead hall here for the soldiers. The duke doesn't permit his men-at-arms to drink in his estate, even when they aren't on duty. But there is a fine tavern in Thorshofn which the officers frequent. I go there now and then. It is called the Troll's Bridge. Tell the proprietor I sent you—he will hire you. Tomorrow, when I get off early, I'll come, and I'd love to meet you there."

"You are too gracious. How can I ever make it up to you, all the good you've done for my family and me? I don't even know your name yet."

"Forgive me, dear lady. Dagfinn Johansen, captain of the guards, at your service." He took her hand and brushed the back with his lips. "It was my pleasure to assist you in this difficult situation. If you insist, I'm sure I can find a way for you to repay my kindness." He looked her in the eyes, a smirk tugging on his lips. "I have to go now. I hope to see you again at the Troll's Bridge tomorrow."

And with that, the infiltration had been achieved, yet in quite a different manner than the conspirators had planned.

CHAPTER SEVENTEEN

Complications

Mae crept through the underbrush at a safe distance from the formidable outer wall that ringed the duke's estate. She was miserable, cold, and wet. The rain had soaked her cloak hours ago. Still, every contact with a tree branch sent another deluge her way. Starting in the north, she had followed the encircling bulwark of the duke's stronghold to the east and south. She could go no further since the estate's western boundary was the bank of Loch Misturvatn.

There was no moat. Instead, the duke's men had stripped an area extending thirty paces from the wall of trees and bushes. The open field provided the guards with a clear line of fire on anyone approaching the fortification. *This has been a complete waste of my time.* Mae wondered if she hadn't been better off working as a scullery maid. Frustrated, she was about to return to Thorshofn when she heard approaching voices. *Guards?*

"Why do we have to walk out here in the rain?" a petulant voice complained.

"Because his lordship is uneasy. You've heard of the attacks?"

Two soldiers walked along the cleared patch. One was old, and the other seemed very young. They marched with halberds over their shoulders, their hoods sogging. Their booted feet squelched in the mud.

Mae crouched behind a bush, and her boot sank deep into a wet mire, icy water pouring over the shaft. She fought to remain quiet despite her whole body shivering from the cold.

"But out here, someone could attack us." The young guard looked around, a frightened expression on his face.

"So?" The old guard stopped and leaned on his polearm. "Do you think the duke cares for the likes of us? We are the least valuable men, haven't you realized?" Wiping the wetness off his face, the older man seemed glad for an excuse to rest and lecture this young sprout. "Regular soldiers with skill and experience defend the outer walls and the main courtyard," he explained. "The inner wall is manned by the elite soldiers who have served long years and have earned the guard captain's approval. And then there is the inner keep." He lowered his voice to impart great wisdom that not everybody was worthy to receive. "That's where the duke and his family reside. Only handpicked soldiers patrol there, all known to the duke. They aren't even allowed to carry crossbows." He coughed with a sickly wet sound, hawked up phlegm, and spit on the ground. "We are the dregs, so we walk here."

"But you have served long years."

"Aye, I was once on the inner wall. But I am old, so the sergeant orders me out here. I am sure he hopes the cold and wet will kill me and free up my bunk in the barracks."

Time to go, Mae thought.

Then, hearing noises behind her, she turned in time to see a wild boar charging, intent on slicing her open with six-inch long tusks for invading his pig wallow. She yelped, shoving mud and water toward her attacker, trying to push the enraged animal off course. Her plan did not work as intended. While she avoided the beast's deadly teeth, the pig's flank rammed into her. Both tumbled out of the underbrush and landed on the grassy field in front of the stunned soldiers.

Yet, the boar wasn't satisfied with dislodging the intruder. Finding its feet, it returned to the attack, and pain shot through Mae's leg as one of the animal's hideous tusks cut her. With a scream of rage and a burst of magic, Mae pushed the large animal away. It flew through the air like a projectile from a catapult, crashing into the older soldier. The impact slammed him to the ground, burying the halberd's blade in his face. The beast, too, seemed injured. It limped back into the forest, trailing blood.

Everything was over in seconds. The young soldier looked, dumbfounded, from the retreating animal to his fallen companion. Finally, he stared open mouthed at Mae. Their gazes met, and she realized his eyes were misaligned and of different colors. Then, the guard turned and ran, shouting about witchcraft. *Damn it!*

Keeping her left hand on her wound, Mae used her right hand to take three sharpened blades from a leather pouch on her belt. She threw the deadly knives after the fleeing soldier, propelled by magic. One missed, one grazed his arm, but the third stuck right between his shoulders, and he went down with a splash.

Mae would have liked to go after him to relieve the young man of his remaining life force. But she had to get out of there. No guard on the wall had witnessed the fight. Still, the shouts might have alerted them. The witch hobbled toward the forest as the young soldier tried to crawl away. He wouldn't get far; Sigri's poison would see to that.

Back under the cover of the trees, Mae tied a hasty bandage around her leg. Luckily, she had left her horse not far from here before embarking on her pointless reconnaissance mission. If she could get there before the soldiers caught up, she had a chance to get away.

* * *

AFTER THE MORNING'S excitement, Renya drove the cart back to Thorshofn. Both Jarne and Sigri would remain in the castle for the duration of their employment. The weather had worsened. Dark clouds sent heavy sheets of rain, and an icy wind blew the torrent sideways, heightening the misery. Still, Renya was glad to leave. The vile comments of these men had gotten under her skin. She might have attacked them herself if Jarne hadn't played the chivalrous knight, defender of women. Still, the idiot could have gotten himself killed. In the end, his gamble had worked out. Renya was glad; she had started to like the foolish boy.

Renya reached the tavern in the early evening after she returned the cart and changed her clothes. Only a few patrons sat at the mismatched tables. The proprietor, Lasse Steensen, was only too happy to hire Renya for her looks alone. He almost fell over backward when she mentioned her reference. The oily man promised her free meals and a copper per night, plus she could keep half of what men gave her extra.

His wife Brunhild was the cook. She promised Renya many more things if the new barmaid got too chummy with her husband. Those were of a decidedly more unpleasant nature. Still, she also promised Renya help if the patrons got carried away. "Call out for me, and I'll set them straight," she said.

Renya started to work and didn't mind it as much as she had thought. The early guests behaved themselves, and Renya delighted in being the undisputed center of attention. She pranced through the room, fulfilling the orders and singing bawdy songs she had learned as a young girl. The patrons clapped and roared their approval and ordered many rounds of drinks.

As Sigri had predicted, Renya learned many interesting facts. The duke did not trust his own soldiers and only permitted six guards in the inner keep at a time. Two guarded the entrance, two patrolled the roof, and two stood outside the duke's apartments. These personal guards came from a hand-selected group of soldiers and were not well liked by their comrades.

As the evening progressed, the men became a bit rowdier. Still, Renya didn't have to call for Mistress Brunhild because she had her own defenses. First, she broke a leg of a chair when its occupant clapped her on the behind. Later, she tripped a drunken fool as he tried to grab her for a dance. And finally, she slapped a man with a bit of magical enhancement after he had touched her breast. The man had crashed into the central pillar and was very slow in getting back up again. After that, the remaining guests treated the new barmaid with much more respect.

It didn't take long, and there were smiles all around again. The tavern keeper had sold many horns of meat and mugs of ale. And the way Renya had handled herself impressed the mistress of the kitchen. The guests loved to hear Renya sing and see her dance through the room. They had stopped pestering her and only grumbled when closing time came around. Taking some of the leftover dinner and a pitcher of mead, Renya walked home in high spirits.

The house was dark and cold, and Renya lit a lantern. Fresh, wet puddles glistened on the floor. Renya followed the trail leading to the loft. Hanging the lamp on a hook in the ceiling beam, she saw Mae lying on the straw, cowered into a ball, and shivering from head to toe.

"Mae, what's wrong?" Then she saw blood mixing with the water pooling around her sister. "By the devils, what happened to you?"

Mae tried to talk, but her chattering teeth rendered her incoherent. It didn't matter; Renya knew what Mae needed. Climbing down, she grabbed all the blankets, cloaks, towels, and tablecloths she could find and brought them back up. Renya peeled Mae out of her wet things and rubbed her dry. The wound looked bad—dirty and festering. Renya wrapped the leg and rolled Mae to a dry spot, burying her under the blankets.

Then she got to work. The day had been long, and Renya was tired. But Mae needed her. Starting a fire, she set water to boil. That done, Renya sorted through Sigri's potions and tinctures, fighting to concentrate despite her fatigue. She found a potion she thought was suitable for cleaning wounds and an ointment that helped fight infections.

For over two hours, Renya labored. She brewed tea, added the potion, and got Mae to drink a few sips. She cleaned the wound, added a poultice, and bandaged the leg again. Finally, when exhaustion threatened to overwhelm her, she extinguished the light. Renya lay beside Mae, sharing her body heat and hoping she had remembered the correct healing methods.

* * *

DESPITE HER WEARINESS, Renya slept poorly, and weird dreams entered her mind. Jarne became the duke and demanded a snowball fight. Mae chased Renya around the castle, riding on a black wolf. She couldn't run fast enough as vines snapped at her ankles and toppled her to the ground. She fought and wrestled, and the guard captain grabbed her shoulder and shook her.

"Hey, Renya, wake up."

Faint light shone through the window. There were no wolves or guards. Instead, Mae knelt by her side, her hand on Renya's shoulder.

"What? Who? Where?" Renya fought to get free of the blankets.

"It's me, Mae. You had a bad dream."

"What? Oh, Mae. Are you all right? Did I wake you?"

"Yeah, you did, when you rolled around like a berserker. With whom were you fighting?"

"Vines, I guess." Renya blinked a few times, shaking her head. "How are you?"

"Alive, I think," Mae answered. "Thanks to you, I believe. My leg hurts like hell, and my head feels stuffed with cotton. But otherwise, I live. What did you give me?"

"I took a few of Sigri's ingredients."

"So, are you a healer too?" Mae asked, astounded.

"No." Renya laughed. "It's too much work to remember everything."

"Then how did you know? You could have poisoned me. Some of Sigri's stuff is dangerous."

"Yes, but Sigri marks it with colors." Renya sat upright. "Green is poison, blue makes you sick, yellow has some weird effects, and red is for healing."

"You're sure?" Mae asked, alarmed. "Wouldn't red be poison?"

"You'd think so. That's why Sigri turned it around; she likes to confuse people. And anyhow, you're still alive, so it must have worked."

"I guess," Mae conceded, not sounding convinced.

"I brought some food and mead from the tavern, if you're up to it."

"I'll have tea. But food sounds good. You can climb down first since I will be slow with my busted leg."

Renya stoked the fire to make tea. Mae hobbled down, trying to keep her weight off her injured leg. The two women sat at the table, eating cold mutton, and shared the previous day's adventures.

"He challenged the castle guards?" Mae asked in shock as Renya recounted the events at the duke's estate.

"Yes, like a valiant knight defending his lady. Sometimes, he is still a little boy believing his mother's stories. But it worked out in the end."

"Except that he has three mortal enemies now. They will want to pay him back for the humiliation."

"Yes, but the captain will protect him if he wants to meet me again." Renya told Mae about the undisguised interest of the captain.

"Can you use him to get to the duke?" Mae asked. "The defenses around the paranoid lord are strong."

"Yes, I heard similar things in the tavern. Nobody gets near him armed unless he approves. You're sure there is no way from the outside?"

"None that I could see. Could you smuggle me in?"

Renya shook her head. "The gate guards check everything before letting anyone enter," she explained.

Mae grimaced. "This is harder than I thought."

"We still have some time. Sigri will come up with something, and your leg needs healing. I'm going to meet the captain tonight."

"What will you do? He'll expect recompense. Your singing won't enough."

"I can play hard to get if I want. The exciting part is the courtship, after all."

"Sure, but he is a soldier. He'll soon get bored of the siege and charge your fortress."

"We'll see." Renya smiled in anticipation of the challenge.

"Yes, but if he wants to...? I mean, if you have to...?"

"I've lain with men, Mae. I don't like it, but I don't like Brussels sprouts either. Don't look so shocked." Renya laughed. "How would I know otherwise that I don't like it? Sometimes, I felt so lonely. You must have felt the same while wandering the land?"

"I wasn't... That wasn't... I was trying to save my brother. And anyhow, this isn't about me. How do we kill the duke?"

"Wait! You and Jarne—that was your first time?"

"I don't know what that has to do with anything." Mae blushed. She tried to get up, but pain shot through her leg and she sat back down.

"Sorry, Mae." Renya looked abashed. "I didn't mean to pry. Let me get you more tea." She refilled Mae's cup. After replacing the kettle on the fireplace, she sat beside Mae and took her hand. "I am happy for you both. You love each other, and you fit well together. That is what counts."

* * *

MORE THAN A week passed before Sigri could leave the duke's estate and return to Thorshofn. She had barely stepped over the threshold when Mae bombarded her with questions.

"How is Jarne? Is he all right? Has he been in another fight? Renya didn't get much out of the guard captain."

"He is fine. Calm down."

Sigri would have liked nothing better than to sit down, drink tea in peace, and rest her feet. The work at the duke's estate had been hard. Her magical ingredients had convinced everybody of her exceptional culinary abilities. Still, the hours were long, and she roamed the estate far and wide to extract information in exchange for pastries.

Hitching a ride to the town with the brewer, she arrived at her childhood home tired and worn out. Yet Sigri could see that she wouldn't get to rest until she had satisfied Mae's inquiries.

"He is guarding the boat dock—Renya must have told you. The captain ordered him there, away from the other guards."

"But he sleeps in the barracks. They can attack him there."

"And so they tried."

"*What?*"

"Relax, your Jarne is quick and can take care of himself. They attacked at night, all three of them. He broke one man's nose and another man's arm. The third ended up with his own knife in his upper thigh."

"Wow," Renya exclaimed as she brought her sister a much-needed cup of tea. "He did this all by himself?"

"Almost." Sigri grinned. "I might have bribed a few of his bunkmates to look out for him. You would be amazed at the power cooks have. Who controls the food controls the men."

"Anyhow," she continued, "to make things worse, the three guards received a whipping, twenty-five lashes each. The sergeant assigned them to forest duty, and they must sleep in the stables. That should prevent further incidents."

"Thank you, Sigri." Mae hugged the tall witch, almost spilling the tea.

"Can I sit down now?"

"Of course, Sigri. Thank you. Sorry for pestering you so, but I am..."

"Deeply in love and worrying yourself sick, I know." Sigri sat at the table, and Mae brought the teapot and a bowl of dried fruits. Renya unwrapped a loaf of fresh bread, still warm from the oven. She broke it into pieces, handing one to each witch.

Renya wasn't working in the tavern that night, as she had known about Sigri's day off. The barkeeper hadn't been happy when she told him. She had become a magnet for customers, and there would be grumbling if she wasn't in. Yet Renya explained that the grumbling would be much louder if she never returned. That won the argument.

During the week of Sigri's absence, guard captain Johansen had frequented the tavern twice. Twice more, Renya had seen him when visiting the duke's estate. Each time, she had inquired about Jarne. The captain assured her that Jarne was alive and well. He had posted the new recruit to a position where Jarne didn't have to interact with many other soldiers. Beyond that, Captain Johansen wasn't keen on discussing Renya's "husband" in great detail.

Instead, he shared some of the castle's best-kept secrets. The ducal estate had seen many changes and alterations over the decades. Only the three-story square tower of gray stone had stood at the lake's shore since before the invasion. Duke Finsgúr's father had ordered massive extensions, ringing the old building on three sides. Yet, nobody had been allowed into those parts of the estate for many years except for a few handpicked guards. Duke Finsgúr did not host guests in his domain. He demanded privacy, security, and secrecy.

Still, a hidden stairway led from an inner courtyard to the keep's tower roof, used exclusively by the duke's most trusted soldiers. Climbing the damp spiral staircase, Renya reached the top, gasping for air. The effort was worth it. The keep's roof offered a breathtaking view of the lake and the surrounding hills. Yet, Captain Johansen had chosen this spot for its seclusion. He ordered the guards away, and Renya knew what was coming.

They kissed, and Captain Johansen—Dagfinn—pushed her toward him, grabbing her back and running his hands up and down her body. Renya played along without encouraging him. She didn't enjoy it. Still, she appreciated that he had washed and shaved. Dagfinn behaved almost well-mannered toward her, which saved him from a long fall with a sudden stop on the rocks below. Regardless, Renya was glad about the icy wind preventing them from taking it further. She had told Sigri and Mae about her discoveries at the first opportunity, and they were impressed by her sacrifice.

Now, it was Sigri's turn. She, too, had something she couldn't wait to tell her sisters. Being the adult in the room, as so often was the case, she had put her own needs off until she answered Mae's questions. Finishing her tea, she put her cup down and cleared her throat.

"I have good news and not-so-good news." Stunned silence followed for a few heartbeats. Then, the two other witches ventured their guesses.

"You killed the duke."

"You know how to kill the duke."

"You poisoned the guards."

"You found a secret entrance."

"You will know when you let me finish." Sigri exclaimed.

"The good news first, please," Mae begged.

"I might have devised a plan to attack and kill the duke, which includes, funny you should mention it, both poison and a secret staircase. It is complex. We must all work together and synchronize our actions. Yet there is a good chance, thanks to all the valuable information both of you have gathered."

Sigri talked for almost twenty minutes, describing her idea step-by-step. Neither listener interrupted her. The tea went cold, and all the food stood forgotten. Mae and Renya absorbed every devilish detail and marveled at the brilliance of her mind.

"But how do we know when it's time?" Mae asked.

"Fire," Sigri replied. "You, Mae, need to signal Renya with a lantern. And Renya will need to set something ablaze. How about the stables?"

"How will you get in?" Renya asked.

"The door guards won't stop the duke from having dinner, even if the stables are on fire."

"Excellent," Mae exclaimed.

"Well, it would be easier if there wasn't the not-so-good news, remember?"

"Oh, troll's booger. I forgot about it," Renya admitted. "What is it?"

"The king," Sigri stated.

"What about him?" Mae asked, bewildered.

"He will be there, too. Few people know about it. He rarely leaves Hagndal these days. Secrecy is sensible, given the unstable situation across the land. Yet, he will be feasting with the duke. The steward informed the chief kitchen staff yesterday."

"Why?" Renya asked.

"I only heard rumors. It might have to do with the uprisings in the north. The king seeks the duke's help. Some speculate about a marriage between the prince and the duke's daughter. But that's irrelevant. Neither his consort nor the prince will accompany the king on this visit."

"What does that mean for your plan?" Mae asked.

"It makes things much more unpredictable, even with my sight."

"So what do we do?" Renya had jumped to her feet and paced up and down the length of the table. For a couple of moments, nobody spoke.

"We do it anyway!" Mae's eyes burned with determination, and her voice was firm, allowing no dissent. "We'll kill the duke and the king. Imagine what this would mean for the people, for us."

"And his black sorceress?" Renya asked. "Won't she be with him?"

"Wouldn't that be great?" Mae's voice grew cold as ice. "It's been too long. I never got to thank her for my gift."

"It will be difficult, and it will be dangerous." Sigri nodded. "But I have to agree with Mae—this is an opportunity we cannot miss."

"Fine with me." Renya clapped her hands together and locked eyes with each woman for a couple of heartbeats. "When?"

"The feast starts in four days. But the first two days will be too hectic with the arrival of the king's entourage. Too much is unknown, and too much can go wrong. Let's do it on the third day of the feast. One week from now, on the fourth hour after sunset. It will be the eleventh day of the eleventh month—Ellefta of Gormánuður—a potent omen."

"Agreed?" Sigri asked.

"Agreed!" Mae responded.

"By the devils, yes. Agreed!" Renya held out her hand, and Mae and Sigri each gripped a wrist. The three women stood united. Clasping their hands in a triangle, they'd ignited the spark of the witches' revolution.

CHAPTER EIGHTEEN

Point of No Return

"Brothers shall fight and fell each other,
And sisters' sons shall kinship stain;
Hard is it on earth, with mighty whoredom;
Axe-time, sword-time, shields are sundered,
Wind-time, wolf-time, ere the world falls;
Nor ever shall men each other spare."[1]

"**T**ONIGHT? THAT MIGHT not be a good idea." The guard captain seemed unaccustomed to defending against Renya's passionate advances. "But you haven't been in the tavern for days."

"We have high guests in the castle and the festivities, you know. I can't leave my post at a time like this. In a couple of days, everything will be different."

"Yes, it will." Renya pouted. "I will be wilted by lack of companionship. If nobody desires me, what is the point? My husband hasn't been home once, and I never see you. Should I end myself?"

"Don't speak like this." He stepped closer and placed his hand on her arm. "You are so different tonight."

"Because I'm lonely. Should I entertain your gate guards? They wouldn't make excuses. Their lust is only too obvious."

"Have any men accosted you again? Tell me their names."

"Of course they have," Renya confessed. "Every time I come here, they strip me of my clothes, run their filthy hands over my body, and do unspeakable things." The captain stiffened in alarm, ready to march to war, so Renya clarified. "With their eyes only, and with their depraved minds. I can read

---

[1] *The Prophecy of the Seeress, Stanza 45*, Poetic Edda, English by Henry Bellows (1936)

their vile thoughts in their lusty stares. But Dagfinn, don't worry about them. Worry about me. Can't you read my mind?"

"Oh, dearest, I thought you weren't... willing. Your husband? I thought you only cared for his position."

"Did my kisses feel unwilling? Did my hands feel unwilling?" Renya placed her hand on his groin and squeezed, causing the captain to jump in surprise. "My husband is kind and loving. But he can be timid, like a little boy. He isn't a man like you—experienced, strong, and forceful. Can't we go up the keep's tower? I don't want to be alone tonight."

"The keep? Tonight?" the captain stammered, torn between desire and duty. "Nobody is allowed... I mean, it must be cold up there."

"I'll keep you warm, I promise."

"We're short of men down here."

"It doesn't feel that short to me."

"Dearest, I've never seen you like this. What has come over you tonight?"

"The moon, Dagfinn," Renya huffed, exasperated. "Women get excited by the full moon." Placing her hand back on his groin, she asked in a sultry voice, "I take it you don't mind?"

"I don't—mind, that is," he gasped, straining to contain his excitement. "Yes, the keep... I mean, the roof. We'd better hurry. I'll send one tower guard down to help." He took her hand and led the way.

Climbing the steep spiral staircase to the keep's roof, Renya wondered if she had lost her touch. Her seduction had taken way too long. She had been on the verge of ripping open her dress in a desperate attempt to convince him of her need. Luckily, it hadn't come to that. How much time was left? Sigri's plan required tight synchronization.

Reaching the roof, Renya felt the icy wind the captain had spoken of. Only men could be so gullible as to believe a woman would want to undress under such conditions. True to his word, Dagfinn sent one guard to augment the soldiers on the wall. The other, he ordered into the little guard shed one level below.

"Nothing of this will be ever mentioned to anyone," he barked. "If I hear the slightest rumors, I will pull out your tongues with hot pincers. Have I made myself clear?"

"Yes, sir. Completely clear, sir."

"Then away with you!"

Renya walked to the battlements and peered out through the crenelation.

The lake lay dark, its surface rippled by the wind, making the reflected moonlight dance over the water. It wasn't even a full moon. Still, Renya was sure her forceful attack on the captain's privates had driven all astronomical considerations from his mind.

Dagfinn placed his cloak like a blanket on the floor beside her. Then, he came up behind her and squeezed her breasts with both hands, pressing his body against her backside. He breathed into her ear, his desire vibrating through his body. Renya wiggled around and started to unbuckle his belt.

"Oh, dearest, how I have dreamt about this."

"Shhh," Renya quieted him. "I'll take you beyond your wildest dreams." The witch thought acting like a pining vixen was bad enough; she didn't need to endure him spouting poetry. She just needed to get his pants down for the charade, and then she would relieve him, but not quite the way he wished her to.

"What is that?" Renya had opened the last buckles when he shouted. A small light bobbed on the water near the base of the tower. *Mae!*

It was time.

Pressing her hand on his mouth, she yanked hard. His lifeless shell crumbled to the ground. Still, she hadn't been fast enough. His muffled cry had pierced the night. Rolling him onto his back, Renya straddled the body and mimed riding him hard when the second guardsman arrived on the roof. From behind the curtain of her whipping hair, she saw the soldier's expression change from alarm to mortification before he turned and ran. *That was close.*

Getting to her feet, Renya pulled her dress straight and looked at the dead captain. His excitement was still visible. She wondered for a moment. He hadn't been too bad a man, and if she was differently inclined...

Then she scolded herself. She had work to do. Peering over the crenelation, Renya saw Mae's tiny boat reaching the dock. *Time for phase two.* The gray witch sprinted to the other side and focused on the stable across the courtyard, over sixty paces from where she stood. She had never exploded anything as big or as far away, but she had also never possessed this much life force. Besides the lustful captain, two unlucky soldiers had contributed to her reserve.

Rubbing her palms together, she hummed, gathering the energy for the strike. The power sizzled in her fingertips, eager to be released. Yet, Renya held back, raising the charge, summoning more and more. Her whole body vibrated, every muscle tense, every sinew taut. The force threatened to tear her apart. When she could hold on no longer, she cried out, a single syllable, an ancient word of power. Three heartbeats, and nothing happened—three heartbeats that felt like an eternity. Then, the stable erupted in flames.

Renya sagged, both in relief and exhaustion. She would rest for a moment before she went below.

* * *

"You can't come in; the keep is locked down. Nobody enters."

"But I have the desserts for his lordship and his esteemed guest," Sigri replied to the stern guard named Morton—at least, she believed so. Over the last few days, Sigri had memorized the faces and names of as many guards as possible. Even the fiercest warrior's façade crumbled when assaulted with her magical pastries.

"Sorry, there is some kind of commotion. We have the strictest orders to let nobody enter."

"The cakes will be ruined; I must serve them hot. I ran all the way over here. You don't expect the duke to forgo dessert because the stable caught fire, do you?"

"There is no exception. Nobody enters."

"Fine," Sigri said, dejected. "These will get cold and rubbery. Preparing them only took me two hours. But I will point to you if the duke's wrath comes down on the kitchen staff. Morton, is it, right? And you are Geirolf? I don't want to blame the wrong people, but I will point it away from me."

"Couldn't we let her in?" Geirolf ventured. "She is right about the duke caring more for his dessert than for his stables."

"Don't say a thing like that," Morton scolded in a carrying whisper. "Not here, if you know what's good for you." After a few seconds of contemplation, he relented. "All right, but only this once. Geirolf, search her."

"Search her? She carries a tray of pastries. Do you think she has an armed assassin hiding under the sugary crust?"

"We have our orders, damn it."

"If you want to see what's inside of the pastries... the two on the left." Sigri pointed with her head. "Those are a little burned. I can't serve them upstairs. You might like something warm on this cold night."

"Yes, indeed," Geirolf exclaimed, "that would be very much appreciated. Let me open the door. I'll take them when you're through. These two, you mean?"

And with that, Sigri was inside. As for getting back out, those two guards wouldn't be a problem, assuming they ate one pastry each.

Sigri walked around the broad stairs to the back corner, where a solid oak door blocked the inner access to the spiral staircase Renya had gone up earlier. Placing her tray on the floor, Sigri knocked thrice. She received the same signal in response. *Good, Renya is in position.*

The door was two inches thick, and a solid metal chain held it closed. The hinges, however, were old and rusty. The green witch pulled a small flask from an inner pocket. Holding a wet cloth in front of nose and mouth, she poured the liquid over the hinges, letting the acid do its work. Acrid smoke rose immediately from the assaulted metal. Sigri needed to hurry before the upper-door guards noticed anything. Dumping the covered cakes on the floor, she gathered the gleaming throwing knives hidden underneath.

The guard was right, Sigri thought. *No assassin is hidden under the sugary crust.* She had entered in plain sight.

* * *

FIVE MINUTES EARLIER, Renya had taken care of the second roof guard. Pushing open the door to his guard shed, she had made the man jump to attention. He looked confused until a concentrated blast of air smashed into his face, shattering his nose and ramming his head hard into the wall behind him. Renya rushed toward him as he slid to the floor and ended his life. Then, she stripped off her dress, revealing black pants underneath. Taking the boots, tunic, and helmet off the deceased guard, Renya dressed as best as possible in the borrowed garments. She needed to stuff the boot tips with wads of cloth to prevent her from sliding around in the large footwear.

Hoisting two crossbows and a quiver of arrows, Renya descended the spiral staircase until she reached the wooden door. She didn't have to wait long. Sigri was reliable and proficient, as always. After replying to the signal, Renya stepped back from the door and counted to one hundred. In her eagerness to join her sister, the impatient witch stumbled in the fifties, skipped the entire seventies, and stopped at ninety-three. She slammed the door with a mighty blast of air. It rattled but didn't open. Only the upper hinge had broken off.

I should have counted all the numbers.

Renya's second attempt broke the door free. Clanging to the floor, the heavy door sent echoes through the keep's vast entrance hall.

"What was that?" shouted one of two soldiers, both guarding the duke's private chambers two flights up.

"Go and look," the second guard ordered. "You have to call for backup. I'll alert his lordship. We need to…" he shouted before a well-aimed throwing knife buried itself between his eyes.

The remaining soldier drew his sword, raised his shield, and looked around in horror. Footsteps approached from below as a third guard lumbered up the staircase.

"We are under attack!" the door guard yelled. "An assassin is in the keep."

"More than one," the new arrival replied. "The door to the tower staircase has been breached. Where did the attack come from?"

"Over there!" The frightened guard waved his shield, pointing toward the dark corner where Sigri hid.

"I'll come up. I brought crossbows." The newcomer held one weapon in both hands, ready to fire.

When only ten feet lay between the two guards, Sigri uttered a shrill war cry and threw another knife. The door guard turned and raised his shield in time for Sigri's blade to hit the wood with an echoing thwack. He never saw the crossbow bolt coming before it punched into his chest. Coughing blood, he sank to the floor.

His supposed comrade dropped the weapon and rushed over to him. The last things the dying man wondered about were the unusually soft hands lifting his face before everything went black.

* * *

Hours before, Jarne had walked up and down the path leading to the boat dock, accompanied by a grouchy old guard. Every day since joining the duke's service, the captain posted Jarne to watch the lake. His companions changed often. Regarded as a tedious task for dimwits and weaklings, the captain reserved this post for soldiers who had gotten themselves in trouble or weren't yet skilled enough for more important positions. Jarne fit both criteria.

"It is cold." Jarne blew in his hands and tried to rub feeling back into his numb fingers.

"Of course. Winter is upon us. But can you imagine standing on the keep's roof tonight? The icy wind would freeze your balls off. Not that there is much to freeze off, mind you."

"What's that supposed to mean?"

"Oh, nothing." The man smirked, displaying crooked teeth. "It isn't my place to judge what goes on between husband and wife. Still, it seems your wife has an appetite you can't satisfy."

"Don't talk like that about my wife. She is a fine woman."

"Agreed! She is a very fine-looking woman. I'm sure she spends the time with the guard captain discussing needlepoint and flower arrangements."

"She wouldn't; she is faithful. She loves me. Look what she smuggled in for me." Jarne pulled a flask from under his tunic. "It's the finest whiskey you can get in Thorshofn."

"You can't have liquor in here!" The old guard stepped back, aghast. "The sergeant will whip you bloody. And if he is in a foul mood, he'll inform the duke. No telling what cruel punishment you'll receive then."

"Who has shriveled-up balls now? It's fine with me if you'd rather freeze. The more for me, the merrier."

"Give me that, boy." He swiped the bottle from Jarne's hand and took a swig. "This is nothing for children. You better stick to milk with honey." Then he let out a laugh, which devolved into a cough. "Oh, this is good stuff. It burns you right through."

Despite trying to put on a brave face, the coughing got worse. Grabbing the wall for support, the guard staggered. The flask slipped from his hand. Rattling and wheezing escaped his throat before his knees gave out, and he collapsed.

Jarne bent down, stoppered the flask, and put it back under his tunic. Then, he dragged the dying soldier by his feet onto the pier, where he rolled the man into the lake. Weighted down by a breastplate and sword belt, the body disappeared from sight. Jarne tossed the flask into the lake as well. Leaning against a wooden pole, he started his most challenging task of the night— waiting in anticipation. The minutes crept by in agonizing slowness while the fear of everything going wrong tortured Jarne's mind. His confidence diminished with every passing moment. Finally, he saw a light bobbing on the lake not far from him. Relieved, he lit his lantern to signal Mae that the way was clear.

Jarne pulled the boat in and helped Mae unload the gear. Before moving inland, though, he encircled Mae with his arms, and they kissed. Everything else seemed irrelevant—the dangerous plan, the tight schedule, and the alarms raised all over the estate. Gasping, Mae broke off the kiss.

"Wasn't there something else?" she smirked. "Some other reason that made me row across a vast lake on a freezing night?"

"It can't be more important than this." And he kissed her again.

"We really should..."

"Yes, we definitely should."

"Get going, I mean." She punched him in the stomach.

"Fine, Witch of Woe." He pouted briefly before grabbing the gear and carrying it to the base of the keep. Stripping off the soldier's tunic, Jarne slipped into the black cloak Mae had brought. He buckled the belt with the throwing knives and hung a crossbow over his shoulder. In the meantime, Mae had laid the coil of rope on the ground and started swinging the grappling hook. She threw, pushing with magic, but her aim was off. The metal hook glanced off the wall and hurtled back toward them.

"Should I do that?" Jarne asked. "I throw, and you push." Mae made a petulant gesture, inviting him to try. He smiled and blew her a kiss. "I couldn't do it alone either, but together, we are an unbeatable team."

He threw as hard as he could, and Mae waited for the right moment to push the hook over the low wall of the duke's terrace. The metal clattered on the stone. Jarne pulled the rope back, and the hook became lodged in the mortar between the blocks.

"All right, master burglar," Mae mocked, "you climb first. And you better hope the anchor holds. I'm not sure I can catch you with magic."

Jarne stole another kiss before climbing up while Mae held the rope steady. Reaching the battlements, he slipped onto the balcony. Light from the duke's study shone through the cracks of wooden shutters.

Mae tugged at the rope, and Jarne pulled her up. They crept forward on either side of the windows and loaded their crossbows.

"This is it. There is no turning back," Jarne whispered.

"There never has been—not for me, anyhow. It took me over a dozen years to figure that out." Mae grimaced. Jarne squeezed her hand, and both continued toward the balcony doors, peering through cracks in the wooden shutters.

"What can you see?" Jarne asked.

"Two men in front of the fireplace." Mae moved her head around to get a better view. "One must be the king—he is quite large. The man with his back to us is the duke. There is a spindly man fluttering around them. A servant? Or there might be two, dressed identically. You?"

"I think you're right. There are two servants. And two guards in front of the door. Different uniforms, though."

"King's guards. Take them out first. Any signs of the black sorceress?"

"Can't see her," Jarne replied.

"Be careful. She is devious. And Jarne," Mae said with urgency, "come here for a moment."

"What?" he asked.

She didn't answer, so he crept toward her. Mae grabbed his face and kissed him. Passion, fear, and excitement pulsed through her body, leaving Jarne dazed and breathless.

"That," she said, grinning. "Now, get ready." Picking up her crossbow, Mae added, "Any moment now. I'll blast the doors open, and you kill the left guard."

* * *

Noises and shouts came from the hallway beyond shortly after Mae and Jarne got in position. First, there was banging and clattering, sounding like an explosion in the bowels of the keep. Then, there was yelling and screaming, much closer this time. Every eye in the room focused on the door, and the guards put their hands on their swords.

"Go!" Mae shouted, sending the shutters flying. Splinters of wood darted everywhere. Jarne fired, and so did Mae, heartbeats later. The first bolt hit one stunned king's guard in the chest. But the second stopped midair as a wall of ice erupted between the soldiers and the assassins. *The black sorceress.* Lurking in the corner, she had reacted with the speed of a striking cobra, forewarned by Mae's use of magic.

Dropping their spent weapons, Mae and Jarne burst into the room. Mae turned left and attacked the sorceress, throwing her poisoned daggers. Hard-pressed to defend herself, the black witch deflected the knives with a bubble of compressed air.

The ricocheting blades bounced in all directions, slicing into the smartly dressed servants and sealing their fates.

Before the sorceress could retaliate, Mae pulled a heavy wooden shield from the wall and sent it hard into the side of her head.

The sorceress went down with a cry of anguish. Still, she wasn't counted out yet. Bracing against the back wall, she thrust the table laden with platters of food and pitchers of drink toward Mae.

Mae crashed into the opposite wall, seeing stars for a second.

Jarne drew his sword and charged toward the fireplace. The rotund man, who must be the king, uttered a piglike squeal. He toppled over backward, landing on the wolf pelt adorning the floor.

The duke, however, sprang to his feet. Spry despite his age, he grabbed the fire poker, wielding it like a sword.

Three king's guards rushed to aid their monarch. Two more had been in the room, unseen by either assailant. Only one was down. These were terrible odds, even if Jarne had been a skilled sword fighter.

Where are Sigri and Renya? he thought. *I could use some backup here.*

Retreating, Jarne threw a knife underhanded. His aim was true, yet the guard deflected the blade with a lightning-fast sword stroke. His companion lunged with equal speed, extending his sword arm in an elegant and fluent motion.

Mae blasted his arm off the deadly trajectory. Unfazed by the use of magic, the guard pulled a dagger from his belt, slicing across Jarne's face. Dumb luck saved Mae's lover. Jarne tripped over the suckling pig, which had been the centerpiece of the evening's banquet. Losing his sword in the fall, he lay defenseless on his back as the guards closed in.

Mae wasn't faring much better; all her throwing knives were gone.

The black sorceress regained her footing and unleashed a torrent of objects. Mae struggled to deflect the attacks. No matter how much she yearned to repay the sorceress's evil deeds, a direct contest of power was futile.

She needed a distraction.

The duke, king, and a lone guard remained huddled by the fireplace. Mae struck the crackling logs with a blast of air, sending a shower of embers flying. Burning debris rained down on all three men, setting their clothes on fire. The flames spread quickly, feasting on tapestries and plush armchairs.

Realizing the king's peril, the black sorceress halted her barrage, allowing Mae to hurl a heavy candelabra across the room, hitting Duke Finsgúr in the back. The duke stumbled forward into the black sorceress's path, and the wrought-iron fire poker pierced the evil witch's leg.

Unnoticed amongst all the chaos, the entrance door opened. Two more guards entered the room, carrying crossbows. They looked small and wore ill-fitting uniforms. The king's hair had caught fire, and he cried out in pain, causing Jarne's attackers to turn.

"To the king!" the taller guard shouted, heartbeats before his head exploded from a crossbow bolt. The second shot hit his companion in the stomach. He fell backward, and Jarne finished him with a carving knife from the piglet that had saved him earlier.

CHAPTER NINETEEN

No Good Deed Goes Unpunished

"The sun turns black, earth sinks in the sea,
The hot stars down from heaven are whirled;
Fierce grows the steam and the life-feeding flame,
Till fire leaps high about heaven itself." [1]

THICK SMOKE BILLOWED everywhere. The hungry fire's tendrils reached the tapestries, furs, and banners decorating the walls. It snapped at the mementos of the Viking clans, setting them ablaze as if to honor the invasion's fortieth anniversary with their violent demise. And in the midst of the devastation stood the black witch, sending curses and debris flying in every direction.

Renya and Sigri had discarded their crossbows and helmets. Together, they attacked, forcing the black sorceress to deflect Sigri's knives and dodge Renya's fire blasts.

The last remaining king's guard tried dragging His Majesty toward the door and beyond, closer to the hallway's breathable air. But the barrage of hurled and reflected deadly objects barred the way, and they hunkered down.

"Where's your crossbow?" Mae yelled over the tumult.

"Outside," Jarne replied, coughing.

"Get it! It's the only way to kill that accursed witch."

"The duke!" Jarne pointed. "He's getting away."

"Cowardly bastard," Mae cursed. "We must hurry. Kill that witch!"

"Go after him. Make him pay!"

"No! I can't leave you. I swore —"

---

[1] *The Prophecy of the Seeress, Stanza 57,* Poetic Edda, English by Henry Bellows (1936)

"Mae," Jarne shouted, "We don't have time!" He coughed. "Go!"

Mae picked up the sword of a fallen guard. Yet still, she hesitated. "I love you," Mae called, voice quavering.

"Love you too. Now go!" Jarne staggered backward as the smoke stole the air from his lungs. With bleary eyes, he saw Mae running toward the opposite door.

Renya, too, had retreated from the room, leaving Sigri engaged in a deadly one-on-one battle with the king's sorceress. Standing in the entrance hall next to the guards she'd killed earlier, the gray witch marveled at the incredible display of her sister's prowess.

All restraints were gone; all masks were down. Sigri held back no longer, no more hiding her abilities. In place of the caring healer stood an indomitable fighter, a witch on a mission. And her raw power pushed the black sorceress to the defense.

Renya reloaded the crossbow but hesitated to attack. The fumes of the raging fire thickened, preventing her from telling friends from foes.

A figure came running toward her. Renya readied her weapon. She was about to fire when the small stature gave her pause. Mae emerged from the room, her arm in front of her nose and mouth, desperate for breathable air.

"Where's the duke?" Mae wheezed.

"Someone fled that way." Renya pointed down the hallway. "Jarne and Sigri, are they all right?"

"Yes, on the balcony. Nobody can survive in there." Coughing, Mae bent over, her hands on her knees. "The last guard is dead. He ran into my sword. Don't know about the king. Watch for the black sorceress," Mae cautioned.

"I'll try," Renya replied, squeezing the weapon in her hand. Behind her, booted feet marched up the stairs.

"More soldiers?" Mae exclaimed.

"Don't worry, I'll take care of them." Renya's eyes lit up. "Get the duke and give him my love."

Mae followed the duke, still catching her breath as Renya turned toward the stairs, facing the oncoming reinforcement. From the corners of her eyes, Mae saw a ball of fire flying from Renya's outstretched hands. Screams and banging followed as the onrushing soldiers tumbled back down the stairs. Renya laughed, wild and furious. She'd always had a special place in her heart for soldiers. Channeling immense power, Renya blasted the ceiling apart. Stone groaned, and an avalanche of bricks rained down on the fallen soldiers, burying their broken bodies.

The noises of the violent battle followed Mae as she hurtled down the deserted hallway. Furniture, furs, shields, and axes lay strewn across her path. She slipped on a goblet and crashed into the wall, causing pain to shoot through her knee and shoulder.

Her head hurt, her lungs burned, and blood ran from a cut on her eyebrow. With an anguished scream, Mae got up and limped toward another staircase leading only up, presumably to the duke's bed chambers.

She had him cornered; there was no escaping now.

A vicious grin twisted her lips as the witch reached deep within, unleashing the seething darkness that dwelled in her soul. Adrenaline surged, the fiery torrent stoking her euphoria, and she bounded up the stairs, taking the steps two at a time.

* * *

JARNE KNELT ON the terrace, fumbling to reload his crossbow. *Much good will it do!* he thought, frustrated. The room was engulfed in a choking, black smoke, smothering any hope of a clear target. Creeping toward the open window, Jarne heard the groan and rumbling of stones echoing through the fog. A rush of scorching air erupted from the balcony doors. Jarne threw himself to the side.

Laughter? Was that laughter he heard?

Then, the wall before him exploded. The blast tossed him in the air, sending him crashing against the battlement. Jarne screamed as white-hot agony erupted in his back. His left shoulder had shattered. His vision blurred, and a deafening ringing filled his ears.

When the dust settled, Jarne discerned two figures standing among the debris, raining curses and destruction upon each other. Soot smeared their faces, and their clothes were ripped to shreds, revealing the landscape of cuts and angry burn marks beneath. Jarne tried to rise, but a torturous jolt spiked through his left side, creating a wave of nausea and dizziness. He groaned, his body collapsing. His right arm landed on a piece of wood. *The crossbow?*

Fighting the crippling spasms, Jarne willed his fingers to explore the shape. The bow was cranked, but the groove was empty. The bolt had to be nearby. He ran his hand across the debris-covered floor, fingers desperately seeking the missing projectile. *Nothing!*

Steeling himself, Jarne jerked his body to the right. Barbed blades twisted in his back, paralyzing his muscles. Tears spilled down his cheeks. Breath by breath, he reasserted control over his broken body. His right hand had found the prize, closing around a wooden shaft the width of a finger. With shaking limbs, he slotted the bolt into the groove.

The witches' battle raged on. Sigri, on the left, struggled to defend against the merciless assault of the dark sorceress.

Gritting his teeth, Jarne hoisted the crossbow onto his knee, pulling his leg up to adjust the angle. He couldn't afford to miss. Senses narrowed to a single point, he focused on the target. His breath slowed.

Wait... Wait... Now!

Sending a silent prayer along with the shot, he fired. The crossbow's jolt unleashed another spasm of torment, causing Jarne to lose consciousness, his reserves utterly spent.

* * *

Sigri had started the fight with an incredible amount of life force. She knew that seeking a confrontation unprepared would ruin their chances. The green witch wasn't cruel. She understood that killing people was evil, even for the greater good. Still, she needed to do evil today because many more people would die if their plan failed. *To forge a sword, you have to break the ore.*

Regretting what she must do, Sigri had laced the tea for the kitchen staff with a strong sedative before harvesting the life force of five women. She saw no other way. The witch had tortured her brain for many days, searching for a better way, like using soldiers instead. Killing soldiers was easy. Only earlier today, the skilled potioner had added a slow-acting poison to the wall guards' midday meal, and many would die in the next twenty-four hours. But she couldn't devise a plan to harvest their life force before they expired.

Brimming with energy, Sigri engaged the black sorceress, and something miraculous happened. Like remembering a forgotten poem, when the opening phrase releases the brain's stranglehold on the memory, the green witch recalled spells and curses to fight her devious foe.

Yet, Sigri was sure those weren't real memories, at least not her personal ones. They felt different, more natural, almost instinctive. Thus, both combatants were well-matched. If the acrid smoke hadn't forced them out, the battle might have gone on until the first witch ran out of energy.

Sigri needed to breathe. Inching toward the balcony, she hoped to trap her opponent in the room. But the king's sorceress had other plans. With an incredible burst of power, the black witch exploded the keep's outer wall, thrusting smoke and debris out over the lake beyond. The fringes of the blast caught Sigri and threw her against the battlements.

Getting to her feet, the green witch was immediately under attack, hard-pressed to defend against a barrage of ferocious curses. She couldn't be running low, not yet. Had the black sorceress held back earlier to protect the king? Regardless, Sigri faced an onslaught of hexes and needed all her skills to avoid fatal injuries.

From the corner of her eyes, she spotted Jarne. The boy had gotten hold of a crossbow and aimed it at the king's sorceress. Fighting to keep her opponent engaged, Sigri threw caution to the wind, attacking with everything she had left, hoping Jarne fired soon.

A twang sounded. The shot's aim was true, yet the despicable black sorceress threw herself backward in the nick of time. The bolt flew on through the smoke-filled room. While missing its intended target, the deadly projectile still ended up killing a witch.

Sigri stumbled, her eyes wide in shock.

Then came the agony—a feeling like a vicious blow slicing her in half. Someone had ripped her beating heart out of her chest and poured icy water through the gaping hole.

Renya!

Sigri knew there was nothing she or anybody else could do. Her little sister, this wild and funny girl, the constant tease with the big mouth and the much bigger heart, was gone forever.

Renya had guarded the entrance. Unable to rejoin the fray, the gray witch prevented anybody from fleeing or reinforcements from arriving.

And the unlucky bolt had found her heart.

She didn't even see it coming. The gray witch felt no pain as she sank to the floor, leaving her sister alone in this cold and brutal world. She died with a smile on her face—the joy of her paying back the duke's soldiers.

Sigri couldn't breathe, couldn't move, couldn't think. Time disappeared, and reality lost its meaning. It felt like only yesterday when she'd taught Renya to walk, to swim, and to use her magic. Images ran through the healer's head in rapid succession—listening to Renya's heartbreak over Katla, consoling her for killing that soldier, confronting their father, and leaving home not knowing where to go. And now, Renya was gone, and it was all over.

Everything!

Sigri exploded. Her raw fury blew the black sorceress off the balcony, sending her tumbling to the icy lake below. The fire behind roared into a white-hot furnace, turning everything to ashes, including the dead bodies.

The reception hall's ceiling collapsed, and the flames shot a hundred feet into the night sky, flaming red like Renya's hair—a funeral pyre worthy of her beloved little sister.

* * *

Reaching the upper landing, Mae stood before a massive wooden door studded with iron bands. The battle had drained nearly all of her resources. Still, Mae doubted whether she could have blasted these doors apart even if she had the energy to spare.

Looking around, Mae noticed a tiny window on her right, barely wider than an arrow slit. Poking her head through, the witch found her way in. Fifteen paces to her left protruded the duke's privy, sending the noble discards down the wall into the lake. If she squeezed through the window and climbed along the outer wall, she could enter from where things usually only exited. The idea was disgusting and dangerous. An icy wind blew in from the lake, and finding purchase on the slippery rocks would be perilous.

Tired, hurting, and angry, Mae's overwrought brain couldn't devise a better plan. She had to risk it. Still, she faced an immediate obstacle. While Mae was slender and nimble, she couldn't fit through the window.

Instead, the witch used her knife to scratch out the mortar between two building blocks. Stepping back, she blasted the rock with all her force. The stone moved but didn't come free. Thrice, Mae repeated the process before the chiseled rock crashed into the lake, leaving the opening wide enough.

Sheathing her bent knife, Mae inched her way to the privy, clinging to the wall like a spider. Slippery filth stuck to the wall underneath the ducal throne. Scouring the wall with blasts of air, the witch was thankful for the decorative stonework providing her with finger holds. With her nose full of the foul smell and her strength almost gone, she squeezed herself through the wooden cutout. Her hands, face, and clothes were caked in filth, but she'd gotten in.

No noises from the room beyond reached her ears. Mae kicked the door open. The duke wheeled around, holding an enormous crossbow. The witch punched him hard in the face with magic. He stumbled, sending the weapon flying. The impact released the shot, and the massive bolt buried itself into the wall next to Mae, splintering an ornate wooden shield. The entire room had been decorated with arms and armament—mementos of his glorious days as a younger, fiercer warrior. Crumpled on the floor, he looked like an old man who had long overstayed his welcome.

Mae snatched a halberd from the wall and advanced. She must have looked frightening and smelled even worse, but the man didn't show fear. Instead, his eyes darted around, trying to find a way to defend himself.

And with the devil's own luck, temporary reprieve came in the form of a younger woman. She rushed into the room through a side door and threw herself on the duke.

"Get away from my husband!" she shouted. "What do you want from him, fiend?"

Mae was flabbergasted. She'd never expected the duke to have a wife who would defend him. Standing open-mouthed, the witch remained unsure of how to proceed while the other woman continued the defense.

"Are you the one who roils up all the villages?" the duke's wife challenged. "Have you killed my husband's soldiers and his servants? He has worked for decades to bring progress and prosperity to these forsaken lands. This is how you thank him?"

"Your husband is an evil tyrant," Mae snarled, finding her voice again. "He kills innocent people whenever he pleases. Prosperity?" She laughed. "He squeezes every last krona out of the people. And when they can't pay their taxes, he has their daughters raped, their wives enslaved, their farms burned, and their sons pressed into the army. Get away from him or share his fate." The witch lifted the polearm like a throwing spear. "My patience has limits," she growled. "He will die. Will you die with him?"

Then the duke spoke, and his words astounded Mae. "Birgith, dearest. Step aside. No harm must come to you." Addressing Mae, he asked, "Will you let me stand up and die like a man?"

Mae stared into his cold and calculating eyes. She nodded. Lumbering to his feet, the duke leaned on the bed's side table, making a show of his age. Yet, despite his surprising concerns for his wife, he ensured she remained in the direct line of fire.

"What do you know about being a leader?" Duke Finsgúr asked, straightening up, his hands behind his back. "Do you think you can rule a country by handing out sweet bread? You call me evil? All men are evil. But most lack the skill and dedication to accomplish more than dream of greatness."

He stared at Mae, pride and righteousness gleaming in his eyes.

"I had to fight my entire life, eliminating my two older brothers to get this title. Every day, I have to deal with the stupidity of a weak king and the cunning attacks of assassins. I must quell uprisings and maintain order. What do I get in return? A stinking witch stands in my bedchamber, threatening my family. How dare you?"

Mae couldn't believe her ears. This man thought he had a right to do what he did. More than that, he believed he was owed gratitude for his actions.

"Don't talk about family," the witch hissed. "Your soldiers came to my house, killed my parents, and abducted my brother. I will not stoop to that level. Only you have to die. Send your wife away. Do it, or she will share in your death."

Mae was done talking.

And so, apparently, was the duke. He grabbed the arm of his dearest Birgith and pushed her aside. But then, in one fluid motion, he raised a hitherto unseen miniature crossbow and fired. Rushed, his aim was slightly off. The bolt sliced into Mae's left arm.

Mae threw her weapon, magic augmenting her strength. Yet, the despicable man wasn't done playing tricks. Maintaining a firm grip on his wife's arm, he pulled his dearest Birgith in front to act as a human shield. The halberd tore into her chest, shredding her lungs and heart. Two feet of bloodied steel exited her back, sinking inches into the duke's shoulder.

Infuriated beyond belief, the witch snatched more weapons and attacked.

The duke jumped over the bed, rolling on the floor to evade her charge.

But he was old. He had nowhere to hide, nobody else to sacrifice. Mae's spear pierced his upper thigh, breaking the bone. He howled in pain, and she howled in madness. The duke crawled on all fours like the beast he was, and the witch nailed his hand to the wooden floor with a sword. Then, she kicked him hard in the face.

Blood and teeth flew from his mouth. Yet still, he was fighting, trying to pull the sword out with his other hand.

Mae couldn't have that. She moved around and kicked him between the legs with all her strength. Erik Finsgúr doubled over and vomited. Picking up an axe, Mae stomped on his free arm and severed his hand with a single blow.

The duke shrieked in agony, realizing he wouldn't get away this time. Picking a mace from the wall, the furious witch struggled to lift the heavy weapon. With a drawn-out war cry, she smashed the spiked ball onto his left leg, shattering the knee into dozens of splinters.

The duke's inhuman screams echoed through the room.

Mae decided she wanted to have nothing of this deplorable being in her. She would kill him. But despite her fatigue, she wouldn't absorb his life force.

Time to end this.

The witch unsheathed her knife. Blood and excrement soiled her hands. In contrast, the blade twinkled in the candlelight, showing off the delicate runes. Kneeling on the heaving and moaning mess that once had been the ruler of the southern province, she pulled his head up by his hair and opened his throat with one forceful slice.

It is done.

"Nooo! You monster!" The high-pitched scream came from the door on the opposite side of the room. Another bedroom?

Mae turned to see a boy and a girl standing at the door, their faces pale, their eyes wide in horror. The girl was taller. She had her hands on the boy's shoulders, trying to restrain him. He jerked free. Picking up a fallen weapon, he ran toward Mae, murder in his eyes.

Mae hadn't noticed the other door earlier. She'd focused all her attention on the duke. Rolling off his corpse, she blasted the boy off course. He stumbled sideways, tripped, and crashed to the floor. His head smashed onto a discarded axe.

Mae had never intended this. She acted in reflex. Could she heal him? Rising to her feet, her steps unsteady, she reached out and gently touched his face. The boy was gone. His eyes, wide and vacant, reflected the horror of his final moments—his hatred etched forever into his dead face.

"Get away from him, witch!" the girl shrieked. "Get away, you evil demon. You killed him! You killed them all! You are a monster!"

Dazed, Mae looked around, trying to comprehend what had happened. *This is not how it was supposed to go. Only the duke was supposed to die.*

Yet, there stood a young girl confronted with the brutal massacre of her entire family. The father lay on the floor with a lake of crimson spreading from his butchered neck. A deadly projectile had impaled the mother as she tried to shield her husband. And a little brother was taken from her forever.

The macabre scene defied comprehension. An evil black witch had ruined the girl's life in a single act of despicable violence. Covered from head to toe in blood and filth, Mae stood amidst the carnage as a grotesque portrait of death's true daughter.

No longer could she hide behind the guise of good intentions. Driven by an insatiable thirst for vengeance, she'd irrefutably become an evil black witch—murderer of families, slayer of dreams—a weaver of nightmares who scarred the souls of innocent girls for life. Her pitiful pretense of *trying to do good* lay in ruins.

Here, in plain sight, was all the "good" she was capable of.

PART THREE

The Quest for Happiness

"Happiness comes from moving toward something. When you run away, ofttimes you bring your misery with you."

– *Myron Lanaklin*[1]

---

[1] Michael J. Sullivan (2012): Heir of Novron

CHAPTER TWENTY

Fallen Heroes

SIGRI STOOD ALONE in the courtyard. An icy wind blew through her tattered clothes, chilling her sweat-covered skin. Behind her, the keep's old tower still stood, blackened and badly damaged.

All other buildings had vanished, replaced by heaps of broken rubble and burned-out timbers. Dark smoke rose from several fires smoldering in the distance, blacking out the stars. Bodies lay scattered everywhere. Yet an eerie silence blanketed the place—the silence of death after a war.

The witch had no recollection of how she'd gotten there—a big hole gaped in her memory. The last she remembered, she'd fought the king's black sorceress when her little sister died. What happened next remained unclear. Sigri assumed some of the guards must have succumbed to her poison. Some buildings must have collapsed due to the burning stable's spreading fire. Still, a sinister voice lurking in the dark shadows of her mind whispered of her hurling curses and raining destruction down on anyone and anything in her path. *What have I done?*

Finding herself alone in a field of destruction, Sigri started looking for her companions. Climbing up the broken steps, she found the boy, Jarne. He lay unconscious on the balcony. Blood and ash covered his face, his cheeks crisscrossed with deep canyons carved by tears. His left shoulder seemed broken.

Sigri dragged him into one of the guest chambers on the keep's second floor. Propping him up in a mighty four-poster bed with opulent drapings, she let him rest. His soot-smeared body soiled the crisp white linens. *Was this the king's bed?* the witch wondered. But the king was dead. He wouldn't reclaim it.

Searching for Mae, Sigri roamed the hallways and climbed the stairs to the duke's bedchambers. There, she stumbled upon the aftermath of her sister's actions. It seemed like Sigri hadn't been the only witch who lost control that night. Mae, too, had obliterated the line between righteous retribution and indiscriminate evil. Seeing the mutilated bodies, the green witch's hope disappeared.

How could it all go so wrong?

A young girl cowered in a corner, horror-struck, rocking back and forth. Sigri assumed her to be the duke's daughter, distraught after witnessing the butchering of her family. The witch approached, taking the girl in her arms. No words existed for a situation like this. Nothing could make this right again. Gently stroking her hair, Sigri relieved the girl of the misery of her life. Better a quick end than endless torment.

Feeling sick to the core, the witch asked herself whether the same logic extended to Jarne. Mae must have run away; she wouldn't return. Caught in the fierce battle between her good intentions and her demonic urges, the black witch hated herself too much to seek him out. *Wouldn't it be kinder to end Jarne, too?* Perhaps. But why should Sigri be kind to him? It had been his stupid idea—the grand plan of the witches' revolution.

With a heavy heart, Sigri trudged downstairs. Stepping outside, she took deep breaths, trying to dispel the horrid smell from her nostrils. Yet here, too, the stink of death fouled the air.

Several fires still smoldered as the sun rose for the first time since Renya's death. Crows feasted on the bodies. The witch dragged some dead soldiers to the estate's entrance. She arranged the bodies in a macabre pattern to frighten off looters. Exhausted, she returned to the keep's tower and slept for a few hours.

In the early afternoon, she returned to care for Jarne. Sigri found food and herbs in the ruins of the kitchen and the attached storehouse. Both buildings had partially survived, as they were fireproof for obvious reasons. The healer bandaged Jarne's shoulder and fed him broth. Her patient remained semiconscious, moaned, and tossed. *Does he suffer bad dreams?* Wiping his face with wet clothes, the witch wondered what about this boy compelled women to care for him.

* * *

JARNE OPENED HIS eyes and tried to orient himself. His entire body hurt. The sour smell of cold ash filled his nostrils. He found himself in an unfamiliar room, darkness hiding many details. Lying on his back, his head rested on a soft pillow, and blankets covered his body. *A bed?* Why was he lying on a bed?

He had been fighting. Smoke and scorching flames caused confusion. Curses flew everywhere. Then, the keep's wall exploded, flinging him through the air, and he crashed into the parapets. His shoulder had shattered. Still, the battle went on, and the black witch attacked Sigri.

The black witch! Jarne jerked, trying to raise his upper body, and excruciating pain shot through his back. Breathing through gritted teeth, he let his body go limp, praying for the spasms to pass.

"I wouldn't do that if I were you." The flat voice sounded from his left. Cold and detached, it sent icy shivers down his spine.

Jarne wanted to see who had spoken, but his broken body objected to the movement. His vision blurred, and the world spun, triggering a bout of nausea. Under all the pain, Jarne felt the sensation of being restrained. Had someone taken him captive? Unlikely. The duke's guards wouldn't place an intruder and assassin in a comfortable bed. Then, his sluggish brain made the obvious connection. Someone had bandaged his shoulder, and the voice was...

"Sigri? Is that you?"

"Yes, I am the one who is still here."

"Where am I?" Jarne asked, not picking up on her strange response.

"Not in hell, Jarne Ólafsson—but you should be."

"What happened?"

"I saved your skin. For someone who is supposed to see the future, I keep making the same mistakes over and over again."

The voice undoubtedly belonged to Sigri, but she sounded strange. Jarne had never heard her speak in such a lifeless tone. Of the three witches Jarne knew, Sigri was the least passionate. She acted with logical precision, calculated the effects of her words before speaking, and remained aloof even in heated discussions. Still, in that moment, her voice reminded Jarne of a corpse that had spent a season or two in a bog.

"Where is Mae?" Silence. "Sigri, where is Mae?" The urgency made Jarne tense, triggering renewed pain.

"Gone." One word, cold and deadly like an icicle, pierced his heart.

"What do you mean 'gone'? Is she...?" Jarne's breathing quickened. He was unable to control his body's shaking despite the agony the movement caused. He needed to know. At the same time, he feared what he was about to hear. Each second of uncertainty burned like a torturer's glowing knife. "Sigri," he pleaded, "what happened to Mae?"

"She isn't dead," Sigri said, her voice straining to cover her pain. "My sister Renya is. She is the one who got killed in your stupid stunt, pierced through the heart by a crossbow bolt."

Jarne's mind froze. Seconds went by before the full realization sank in. He had fired a crossbow bolt, aiming at the black witch. And he had passed out, not knowing if he had hit his mark.

"Sigri, did I...?" Jarne's voice was meek, a child pleading with his mother, desperate to hear that all would be well again. But he wasn't a child, and comforting Jarne was the last thing on Sigri's mind.

"Of course you did!" she hissed. "But not with your unlucky shot. You took two sisters away from me by setting us on this path, by convincing us to start your foolish revolution, by insisting that good could come from doing evil."

Jarne didn't know what to think. Too much was going on. Was everything his fault? Right then, he couldn't focus on that. Right then, he needed to have clarity.

"What are you saying? Where is Mae?" Jarne's heart tried to jump out of his ribcage. Sigri, on the other hand, had calmed down again.

"Mae fled. I believe she's running away from herself. She'll try to get as far away as possible—maybe even leaving Heilladur—or further. It isn't easy to outrun your own self-blame. But wherever she goes, neither of us will ever see her again."

"I don't understand."

"Of course you don't!" A harsh, mirthless laugh escaped her mouth. "You know, I considered not healing you." Sigri let the statement hang in the air for a few heartbeats before continuing in an icy tone. "I've lost so much in this fight. I was close to taking your life as repayment."

"You wouldn't, Sigri." Jarne rolled on his side, facing the green witch, despite the stabbing pain in his shoulder. "We are friends."

A force of air hit him like a battering ram. Jarne was flung from the bed and crashed onto the floor. Sigri strolled over and looked down, revulsion and hatred on her face.

"No, you are nothing to me. I spared you because death would be too easy for you, after what you've done." She grabbed the front of his shirt, pulled his face toward hers, and looked him straight in the eyes. "I wish you a long and painful life. May all your faults and mistakes haunt you day and night. May your existence be a never-ending misery. I've lost two sisters, thanks to you. Curse you, Jarne Birger Ólafsson." With that, Sigri dropped him to the floor and left the room, slamming the door behind her.

* * *

SIGRI WALKED DOWN the hall, breathing rapidly and trying to calm the raging fire in her chest. The sulfurous smell of smoke became more pungent as she neared the ruin of the duke's reception hall. Climbing over the rubble, she made her way toward the collapsed staircase.

Sigri hadn't lied; right then, she hated Jarne. Still, she didn't hate him as much as she hated herself. The attack had been *her* plan. He was a silly boy who believed in fairytales like Mae and Renya. Both her sisters had oftentimes acted like hot-headed children despite their age. Sigri was the only responsible adult. Yet, she, too, had been swept away in fantasies of victory and glory.

From her elevated vantage point, the last remaining witch surveyed the fruits of their "glorious victory." In front of her lay a devastation of epic proportions. Only the keep's old tower had survived, charred and blackened. The battle had destroyed all other buildings. Hordes of warring giants must have rampaged through the estate.

Nobody would believe three witches and a silly boy had caused all the death and destruction. Sigri couldn't believe it either, despite her own recollections. Still, the truth wouldn't matter. The few survivors had fled in terror, spreading the word of fighting demons and evil witchery.

Following a precarious path over heaps of crumbled stones, Sigri clambered down to the courtyard level. Despite her anger and sadness, the witch didn't want Jarne to die. Still, she was sure she never wanted to see him again. His life was his responsibility.

And mine? For the first time in her life, Sigri was alone. She could do whatever she wanted. The prospect frightened her.

* * *

TWO DAYS EARLIER, Mae had fled from the duke's bedchamber, haunted by the painful accusations of his daughter. Slipping out of an ornate window, she climbed the rough outer wall three stories to the tower's base. If she only could have fallen to her death, everything would have been over. Yet the devil's own luck was on her side.

Reaching firm footing, her fingers felt numb, her shoulders ached, and her many cuts and bruises threatened to overwhelm her. Mae sank to her knees, the night's horrors catching up. She retched, emptying her stomach.

"Who goes there?" The call pierced the night. The black witch hadn't heard anybody approaching. Forcing her punished body back onto her feet, Mae looked for a weapon, but there were none. She'd left her knife next to the duke's corpse.

Two soldiers approached. They looked ill, struggling to hold each other up. Sick clung to the front of their uniforms. *Sigri's poison must be doing its work.* Mae retreated toward the uneven rocks at the lake's shore, annoyed by the guard's dedication to pursuing an intruder despite their condition.

As she'd hoped, the taller soldier toppled on the uneven ground, dragging his comrade down. Mae was on them, hitting the big man in the face with a rock, breaking his nose. The second soldier grabbed her wrist, and she bit his arm. Tasting blood, she used the contact to suck his soul from his body. His corpse fell across his taller comrade, pinning the man to the ground. Mae spat and wiped the blood from her lips before relieving the broken-nosed guard of his suffering as well.

After the scuffle, the black witch fled north. She hiked through the forest and toward the mountains. For two or three days—Mae couldn't say for sure— she walked. Time had blurred. Exhausted and devastated, she'd abdicated control to her baser instincts, desperate to escape the scene of her crimes. The witch slept little, fearing her dreams. As time passed, her conscious self resurfaced, reasserting command, and Mae hatched a plan. She would travel through the Copper Mountains to the craggy shore beyond.

Cresting a hill, the witch finally spotted the sea to the north. The sun had already disappeared behind the Smoking Mountains, stealing the color from the waves crashing against the cliffs. If she continued the entire night, Mae could reach the water's edge by morning. *That's as far as I'll go.* She wasn't in a hurry. Still, the full moon would rise soon, providing more than enough light to guide her path down to the ocean.

Mae followed a steep and narrow ravine until she arrived at a wide beach of black sand. The moon had risen high, making the wet sand glisten in the pale light. Dotted with lighter crystals, the beach mirrored the starry sky above. The witch couldn't discern where the water started nor see the horizon. In front of her stretched eternity.

She'd come to the end of the world—the end of her world.

Looking around for stones to fill her pockets, Mae felt her inner demon stirring. Would she be able to walk into the icy sea, or would she again lose control? Which side of her would win the fight? *There must be a better way!* To her right, sheer cliffs rose in the distance. Trudging through the wet sand, she searched for a suitable spot.

An hour passed. In the east, a purple band announced the sunrise. As Mae walked on, she came upon a wall of vertical basalt columns standing tall in perfect formation. A narrow waterfall sent a spray of glittering droplets over the cliff's edge, marking the mountain stream's violent demise.

The wetness gave the black columns an elegant glow in the early morning light. Mae marveled at the beauty of the scene. The water's sacrifice turned the cold, black pillars of unforgiving stone into a stunning backdrop for an illustration of nature's fundamental law: *Everything must end, but nothing is wasted. It becomes part of something bigger.*

She smiled as she climbed the regular blocks next to the waterfall. The first rays of the sun crested the horizon. Mae couldn't have asked for a more beautiful setting. She took off her shoes and walked along the brink toward the stream. With her head held high, the witch stepped forward, letting her toes feel the edge. A steady breeze blew salty air into her face. She didn't mind. She didn't feel cold; she didn't feel fear.

Mae raised her arms wide to embrace the wind. Relaxing her shoulders, she let her fingers play the air's invisible strings. This is what she needed to do. This is what she wanted to do. Calm spread through her body, and she thanked the Norns for guiding her to this spot. The witch had found something that was black, yet still, it was beautiful.

Thinking of Jarne, Mae let go.

CHAPTER TWENTY-ONE

No Way Home

THE RAIN AND sleet, which had persisted over the last couple of days, finally lifted as Sigri approached Thorshofn from the north. Her cloak was soaked, the hood plastered to her head, her legs caked in mud up to her knees. Despite the dampness, the salty sea breeze carried a foul smell of smoke. Sigri doubted that benevolent cookfires alone could cause such a pungent odor. Rounding a corner, the vista of the town below opened, confirming Sigri's suspicions. Strewn all over the city, dark blotches marked burned houses. She wondered if any building in Thorshofn would still be standing if it hadn't been for this month's unusually wet weather.

The town had no protective wall nor guarded gatehouses. Most buildings stood close together with low wooden fences in between, preventing livestock from escaping or wild animals from entering. The proximity to the duke's estate and the headquarters of his guards had always been sufficient to guarantee Thorshofn's safety. As the province's premier hub for commerce, the town had grown around the name-giving harbor. The King's Road, on which Sigri stood, flowed like a mighty river through its center, allowing the unhindered traffic of goods—from Hagndal in the north to Makevinger in the south.

A lot had changed since Sigri had left a few days ago. Oxcarts and heaps of lumber formed barricades blocking the trade artery. Behind those, she spotted men guarding the town's entrance. The news of the duke's death must have traveled fast, and the signs didn't bode well for the current state of affairs.

Sigri wasn't keen on being searched, questioned, and detained. Instead, she left the road and circled the town through the dense forest that covered the hills. She knew the area well, having wandered these woods often as a young girl while exploring her magic. It didn't take her long to reach a spot where a sheep barn with loose boards on the back let her enter. Stepping out the front, Sigri stood in the quiet street of her childhood home. Here, too, traces of violence were visible. Doors hung half open, and many possessions lay broken and scattered in the street.

Sigri reached her father's house. The front door had been kicked in, the hinges broken, and the frame splintered. Inside, a scene of looting and senseless vandalism greeted her eyes. The chests and cupboards lay turned over. The intruders had spilled her herbs and powders all over the kitchen floor. A trail of blood led toward the small backyard.

Rummaging through the debris near the hearth, Sigri found the wrought-iron fire poker and hefted it like a weapon. She stepped outside. A middle-aged man lay in her backyard, propped against her storage shed. His legs looked broken, and large amounts of dried blood covered his face and neck. Despite the severe injuries, he was breathing, a faint moan escaping his lips with each exhalation.

"Who are you?" Sigri questioned without any trace of compassion. The man looked around, confused. Then he saw Sigri looming over him.

"Water, please," he croaked, his voice rasping like gravel sliding down a mountainside.

"This is my house. I don't remember inviting you. One more chance. Who are you?"

"I am..." He cleared his throat. "Borger... My name is Borger Raknarsson. I'm a dock master."

"You're in the wrong part of town, Borger. The harbor is near the sea, not in my backyard. What are you doing here?"

"Please, water. Have mercy."

Sigri glared, considering kicking his injured legs to make him answer. Instead, she grabbed the only surviving pitcher from the kitchen and walked down the street to the well. Some idiots had broken the well's bucket; only the handle dangled from the chain. Sigri used her belt to tie the pitcher to the chain. Lowering it carefully, she filled it with water. On her way back, she wondered about the deserted street. It was mid-morning, yet nobody was around. No noises came from the houses.

"Drink and answer my questions," Sigri demanded after handing Borger the pitcher. "What happened?"

The man gulped mouthfuls of water, spilling large amounts over the front of his ripped and bloodstained shirt. Impatient, Sigri took the pitcher away.

"The duke is dead," he whispered. "They say evil witches killed him. Demons destroyed the estate and killed everyone. It was terrible, they say."

"I don't care about the duke," Sigri interrupted. "What happened here?" Her gray eyes glared with fiery intensity.

"People argued about what to do," Borger explained. "Some wanted a council of elders; some argued for trial by combat to pick a new chieftain."

Sigri lost her patience. She kicked his broken leg. The man screamed. "I'm not interested in the meeting records. Get to the important points."

"There was fighting," the man whimpered. "Three groups formed. It was bloody and brutal."

"Which group did you fight for? Not the winners, I take it?"

"How do you know?"

Sigri sighed; it couldn't be more obvious. Still, she saw no need to explain that one and one made two. Resting the poker on the man's leg encouraged him to keep going.

"Halmar Jonsson, the town's cooper... He gathered the biggest group. I joined up with him. There is safety in strength," the man wheezed. "Most people fled. There was raping and looting. Men can be beasts when their blood is up."

"You don't say." Sigri sneered. "So, the other two groups joined forces."

"You already know?" Borger asked, bewildered.

"I don't, but it seems obvious. Still, that doesn't explain why you are in my house."

"They attacked me," the man coughed. "When Halmar died, his group disbanded and..." More wheezing followed. Sigri handed Borger the water pitcher, and he drank. "The winners took over the town," he continued. "Calling themselves magistrate of the free city and captain of the guard. They promised to end the violence, hanging any looter or rapist."

"So, did you rape or loot?" Sigri asked, showing little patience with his long-winded explanations.

"I did nothing of that sort. I helped people," he huffed in indignation. "They came upon me, a group of five. I had injured one in the fighting. He and his friends took cruel revenge. When they left me for dead, I crawled into your house."

Sigri didn't bother pointing out that the blood traces started inside her house. She had heard enough. Everything implicated Borger being caught in the act of looting. Her thoughts must have been visible on her face. Thus, with panic in his voice, he rushed on.

"I can help you if you help me."

"*You?* Help me?" Sigri asked, her disbelief evident.

"To get away. This town is dangerous for a woman. I know where horses are."

"I'm not going anywhere," she said. "This is my home."

"That's folly. A woman alone? They'll come and do things to you. All the herbs in this house. They'll call you a witch, and you'll burn at the stake."

"You said evil witches killed the duke and destroyed his estate, killing everyone?" Sigri knelt beside Borger, taking his hands in hers.

He nodded. "Aye, fiends from hell with terrible powers."

"Good thing, then..." She smiled. "That I'm one of those."

Sigri squeezed his hands and drained his life. She would need to bury the body and fix the front door before making herself at home.

* * *

JARNE PICKED HIMSELF up from the floor. Pain flared all over his body. The vicious double blow of Sigri's revelations and her attack may have caused more damage than the explosion inflicted.

Jarne was no stranger to injury. Still, for the first time, he feared he might not recover from this. Mae was gone. Renya was dead. And Sigri, who could have been his ally in finding Mae, hated him from the bottom of her heart. Should he go after her? Console her? He couldn't manage it. Neither was he able to follow her in his condition nor was the time right. Sigri needed time to grieve, and so did he.

Jarne dragged himself back into the bed and let the exhaustion take him. It was dark when he woke the following day. Keeping his eyes closed, he hoped against hope that everything had been a bad dream. He would find himself in the cabin in the woods, Mae beside him. Deep in his heart, Jarne was still that boy who demanded happy endings to all his stories. Yet, the pain in his shoulder was real, bringing him back to reality.

The faintest glow of predawn light brightened the horizon outside his window. Jarne sat up, stiff and bruised, trying to clear the fog from his head. His feet touched a basket beside the bed. Straining to bend down, he pulled the object closer and explored its content. *Food!* There was a loaf of bread, a wedge of cheese, and something that smelled like smoked sausages.

Jarne surveyed the room for more surprises. A pewter pitcher stood on the table beside the fireplace. He hoped it contained water; he was so thirsty.

Hobbling across the room, Jarne smelled ale. He drank deep, lifting the heavy pitcher one-handed. Sigri had left him food and drink. She had also cared for his injuries. Despite her undoing much of that treatment by smashing him onto the floor, Jarne couldn't help but smile. Sigri didn't hate him, not entirely.

With the edge taken off his thirst, Jarne felt a different urge. He looked around for a chamber pot but couldn't find one. Steadying himself against the wall's polished stones, he shuffled toward the collapsed reception hall. Fading stars greeted him where the hall's vaulted ceiling used to be. Carefully, he inched out into the open and relieved himself—urinating on the ruins of Duke Finsgúr's glory.

Returning inside, Jarne followed the corridor and up the staircase to the duke's bedchambers. An awful smell greeted him. Still, it paled compared to the horrific scene of the mutilated bodies. His stomach heaved, forcing Jarne to his knees as he vomited the ale across the wooden floorboards. His brain fought to reconcile the perpetrator of this gruesome massacre with the loving woman he knew Mae to be. There had always been a darkness in her; she called it her *evil*. Jarne had denied its existence. He could no longer. Mae was a black witch. In front of him lay her handiwork—a demon's masterpiece.

Jarne crawled away from the puddle of sick toward the small window, the sour stench masking the repulsive smell of decaying corpses. Drawing deep breaths of the fresh air, he slumped against the wall, and his spirit collapsed. How could he go on? His body was in pain, and he felt ashamed, frightened, and disgusted.

Jarne sat there for a long time, unable to get up, until he heard voices from the courtyard below. *Mae? Sigri?* No, the voices sounded like men. They argued. Jarne strained to understand the conversation. He caught words like treasure, demons, witches, and coward. It didn't take a genius to deduce the meaning. Those men were looters, debating whether the potential spoils would outweigh the dangers.

Roused by the unexpected intruders, Jarne pushed himself to his feet and shuffled back into the duke's chambers. Holding his right arm in front of his mouth and nose, he entered one of the smaller bedrooms where the windows faced the courtyard. The men worried about confronting evil spirits. Jarne would use their anxiety to his advantage.

A brass bed-warming pan with a long wooden handle lay in one corner. Raising the heavy object, Jarne gritted his teeth and banged it against the wall. Howling in pain and frustration, he kept hitting and smashing things.

When the agony threatened to overwhelm him, Jarne dropped the bedpan. It clattered to the floor, the ornate lid warped and dented. The ruse had worked. Jarne saw three men running for their lives, fleeing the estate like the devil chased them.

Jarne leaned against the wall. In fighting off the intruders, he had regained some clarity. He couldn't stay here. More men would come, tempted by the duke's treasures. He needed to leave while he could. Where should he go?

One fact was certain: Jarne would search for Mae. If it took all his life, he would never stop looking for her. But where to begin? Their hut in the Deepwood forest seemed the best location, followed by the Witches' Castle. In the winter, Jarne would need more than a week to reach either destination. Without horses and travel gear, he wouldn't survive the journey. Jarne required a safe place to rest, heal, and make better plans. The house in Thorshofn was closer. He could reach it in one day. But Sigri must have gone there. That left him with no other option. Jarne would go to Kristiansund, his home village.

The villagers had never been especially friendly. Jarne remembered that nobody had helped when his mother got sick. But he would arrive with good news. The duke was dead. The villagers must surely welcome the hero who liberated them from the tyrant. Jarne would talk to them about the role of the witches, changing their minds about magic. Then, he could convince Sigri to help him search for Mae.

All the hardship, Renya's sacrifice—everything would be worth it in the end.

* * *

"I am telling you, it was witchcraft. All those men, dead where they stood," the small man in a gray smock insisted. He stood beside the smithy with hunched shoulders, wringing his hands in front of his chest. His large front teeth gnawed on his lower lip, giving him the appearance of a rodent planning an attack on food left out in the open. "Must have been a dozen. I heard about covens of dark witches."

"Bah, nonsense," replied the tall, blond man opposite him. His shoulders were broad, and he wore a sleeveless shirt despite the chill air. Sweat glistened on his muscled arms as he beat the glowing iron with his hammer. "Where would you hear something like that? Did the mackerels whisper to you? Or did you meet a mermaid? More like you heard it murmured from the bottom of your bottle."

"You haven't seen it, Ulfir—bodies arranged in evil symbols."

"And neither have you, Arnulf Egberson."

"But my sister has. She worked in the duke's services. What she saw... It frightened her out of her wits."

"Some say there wasn't much wit to start with. Didn't she insist headless riders stole Farmer Holgrim's horses?"

"That was years ago," Arnulf interjected, "and someone stole those horses." Ulfir Pederssen, the village smith, shrugged and continued working the iron. "I am telling you, Ulfir. It was witches. And they are on the loose."

"He is right, you know." Jarne stepped closer.

It felt strange to stand in his home village, like turning back time. Little had changed. The same windswept wooden houses stood clustered around the fishing harbor. The same tiny boats rocked on the gray water. If anything, the village felt smaller, less important. A dust devil danced over the dirt-packed village square, and the breeze made Jarne shiver despite his thick coat.

Jarne had recognized Ulfir. The son of Kristiansund's old smith was the spitting image of his father. He didn't recognize the shorter man, Arnulf. Both men turned toward him, suspicion and mistrust on their faces.

"Who are you?" the smith asked.

"Jarne Ólafsson. I used to live in this village," Jarne answered with a friendly smile. Neither man reacted to his attempt at levity.

"Uh-huh," the smith grumbled, "and when was that?" He rested his hammer on the anvil while his grip on the smooth wooden handle tightened. "I don't remember you. I've lived in this village my entire life."

"Wait a moment," the other man said. "Ólafsson... You're that boy. Olaf Jonsson's son, or at least, his whore wife's brat. The bastard." Turning to Ulfir, he explained. "He was born a few years before you served in the duke's army. Later, he kept to himself. Nobody liked him. But didn't you die on the day your father was killed?"

"I didn't. I was injured, but I survived. Nothing much has changed here, not even the disgusting lies about my mother." Jarne stood straight and looked into the smith's eyes. His right hand resting on the sword's hilt—he strove for an impressive, worldly pose. Yet, the fact that his left arm rested in a sling marred the impact.

"Then why come back?" Ulfir asked with unexpected venom in his voice. "And what do you know about witches?"

Jarne wondered where all the animosity came from. It couldn't just be their misgivings against strangers.

"I was there. I fought with the witches. I planned the assault with my three friends. Together, we killed the duke, the king, and most of his soldiers."

Arnulf's laughter rang across the square, sounding like the bleating of an angry goat. But Ulfir remained quiet. He let go of the hammer and the iron rod and stepped out of the smithy toward Jarne. Approaching in slow and measured steps, he narrowed his eyes as he addressed the returned traveler.

"*You* fought with witches? *You* killed the duke?" the smith asked.

"I fought side by side with three witches. I killed many soldiers. And Mae, my... wife..." Jarne couldn't come up with a better word. But why not. They had lived together, and he loved her. "She killed the duke."

"You've wedded a witch?" Ulfir's stare grew even more hostile.

Jarne didn't like the direction the conversation took. He had expected elation about the duke's death and gratitude for his involvement.

"You know, I think I remember you," the smith said. "You were that little runt, stealing and always up to something."

Jarne tensed; this had been a mistake. He slid his left foot back, widened his stance, and prepared to draw his sword as he had been trained in the duke's guard. Both men sized each other up. Then, the smith punched him hard, sending Jarne sprawling.

"You and the witches caused the soldiers to come here and kill my father." Ulfir knelt beside Jarne, the smith's large hand squeezing his neck. "So I got news for you." Ulfir picked up a rock. "I am delighted you came back. And now, I'll make sure you'll never leave."

"Don't kill him yet," Arnulf shouted.

"Stay out of this. He has to pay for my father's death," the smith growled.

"And so he shall, but we don't know where the wind will turn."

"What's that supposed to mean?" Ulfir asked.

Arnulf shuffled closer, still wringing his hands. "There might be a new nobleman soon. If we handed over the criminal who killed the duke? That could be beneficial. He could be tortured to reveal where the witches are. We might even get a reward."

"And what if the witches come looking?" Ulfir asked. "It seems too risky."

"Wouldn't we be glad then that we haven't killed him? We'll say we took him in, offered our hospitality, so to speak."

Arnulf spoke with an oily voice, making no effort to disguise his insincerity. Still, Ulfir furrowed his brow.

"Where would we keep him? He's not staying in my house."

"We'll put him into the ruins of the old mill. Nobody uses the building. I'm sure you could make manacles and a chain to keep him… safe?" Arnulf asked.

The smith dropped the rock and got back up. Jarne gasped for air, the renewed pain in his shoulder preventing him from rising. The smith dusted off his hands and nodded to his friend.

"All right, we'll keep him there. I can always kill him later." An evil grin appeared on the smith's face before he kicked Jarne's head hard, and everything went black.

CHAPTER TWENTY-TWO

Dark Secrets

MAE WAS IN hell. The musty smell of damp earth filled her nose, and the shrieks of tortured souls drilled into her brain. She was freezing, her head felt twice its usual size, and someone or something hit her aching ribs with wooden beams in irregular intervals. She knew she deserved to be in hell, her torments duly earned through all her evil deeds. Still, she never thought that it would be so cold.

Mae heard a deep and pained moan. Only when her parched throat complained did she realize she had made the sound. She wanted to open her eyes, lift her head, look her captors in the face—if they had one. But she couldn't find the strength. Another blow rattled her body. Mae cried out, turned her head, and saw booted feet inches from her nose, tapping a rhythm.

"Einar, she is awake," an excited voice called out.

The noise sent a stab of pain through her brain. Detached from the agony of her body, Mae's mind marveled about her utter misconceptions of hell. Not only was it much colder than expected, but the demons sounded like village boys.

"Come over here and take the reins. I'll see to our guest." That voice was deeper, gravelly, with authority. Yet it carried no discernible menace. The owner of the bouncing feet stood up and walked out of Mae's line of sight.

Her world swayed from side to side as the two speakers switched positions. Mae closed her eyes again. She had no strength to fend off any assault. She couldn't even muster emotions like fear or apprehension. Lying there, she waited to dissolve and disappear.

It wasn't to be.

Calloused hands touched her cheeks and lifted her head, tilting it forward. Something leathery and wet touched her lips.

"Drink, at least a little," the deep voice said, almost sounding concerned.

Mae obeyed. Cold water gushed into her mouth. She tried to swallow, but there was too much liquid. She gagged and spluttered.

"Easy. Take it slow. You need to drink, but you need to breathe, too." The waterskin touched her lips again, and that time, Mae managed to gulp down a few mouthfuls. "That's enough for now. Let's see if it stays inside."

"Where am I?" Mae croaked.

"On an oxcart. We're traveling on the Western Road and should reach Hestavik by tomorrow."

Mae heard the words; she understood their meaning in isolation. Together, they didn't make any sense. She needed more information. With an effort, she reopened her eyes. Blinking moisture away, Mae regarded her environment. She was lying on what looked like burlap sacks on hard wooden boards. Above her stretched a gray sky, and a wrinkled face shielded her eyes from the sun. It didn't look like any perception of hell she had ever entertained. That left her without a reference point.

"Help me up," Mae muttered, her voice hoarse from lack of use.

"You're sure? You're pretty beaten up. Your entire body is a purple bruise."

Mae glared. The speaker shrugged and pulled her upright. She hissed. He had been right about her body hurting. Still, she couldn't have a meaningful conversation lying on smelly turnip sacks. He, too, sat down and wiped his large hand over his face. They rode on a dilapidated wooden cart. The shrieking came from the wheel bearings missing grease, and the bumps in the road had hurt her ribs.

"The name is Einar Ingulfson. The young lad up front is Holger Bjørndahl."

"Mae... I mean Mette. Mette Einarsdóttir."

"Not mine, I take it?" he chuckled. Mae felt confused, being slow on the uptake. Then she rolled her eyes.

"My father died many years ago."

"My apologies." He nodded in respect, and a brief silence fell.

Mae took the opportunity to regard him closer. He was an older man—over forty, lean but tough. His short-cropped hair was gray, while his beard held faint traces of red. Several old scars adorned his wrinkled face, and his nose had been broken more than once. He had seen rough times. However, his steel-blue eyes exuded curiosity instead of menace. He wore the cloak of a soldier over shabby peasant clothes. A knife hilt protruded from his belt, another from the shaft of his boot. As his hands rested on his knees, Mae spotted the faded welts of a branding scar. He followed her gaze.

"I was a slave in the copper mines, and so was Holger."

Mae detected the slight tone of a challenge in his voice. She looked him in the eyes, her expression void of judgment, and returned his honesty.

"I'm a witch." Mae didn't know what made her say it. She was beyond caring. If he was dangerous, so was she. Regardless, his reaction surprised her. Instead of shying away in fear, he laughed out loud.

"Did you hear that, Holger?" he chuckled. "I told you so."

"How... What?" Mae stammered, dumbfounded.

"I take it you don't remember much?"

Mae shook her head, regretting the motion as searing pain spread from her temples, triggering nausea.

"All right," he said, adjusting his perch to settle in for a longer explanation. "Yesterday, after nightfall, you walked into the mining camp, more dead than alive. Your clothes were wet and torn, your skin blue, your stare blank. You looked like a corpse three weeks dead."

Mae nodded slowly and held her hand out for the waterskin. After she drank and wiped her mouth, Einar continued.

"News of the duke's death had reached the camp that day. Some soldiers ran, leaving weapons and uniforms behind. Others weren't so fortunate." His face broke into an evil grin at the memory. "We took what we could. I had just claimed this cart when you stumbled into our midst."

"The others let you have the cart?" Mae asked.

"I needed to substantiate my claim." He spread his large hands, the knuckles still red and raw. "Most knew me. Some might even have feared me." Another grin followed. "That's why I could take you out of there, bring you to safety."

Mae gawked, open mouthed, bewilderment in her eyes.

"See, you walked into the camp, and all of a sudden, you dropped—like a puppet with the strings cut. I thought you dead... most did." Einar held out his hand for the water, and Mae obliged. "Wish it was something with a bit more of a bite," he grumbled after a long pull. "Regardless, one man approached. Don't remember his name. He turned you over, and you were still breathing. Only, well, your shirt... it was ripped to shreds, and your chest was bare." He looked apologetic, almost embarrassed.

Mae looked down and realized she was wearing a soldier's tunic, a pair of rough woolen pants, and boots that weren't hers. She raised her gaze back to Einar's face, her eyes wide open in disbelief.

"These men, some had been slaves for years. They hadn't had a woman in all that time." Einar cleared his throat, looking uncomfortable. "I mean, you're young, still a girl. But this chap, he got some ideas. Grinning like a fool, he knelt beside you and squeezed your breasts. No telling what next. You lay there, not moving, and then your hands grabbed his face. And then it was *him* crumpling. Only, he was dead for real."

Mae didn't remember any of this. Her last memory was of the waterfall, the black beach, the sunrise, and... her attempt to kill herself. Somehow, she must have survived. Her inner demons had taken over, walked her back to the mining camp, and defended her life. Einar was spot on with the metaphor of the puppet. Mae's mind hadn't been in control—her curse had been the puppeteer. All this became crystal clear to her in a matter of heartbeats. Still, his actions didn't make any sense.

"You saw me kill a man. You knew I was a witch... with black magic. And you took me along? Rescued me?" It all felt so wrong. "*Why?*"

"Don't know about black magic. But that's beside the point." Einar bent forward, a sad little smile on his lips. "I would have died in that mine. There was no escaping. We tried an uprising. The duke's wrath was terrible. I'd lost all hope." Wiping a trace of moisture from his eyes, he took a deep breath. "They say witches killed that bastard whoreson of a duke. They say witches butchered him and the king and his soldiers. There ain't many witches around. Even if you weren't one of them, I wouldn't have you harmed. I'm grateful for what you or your sisters have done."

* * *

THEY TRAVELED FOR most of the day until the light faded. Spotting a cluster of trees not far off the road, Einar called a halt.

"We'll stop there," he said. "Best if nobody spots us from the road at night. These are troubled times."

"Won't they see our fire?" Holger asked, fearing another cold night.

"We'll keep it small."

Mae and Holger climbed off the cart, and Einar steered it toward the intended campsite.

"Let's see if I can find us some dinner," Holger said, taking a bow and arrows from the cart and sauntering off into the wilderness.

Einar started to collect wood for the fire, sending a stern look in Mae's direction, forbidding her to help. She felt useless but grateful. After he had gathered an armful of good-sized branches and smaller twigs, he built up a cone-shaped structure. Then he stepped back and looked at Mae, mischief twinkling in his eyes. She returned his gaze, confused.

"I have a steel dagger. I might even find some flint. But I was never good with that," Einar confessed, the sheepish grin broadening on his face.

"You want me to?" Nobody except her closest companions had ever asked her to do magic, and never in such a casual setting. She felt a little apprehensive. Still, they needed a fire, and Einar had seen her do much worse. Mae closed her eyes and rubbed her palms together. Her body hurt, but she had plenty of life force to fuel her magic, thanks to the groping stranger. With a clap and a shout, the witch ignited the wood pile, conjuring a bonfire much larger than she had intended. "Oops," she said.

Einar laughed. "Not to worry, not to worry."

Holger returned an hour later, carrying two plump ptarmigans by their feet. Mae insisted on helping with the preparation, and not long after, the game birds roasted over the fire. Einar took crispbread and hard cheese from the wagon. All three ate in silence while the fire burned low.

Mae felt better. She leaned against a tree stump, stretching her feet toward the glowing embers and pulling the sacks like a blanket around her shoulder. From time to time, both men looked at her, curious to hear her story but not daring to ask outright. Mae took a deep breath and began.

"You are right; I killed the duke." Her voice was flat. "My sisters and I planned the assault for weeks. We infiltrated his court, then struck at the right moment. He was an evil man. I was certain he deserved to die."

"You won't hear complaints from us," Einar declared, and Holger nodded.

"It didn't go well." Mae's voice quavered. "I lost control; too many died. His servants, his family... his children."

Choking on the last word, Mae lowered her head. In her mind, she was back in the tower room. Blood was everywhere, the boy lay dead, and his sister denounced Mae for the evil monster she was.

"Innocent deaths are a heavy burden." Einar struck a consoling tone. "I'm sure you tried to do the right thing, a *good* thing."

"That's the story of my life!" Mae's mirthless laugh cut through the night. "I try to do *good*. And every time I try, death follows ... innocent people pay the price."

Her throat closed as tears welled in her eyes. Pressing her clenched fists into her lap, the witch stared into the glowing embers, trying to suppress her body's violent shaking.

"I caused endless suffering—even to people I never met," Mae whispered after a long pause. "For years, I have carried this black curse. I've tried to ignore it, to deny it, to fight it, and even to channel it. I wanted to use my magic for good. Only evil followed."

Mae glared at them, moisture sparkling in her narrowed eyes.

"Killing is the only thing I'm good at. I killed a king, for devil's sake," she shrieked, "and a duke, many noblemen, ... and even more children." She slumped, burying her face in her hands. "Only one evil fiend escaped, only one killing failed, only one target survived, still poisoning the world. The one who needed killing most—I failed to end her ... myself."

Heaving sobs racked her body, rendering her incoherent.

The men shared glances, yet neither approached her, laying an arm around her shoulder, telling her all would be fine. They were hard men. Without meaning to, they'd saved a black witch. What would they do now? Would they finish what she couldn't? Would they kill her?

"I killed my wife," Einar said after a long pause. "That is how I became a slave. I had found her with another man. I beat them to death. First him, while she watched, then her." He looked at his hands as if he could still see their blood on his fingers. "I expected them to hang me. I didn't fight the arrest. Instead, they made me a slave."

Mae looked up, confounded by his tale, her eyes red and puffy. Was that supposed to make her feel better? Had Einar seen her story as an invitation to engage in a competition of bygone horrors?

"I didn't have to kill her," Einar continued with a faraway look. "I didn't even like her much. We wedded young; our parents arranged it. I could have let her go, and I would have been free, too. But I always had this anger in me, something driving me mad." He poked the embers with a stick, shooting sparks in the air. They shone bright for one heartbeat before the fire in them burned them to ashes, and the wind carried them away.

"You can't change what you have done, Mette." Einar looked at Mae. "That's in the past. You can't even change who you are. Your past has formed you. You can only choose what you will do. And thus, you define who you will be." He held her gaze, his striking eyes glowing in the firelight. "The blood of my wife will always be on my hands. But when I was sent to the mine, I chose to act differently. Instead of my anger controlling me, I chose to control my anger."

"I don't know if I have the strength," Mae croaked. "I don't know what for?"

"How about that boy of yours? Yarmo? Was that his name?"

"How... do you know? His name is Jarne. But how...?" Mae stared at Einar, everything else forgotten.

"So, where is he?" Einar chuckled. "We couldn't make out much of what you said when you were unconscious. But that name, you said it quite often."

"I don't know," Mae admitted.

"You need to get better, Mette. Heal your injuries and put some meat on those bones. And then, I would suggest you go looking for that Jarne. Everything else... Well, as I said. It is your choice."

* * *

MAE TRAVELED WITH Einar and Holger until they reached Hestavik. There, she bade the two men goodbye. While unsure about her path forward, something seemed to draw her home—to the cabin in the woods, where everything had begun. Mae hoped Jarne would be there. Wouldn't he go home after the fight to look for her? *Is he still alive?* Mae felt horrible about running out on him and her sisters. She couldn't think. The witch needed a place to rest, and the devious Norns had sent her close to her childhood home. That must have been a sign.

Walking into the Deepwood, Mae pondered Einar's words of the night before. He'd claimed there was a choice. But how could she choose what to do? He knew nothing about her curse and the terrible price for her continued existence. *He doesn't need to.* Mae made her choice. She would use all her energy to remove the black curse from this world. This curse was the reason for all the horrors Mae had inflicted. She would hunt every last black witch. Then, she would find a way to end her inner demons once and for all.

Twilight had fallen when Mae reached the clearing near the stream where she had grown up. The house stood there, crooked as it had always been. No smoke rose from the chimney despite the chill air. Getting closer, she saw the flickering of a candle inside. Somebody was home. *Jarne!* Mae sprinted the last few steps and pulled the door open. Despite the burning candle, the hut felt dark and repulsive. A foul smell she couldn't place filled the air—a mixture of herbs and rot.

"Jarne?" Mae called, standing on the doorstep.

"I'm afraid not." The voice sounded weak, old, and sick. An icy shiver ran down Mae's spine. She knew that voice; she'd heard it before, a long time ago. Could it be?

Mae stepped in and looked around. She didn't carry any knives or other weapons. Should she look outside for the wood axe? If her suspicion was correct, mundane weapons would be of little use.

On the bed lay an emaciated figure, the foul smell emanating from her direction. Herbs and powders covered the wooden table, and a blackened cauldron hung over the cold fireplace. The single candle burned on a stool beside the bed, allowing Mae to make out the occupant's face in its sparse light. Familiar but also horribly altered, the king's black sorceress had aged decades since Mae had seen her last. Her raven-black hair had become white and brittle. Yellowing skin stretched like parchment over protruding cheekbones. Still, her sunken eyes exuded the same menace as ever.

A skeletal hand rose, and Mae blasted it with a concentrated punch of air. The arm smacked against a wooden beam, breaking bones as a dirty handkerchief fell to the ground. The black sorceress coughed, spewing drops of blood from her withered mouth.

"That was quite unnecessary, Mae," the other woman stated. "Did I get the name right? It is Mae, isn't it? There was a lot of shouting and fighting last we met." She coughed some more, a sickly sound escaping her lungs. Letting her mangled hand fall onto her blanket, the sorceress showed no signs of pain, nor the slightest interest in the state of her limb. "I couldn't harm you even if I wanted. I don't have any magic left. And as you can see, I'm no match in a catfight, not even against a scrawny creature like yourself."

Mae narrowed her eyes, not trusting a word this demon uttered. Walking over to the hearth, she grabbed the fire poker. The emaciated witch shook her skull-like head with a faint echo of her old superiority.

"What a dull instrument to resort to. You *are* a witch. Never properly trained, I give you that, but still, you've had your powers long enough."

"And now I'll use them to end you, black witch!" Mae had found her voice.

"End away." The sorceress chuckled, which turned into a fit of coughing. "But that'll change nothing. I'm not a black witch, not any longer. You are." She smiled. "Why don't you sit? You look like you've seen a ghost. I'm not that either—not yet."

Mae stared in disbelief at the wasted form of the woman who'd cursed her in this cabin over a dozen years ago. After all this time, she had the chance to pay her back, to kill her. *Do it, now!* Who knew what tricks this fiend had in store. Still, Mae couldn't bring herself to it. What if her words were true? Mae needed to learn more.

"My name is Bergrún by the way, Bergrún Lilith Gullveigardóttir. We don't want to get confused on who is a black witch and who isn't."

"You are," Mae blurted. "You are the cause of it all."

"Hardly. You give me too much credit."

"You cursed me to this existence, and now I will end you."

"Believe me, I didn't do that on purpose. Especially when I see how you have squandered your gifts. I had to fight for them; I had to kill for them. You got them handed on a plate. And you remained an ignorant child, forever whining about how unfair your life has been." Bergrún became agitated, narrowing her sunken eyes. "I watched you from a distance all those years—your pathetic attempts to deny what you are. I couldn't have chosen worse. I could never guide you on your rightful path. Still, one hopes..."

"You what...? No, you lie!" Mae shouted, but she was shaken. *What's all this?*

"Sit or don't sit. Kill me or don't. I grow weary of this." Bergrún sighed, accompanied by a dry rattling in her chest. She tried to make a dismissive gesture, but her broken hand didn't cooperate. "See, I'm not long for this world. But all that knowledge of seventy-five years, the accumulated wisdom of Death's Daughters... Will you let it go to waste?"

* * *

MAE'S CURIOSITY HAD won out, even though she didn't trust the source. She sat as far away as she could and listened to Bergrún's tale, straining to detect treachery. Yet try as she might, Mae couldn't stop the powerful magic of a gripping story.

Bergrún was born on Heillaður thirty-five years before the Viking conquest. She grew up in a small fishing village on the western coast, always knowing she was special—destined for greater things despite her family being poor. She had no friends. At age twenty, she fancied a young man from a well-respected family. He rejected her because of her poverty. Humiliated, she ran away, swearing revenge.

After years of roaming the land, she found one of the five black witches and begged her for help. The witch saw her passion and potential. She offered Bergrún an apprenticeship. Bergrún accepted, but she soon hated working for the old hag. One night, she knifed the black witch in her sleep, thus absorbing the curse.

Flushed with power, she returned to her village, where she butchered the young man and his entire household. Taking all their possessions, she tried to set up her kin as the most powerful family. But her parents were appalled. They pleaded with her to repent her sins. Infuriated, the black witch burned the entire village, killing everybody, including her parents.

Bergrún went into exile. She traveled among the forbidden isles for seven years to learn all she could about witchcraft. During that time, she hatched the plan to invade Heillaður but couldn't convince men to follow her. She was a woman, after all.

Frustrated, she persuaded Harold Svenson, an ambitious Viking chieftain, to invade Heillaður, promising to aid his conquest with her dark magic. In return, she insisted the new king heed her council and outlaw magic to kill off any opposition. When her influence over the king waned, she started grooming a successor, ensuring a weak and malleable man inherited the throne. Bergrún still needed a male strawman puppet despite all her cunning and power.

"And I would have lived happily ever after," she cackled, "if I hadn't crossed paths with you."

"I'd feel sorry," Mae snarled, "if you hadn't killed my family and cursed me!"

"But I didn't kill your family—the duke's soldiers did. And I wouldn't have cursed you if you hadn't attacked me."

"Oh? You would have let me go? Because of the goodness of your heart?"

"No, silly girl! Weren't you listening? I'd have taken you along as my slave. But by cursing you, I gave up my power," Bergrún hissed, earning her the worst coughing fit. Mae didn't offer her water. Getting her breathing under control, the sorceress continued in a rasping whisper. "Each curse can only possess one woman at a time. There can only be five black witches because Death had five daughters in the beginning." Bergrún's eyes burned with intensity as she divulged the dark secrets.

"Then why give it up if you loved it so much?" Mae asked with scorn—but also genuine curiosity.

"I had no choice. Somehow, you broke my binding and plunged that knife into my chest. I would have died. I took some of your vitality in cursing you—enough to heal me."

"You could have killed me afterward, taking back the curse."

"The world doesn't work that way. The curse requires strength. When I killed my mentor, it chose me for my boldness. But in giving it to you, I proved myself unworthy."

Mae's head was swimming. Too many thoughts floated around, bobbing and bouncing against the new information. Was everything a lie? But why drag this out? If the black sorceress... if *Bergrún* had a plan, wouldn't she have acted on it by now?

"So what are you now?" Mae asked, disgusted by even talking to this demon.

"A shadow of myself. A witch on borrowed time. Every bit of magic I've performed since I cursed you has drained my life. Nothing can refill it. I had to live off my reputation. The fight in Duke Finsgúr's estate was too much. Broken, powerless, and hated—I needed to get far away from everybody. That's when I remembered your lovely, isolated house. I managed to get here with the last ounce of my strength. And this is the end of the road for me."

"Yes, it is." Mae stood up. "That might've been the only true thing you've said to me all evening."

"Believe what you want, but heed my warning. The black witch of Urðr, she has become too dangerous. She'll come for you next. I had plans to deal with her. Now, you must..." Bergrún coughed.

"I'll see to her after I'm done with you." Hatred hardened Mae's voice. "I will eliminate this vile curse for good."

"You can't destroy it. The curse will live on. Give it up, and you'll end up like me." Bergrún spoke in a rush, telling fantastic tales about the secrets she had learned from the mentor she murdered. Her words could have explained so much of what Mae had experienced during the years of her damned existence. But at that moment, Mae couldn't wait for her to finish.

She hated Bergrún's loving tone when referring to the powers. The black sorceress feared the disappearance of her knowledge more than she dreaded her own end. Mae, on the other side, yearned for the curse and all the stories about it to vanish from this world forever, together with the woman who had ruined her life.

"You are what you are," Bergrún implored Mae, "and you will be a black witch 'til the end. You have no choice."

"Oh, I *do* have a choice." Mae stepped toward the far corner of the house and returned with a large pitcher, its opening sealed with wax. She hit it with the poker, cracking the top. Liquid spilled over her hands and onto the ground. Bergrún followed her every move with her eyes but didn't say a word.

"I hope you'll burn in hell, Bergrún." Mae stepped closer. "But if they're out of firewood, let me help." Mae threw the pitcher and propelled it with magic. The jug hit the wall above Bergrún's head, bursting apart and showering her in lamp oil. When the flood of flammable liquid reached the candle, half of the hut erupted in flames, including the bed and its withered occupant.

Mae stepped back, ensuring that there would be no escape this time. As Bergrún's shrieks grew unbearable and the flame's scorching heat seared Mae's face, she left the hut. Yet she remained close, watching her entire past—the good and the bad—being consumed by fire.

CHAPTER TWENTY-THREE

Renewed Alliance

After raging for two hours, the fire burned low, and so did Mae's euphoria. She'd felt incredibly powerful and righteous, annihilating the evil sorceress who'd ruined her life—like an avenging angel. A memory stirred of Renya calling her that once. At long last, Mae had fulfilled her sacred mission.

The black witch had achieved the near impossible. She and her sisters had overthrown the foreign invaders' tyranny of forty years. The king and the duke both died at their hands. Mae had made them pay retribution for the death of her family. And finally, her burning hatred of her dark curse had incinerated the king's black sorceress. Shouldn't she feel elated about completing her vendetta?

Yet, as Mae stood there, alone in the dark forest, she only felt drained. Her body ached. Tasting the ashes in the air, her mental state closely resembled the burned-out husk of her childhood home. Her father had built the cabin. Her mother had given him two children. Together, they'd raised a family and forged a happy life in these woods. What had Mae ever built? What good had her actions wrought? Had she made the world a *better* place? For her? For her sisters? For the people of Heilladur?

Hate had dominated almost her entire life, driving her with a single-minded focus toward the destruction of her foes. What was her purpose now? Mae needed to rest for a few hours. She felt too worn out to think. She missed her sisters, and most of all, she missed Jarne. How could she find them? Were they still alive?

Sinking to the ground beside the empty chicken coop, the witch pulled her cloak tight. As the fire died, leaving only the ashes of her former life, the cold crept up on her, seeping into her bones. Why hadn't she taken any blankets, clothes, or other useful items from the hut before burning it?

Sigri would have thought of that. Everybody would have! Mae hated her impulsive behavior. She deserved a cold night in the open as a reminder to think before acting. At least the rain had stopped. Pulling her hood over her eyes and wrapping her arms tight, the witch let the exhaustion take her.

The following morning dawned gray, the air smelling of snow. Mae got to her feet. Her muscles felt stiff—brittle like stockfish left in the open for too long. Her head hurt. She'd dreamt of a storm, winds whipping the sea into a fury, and her tiny boat crashing against a rocky shore. That couldn't be a bad omen, could it? *No time to worry about silly dreams.* She needed to find Jarne, Sigri, and Renya.

The witch had harbored a tiny hope to find Jarne here, in their cabin in the woods, where they'd tried to live a normal and happy life. His absence must mean the three stayed together. They would have gone back to a safe location. Pondering her options, Mae decided against the Witches' Castle. Renya had hated it there. The Guðmundsdóttir sisters yearned for a life among regular people. That made the house in Thorshofn the most probable location.

Starting her journey, she realized it would take her many days on foot—too many. Already cold and hungry, she didn't relish spending more nights in the open. Winter had almost arrived. Instead, she would sneak into Hestavik and "acquire" a horse and some provisions. Mae didn't steal from poor folks if she could avoid it. Yet, given her predicament, she saw no other option.

Am I not owed a little compensation for ridding the people of the tyrants? Walking the familiar path to the fishing village, Mae smiled to herself, imagining how Jarne would support her argument.

* * *

"I DIDN'T THINK I'd ever see you again." Sigri's voice startled the intruder. Having spotted light through the windows, the witch had circled the house and entered through the back door. She saw candles burning, a fire crackled in the hearth, and a figure slumped over, resting her head on the kitchen table next to a forgotten mug of tea.

"Sigri!" Mae shouted, scrambling to her feet. She rushed to engulf her sister in a fierce hug. Stupefied, Sigri dropped the basket of vegetables she was holding. When Mae didn't let go, Sigri returned the embrace.

Both women started to laugh and cry, holding each other for solace. A long moment passed before Mae released Sigri. She looked at the tall witch, tears glistening in her eyes and a nervous smile on her lips.

"Where is Jarne?" Mae asked, her voice trembling. "And Renya?" she added.

"Jarne survived. He injured his shoulder during the fight. There was an explosion. I cared for him, but we went our separate ways." Sigri paused, and Mae's eyes widened in shock, apparently reading the answer to her second question on the green witch's face.

"No!" Mae wailed, raising her hand to her mouth. Sigri picked up the basket and stepped over the threshold. She deposited the food on a shelf next to the hearth. Standing motionless with her back to Mae, she confirmed Mae's fear.

"Renya is dead. She died fighting. You went after the duke. There was confusion, fire, and smoke. Curses flew everywhere." Sigri took a labored breath. "It was quick; she didn't feel pain." Her voice cracked on the last words.

Mae had closed the door and approached. Sigri turned, squared her shoulders, and lifted her chin. Her regal posture and stiff upper lip stopped Mae. She stood as the embodiment of poise and composure, and it was a lie. Mae's expression mirrored the despair in Sigri's eyes. Instead of embracing her sister, the black witch took her hand. A tremble tugged on Sigri's stoic façade.

"She died fighting soldiers," Sigri repeated with pride. "Renya had always hated the duke's soldiers. She never told you, but Renya supported your plans more than you thought. I only wanted a normal life, not bothering anybody and not being bothered. But Renya, she wanted to fight back. She wanted to be like you."

Sigri broke. Flinging herself into Mae's arms, she cried bitter tears. Since her sister's death, she'd kept herself distracted, pushing the pain away. She'd cared for Jarne. Then, she returned home and repaired her house. Sigri hadn't let the reality of her beloved baby sister's passing sink in—until now.

Mae hugged her back, lending her strength. Ushering her sister to sit at the table, Mae brewed a fresh cup of tea. She added honey and wished there was whiskey. After refilling her cup, Mae sat in silence. Twice, she opened her mouth to speak. But the right words seemed to elude her. Instead, Sigri started talking, letting it all out.

"When I felt her die, something in me broke apart. I don't know what happened next. I must have killed many people. The black sorceress and the king, soldiers and servants—I found myself surrounded by dead bodies."

Sigri spoke about everything she could remember, detailing the events she had pieced together. Mae cringed when the tall witch talked about her discovery in the duke's bedchamber. Yet, there was no judgment. In her detached and analytical voice, Sigri stated the plain facts, including her mercy killing of the duke's daughter. Mae listened without interrupting.

Next, Sigri told Mae about Jarne, his injury, and Sigri's care. She didn't mince her words, admitting she had lost her temper. She only withheld her suspicion about his crossbow bolt killing Renya. Mae didn't need to know. He'd tried to save Sigri, and she'd forgiven him.

Anyhow, Renya had known about the risks of their insane plan. The gray witch joined the conspiracy willingly. Nobody forced her. To assume Jarne, Mae, or Sigri were responsible for her death was presumptuous, demeaning Renya's sacrifice.

"It's getting late." Sigri wiped the moisture off her face. "I should prepare dinner."

"Let me help. What can I do?"

"Why don't you get water from the well?" Sigri suggested. Mae jumped to her feet and grabbed the water buckets. "And then, it's your turn," Sigri called as Mae was about to leave the house. "I want to know what happened to you."

* * *

Throughout the preparations and the evening meal, Mae relayed her adventures. Sigri listened in fascination, letting her dinner get cold. Mae could almost see her sister's brain laboring to make sense of it all.

"So, she got away from me?" Sigri asked. "You believe her then, all those fantastic stories?"

"Bergrún told me what she believed to be the truth," Mae replied. "I'm certain. She wanted me to know. Her biggest fear was all her knowledge dying with her."

"Perhaps." Sigri furrowed her eyebrows. "But how does that help you? According to her, you can't get rid of your curse."

"But I can rid the world of it. Only three black witches are left, and I know where to find them." Mae's eyes shone with fervor. "There won't be salvation for me, but I can prevent others from sharing my doom."

"How? Even if you find and eliminate the other black witches, the curse will live on in you," Sigri said, her fingers massaging the bridge of her nose. "Maybe you could go into exile?"

"And bring the curse to other lands? Are the people there less deserving of a happy life?"

"You're right," Sigri agreed. "That's not a solution."

"I need to travel to the Sister Islands," Mae declared. "Will you help me? When I'm the last black witch, we'll find a way to eliminate my curse."

"Is that what you want?" Sigri looked into Mae's eyes. "What about Jarne?"

"What about him?" The question irritated Mae.

"You and Jarne, don't the two of you deserve a happy life together?"

"I can't go on like this. I tried, Sigri. I tried it all." Mae needed her sister to understand. "Thirteen years I've carried the curse—thirteen years of killing!" Mae's voice rose, and she took several deep breaths. Struggling to suppress her anger and frustration, the witch continued. "In the beginning, I ignored my dark urges until my inner demons overpowered me. I ended up killing an entire family—five innocent people. I can't live with that."

"And you didn't," Sigri objected. "After understanding your curse, you changed. That's why you only targeted evil people like those who'd murdered your family." The green witch leaned across the table, taking Mae's hands in hers.

"But random people paid the price," Mae replied, looking Sigri in the eyes. "Didn't the soldiers I butchered have families? What about the women the duke hanged after our failed ambush? Remember the innocent people he executed in Makevinger!"

"The duke was a despicable tyrant," Sigri interjected. "We killed him as punischment for his cruelty."

"And his children? His servants and his guards?" Mae stood, raising her hands in frustration. "We even killed his horses. That is too much, the price these innocent bystanders paid. The world is better off without me and any women of my kind."

Mae paced in front of the table like a caged bear. Her heart pounded a furious rhythm. Clenching and unclenching her hands, the black witch wrestled with the demonic voices in her head, relentlessly urging her to kill. Swallowing hard, she sat down and wiped her eyes. "Jarne, too," Mae whispered, fighting to keep her voice steady. "He is better off without me."

A flicker of pain crossed Sigri's face, mirroring the anguish in her sister's voice. Her lips pressed into a thin line, the healer sat motionless like a statue while her gaze followed the black witch's every move. Mae glimpsed a tear threatening to spill. Drawing strength from the silent support, the black witch slowed her breathing, placed her folded hands on the table, and relayed the thoughts that kept her mind spinning since her conversation with Einar.

"What if the Norns placed that curse on me for a reason?" she asked.

"What do you mean?" Sigri replied, a note of surprise softening the tension in her voice.

"Einar told me I had a choice. What if he was right, and I've chosen wrong all these years?" Mae leaned toward her sister. "I wanted my brother back, so I killed soldiers. I wanted revenge for my parents, so I went after the duke. I believed in Jarne's dream, so I pulled you into this fool's errand of a bloody uprising. Have you never wondered why killing men doesn't solve anything?" Mae asked, but she didn't wait for an answer. "Evil begets evil!" the witch shouted. Raising her hands in apology for her outburst, she continued in a calmer tone. "Men don't need us for the killing. They're more than capable of doing it themselves."

"If you say it like that, it's hard to argue with your statement," Sigri said, her brow furrowed. "But if killing men was the wrong choice, what do you think is the right one?"

"Eliminating the curse, of course," Mae replied without hesitation. "The curse is at the root of everything. It was the reason for clan wars, the Viking invasion, the troubles on the Sister Islands, and, of course, the countless lives lost to sate the appetite of black witches. I've murdered people because of the curse, and even you and Renya were encouraged to take lives since you helped me with my misguided vendetta."

Sigri averted her gaze, battling the blush of embarrassment spreading over her cheeks.

"I don't blame you," Mae said, shaking her head. A sad smile curled her lips. "Your calming influence on me has undoubtedly saved more lives than you have ended. No! The fault is mine. My blinding rage and self-pity have prevented me from seeing the obvious."

"Which is?"

"Why the Norns chose me! For centuries, the curse has endured because witches yearned for unlimited power. Every time the demons found a new host, the new black witch rejoiced in using dark magic to spread fear, gain influence, and increase her status—until somebody else took the curse from her." Mae halted for one deep breath before professing, "All I ever wanted was my ordinary life back! The curse came to me by accident. Bergrún saw no other option for saving her life. But I never wanted power, not even to use it for the greater good. Sadly, it took me so long to realize.

"I am willing to die to end this curse. Hell, I've already tried to kill myself," Mae admitted, a bitter laugh escaping her lips. "But the time wasn't right. I have unfinished business. That's why I've survived. The Norns weren't done with me. First, I need to eliminate all other black witches. Only when I am Death's last daughter will my own death break the curse for good."

Sigri sat open mouthed, her eyes wide in astonishment. Mae knew she'd convinced her sister. The green witch couldn't deny the logic of the arguments. Despite discussing her own end, Mae felt elated. She'd finally unraveled the mystery. The Norns were never wrong. They'd placed the murderous curse next to an innocent heart, knowing that Mae would never accept what she had become. If they had only given Mae the wisdom to find her purpose earlier, much hardship could have been averted.

"I don't know what to say," Sigri admitted.

"Will you help me?"

"If that is what you want to do."

"It's what I need to do!" Mae insisted.

"Then yes, of course! I'll help you eliminate all remaining black witches. And I'll find a way to end the curse inside you."

Sigri took her sister's hands. Tears glistened in her gray eyes. Still, Mae believed she could see the green witch's mind working. Was she already formulating a plan, weighing the options, and choosing the next steps?

"One more thing," Mae said. "When I am... When we have succeeded, will you look for Jarne and tell him what I did? He needs to know why."

Sigri stood, walked over to Mae, and kissed her forehead. Clearing her throat, she whispered, "I will ensure Jarne doesn't have to live with the uncertainty of where you went." Straightening and wiping her face, the tall woman continued, "We should get some sleep. The morning will bring new answers. There are blankets on the hayloft." Then, she walked to the backdoor, taking the lantern to the outhouse.

"Thank you, Sigri," Mae called after her.

* * *

MAE FELT LIKE she'd gone to sleep only moments before when Sigri shook her shoulder.

"Wake up, Mae. We have to hurry."

"What's happening? Where is the fire?" Mae mumbled, turning away from her annoying host and trying to go back to sleep. Sigri wanted none of that. She ripped Mae's blanket away and dragged her toward the ladder.

"Get up! There's no time to lose!" Sigri shouted.

"It's dark. It's cold. What's gotten into you?" Mae started to get angry.

"Jarne!" One word made Mae jolt upright, searching Sigri's face in the dark.

"What about him?" Mae wanted to grab hold of her sister, but Sigri had already clambered down the rickety ladder. From below, she shouted.

"Get down and get dressed. We need to rescue him!"

"What are you talking about?"

"He is going to be executed at midday."

"What... Why... How do you know?" Mae stuttered, dumbfounded.

"Do you want to waste time discussing the ways of the world? Or do you want to rescue him?" Sigri huffed. "I've foreseen it. I'll tell you about it on the way. Get going!"

Mae rushed down the ladder, almost falling. Flustered, she needed three tries to get her pants on, and she mixed up her boots. Finally, she stood, fully dressed and ready to leave. Sigri handed her a belt with throwing knives and a crossbow. Then, Sigri took a sword, a dagger, and another crossbow, pushing a flabbergasted Mae out of the door.

"You could outfit an army with your stockpile."

"There's been a lot of fighting. I gathered up what I could find. The dead men didn't need them any longer."

"Where are we going?" Mae asked, hustling to match the strides of the taller woman.

"The stables—we need fast horses. Be ready to fight. Sentries guard the animals day and night."

"Are you sure about this? What have you seen?"

"Jarne is in Kristiansund, his home village. I've seen glimpses over the last few days." Sigri's voice was strained as they rushed over uneven cobblestones. "Last night, the vision became clearer. He's gotten himself into trouble. The villagers decided to burn him for witchcraft."

Fury replaced Mae's confusion. She sprinted ahead. Rounding the last corner, she spotted two tired guards standing beside the stable's double door, leaning on long wooden poles. Mae's right hand went to the throwing knives. Then, she reconsidered. She'd killed enough men for one lifetime. Letting go of the blades, Mae punched the first guard's head with a blast of air, knocking him out. His companion barely had time to scream before Sigri dealt him a similar blow.

A dozen horses stood in individual stalls, their saddles and bridles aligned on wooden benches. Sigri pointed to two swift-looking coursers. Mae opened the first gate and threw a blanket onto the animal. The horse didn't stir or shy away, thanks to Sigri's touch on the beast's mind. Moments later, the mount was saddled and ready to go.

Mae proceeded to the second stall when shouts and running footsteps disturbed the quiet night. Abandoning the horse's tack, she jumped onto the animal's bare back, grabbing the mane and kicking its flanks. Four men rushed toward the stables, struggling to pull on jackets and strap on weapons.

Mae galloped through their midst, scattering them like birds, with Sigri following shortly behind. The two witches sped north on the King's Road. Near the town's exit, Mae wore off the road and cleared the five-foot fence that had replaced the makeshift barricade. She didn't spare a single thought for the danger of jumping without a saddle.

Urging her beast onward, the black witch's mind was focused solely on getting to Kristiansund and saving Jarne.

CHAPTER TWENTY-FOUR

Kristiansund

The sunrise signaled the long-awaited end of another cold and wet night. Jarne sat on a pile of straw, bruised and filthy. He had crawled to the driest part of his cell. The room, which used to be the storeroom of the old mill, didn't quite deserve that name. While the solid walls were built from river stone, a large hole on the opposite side opened to the world beyond. A fire had destroyed the building's upper floor several years ago. Since then, the ruin stood unused, exposed to the elements, at the southern boundary of Kristiansund.

Still, Jarne couldn't escape his prison. Crude manacles encircled his ankles, and a four-foot chain extended to a hook in the wall. The first night of his captivity, he'd lain shivering on the bare dirt floor before some villagers brought a bundle of straw and a thin blanket. Over the following two days, he received food, water, a second blanket, and a bucket to relieve himself. Yet, nobody talked to him. His jailers only gazed at him, some with mistrust and glee, others with curiosity and pity.

This morning, he was presented with a veritable feast. A plate of cold mutton, dried fish, stewed vegetables, and dark bread lay before him on a wooden tray next to a chipped pitcher of ale and a shriveled apple. Jarne had lost weight since the attack on Duke Finsgúr's estate, having spent several days either unconscious or kept prisoner. Still, he had no appetite. This was to be his last meal. At midday, they would drag him from this miserable excuse for a prison and burn him at the stake for witchcraft. Him? There was irony in it somewhere.

Jarne had dreamed of changing the people's superstitious fear and hatred of witches. Sadly, his vision collided with Ulfir Pederssen, the village smith. The man had strong arms and stronger prejudices, believing in the superiority of men and the rule of the powerful over the weak.

Jarne would likely have died of exposure or starvation if it hadn't been for Frigga Pedersdotter, Ulfir's estranged older sister. The village's midwife objected to the cruel treatment of the prisoner and demanded a public trial.

Standing before the assembled villagers the previous day, Jarne was eager to convince everyone to welcome witches back into their midst. Yet, the five village elders followed Ulfir's reasoning to a man, condemning him to death. All through the following night, the last night of his life, Jarne had lain awake, revisiting the interrogation in his mind.

"Jarne Ólafsson, do you consort with witches?" the village baker had asked. Asger Svendsen was a stocky man. He was going bald, and sweat glistened on his forehead as he presided over the trial. The entire village had gathered in the square. Jarne stood at the center, his hands and feet bound, facing the elders' stern faces. The five men sat on wooden benches in front of the smithy, the baker at their center.

"Yes, I befriended three witches," Jarne stated without hesitation. Standing straight, his head held high, he spoke with a steady voice. "Together, we attacked the ducal estate. Their names are—"

"Befriended?" the baker interjected. "Aren't you wedded to a witch?" A murmur rose from the spectators. Someone booed, and others shouted insults. "Do you fornicate with all three witches?" Asger needed to raise his voice.

"I do not fornicate," Jarne replied with indignation. "I am wedded to Mae, one of the witches. The other two are—"

"These witches killed the duke?"

"Yes, the duke and the king," Jarne declared with pride, hoping for gratitude and a chance to finish a sentence.

"Wielding dark magic?" the baker pressed on.

"They fought with honor, not resorting to dark magic."

"Can you cast spells?" the man to Asger's left asked.

"No," Jarne replied, wondering if he should lie. Maybe they would be afraid and let him go.

"Then how can you tell if they used dark magic?" The speaker's voice was high-pitched and discordant. With his greasy black hair and large, hooked nose, he reminded Jarne of an ill-tempered raven.

"I was there. I saw them use magic."

"Did these witches kill innocent people?" Asger asked, giving Jarne no time to elaborate.

"What do you mean?" Jarne asked.

"Isn't it true that servants were killed? And the kitchen staff?"

"Some might have died in the fight. But—"

"And the duke's children?" another elder asked with a voice brittle as dry straw. "A boy and a girl?"

At that, the villagers cursed and yelled vile insults. They might have killed Jarne if Ulfir and two other strong men hadn't guarded the accused.

"I believe they died in the fighting. It was like war," Jarne shouted over the noise. "Innocent people may die in war. The duke and his soldiers had done much worse atrocities."

"So you call the witches' evil deeds an atrocity?" the raven cawed.

"No, I was saying..." But he didn't know what. Jarne wasn't as good with words as he had imagined. It shouldn't matter. Couldn't these people appreciate what the witches had done?

"Have these witches killed in the past?" Despite Asger's strong voice, the baker needed to bang his rolling pin several times onto the table to reassert control and order.

"They have been fighting evil men, like the steward in Makevinger," Jarne replied, realizing his mistake too late.

"Are you saying these witches caused the massacre of Makevinger?" Asger stood, pointing an accusing finger. Renewed outcries and insults came from the villagers, and a clump of mud struck Jarne's face.

"I meant to say that—"

"Did these witches attack the duke three years ago?" Asger shouted over the tumult. Jarne remained silent. "Did they?" The smith hit Jarne on the back of his head, ensuring he answered the question.

"Yes," Jarne said, defeated.

"Were you involved in that attack?"

"Not with the witches."

"But were you involved?" This time, the raven asked in a softer voice, dripping venom. "You stole Farmer Holgrim's horses, didn't you?" Another silence, another slap on the head, and another condemning response.

"I only wanted to borrow them," Jarne pleaded. "My mother was sick. We needed the money!"

The uproar from the villagers became deafening.

"I call for a vote of conviction." Asger Svendsen stood and raised his voice. "For witchcraft and evil deeds against the people of Heilladur."

"But we freed you of the foreign tyrants!" Jarne shouted to no avail.

Five hands rose at once.

His guards dragged Jarne away while the villagers pelted him with dirt and stones, rotten vegetables, and horse manure.

* * *

At midday, the sun hid behind an overcast sky. Jarne stood on the hastily stacked pile of wood. His head held high, he let his gaze wander far above the gathered spectators, watching darker clouds drifting in from the sea. A few forlorn snow flurries danced in the air, unsure where to settle and melt. Icy gusts of wind pulled at his tattered shirt, raising goosebumps. Jarne didn't mind; he would be warm soon. The familiar scent of brine and seaweed filled his nose, reminding him of all the adventures he had dreamed up as a little boy. Jarne was home. If he must die today, this wasn't a bad spot.

He hadn't resisted when they dragged him from his cell and tied him to the trunk of a pine. It, too, would burn and die before its time, sap instead of blood oozing from its wounds. Nobody had asked for any last words. And even if they had, he wouldn't have spoken. Jarne didn't spare a single thought for the villagers. These people were set in their misguided ways, preferring the cruelty of foreign tyrants over the companionship of valuable allies.

Instead, Jarne thought of Mae. Where was she? Could she forgive herself? Could she forgive him for not finding her? Would she learn about his death? He hoped not. Her wrath would be terrible; nobody in this village would survive. Maybe the fear of witches wasn't all that misplaced. He didn't want her to kill for him, knowing how much her conscience made her suffer.

He wanted her to be happy; he'd always wanted her to be happy. Jarne hoped she remembered him, the years they had spent together. Tears welled in his eyes. They shouldn't see him crying. This was private, not for them. Anger rose, and in defiance, Jarne shouted.

"Get it over with! Purge me from your fine village before I summon evil spirits to haunt you!" That got everybody's attention. Ulfir Pederssen stepped forward and threw a bucket of whale oil, splashing Jarne's face and soaking his clothes.

"Flap your vile tongue all you want! Soon enough, you'll sing a different tune. I can't wait to listen to the melody of your screams." He stepped back to grab a torch.

Jarne sputtered, spitting out the rancid liquid. At least the fire would be quick to engulf him. Blinking his stinging eyes, he watched the angry smith approach, the torch held high. Jarne couldn't hold back his panic any longer. The fear of pain and death had finally broken through his stoic façade. Clenching his hands into fists, Jarne squeezed his eyes shut, and his breathing quickened. Would he feel, hear, or smell the flames first?

He heard it. But instead of the whooshing sound of an igniting blaze, a twang and a thud reached Jarne's ears, followed by a scream and the sound of a body falling to the ground.

Jarne opened his eyes. The smith lay in the dirt, his torch mere inches from the woodpile.

Shock and surprise were etched onto the villagers' faces as a slender figure in dark clothes darted from behind a salt-bleached boathouse. Rubbing her hands as she ran, Mae shouted an incantation and clapped once. A ball of piercing bright light erupted in midair, followed by thunder.

"The witches are coming!" someone shrieked.

Pandemonium broke loose.

Most spectators ran away, seeking places to hide. Others grabbed wooden poles, axes, or anything else they could use as a weapon. They huddled together, unsure if they should defend or attack. Those men weren't warriors; they were fishermen and farmers. Arnulf Egberson stood among them, urging the villagers to attack Mae while hiding behind their ranks.

A second figure emerged. With her hood raised, the wind flapping her cloak gave Sigri a mysterious air. Arnulf pointed, and Sigri channeled the wind, punching him to the ground. That did the trick. The men dropped whatever they held and scattered like sheep discovering a wolf in their midst.

Mae had almost reached Jarne when Ulfir stirred again. The bolt had lodged in his lower back, puncturing his left kidney. Blood gushed from the wound. Still, the man was alive and determined. Grabbing the torch in his right hand, he tried to crawl forward. His legs didn't work.

Frustrated, he rolled on his injured side, and with a roar of agony, he tossed the torch onto the pile. Mere feet separated Mae and Jarne when the torch struck Jarne's leg. His eyes had found hers.

For the tiniest moment, their gazes locked—communicating love and despair, shame and forgiveness, hope and sadness.

Then... nothing happened. The cloth-wrapped wood bounced off Jarne's leg and plunked onto the pile. Jarne looked bewildered until he saw Sigri. Facing him, the green witch stood with her eyes closed and her hands out in front, palms raised. She must have snuffed out the flame in the nick of time. Jarne breathed a sigh of relief, which turned into mortification as he felt warm liquid running down his leg.

There was no time to worry. Mae had frozen for one second before jumping onto Ulfir's back. Grabbing a handful of hair, she yanked his head back. With her right hand, Mae snatched a knife from her belt, intending to open his throat from ear to ear.

"NO!" Jarne shouted. "Don't kill him." Mae looked up with anger and vexation. Holding her gaze, he added, "Please, Mae, don't."

Shaking her head, Mae rammed Ulfir's face into the dirt, knocking him unconscious. Taking two strides, she jumped onto the woodpile and kicked the unlit torch away as if it were a venomous snake. Then, she seized Jarne by his ears and kissed him violently, burning him with her passion more fiercely than the pyre could have.

It was heaven; he could die now—a happy man.

Mae had other plans. Resurfacing, she slit his bonds. Pain shot through his shoulder, but Mae was there to catch him. Slowly and carefully, the two stepped off the woodpile, and she lowered him to the ground. Meanwhile, Sigri approached the injured smith and analyzed his condition.

"Can you save him?" Jarne asked.

"Save him?" Sigri looked taken aback. "Are you sure?"

"I think so," Jarne grunted as another stab of pain ran through his back. Gritting his teeth, he explained. "He lost his father because of our ambush three years ago. We would never be friends, but his hostility stemmed from pain. Please, Sigri, try to save him."

She, too, shook her head. Jarne would never change. He would forever remain a silly boy with outlandish ideas, like overthrowing Duke Finsgúr. Kneeling beside the unconscious man, Sigri lifted the smith's bloodstained shirt. Then, she turned around, facing the village houses.

"If you want to keep this man alive," the healer shouted, "you'd better bring me some bandages, boiling water, and needle and thread." Nobody moved. "Fine with me," she added with a mocking tone of levity. "He just tried to murder my friend. I'm content to watch his life bleed into the dirt."

"You'll help him?" an unseen woman called.

"Not my first choice. But this idiot insists on it," Sigri replied.

A broad-shouldered woman stepped into the open, her resemblance to the fallen village smith undeniable. She looked from Sigri to Jarne, then to Mae, and back to her brother.

"He's an idiot, too," she shouted. "That's men for you. Still, the village needs him. I'll get you what you need."

* * *

"THIS IS ALL I can do at the moment." Sigri had removed the bolt from Ulfir's back before she cleaned, stitched, and bandaged the wound. "Call some men to carry him to his bed," she said, wiping her bloody hands on a rag.

A dozen women surrounded Sigri. Frigga had been the first to bring her the items she required. But as the healer worked, more and more women approached. Mae had tensed. Sitting with Jarne ten feet away, she eyed every new arrival with mistrust. Still, the black witch reserved her open hostility for the men huddled together in the distance, hiding in the shadow of their houses.

"It would be good to mix a poultice to prevent an infection. Is anybody in this village knowledgeable with herbs?"

"I'm the midwife," Frigga stated. "I learned some from my mother."

"He's your brother, isn't he?" Sigri asked, regarding the sturdy woman.

"Not my first choice, either" she replied, and Sigri chuckled. An awkward silence followed. Then, to everybody's surprise, Frigga posed a question. "Can you teach me?"

"There is no time. It's already late, and the way to Thorshofn is long."

"You could stay in my house," Frigga suggested. "There is a spare room. I've lived alone since my husband died."

"We're not staying here," Mae hissed.

"I have to agree with my sister," Sigri said. "I'm not planning to give you a second chance of burning my friend together with us."

"Nobody will harm you. He is to blame." Frigga pointed at her brother. "Bullying everyone into condemning Jarne."

"Is that so?" Sigri's voice chilled to ice while her hand rested on the hilt of her dagger. "Maybe you should have told me before I tended his wound."

"I told you my brother is an idiot," Frigga replied, ignoring Sigri's insinuation. "I would like to see if this one was smarter." She pointed to Jarne. "He told everybody you were good people." Both witches turned to Jarne, exasperation in their eyes. He grinned like a fool, feigning innocence.

"Both men need rest," Frigga declared when Sigri's gaze had returned. "I offer room and protection. I might even find some clothes that would fit Jarne. You can stay as long as you need with the blessing of the village women."

"Why?" Mae demanded.

"I knew his mother," Frigga explained. "She was a kind woman despite her no-good husband causing her grief. I admired her." She looked at Jarne, a hint of compassion softening her rectangular face. "My brother never gave you a chance, and the doddering old men in this village went along with him. The women can do better." The midwife took a deep breath and returned her gaze to Sigri. "We can learn from you. I've seen too much sickness and death because I don't have the skills. I'd like you to teach me, and teach anyone who wants to learn."

* * *

JARNE AND THE two witches stayed in Kristiansund for almost six weeks. The first couple of days were tense. Mae didn't allow anybody near their temporary residence, and the villagers feared waking up transfigured into newts or toads. To defuse the tension, Sigri taught a few women about healing, preventing infection, and brewing various teas for minor ailments. She didn't detect any magic among her pupils. Still, some women had an aptitude for the topic, like Frigga. She could sense illnesses and possessed the right instincts for treating those.

Jarne got better, but the progress was slow. The beating and his captivity had undone Sigri's prior ministrations. The healer needed to break the bone again to reset it. As his muffled screams of pain reverberated through the house, Sigri required Frigga's help restraining Mae from killing the village smith. Once Sigri had immobilized Jarne's arm, she ordered him to rest. Mae never left his side.

After days of pleading, Sigri allowed her patient to leave the bed for a few hours. Mae and Jarne walked in the forest and along the beaches. Roaming the realm of his childhood adventures, the two lovers talked, laughed, and enjoyed each other's company. Mae told him everything she had learned. Jarne sat and listened, fascinated. He had always loved a good story. And this one combined all the required ingredients—mystery and magic, ambition and betrayal, tragedy and adventures in foreign lands.

"So, the curse was brought into the world," he asked, "by the original five black witches?"

"Yes. Well, they weren't black witches then," Mae replied. "According to Bergrún, all magic came from the huldufólk—the hidden folk or elves, as some call them. They taught women and men how to use the powers of nature. They might even have mixed with humans. But that was long ago. When some women—witches, you might say—got too greedy and wanted more power, the huldufólk withdrew, disappearing from this world. Still, they'd laid the foundation of understanding the flow of energy." Mae closed her eyes, trying to recall all the details.

"Among the witches," she continued, "were five especially power-hungry women. They were sisters or cousins, I don't remember. Together, they traveled to Mount Snæfell, a volcano on Urðr, the largest of the three Sister Islands. Rumors claim its crater is the entrance to the underworld. There are unimaginable amounts of power in the fiery depths of the world.

"The five witches gathered around a vent from which sulfurous steam rose. Linking hands, they chanted for days without rest, entering a trance. With their combined life force and the power of their burning ambitions, they summoned a being from beyond the veil that separates the realms. Released into this world, the demon took possession of these five women, turning them into the first black witches. That's why they are called Death's Daughters."

"And that's where we are going, to Urðr?" Jarne asked.

"We might as well start there. According to Bergrún, the black witches couldn't stay near each other. The curse made them aggressive and territorial. They spread out. Two returned to Heillaður, settling in the far north and the deep south. The other three settled each on one of the Sister Islands—that might be where the name comes from."

"So there's another black witch on Heillaður, besides… I mean…" he stuttered.

"Besides me, you mean?" Mae asked, trying to give him her best black witch's glare. "No, not anymore. Bergrún learned from her mentor about a clan war many years before the invasion. The two witches fought, one killing the other, absorbing the curse."

"But that makes you…?"

"Double-cursed, yes." Mae gave him a sad little smile. "Doesn't make a difference."

Silence.

"It does," Jarne said with a sudden burst of excitement. "Only three black witches are left, and you are stronger than them." Sitting up straighter, he asked, "When do we sail?"

"We?" Mae asked in mock confusion. "Why would I take you along?"

"To captain your ship, Your Witchiness. You need someone with maritime experience."

"I do," she shrugged. "But what does this have to do with you?"

"Am I not the best skipper you ever sailed with?"

"I've only sailed once in my life."

"Twice, forth and back," Jarne corrected, smiling.

"Yes... But that makes you also the worst skipper I ever sailed with."

"So, when are we leaving?"

Mae stood and turned around, all levity draining away. "You need to get better first," she said, straining to keep her voice from cracking. "It's getting late. We should head back."

He could be so naïve, seeing it all as a great adventure. Leaving would mean fighting, and killing, and dying. Mae knew there was no other way.

Right then, they had a taste of a different life—living as a couple in a small fishing village among regular people. Sigri enjoyed teaching, and the witches didn't have to worry about dukes, kings, or evil sorceresses. Mae wanted this to last forever. That was why she must leave soon, or she wouldn't have the strength to do it. Should she sneak away alone and leave Jarne and Sigri behind to live a happier life?

"We can go back, if you like." Jarne got to his feet and took Mae's left hand into his right. "I'll go wherever you go. I'll never let you out of my sight again, ever!"

CHAPTER TWENTY-FIVE

Sailing South

MIDWINTER HAD LONG passed before Jarne and the witches were finally ready to start their journey. Sigri had done an incredible job of teaching the village women. She helped with a complicated birth, stopped the spread of the chills, and tended to a boy who had been bitten by wild dogs. In addition, the village smith recovered. Many had expected him to die of slow poison the witches must have mixed in his medicine.

As reparations for the attempt on Jarne's life, Mae demanded a seaworthy knarr to be outfitted for an extended voyage. The villagers' initial grumbling dissipated when Sigri offered to pay. She had taken a pouch of coins from the king's bedroom. Yielding under Mae's stern gaze, the fishermen agreed to part with the largest boat. They made some modifications for storing provisions and even offered advice on the journey.

"The wind is strong from the east this time of year," explained a toothless sailor named Søren, while his companions nodded. "Hug the coast past Makevinger and steer east by southeast. Else, the wind will carry you into the west before you get near the islands. There ain't nothin' there but the endless sea."

"And stay away from Sculd," another man warned. "That island is cursed. Who goes ashore never returns."

"Aye," Søren agreed. "Rogård is right. My grandfather told me the tale. When raiders from the south came to the island, they encountered an evil witch—pardon me."

"Go on," Mae prompted, giving him her best bone-chilling leer.

"As I was saying... the witch, she had done away with most of the folks by the time a young archer shot her through the heart. The moment she died, the archer fell ill, jerking and threshing. He was dead two days hence, dried up like all life was sucked out of him." Søren paused for dramatic effect. "When he died, the man beside him fell to the ground, doing the same jerking and threshing. That's when the others ran, spreading the tale of the island's curse."

"Must have been the witch. Dying, she cursed the land," Rogård stated to renewed nods from all men present.

"Good thing you didn't try to kill me," Mae remarked, sending a wave of shivers through the men, and they excused themselves, almost tripping over each other.

"What do you make of it?" Sigri asked when the villagers had gone.

"Sounds like the archer killed a black witch, and the curse poured into him. But why did he die?"

"I had wondered…" Sigri said, deep in thought. "Can a man carry the curse?" Mae gaped. "Perhaps the curse drained his life," Sigri speculated. "I've never heard of a male witch. Seems like men can't handle this power."

"But why did the next man fall ill?" Mae asked. "He hadn't killed the archer."

"The curse must have switched hosts, possessing whoever was near."

"So, there's no way to end it?" Mae slumped.

"When nobody is near," Sigri ventured, "the curse could disappear,"

"But they said everybody who steps ashore dies." Mae sounded worried. "What if the curse clings to the land?"

"These are fisherman's tales. You can't believe everything."

"We need to go there, Sigri. I'll need to step ashore. If the curse is still around, best that I absorb it, if possible."

"Let's not be hasty. We'll have lots to prepare. We can plan once we set sail."

A few days later, the three travelers stepped aboard the *Wayfinder* to start their voyage. The sun peeked over the horizon, promising a calm day. Friendly waves wrinkled the gray sea. The village men had stored water and provisions for a two-week journey on the boat. The women provided warm cloaks and blankets.

It almost seemed like the inhabitants of Kristiansund were happy to see the witches leave. Only Frigga and an old woman came to the dock to see them off. Jarne had already taken his position. His shoulder had healed, and his spirits were high. Mae, on the other hand, tried to hide her trepidation. She expected to never return to Heillaður.

"Mayhaps you could use this?" The old woman offered a sealskin-wrapped bundle to Sigri. "It's been in my family for many years, hidden. We were afraid someone might find it."

"A book?" Sigri asked, taking the heavy, rectangular object. The woman flinched, ducking her head between her shoulders like a turtle retreating into its shell.

"Aye," she said. "I couldn't read it—didn't want to. Where the wolf's ears are, the wolf's teeth are near."

"I'll bear that in mind." Sigri smiled. She stepped on board, and Frigga tossed her the line.

"Fair winds and fair fortunes whereever your journeys may take you," the midwife called as she pushed the boat away.

"And fair fortunes to you," Sigri replied. She smiled again. "Keep the men guessing what I taught you, and they'll heed your counsel more often."

* * *

The travelers made good progress. After some initial scrambling, Jarne got into a rhythm. The steady wind and the calm sea near the shore made for smooth sailing. Still, Mae's stomach wasn't happy with the rolling motion, and Sigri gave her a potion to ease the sea sickness. Mae was thankful. Despite that, her face looked pale with a greenish tint.

Jarne manned the rudder and shouted commands like a seasoned captain, cracking jokes about landlubbers and sand crabs. Seeing this discrepancy in well-being, Sigri "accidentally" poured half a bucket of icy water over his head. That shut him up.

Besides her brief prank, Sigri usually picked the driest spot and leafed through the book in reverence. Indeed, it turned out to be a book of magic, and Sigri could read it. Fascinated, she read for hours, summarizing some sections for her companions.

"This is a marvelous book," Sigri said. "There are stories, recipes, spells, and sections on nature. It's a treasure trove. Some paragraphs explain what I already knew, while others are new. If I can believe the writing, we have used only the tiniest part of our abilities."

"Such as?" Jarne asked.

"I knew I could influence animals, and even men to some extent. I can enter their minds and make them do or feel what I want. But the book claims one can have much finer control, down to individual muscle movements." Sigri turned a page. "It says here: 'The body shall heed thy command, may it be the arm striking a foe or the heart stopping its meter.'" Sigri froze, shocked.

"No wonder that old hag hid the book," Mae scoffed, her condition not helping her mood.

"But if this is true..." Sigri trailed off.

"It's a tool," Jarne stated, "like a knife. You can slice bread or slit someone's throat with a knife. The tool is neither good nor evil. You have to be careful how to use it."

"Thank you for your wisdom," Mae replied, her voice laden with sarcasm.

"You're welcome. And speaking of wisdom. Sigri, you should teach Mae to read. This knowledge could make all the difference when we return."

Sigri looked at Mae, the question clear in her eyes. Mae shook her head the tiniest bit. She hadn't told Jarne about her plans. And it wasn't up to Sigri to raise that topic either. He would find out in time. Mae turned away, looking longingly toward the steady shore, willing her stomach to settle.

"Another time," she said. "Right now, I am not taking anything in."

The sea became rougher on the third day of their journey. They'd sheltered for the night in a bay near Cape Draugr before steering into the wind. Sailing out in the open sea, the waves reached ten feet or more. The constant tacking made the boat's motion worse. Mae clung to the railing, pained by the heaving of her empty stomach. Sigri fared better but lacked the strength or experience to help with the sailing.

Jarne gritted his teeth. Drenched in the icy ocean spray, his shoulder ached. He pulled the sheets with one hand while keeping the rudder true with the other. His legs started to cramp as he pressed hard against a board to hold him in place.

The wind got stronger as their journey progressed. On the fourth day, dark clouds gathered in the east, promising worse yet to come. They had lost sight of Heilladur but couldn't see the Sister Islands yet. Jarne could only guess the course, wishing the witches were able to control the weather.

"The sea might get a little rougher," he shouted as the ominous wall of storm clouds approached.

"A little rougher?" Mae shrieked, fury and misery coloring her voice.

"We need to lower the mainsail," Jarne called. "Sigri, loosen the halyard." Sigri sat at the bottom of the boat, cradling her wrapped magic book like a baby, her eyes wide with apprehension. "Sigri, the rope," Jarne shouted again, his voice all but carried away by the rising storm.

Mae released her death grip on the railing and crawled to the bow to loosen the halyard. The mainsail lost tension and started flapping, smacking Sigri in the face. That shook her from her temporary paralysis.

"Pull the downhaul." Having no idea what the downhaul was, Sigri grabbed the first rope she could reach. Mae came to her aid, and moments later, the sail canvas lay folded on the deck. Jarne tied off the rudder, brought the yard in, and secured the mainsail.

"Sit as low as you can and tie a rope around your waist," he suggested, resigned. "We have to weather the storm. We can do nothing else; we're in the sea god's hands now."

The storm front reached them minutes later. Icy sea water gushed from below, while hail pelted them from above. The waves grew wild, tossing the boat about like a toy. Sheets of rain obscured all vision while the wind howled with demonic voices. One moment, the angry sea lifted the boat high. Then, it crashed down into the trough, jarring their bones.

Again and again, the torture repeated. Mighty breakers washed over the deck, tilting the boat so far that Jarne feared they would capsize. For hours, the storm raged. Every single bone in Jarne's body hurt; every single muscle burned. Still, he held on, and so did Mae and Sigri.

Jarne had lost track of time when the boat shuttered, the jarring impact accompanied by angry scraping sounds. When the next wave crashed into their vessel, wood cracked, and boards splintered. They had run aground. Jarne lifted his head above the railing. He couldn't see land in the stormy darkness.

"Untie yourselves!" he shouted. "We've hit a reef."

Jarne fumbled with the knots as another powerful wave smashed into the boat. The hull cracked, and water foamed through the breach. Jarne was thrown onto the deck, feeling the water rising. When he finally managed to loosen his rope, Jarne pushed himself to his feet and staggered toward Mae and Sigri.

Then, he watched in horror as a twenty-foot wall of water approached. The monstrous breaker crashed over the shattered vessel, ripping the hull to pieces and throwing the three travelers into the churning surf like flotsam.

* * *

The turbulent waters tossed Jarne around, robbing him of all sense of direction. His hip smacked into the rocks. Debris from the ship grazed his scalp before the next breaking wave rolled him onwards. The icy water bit into his skin. Flailing his arms and legs, Jarne pushed toward a faint light, hoping that this way was up. The storm-darkened sky and the foaming froth around him made it difficult to determine the right direction. His lungs burned, screaming for air.

When his feet touched a solid object, he pushed with all his might, and his head broke the surface. Ecstatic, he gulped in the salty air, sputtering as spray found its way into his windpipe. A large piece of the ship's shattered wooden hull floated past him. Jarne grabbed on, hoisting his upper body onto the heaven-sent life raft.

He looked around, searching for Mae and Sigri. The elements had propelled him to the leeward side of the reef, where the sea fought less violently. Still, the waves reached three feet or higher, blocking the view. Jarne called out. He shouted until his throat burned. Only the howling wind responded, aided by the rolling thunder of the waves crashing against the rocks.

Cresting another wave, he saw debris floating all around him. Then he spotted a lumpy shape to his left. A body? Jarne kicked his feet, steering in that direction. Harder and harder, he kicked, straining his muscles to the breaking point, willing his raft to close the distance.

He reached her in the nick of time. She had fallen unconscious. Her grip slackened, and she started to slip off the barrel lid she had clung to.

Jarne let go of his island of safety and paddled the remaining ten feet. Rolling onto his back, he cradled her in his arm, fighting to keep the witch's head above the water. Jarne struggled to return. They needed to reach the floating aid he had left behind. Holding on to the woman's head by her hair, he extended his other hand toward the platform of splintered boards. The tips of his fingers grabbed a tenuous hold.

Jarne hung for a few seconds, catching his breath and providing a human bridge between drowning and salvation. Then, he managed to pull her close. Even with the lift from the waves, Jarne needed five tries to shove the unconcious woman onto the raft, bruising her back and shoulders. He swallowed several mouthfuls of water.

In the end, Sigri's back rested on the boards, her nose and mouth above the water line.

Jarne's exhaustion reached the point where his muscles started to refuse orders. He shivered, cramps torturing his legs. With a last-ditch effort, he hoisted his upper body onto the raft. Clinging to a crossbeam, he let the current push them ashore.

One last time, he shouted Mae's name, his pitiful croak lost in the sounds of nature's ferocious battle.

He might have drifted in and out of consciousness before the rocking motion's absence alerted him to the change. They'd reached a beach. It was still dark. Clouds covered the sky, hiding the stars. Weary, Jarne dragged Sigri up the dunes, her feet leaving two deep gouges in the wet sand. When his legs refused a single extra step, he plunked down, letting go of her shoulders.

Jarne's body aching, his tired eyes swept over their surroundings. It was too dark to make out much. Below, the sea washed forth and back over the sand, making the ocean's destructive force look whimsical. On his left, the terrain rose, visible only as a darker shadow blocking out the cloudy sky.

And from his right, a light approached.

"Help!" Jarne shouted, digging into the last ounce of his energy. "Help us. Over here!"

The light bobbed toward them. Jarne hoped it was Mae, his brain ignoring the improbability of her having found a torch. Getting closer, the light split into two. *Must be a patrol.* Jarne couldn't summon any anxiety. He was frozen to the core and exhausted beyond words. He hadn't done these men any harm. Why should they be hostile? He waved his arms and shouted again.

"Help! We're over here."

A dozen men closed in, surrounding Jarne and Sigri. From their midst, a hooded figure emerged, raised a long rod toward his mouth, and blew. Jarne felt a sting on his cheek. Touching his face, he found a dart sticking there, numbness spreading rapidly.

"What's going on?" Jarne shouted.

He struggled to his feet and fumbled for his belt knife just before his legs gave out.

* * *

SIGRI'S HEAD SWUNG left and right with an uncomfortable bounce. Was she still drifting in the ocean? This felt different. Her neck complained about the weight of her head, and her shoulders ached, pulling on her bound hands. Why were her hands bound? Without opening her eyes, she could feel the rough rope cutting into her wrists. She heard noises, too: footfalls on dried leaves and men talking. The witch risked opening her eyes. The world was upside down, feet trampling in the sky. Below her, the dawn's faint light illuminated a canopy of bare trees.

She needed several moments to make sense of the unexpected visual information. The world wasn't upside down, she was—hanging like a killed deer tied to a pole. This didn't seem like a rescue. Someone had taken her captive and carried her along a forest trail. *What happened?*

Sigri opened her eyes again. Her world swayed with every stride of the men, giving her a headache. A weird numbness spread from where the leather strap of her hidden herb pouch crossed her chest. It felt like the poisonous sting of an insect. Blinking her eyes to clear her head, she tried peering past the stomping legs. She couldn't see anything. Suddenly, one of her captors tripped, smacking her lower back onto the ground.

"Skítr!" the fallen man yelled. The carrier up front halted, turned, and lowered Sigri's shoulders.

"By Thor! What are you doing, idiot? Want to push me off the mountain?"

"I tripped, rassgat. It's dark." The fallen man stood back up and rubbed his bruised knee. Grimacing, he turned to his comrade. "If I wanted to shove you off the path, I'd do it to your face and without hurting myself. What came over that old hag," he continued, "ordering us to run up this hill in the dark?"

"Why don't *you* ask her, Mækir? With these two catches, we are off the hook for half a year. Your ass can buy us three more months."

"You'd better hope I'll not offer your worthless skin, Ragnar. Your wife's and children's, too. But even that I would do in daylight."

"Must be the woman," Ragnar speculated, ignoring the older man's threats. "She told us to catch that woman. Maybe she craves female company for breakfast."

"Are we staying longer?" someone shouted from behind. "The men want to start a fire."

"A fire?" Ragnar bellowed back. "Are there only idiots on this raid? We'll move on as soon as my elderly brother has recovered."

"I give you elderly when I split your skull and ravage your daughters," Mækir replied, the threat only thinly wrapped in brotherly banter. "Get going, then."

"You'd better keep up, you spineless maðkar!" Ragnar shouted to the men behind before he and his brother hoisted Sigri's pole and continued up the mountain path.

The witch had remained silent and motionless throughout the exchange, her mind working to piece the information together. She wasn't the only captive. Given that Ragnar had mentioned "that woman," she deduced that these men only knew about one witch. Jarne must be the second hostage, likely bound and carried in the same way as she.

An "old hag" had ordered these men to hunt for a woman. Could that be a black witch? Sigri was certain. What else could the calculation of three months per sacrificed prisoner mean? The black witch must have felt Mae's arrival and sent the men to catch her. Thus, the moment the men delivered

Sigri, the old hag would learn about the presence of a second witch on this island. She needed to get away and warn Mae.

The men wheezed from exertion as they climbed the steep trail that clung to the mountain. The path was narrow, the terrain rising on one side and falling away on the other.

Sigri concentrated on Ragnar, the younger man in front. Sensing his presence, she reached into his body. She didn't dare to insert a command into his mind. Most people could detect the mental intruder and became suspicious of their thoughts and feelings. But she'd learned much from the book during their sea voyage. She had even reached into Jarne's body without his knowledge to train her awareness. Now, she had found a deserving target for a practical experiment.

The conditions were far from perfect. Sigri was trussed up like an animal. Her bouncing head throbbed, her bruised body ached everywhere, and the cold muddled her mind. Still, her ordeal had put her in an unforgiving mood, making her reckless.

Curling her fingers, she sent her mind searching for the right strings to pull. Having found them, she visualized living flesh becoming butchered meat. Muttering words of power, she spread her fingers in an explosive motion. Ragnar stopped mid-stride, keeled over like a felled tree, and tumbled down the mountainside, dragging the captured witch along.

CHAPTER TWENTY-SIX

Queen of the Island

BRUISED AND EXHAUSTED, Mae dragged herself onto the porous lava field that formed the island's jagged coastline and collapsed. The razor-sharp rocks bit into her hands and cheeks, and the smell of rotting seaweed filled her nostrils. Mae didn't mind. Simply breathing was a joy.

How am I even still alive? she wondered.

The witch hadn't gotten the rope untied before the waves smashed the boat to splinters. Plunged into the violent waters, the beam anchoring her rope's other side had gotten stuck, keeping her submerged. The angry waves rolled Mae forth and back over the reef like a rag doll.

With the air knocked from her lungs by the initial impact, the black witch felt the freezing water smothering her like death's embrace, welcoming her to her watery grave. All thoughts of magic fled her mind.

Crossing her arms and hugging her shoulders, Mae tried to prevent more painful collisions with the rocks. That was when her hand touched the knife dangling from her belt. A fresh burst of energy surged through her body. Grabbing the blade's worn wooden handle, she cut the rope with a single slice.

Mae flailed her arms and legs until her head broke the surface. Gasping, she breathed the glorious life-giving air. Every bone hurt, every muscle burned. Still, the witch reached the shallows, paddling like a dog, and escaped the ocean's deadly grasp.

Her euphoria lasted less than a minute, until a stab of anxiety pierced her heart. *Jarne! Sigri! Did they survive?* Pushing herself to her feet, Mae looked around.

The night was pitch dark. Still, dawn couldn't be far off. Where should she go, left or right? She was exhausted, her body bruised, and her knees wobbled. Closing her eyes to gather her energy, Mae tasted a foul taint in the air, much worse than decaying kelp. She turned inland, and the odor got stronger, twisting her guts and raising the hairs on her neck. A pungent stench of death and darkness emanated from the heart of the island.

Mae had never experienced anything like this. Rumors proclaimed black witches lived on the Sister Islands. Had Mae come to the right place after all? Could a black witch's presence be the source of this vile sensation?

Mae felt appalled, yet simultaneously, she was drawn near, eager to fight for superiority. Her pulse quickened. Adrenaline pumping through her veins cleared her mind. If she could sense another black witch, that woman must feel it, too, making a confrontation all but unavoidable. Without a conscious decision, Mae moved toward the direction whence came the stink.

Despite her cuts, scrapes, and bruises, the witch sprinted over the uneven ground. An angry fire had kindled inside her, dulling her aches and propelling her toward the center of the accursed island. Cutting through the forest, she came across a path leading up the mountain. The sparse moonlight revealed the track to be steep and well traveled. Mae followed the trail, her feet struggling to keep in step with the ferocious pounding of her heart. Her tortured muscles burned.

Yet Mae relished in her bodily pain, letting the aches stoke the fury rising inside her. Rounding a corner, she spotted men ahead, carrying what looked like killed deer on wooden poles. Instinctively, she sped up to close the distance.

She had almost caught up with the group when a commotion drew her attention. The leader had tripped. Veering off the trail, he stumbled down the mountainside, crashing through the low underbrush and bouncing off trees. A scream ripped through the darkness. *Sigri!* It must have been her. Those men didn't carry deer. They'd taken her friends captive, and one had dragged Sigri with him as he fell.

Three men broke off, descending with caution, while the remaining group rushed onward. Mae needed to make a decision. Did she follow Jarne's captors, or should she rescue Sigri? Letting the larger group go, the black witch cut through the underbrush, weaving between the trees, her footfalls muffled on the moss-covered ground.

The three men had spread out, each looking for a different route down, making her hunt much easier. Two strides away from her first target, the witch jumped, tackling her prey. She buried her knife in his neck before he realized what had happened. Her other hand grabbed his ear like a handle. Nails digging into the cartilage, she drained his life force. He was dead before he hit the ground, snapping branches as he fell. Mae used her momentum to get back onto her feet.

"What was that?" the second man shouted, giving Mae a beacon to home in on. "Håkan? Are you all right?"

"He's dead," she crooned, "and you're next!"

"Who are you? Show yourself!"

"Death!" the witch hissed as she barreled into her next victim. Ramming her shoulder into his belly, she buried her knife deep between his legs.

He crashed to the floor, screaming in agony. Mae ripped the knife free and licked the blood off the blade. Convulsing on the ground, he rolled on his side. But Mae wasn't done.

Possessed by an irresistible desire to hurt and kill, she jammed her knife to the hilt into his left eye. Using the handle to tilt his face upward, her free hand almost caressed his cheek as she drained him.

The third man abandoned the chase of his fallen comrade. Drawing a sword and a dagger, he positioned himself for a fight. Mae laughed out loud, her high-pitched cackle scaring birds into flight. *Could these idiots make it any easier?* Brimming with energy, she punched his face with a blast of air, sending him tumbling. With another quick spell, the witch broke a branch off the tree above him, pinning him to the ground.

He struggled to lift the tree limb, almost getting free.

Mae rushed toward him. But she got careless, lost her footing, and fell.

Hammering her knife down to grab hold of dirt or roots, she inadvertently sank her weapon deep into his upper thigh. It wasn't enough to provide Mae an anchor. With her feet unable to find purchase on the wet leaves, she slid down the mountain, ripping the knife free. The blade sliced his femoral artery three inches open. Hot, red blood gushed forth like an erupting volcano, bleeding him dry in seconds.

Twenty paces below, a thicket of brambles stopped Mae's descent. She crawled on all fours to climb the steep hill, eager to harvest her prize. He was dead. Frustrated, the witch kicked his lifeless body.

Fury surged through her veins, stoking her burning desire for violence. Her whole body trembled. Cursing and spitting, the black witch scraped the dirt and blood off her hands and checked her weapons. She was about to follow the other group of men when she remembered her fallen friend.

What has come over me? Where does this bloodlust come from? Mae shook her head in disgust. Clenching her fists, she inhaled deep breaths, willing her dark urges to yield control.

It's this island—the other black witch! Her proximity aggravated Mae's curse, roiling her inner demons and bringing out the worst in her.

Mae squeezed her eyes shut. Her stomach churned. Her heart pounded like a war drum. With every breath, she fought against the darkness. Sigri needed Mae; Jarne needed Mae. Holding on to those thoughts, the witch felt her rage ebbing. Her muscles relaxed, and the red haze cleared. She almost welcomed the resurfacing pain from her numerous scrapes and bruises.

"Sigri?" she called, her voice shaky.

"Here," a faint voice sounded from her right.

Mae half ran, half slipped into that direction.

"Keep calling," she shouted, "and give me your location."

"I'm here. Can't move. Over here!"

Mae saw her. Sigri had gotten wedged between a tree root and a large stone. Her arms and legs stuck up in the air, making it easy to cut the bonds.

"Anything broken?" Mae asked, not wanting to inflict more harm by pulling too hard.

"Everything," the green witch responded. "Pull me out. We need to rescue Jarne. Mae, there is a black witch on this island."

"I know," Mae groaned, straining to free her sister. Her sweaty hands slipped, and she tumbled backward. Getting up, Mae continued, "I can feel her. My curse reacts to her essence. I almost lost control. I need to kill her."

"Pull me out first," Sigri implored. "We need to talk. I have an idea."

* * *

Helgrid Sigurdsdóttir was an imposing woman. She had already been tall and squarish as a child, causing the other children to call her names, like monster or bear-woman. Her body had filled out in her youth, developing an ample bust and broad hips. Now, during her middle years that would last forever, she had grown to an immense size.

Helgrid liked it that way. She savored even more that nobody dared to call her anything except "Your Majesty." Not to her face, at least. Behind her back, they still might call her a monster. But these days, the black witch had earned that title.

The witch sat on her throne as the morning sun crept over the crater rim, painting long shadows across the floor of volcanic ash. Open fires crackled on either side, and torches outlined the oval caldera. Two blackened wooden poles stood to the sides, decorated by the charred remains of human bodies. The witch looked forward to changing the ornaments soon.

Usually, the island's queen didn't rise before noon. But she'd woken in the middle of the night, alerted by the presence of another black witch. Immediately, Helgrid commanded a hunting party to "invite" the unexpected visitor to a private audience. With her gaze fixed on the only entrance, she waited. The men would return soon—what an exciting morning!

Not long after, footsteps echoed in the lava tunnel leading to Queen Helgrid's lair. The hunting party had arrived. Yet, the island's ruler did not feel the presence of her expected guest. When eight men rushed into the caldera, they carried only one male captive. The lead hunter approached and went to one knee.

"Your Majesty," he greeted, lowering his head.

"Where is the woman?" she asked.

"We captured her, Your Majesty. But Ragnar tripped and slid down the mountain, dragging her with him. Mækir and two other men went after him. They will follow soon."

"Stand!" Helgrid barked, and the man obeyed. "The woman fell down the mountain, and you did not help to retrieve her?" she asked, her whisper dripping with menace.

"I thought, Your Majesty, we had the male captive... I thought bringing him to you as fast as possible was wise."

"You thought I would want *him*?" the queen asked. "You thought I would be glad for your initiative? Do you desire a reward for your *thoughts*?"

The man blanched, unsure how to answer the question.

"Your Majesty..." he stammered.

The black witch tilted her head and looked into his eyes, seeing panic rising. "Do you want to know what I think?" she asked, in a voice soft as silk. "I think you *do* deserve a reward."

Smiling, she incinerated him where he stood. His screams lasted almost a minute before his smoking husk fell silent, emanating the lovely smell of singed hair. Helgrid watched the other men shaking in fear, yet nobody ran. They knew better. She could kill them all. But she didn't need to. They'd brought her a hostage, and this bargaining chip would draw her prize nearer.

"Tie the prisoner to one pole and get some rest. I will need you later." The island's queen could appear merciful when she needed to. Push even a skittish animal too far into a corner, and it will attack. Relieved, the men tied Jarne's hands to a metal ring and prepared to withdraw when Helgrid spoke again. "You do know you disappointed me, don't you? I am sure at least one of you feels so overwhelmed with remorse that he gladly offers himself as recompense for the entire hunting party's failure."

The men looked at each other, frozen for two heartbeats. Then, a scuffle broke out, alliances forming in seconds. Soon, six men had wrestled the seventh into submission. Bruised and bloodied, the unlucky man crawled to the foot of her throne, reaching a shaking hand toward her.

Queen Helgrid descended in measured steps, allowing her protective sphere to engulf his hand. With a swift motion, she rammed the steel tip of her staff down, nailing his hand to the wood. He screamed, displeasing her, and she pulled the air from his lungs. His body convulsed in silent agony. The black witch touched her bare foot to his bleeding hand and accepted his sacrifice.

"You may leave," the queen commanded, leaving bloody footsteps on the stairs to her throne. "Next time, I won't be so forgiving. Fail me again, and your children will pay the price! I'll crush their tiny skulls while you watch."

Had she made that threat already this month? After so many years as the island's absolute ruler, devising novel threats became harder and harder.

* * *

HOURS PASSED. QUEEN Helgrid remained on her throne, embodying the image of a serene ruler contemplating the burden of leadership. Servants brought food and ale, fed fresh logs to the braziers, and opened a parasol to shield the queen from the sun's glare. She ignored them.

The black witch sat motionless. Her fingers steepled, her eyes focused on the entrance as the sun began to near the western crater rim. Yet her semblance of calm was a lie. She could feel *her* approach. The queen had sensed her visitor circling the caldera. But now, the other witch had entered the lava tube. The final contest was moments away. Would she be wary of a trap? Would she attack? Why else had she left her fortified home on Heilladur? She must not know about Helgrid's past deeds.

Well, she would learn soon.

With a wave of the queen's hand, the torches flared, burning bright blue. A snap of her fingers caused two guards to take positions on either side of Jarne, pointing their swords at his neck. The stage was set.

The faint echoes of feet crunching on gravel broke the silence. As the sound grew steadily louder, shadows stirred in the tunnel's semi-darkness. Finally, a figure stepped into the torch-lit caldera. She was small, little more than a child. Wrapped in a shapeless gray cloak, she wore black pants and a black shirt. Queen Helgrid could see the rips and tears caused by her uncomfortable arrival and her harrowing escape from capture.

She stank. Many years had passed since the island's ruler last faced a black sister in person. Fridhold's smell hadn't been that strong. But then, this scrawny creature carried two-fifths of the curse, bringing it to Helgrid all the way from Heilladur.

"Welcome, sister, to my humble abode," Helgrid called. "I am Helgrid Sigurdsdóttir, Queen of the Sister Isles, Foremost of Death's Daughters, and soon to be Ruler of the World. I hope you had a pleasant journey." The queen smirked. "So nice of you to visit. It's been too long since I last met one of our kind."

Mae stepped into the circle of firelight but halted ten paces from the entrance. She didn't reply.

"We found your pet," Helgrid mused, pointing to Jarne with a lazy wave. "He looked like a drowned rat when my men invited him. I assume you're here to thank me." The queen shaded her eyes, gauging Mae's reaction. "Please, do come closer. Let me embrace you. How I yearn to receive the present you brought. You must be exhausted. Why don't you rest by my side... *forever!*" she hissed. Leaning forward, she added, "I might even let *him* live."

Jarne shook his head and screamed into his gag, willing Mae to retreat.

"No, thank you," Mae replied, her voice calm. "I came for you. Since I'm here, I have no further need of my helmsman." Mae looked around, scanning the shadows. "I'm sure one of your twenty thugs can steer a boat. After we're done, I'll pay my respects to our remaining sisters."

"Oh, child," the queen laughed. "I wondered why you braved the treacherous sea voyage? You don't know!" Helgrid threw her head back. Her booming laughter rebounded from the crater walls. "How I hate to destroy your illusions," she jeered, wiping tears from her eyes. "There are no other black witches. I took care of them years ago after the curse on Sculd took me." Gripping her throne's armrests with beringed fingers, Helgrid continued in a carrying whisper, "You and I, we're the last of Death's Daughters. And in a heartbeat, I'll be the last of them all!"

Without warning, the queen sent the burning braziers flying in Mae's direction. She waved her arms in wide arcs, pulling obsidian crystals from the crater wall. A barrage of deadly projectiles sped toward her challenger. Mae stood tall, never taking her eyes off her opponent.

The sound of splintering glass filled the open space as the hurled objects bounced off a shimmering sphere surrounding the new arrival.

Laughing, Mae slapped her palms together, causing a ball of blinding light to explode in midair. Taking advantage of everyone's diverted attention, the slender witch propelled two throwing knives into the foreheads of the men guarding Jarne.

"In that case," she shouted as the guards toppled backward, "I'll stay here. Take over your island kingdom, so to speak."

"Impressive!" Helgrid stood, clapping her hands trice in a slow rhythm. "No wonder that weak king kept you as his guard dog. How does it feel to jump at the commands of a lesser man?" she sneered. "You'll find me a harder nut to crack." To underscore her lack of concern, the queen plucked an apple from a plate beside her and bit into the fruit, juice spilling down her forearm.

"Here is a suggestion," Mae hissed, taking a few strides toward her foe. "Why don't you choke on your fruit and die! I never served the king. I killed his sorceress less than a season ago, burning her alive."

Whirling on the spot, she summoned the wind. A cloud of dust and debris sped toward the so-called queen of the island. With her opponent's sight blocked, Mae aimed a pulse of air at the center of the other witch's defense.

The impact sent the queen stumbling backward. Plunking down hard on her throne, she dropped her fruit. Her head smacked against the ornately carved backrest. Dazed, Helgrid touched the back of her head. Her fingers came away bloody. Mae saw murder burning in her eyes, replacing the earlier false levity.

"You think you can beat me?" Helgrid snarled. "You might possess power, but no finesse. So much potential. What a pity; it all ends here."

A ball of fire shot from the witch queen's hands. To Mae's horror, the attack sliced through the protective shield like a hot knife through butter. Dodging at the last second, the slender witch felt the searing heat of a near miss. A second fireball hurtled her way. Mae ran, jumped, and rolled.

"Is that all you have!" she shouted in defiance after the third incendiary projectile exploded on the crater wall behind her.

Mae stood straight, grimacing to mask the pain from the splinters of volcanic rock pelting her back. Still, she couldn't outrun the attacks forever. One lucky shot might end the confrontation at any second. Widening her stance, Mae clenched her fists and narrowed her eyes.

Helgrid looked perplexed before a grin spread across her face.

"Good girl," the queen jeered. "Realized you can't hide?"

Flexing her fingers, she prepared to unleash another fiery torrent. Mae was ready. With a viper-quick motion, the younger witch sent a pulse of air toward her opponent, channeling all her power into the attack. The spells collided in a ferocious explosion mere feet from the queen's throne.

Sparks and burning debris burst in all directions, showering the rotund witch. Helgrid's hair caught fire, as did the lace collar of her extravagant dress. Screaming in rage, the witch queen summoned the wind to smother the flames spreading all over her body.

"Is that enough finesse for you?" Mae taunted.

Bent over from exertion, she breathed hard. Still, her eyes remained fixed on her adversary, burning with the fiendish desire to kill and destroy.

How must it feel to be the last black witch? The sudden thought took hold of Mae's mind. Deep inside her, the irresistible urge grew to take the power for herself, to combine the curse for the first time since its release into the world. She'd be the last—the deadliest of Death's daughters.

"You cretin!" Helgrid spat. "You think you won 'cause you countered one of my spells? You've no idea what you're up against."

Smoke rose from the queen's head and shoulders. Her massive bosom rose and fell, causing the torches to flare in time with each fuming exhale. Helgrid squeezed her staff so hard the wood cracked.

"You're like your sisters before, not grasping a black witch's true power," she shouted, her voice booming like thunder. "You think your magic spells are your best weapon? No—it is fear. Now, fear me, little girl!"

The queen raised her staff like a weapon, and the score of men hidden in the shadows attacked.

* * *

MAE SNARLED LIKE an angry beast. She'd stepped into the trap. Helgrid's attacks had driven her into the open, herding her toward the center of the caldera. Blinded by the raging fury of her inner demons, she'd ignored the danger of being surrounded until it was too late.

Pulling her knife from her belt, Mae crouched. Three men threw javelins as they approached. The slender witch's resurrected shield deflected the weapons but couldn't block them. One spearhead pierced her cloak, and another grazed her right cheek.

The remaining attackers drew their swords and closed in. Mae rolled and punched with air, causing men to topple backward. Still, they kept attacking. These men seemed accustomed to the use of magic. Broad shields blocked the brunt of Mae's blasts, while sword thrusts and obsidian crystals hurled from slings relentlessly challenged her defenses. Grabbing a fallen spear, the witch whirled in a circle, using blade and magic to repel the attacks.

She needed to get through these men.

The island's queen sat on her throne thirty paces away. Whenever Mae's back was turned, Helgrid continued shooting fireballs into the melee, unconcerned about whom she hit.

Seeing the eyes of an attacker widen in fear, Mae ducked in the nick of time. She felt the scorching heat as the fireblast engulfed the unlucky man. His screams chilled her bones, giving his comrades pause.

Mae seized her chance, piercing one man through the neck with a spear. Pulling the weapon free, she rammed the spear-butt into another man's abdomen. With her back to the crater wall, Mae summoned the burning braziers, creating a wall of fire between her and the men.

"Do I have to do everything by myself?" Queen Helgrid screamed. Hell's fury blazed in her narrowed eyes. An aura of darkness surrounded the witch queen as she wove her hands in intricate circles.

For two heartbeats, nothing happened.

Then, racer-sharp basalt spikes erupted from the ground under Mae's feet. She jumped and rolled, blood spilling from her shredded pant leg. Howling in pain, she moved in erratic patterns, not giving Queen Helgrid a target. In front, the men stood shoulder to shoulder, forming a wall of shields and spears.

Mae was cornered. In desperation, she raised a whirlwind, sending stones and debris into the faces of the attackers. Obscuring Queen Helgrid's view with a wall of dust, Mae bolted toward the throne, her only hope to end this now. But her ruse was cut short.

The earth shook. All across the caldera, jagged blades of stone erupted, forming a deadly barrier. Barely avoiding the lethal spikes, the harried witch was forced to retreat.

Mae's eyes stung. She tasted blood. Every muscle burned, every breath a ragged gasp. The witch limped, one hand pressed against a gash on her side. Frantically, her gaze darted across the ravaged battlefield. Some men were dead. Too many were still alive, and her enemies closed in.

Unseen, one warrior snuck behind Mae. He raised his weapon for a deadly blow. Then, he stumbled, and his lifeless body hit the ground. Mae hadn't even realized his approach. A second man fell. Then, a third clutched his chest with a scream of pain. The unexpected development gave the remaining warriors pause. Mae used the heaven-sent respite to gather the last ounces of energy.

With an ear-piercing battle cry, she pushed out in all directions, swiping the men off their feet. Pulling loose rocks from the crater wall, she pelted the fallen warriors with an avalanche of fist-sized stones.

"Get out of my way," Mae yelled. "This is between Queen Helgrid and me. Mortal men have no place in this fight."

Slow and weary, only half of the men clawed their way from the rubble. Amidst them stood the slender witch, covered in ash and blood from head to toe, bruised and exhausted. Yet her eyes blazed devilish red, her furious gaze stealing the air from their lungs. The witch's body trembled with a rage so potent the very earth thrummed beneath her feet.

The men stood frozen, suspended between two terrors—the black witch queen they served and the terrifying specter before them.

"This ends now!" the island's queen shouted, her amplified voice echoing from the crater walls.

Amidst the chaos, she'd moved toward the pole where Jarne stood. Pulling his head by the hair, the witch pressed a gleaming knife to his throat. An eerie silence fell. Only the torchlight dared to move. Helgrid had Mae's full attention. The two black witches stared at each other from opposite sides of the caldera, murder in their eyes.

"Bind her and bring her here," the witch queen barked. "She will not resist. Isn't that so, *Mae*? It was quite amusing to break into his mind. What passion, what devotion... what love," Helgrid sneered. With great hesitation, the remaining men inched forward.

Mae's gaze flicked to Jarne. She needed to save him. He was the most important person in her life. She'd sworn to take care of him—never to abandon him. She would gladly die to save his life. Mae needed to surrender. There was no other way. Hope drained from her body with every drop of blood hitting the dirt.

"I'm sorry, Jarne," Mae whispered. "I can't!"

Through the haze of pain and fear, Mae recalled her mission, her promise, her last remaining purpose. She came here to break the curse by killing every last black witch. Surrender only led to more pain and suffering. The island's black witch would kill Jarne—or worse. No victory lay at the end of such a path—no happily-ever-after.

Mae clenched her jaw as she steeled herself for the attack. Sliding her right foot back, she widened her stance for increased leverage. Her right hand moved toward the pouch with the poisoned throwing knives.

Time seemed frozen. Mae stood in the eye of the hurricane. Her breathing quieted. Ice had replaced the magma in her veins. Her nerves had become bands of steel. She was ready to fight, ready to kill—ready to sacrifice the only person who mattered for the greater good.

Mae saw Helgrid's expression change from triumph to trepidation. Looking Jarne in the eyes, she felt his acceptance replacing fear. The air vibrated around the determined witch as she gathered the energy for the strike.

Suddenly, a dart struck Mae, fired from the shadows of the lava tube.

She staggered, forcing the men to retreat. Clutching at her neck, Mae tried to dislodge the projectile, but her body betrayed her, and she crumpled to the floor.

"Bring her!" Helgrid commanded, her voice quivering. "And then leave us. My guest was right. This confrontation is beyond mortal men. And," she added with noticeable relief, "it's beyond silly girls." Sheathing her knife, Helgrid returned to her throne.

Two warriors rushed to grab Mae under the arms. They deposited the defeated witch in the dirt before the queen's feet. Then they scrambled toward the exit, eager to be as far away as possible from this horrid place.

As the men fled, dragging their fallen comrades along, a hooded figure with a blowpipe stepped into the caldera. Standing tall, face hidden in the shadows, the figure's pale-gray eyes surveyed the scene.

"Ah, yes," the queen acknowledged the new arrival, "you may stay. You earned that privilege." Rising from her throne, she lifted her arms toward the sky, striking the pose of someone accepting a heavenly blessing. "I want stories to be told and songs to be sung. But stay back there!" she ordered, ensuring she remained beyond the range of the figure's blowpipe.

"Stories make all the difference," she mused. "They transform a knife in the back into a heroic battle. An almost defeat becomes a sly ruse. Who can untangle the weave of truth from the whispers of legend? Neither Fridhold nor Ylva are still among us. I am!"

Stepping off her throne, the queen gave Mae's body a dismissive prod with her bloody foot.

"I am here to take it all!" she shouted, her voice booming like thunder in the empty space. "The world will remember me for combining all five parts of death's gift. What really happened, who cares? The truth dies with this unconscious girl." Looking at the hooded figure, she shouted, "But you! Tell a great story about my victory. Speak about the epic battle and how my sly cunning overcame her feeble trickery. Spin a tale of suspense and surprise."

"Oh, she will," Mae whispered as she grabbed Helgrid's ankle. "Here's a surprise for you."

Then she drained all life from the Queen of the Sister Isles, absorbing the entire curse and becoming Death's last remaining daughter.

CHAPTER TWENTY-SEVEN

'Til Death Do Us Part

"Much have I fared, much have I found,
Much have I got of the gods:
Whence comes the sun to the smooth sky back,
When Fenrir has snatched it forth?"[1]

As the island's witch queen fell lifeless to the ground, Mae had barely enough time to rejoice in the success of Sigri's plan before the black curse surged into her. White-hot knives stabbed into her brain. Her muscles spasmed, and her insides writhed like serpents in a pit of fire. Convulsing on the ground in agony, her bloodcurdling screams shattered the quiet of the empty space.

Sigri had rushed to Jarne, cutting his bonds, but she wished she hadn't. He fought her to get to Mae, his own suffering etched into his face. Sigri couldn't hold him back. Nothing in the world could. Only Mae had the power to do so.

"Stay back," Mae shrieked. Her unnaturally high-pitched scream could have woken the dead.

Sigri covered her ears in pain.

"I'm not safe," Mae wailed between jerks of her body. "Not in control."

Jarne stopped in his tracks twelve feet away, his whole body trembling.

Sigri couldn't begin to comprehend the torments her sister was enduring. Yet her analytical brain couldn't help but wonder how lucid Mae's mind seemed while unimaginable agony assaulted her body.

Mae's limbs kept twitching, accompanied by grunts and groans. Then, a

---

[1] *The Lay of Vafthrudnir, Stanza 46*, Poetic Edda, English by Henry Bellows (1936)

piercing wail escaped her lips, and she slumped like a ragdoll. Jarne could not hold back any longer. He rushed toward her, pulling her body into his arms. Kissing her forehead, he stroked her hair. Tears ran down his cheeks, and he rocked back and forth.

Sigri didn't know what to do. Should she approach Mae to offer her healing, or should she leave the two lovers alone? She had just decided to walk away when the black witch's body stiffened.

Mae grabbed Jarne by the throat with a viper-quick motion, her pupils glowing devilish red. Sigri yelped in shock, but Jarne didn't move; he didn't fight. He looked back into Mae's eyes with sorrow and patience. She squeezed his neck, baring her teeth. He reached a shaking hand to touch her cheek.

Sigri stood rooted to the spot. She should do something.

When Jarne was on the brink of passing out, Mae came to her senses. The red glow in her eyes vanished, and she pulled her arm back, looking horror-struck at her treacherous hand.

"Oh, mother of all, what have I done?" she cried.

"Shhh," Jarne croaked, "you've done nothing. You came back to me."

He hugged her close, and she melted into him, both crying tears of pain and joy. Sigri left them.

Wiping the moisture from her eyes, the healer started exploring the lair of Queen Helgrid.

* * *

"Wasn't there anything in the book?" Mae snapped with more aggression than Sigri deserved.

"I didn't read every page," the green witch replied in her usual calm tone, not displaying the slightest irritation from Mae's unwarranted aspersions. "But I skimmed through the content. I saw very little about black witches. Between what you learned from Bergrún and Helgrid's boasting, we must be the most knowledgeable people on that subject."

After returning from her exploration, Sigri had ushered Mae and Jarne into the luxurious cave apartments of the island's former ruler. A narrow, unassuming crack in the crater wall led to a series of sizable caverns. Formed by the volcano's fiery blood, these rooms had been extended by laborers to hold the bounty of countless shipwrecks. Chests and barrels filled with clothes, spices, weapons, and other treasures stood among furniture made from driftwood. Oil lamps only partly illuminated the vast space, their dancing shadows increasing the sense of mystery.

Seating Mae on a thick seagrass mattress, Sigri had tented to her sister's numerous injuries. She'd cleaned, stitched, and bandaged while Jarne wrapped Mae in a warm woolen blanket and held on to her.

Pouring her magical energy into the black witch, the healer was glad for the surplus she had harvested from the dying warriors. Once the worst wounds had been treated, Sigri sent Jarne to fetch food and drink from the store-rooms deeper in the mountain. A light breeze circulated through cleverly placed ventilation holes, keeping the elements out while providing plenty of fresh air.

Mae shivered. In some part of her brain, she appreciated Sigri's efforts to care for her body's needs before they discussed what to do next. But the effort was futile. The black witch felt too wound up. Clenching and unclenching her jaw, her eyes darted around the room like a flock of frightened birds. Her feet tapped a nervous rhythm on the wicker carpet, mirroring the erratic fluttering of her heart.

"But what do we do?" she moaned in frustration.

"We should rest," Jarne suggested. "We've all been through a lot. Our minds will be refreshed in the morning, and we'll find the answers."

"I can't rest," Mae shrieked. Taking three deep breaths, she tried to force her anger down. Closing her eyes, she slowed her heartbeat. In a calmer but strained voice, Mae explained, "I can't rest, Jarne. This curse... It's too powerful. I can barely control it. Hell, I can't control it at all!" She laughed a mirthless cackle. "I attacked you, almost killed you. If I fall asleep, none of you will ever wake again."

"Perhaps," he said, not shying away from her. "But the curse is like an illness. If your body is weak and exhausted, you don't have the strength to fight it either."

"So you're an experienced healer now?" Mae's voice was filled with scorn for this naïve boy.

"No," he replied, "but I know you, and I listened to your accounts of the time after we fought the duke." He turned toward her and took her hand. She offered only token resistance. "You said the curse took full control of your body after you fell down the waterfall," Jarne continued, avoiding the word "jumped." Mae cringed, trying to pull back, but he didn't let go. "You gave yourself over to the curse in the duke's apartment like you did that night in our cabin in the woods."

This time, Mae did pull her hands free. "Is that supposed to make me feel better?" she scoffed. "It doesn't!"

"Actually, it should. All these times, you were alone, hurt, frightened. When your soul is vulnerable, the curse has an easy time dominating you. But you aren't alone now." Jarne retook her hands, looking her straight in the eyes. "You have us, and we'll keep you safe."

Moisture pooled in Mae's eyes. She averted her gaze in shame, but at the same time, she squeezed his hands harder. Sigri hadn't spoken the entire time. Fascinated, she observed the exchange, marveling at Jarne's audacity of confronting Mae with her most heinous deeds in her current condition. Still, she couldn't deny the wisdom and success of his actions. Moving closer, she laid her hands on Mae's and Jarne's, expressing her total agreement without saying a single word.

"I'll take the first watch," Sigri said after several moments of silence. "I'll wake you, Jarne, in four hours. Get some rest."

"I should move away," Mae interjected. "Isn't there a room we can lock?"

"I don't think that is a good idea," Sigri replied. "I have to agree with my fellow healer." She gave Jarne a respectful nod, her gesture only slightly marred by her struggle to keep her face straight. "Physical contact with another person will instill a sense of warmth and security while you sleep."

"But what if I lose control and someone is near?"

"I harbor no illusions that a locked door would be any protection. No, Jarne is right. To keep *you* in charge, you need to know that we are near and care for you. That we love you, Mae."

Mae pulled herself to her feet and hugged her sister, muttering thanks. Jarne stood, approached, and embraced the two women. Both witches lifted one arm and included him in the circle.

* * *

MAE SLEPT WELL past midday. Both Jarne and Sigri had stood watch, changing positions twice. Some islanders had approached in the early hours of the morning. Sigri chased them away by projecting the feeling of burning pain. Amplifying her voice, she warned them never to return unless they wanted all their families and kin to die. The men fled head over heels, leaving Sigri to enjoy a moment of serene quiet before daybreak.

With the sun nearing its zenith, Jarne decided to eat outside under the open sky. He carried stools and tables into the caldera. Queen Helgrid had lived a luxurious life, having the islanders fill her storerooms with cheeses, meats, nuts, dried fruits, ales, and mead. Jarne took a little of everything. He knew from experience that difficult topics were best discussed on a full stomach. He only regretted that they had no bread. The islanders must have provided their queen with fresh baked goods daily. After Sigri's warning, that source had dried up.

Mae stepped out, leaning on Queen Helgrid's staff. She wore a brocade robe over thin, silken undergarments, having discarded her ripped and blood-stained clothes. The robe was several sizes too large, giving Mae the appearance of a child dressing in her mother's clothes.

Jarne smiled, and she smiled back. Then she closed her eyes, raised her head, and let the sunshine warm her. Her face, still marked from the recent struggles, had lost some of the tension and anxiety.

Sigri, too, had changed. She'd found a dress of pale blue. Simple yet elegant, it complimented her tall and slim figure. Jarne looked down on himself.

"I'm wearing rags while both of you are dressed for a feast," he bemoaned.

"That's quite all right." Sigri smiled. "The serving staff should never rival the ladies of the house."

"Serving staff? What happened to 'fellow healer'?" he asked.

"Did I say that? You must have misheard me."

Mae closed the distance and took him in her arms, kissing him.

"Not to worry," she whispered, "noble ladies are known to sometimes dally with the stable boys."

He started complaining, but then he realized that her robe had fallen open, offering delightful views. She followed his gaze, closed her robe in mock bashfulness, turned on the spot, and hobbled toward the table laden with food. He followed, dazed and muttering under his breath.

"Servant, stable boy—beautiful women think they can get away with everything."

"Of course," Sigri mused, "but thank you for the compliment, nonetheless."

The jovial mood persisted throughout the meal. Yet, as the sun neared the crater's rim, the lengthening shadows touched the three friends, chilling their high spirits. Reading the change on Mae's face, Jarne attacked the topic head on.

"What is it you want, Mae?" he asked.

"What do you mean?"

"Sigri and I, we can't know how you feel. We want to help you." He looked to Sigri, seeking reassurance. She nodded, and Jarne continued. "To find a way forward, we need to know what you want."

"It's not about me. It's about the curse. It must be destroyed."

"Why?" he asked, infuriating Mae further.

"Don't play stupid with me." she growled. "Nobody believes your simple-farm-boy act."

"I didn't grow up on a farm." Jarne tried the feeble joke but changed his tack when he saw Mae glaring daggers at him. "Still, it *is* that simple. Hear me out," he added when Mae rose from her seat. "You said you wanted to prevent other women or men from sharing your fate. You wanted to stop there being any new black witches. You are the last. Unless you curse someone, there won't be another black witch." Jarne stopped, letting his words sink in.

"The curse will pick a new vessel when I die, whether I want to or not."

"Then don't die." No sarcasm colored his words, and no levity softened his face. He was dead serious.

Mae could feel the longing emanating from him. He loved her and wanted to be with her, regardless of the price. Her hand touched his, and she looked him in the eyes, softening her tone.

"I can't, Jarne. I can't live with killing innocent people. And innocent people will die," she added when he was about to object. "Remember Makevinger? Remember the duke's estate? We tried so hard to use evil for good—it never worked." She took a deep breath and told him what she should have told him long ago. "I love you, and I want to be with you. But I can't."

"What do you say?" He rounded on Sigri. "Talk sense into her."

"What would you do in her stead, Jarne?" Sigri asked. "Could you sleep easy with the guilt? Mae told me long ago, before we moved to Thorshofn, that she needed to end the curse. It became more urgent after the horrors of the duke's estate. Other people can choose whether to be evil or good. Not her, and that's torturing her."

"And you didn't tell me?"

"I didn't want her to tell you," Mae clarified. "Maybe, with time, you might have found someone else. I can't give you children."

"I don't care about that."

"But you should. You will be a wonderful father."

Silence.

"I hoped I could find a different way to break the curse," Sigri ventured.

Jarne looked at her, an ounce of hope glimmering in his eyes. But Sigri shook her head.

"So what then?" Jarne snapped, anger tainting his voice. "You'll try to kill yourself? Again?" he barked, acknowledging the nature of her "waterfall" for the first time. "What would that accomplish except for laying a trap for anybody stumbling onto that spot. The curse clings to the land, remember?"

"Sigri thought I could go into exile, far away. I'll die on an uninhabited island somewhere in the vast ocean."

"That won't work," Jarne argued. "How would you find such a spot? When you get too weak, the curse will take control, steering you toward promising hunting grounds."

"I might have an idea," Sigri said. Both pairs of eyes turn toward her, hope in the green and betrayal in the blue. "The curse would need to go where nobody could follow."

"That's impossible," Jarne huffed. "If Mae can go there, so can anybody else."

"Let me rephrase. The curse must go to a place nobody can return from."

"Where?" Mae and Jarne asked in unison.

"The bottom of the ocean."

* * *

Sigri's plan was simple and brilliant. She'd considered every angle and facet, weaving them with her knowledge and skill into a meticulous procedure.

"The curse only leaves its host under two conditions," she explained. "Either by passing it on or when the bearer dies. Mae doesn't want to pass on the curse."

"Of course not," Mae declared. "What would be the point in that?"

"What indeed?" Sigri asked under her breath. "In that case," she said more loudly, "the curse bearer can't die with anybody being near. My plan is to send the curse out into the open sea. If we use a boat with a tiny hole in the hull, it'll sink before reaching another island, taking the curse to the bottom of the ocean."

"Won't the curse make me fight against drowning?" Mae asked. "I could turn the boat around or swim or something."

"That's why we'll use potions. I can brew something that'll make a person sleep for twenty-four hours. Enough time to sail many leagues, especially with the strong wind."

"We need a boat," Mae said.

"I'm sure I can persuade the islanders to provide one."

"Of course!" Mae exclaimed. "They will be happy to see a black witch leave. When can we do it? How long do you need to brew a dose of your sleeping potion?"

"Two doses," Jarne spoke for the first time since Sigri had started talking.

"Absolutely not!" Mae looked outraged at Jarne. "You are not joining me. You have your whole life in front of you."

"It's no life without you."

"Of course it is. What would you have done if I hadn't found you in Kristiansund?"

"I was a kid then."

"Not then—now!" she shouted at him. "Seven weeks ago, when we stopped your execution."

"I would have burned," Jarne replied.

Mae jumped to her feet, anger glowing red in her eyes. Raising his hands in an appeasing gesture, Jarne answered Mae's underlying question.

"After we split in the estate and Sigri tended my wounds, I vowed to look for you. If I had to travel to the end of the world, I would never have stopped looking for you."

"And if you hadn't found me?" she challenged. "If my plan at the waterfall had succeeded?"

"If I had turned every stone and climbed every mountain... If I had no hope left, I would have killed myself, like I'm willing to do now. You have exchanged years of pain and dread with weeks of bliss and happiness by finding me. I'm grateful for that."

Mae shook her head. Her gaze landed on Sigri.

"You talk sense into him. Make some incontrovertible arguments."

"I'm not getting in the middle of that. I told you in the mountain meadow that he wouldn't accept it."

"And I told you he doesn't get a say. It is *my* life."

"But he's not arguing about your life, Mae. Jarne talks about his own. Maybe in that case, *you* don't get a say?" Sigri stood. "We have a few days yet. I need to brew the potion. For now, I'm going to acquire a boat. Don't do anything foolish." She looked from Mae to Jarne and back. Shaking her head, she added, "I forgot who I was talking to."

* * *

SIGRI MANAGED TO accomplish her task much quicker than she had expected. Halfway down the mountain, she came upon a group of six men arguing about whether to attack or respect the new masters of the mountain.

"I'm not tolerating another cabal of witches," one man shouted. "The old hag got killed, so these ones can be killed too. We have to rid our island of their kind."

"Keep your voice down," another man cautioned in a carrying whisper. "You'll bring them down on us."

"I'm afraid he already has." Sigri's voice carried, freezing the men in place. The first man drew his sword and turned toward the threat.

"Then I'll rather die fighting than be ruled by evil witches!" he snarled.

"That is folly," Sigri declared as her blast of air sent him tumbling down the mountainside. "You can't fight us. Well, you can, but you will lose."

The five remaining men cowered. Sigri let the threat hang in the air for a long moment, looking at each man with her icy stare.

"But why risk your lives?" she added in a conversational tone. "When we're going to leave you anyhow."

"You will be leaving?" the cautious man asked.

"Yes, in about one week. We require two boats. One smaller vessel with a large sail must be moored in an isolated bay on the island's western coast. Is there such a place?"

"Aye, Lover's Bay."

"That'll work just fine. The other must be a longboat, capable of sailing to Heilladur. Stock provision for three weeks and moor it in the east."

"At Austurfjord?" the man volunteered. In quick succession, Sigri blasted the men to either side of the speaker off their feet. She didn't use extensive force. Still, she wanted to make a point.

"Make sure these spots are suitable," she warned. "Prepare these boats well. Do not try any tricks with me. Remember your old master? We snuffed her out, crushed her like a bug. What do you think we'll do with you?"

"It will be done, mistress. Your Highness, I mean. Forgive us our insolence." The man's voice squeaked like a mouse Sigri had trodden on.

"From tomorrow on, I'll expect a progress report at sunrise. Send one man and one man only. Bring maps if you have them. Oh, and fresh bread and cheese," Sigri added. "Do I make myself clear?"

"Yes, of course. Perfectly clear, Your Highness."

"The faster you work, the faster we'll leave. Now, off with you." Sigri amplified her last words with magic. Sending another blast of air, she knocked all five men to the ground, including those two who had just gotten back to their feet.

* * *

Returning well after dark, Sigri found the caves quiet but neither cold nor empty. The oil lamps had burned low, and she spotted Mae and Jarne in the muted light, sleeping arm in arm. Sigri was glad despite the image sending a stab of loneliness into her heart. She wanted the two lovers to enjoy each other's company before their time was up—before Sigri needed to destroy the curse.

Slipping into an adjacent room, the green witch climbed into a hammock, letting her thoughts sway with the gentle rocking motion. Where was Renya now? Did she watch over her sister? Would she agree with Sigri's plan? Sigri had been confident earlier. But now the doubt came. There were dangers and pitfalls. She could ruin everything.

Give me strength, Renya, she thought. *You have always been the stronger woman, the more courageous witch, the better person.*

Mere moments later, Sigri started. Somebody stood beside her in the dark.

"Shhh, Sigri. It's me," Mae whispered.

"Mae, don't do that. You could have killed me."

"Sorry. I needed to..."

"Talk?" Sigri completed her sentence. "I expected as much. Let me get up." Sigri rose from the hammock. Getting to her feet, she moved to light the lamp.

"No," Mae said. "Leave the lamp."

"It's dark!"

"Take my hand. My eyes are adjusted. And take this." Mae handed her a cloak. "It's a clear night. The stars are beautiful."

"Stars? Seriously?" Sigri slipped into the cloak and took Mae's hand.

They tiptoed past Jarne, who slept with a rolled-up blanket in his arms. Sigri smiled.

Stepping out into the open, Sigri had to agree with Mae. Inside the dark rim of the crater, an incredible number of brilliant pinpricks covered the night sky. The white band of the densely packed stars ran through its center, marking a path so solid-looking that Sigri could have stepped onto it and walked among the endless field of lights.

"It's beautiful," she whispered.

"Yes, it is," Mae agreed, battling emotions. "The world is beautiful; life is beautiful. Jarne must not lose this, not for me."

"He does not want to live without you." Sigri looked at her fellow witch.

"He does not know what he wants. He's too young," Mae snapped. "And anyhow, it's not up to him."

"How do you make that out?"

"Because you will tell him." Mae looked into Sigri's face, her jaw set, her eyes firm. "Tell him my last wish. I want him to live. I need him to live. He must move on—not forget me, but take the good we had with him. And find someone to love like he loved me."

Mae's voice broke. Sigri saw the reflected stars in Mae's eyes getting fuzzy, distorted by her tears.

"He can't refuse my wish," the black witch whispered. "If he has children, he should tell them stories about us, about me." Mae clenched her fists, and raising her voice, she spoke through gritted teeth. "Swear to me, Sigri. Swear that you won't send him with me on that boat."

"Mae, I would never…"

"Swear it, Sigrid Runa!" Mae urged. "Swear by your sister's soul. He will come to you and ask you to send him to his death. You cannot do it. You must not do it."

"Mae, I swear it. By Renya's soul, I do swear not to send Jarne with the black curse to his death. He will not be on the boat that carries the last black witch."

"Thank you, Sigri. Thank you for everything. I wish I had been a better friend." She threw herself into the arms of the taller witch.

"You are a good person, Mette Annegret Einarsdóttir. You are a good witch and a good friend. You deserve better." Sigri stroked Mae's hair. "I would do anything for you. I love you."

"Love you, too," Mae's muffled voice replied, holding her sister.

There they stood together for a long moment, two tiny lights in an endless sea of darkness.

* * *

Sigri managed to sleep for a few hours before her second visitor shook her awake. He was more careful, knowing the dangers of poking a sleeping dragon or witch. Sigri turned toward him.

"Let me guess," she said.

"I need to talk," Jarne replied, ignoring the undertone. "Can you step out with me? Mae is fast asleep."

Sigri got up, took her coat, and followed him outside. She could have sworn she saw Mae's eyes opening an infinitesimal gap. After all, Mae had warned Sigri about Jarne's plan and made her sister swear to save him. Why not go along with the charade?

The stars had disappeared behind low clouds, giving the place an otherworldly guise. Jarne moved further away from the opening than Mae had.

"Sound carries further in the fog," he whispered. "Mae suspects me of doing what I am doing. Still, I don't want her to overhear our conversation."

"You know that Mae knows?"

"Of course. I'm not as naïve as you think."

"You don't know how naïve I think you are." He looked at her, confused. "Exactly," she mused.

"Mae wants you to leave me behind?" he asked when they had reached the other side of the caldera. There was no question in his statement.

"Yes."

"Did she make you swear?"

"Yes, she did," Sigri replied, surprised.

"But she didn't ask you to watch over me for the rest of my life?"

"No, why would she?"

"Because I'm going to kill myself the moment I wake up and find she is not with me."

"You can't! Her last wish..."

"Haven't heard a last wish yet. But here is mine. I do not want to live without Mae, not for one second. I would prefer to rest beside her at the bottom of the ocean. It must be easier for our souls to find each other when we're near. But I'll find her anyhow."

"What are you saying?"

"I'm not asking you to break your oath. Instead, swear that you will not let me wake without her. Knife me, throw me in the ocean, drain my life—I don't care. Don't let me wake without her." His voice broke. "I want to go to sleep beside her, knowing I'll be where she will be when the potion loses its effect. Swear to me, please."

"I underestimated you, and so did Mae. Jarne Ólafsson, I'm sorry for what I said back in the duke's estate. I wish you love and happiness wherever you will be."

She looked at him with tears in her eyes. He looked back, fighting the emotions yet determined to hear her say it.

"I swear, by my sister's soul, I won't let you wake without Mae by your side."

"Thank you, Sigri. I wish you were my sister."

"But I am, Jarne. I always wanted a little brother." She hugged him, and he hugged her back. "Promise me one thing in return."

"What is it?"

"Use the time the two of you have. Let tomorrow be a concern of another day. Let yesterday be a story from another life. Live in the moment, care for each other, and keep smiling."

"I will, I promise."

CHAPTER TWENTY-EIGHT

Into the Blue

"A measure of wisdom each man shall have,
But never too much let him know;
Let no man the fate before him see,
For so is he freest from sorrow."[1]

S CRUNCHING UP HER face, Sigri hunched her shoulders and continued telling her story in a convincing imitation of a simple old man.

"'Why this? It's my lucky shoe,'

"'But... that's a left shoe?' the raven cawed."

Mae laughed out loud. Not only had Sigri cawed like a raven, but she'd also bobbed her head as the bird would do. Jarne shushed her, eager to hear the end of the story.

"'Aye, that it is. Ain't that lucky? My good wife bought it me, as I was in the war.'

"'How can it be lucky?' the raven asked. 'You don't have a left foot.'

"'That I don't. A Viking axe split me leg. The butcher had to cut it off.'"

Sigri made a sad face so silly that Jarne, too, had to laugh.

"'So, doesn't that make it an unlucky shoe?' The bird looked confused.

"'Nah! See this one here?' The old man pulled the shoe from his remaining foot.
'Its twin is worn and weary, frayed and faded, torn and tatty, crushed and crinkled.
While this one still shines as new—after all those years. I'd consider that lucky.'

"'Is your good wife still with you?' the raven asked, already guessing the answer.

"'Ooh, no! She left me, went with the shoemaker. But the lucky shoe, that'll
stick by me forever.'"

Mae and Jarne applauded, forcing Sigri to rise and take a bow.

---

1 *The Sayings of Hár*, Stanza 56, Poetic Edda, English by Henry Bellows (1936)

"One more round," Jarne demanded.

"Not tonight," Sigri replied. "I have to admit, your game was more fun than I expected. But it's time for me to go to bed."

"But I'm not tired," Jarne complained, like a small child.

"And neither am I," Mae whispered.

"Then why go to bed?" Jarne asked. Mae gave him a look. He looked dumbfounded for two heartbeats before blushing deep red.

"Good night," Sigri said, grinning. "Tomorrow, we'll start early."

The three friends had decided to make the best of the little time they had left. Sigri changed the room assignments, providing the two lovers more privacy. Yet, all three had spent every waking moment together. They prepared the meals, completed chores, roamed the surroundings, and engaged in activities of their choice.

Today, Jarne had been in charge. He devised a game where one player chose two random objects from the treasure hoard in the cave. The next player imagined a setting, and the third had to tell an exciting story. Jarne loved stories, and he was good at telling them, too. Mae sometimes struggled, needing to ask the audience for prompts to continue. But Sigri was the unrivaled master of storytelling. She'd often spun tales for her little sister's amusement, and the game reminded her of happier times.

With six days left, each friend got twice the chance to select the day's activity. Mae chose tracking and trapping on her first, and a hike down to the sea on her second. She'd explained that physical exertion helped her ignore her dark urges. Nobody objected.

The day before, Jarne had suggested baking pies together. Yet, lacking all the right ingredients and a proper oven, the experiment resulted in an unappealing, sour-tasting mash. Frustrated, Jarne pelted Mae with blueberries. The witch glared at him, creating a tense moment. After two heartbeats, she retaliated with a wicked smile, triggering the world's most epic kitchen fight, with dough and fruit paste flying everywhere. As "punishment," Sigri doused Jarne with a bucket of icy water and banned him from the kitchen henceforth. He didn't mind. Still, he picked the safer story game on his second day.

Sigri surprised everyone by wanting to teach Mae and Jarne to dance. Having found a scuffed and battered talharpa among the cave's treasures, Sigri started to sing and play. She had a beautiful voice, which compensated for her beginner-level musician's skills. Mae and Jarne started out slow, awkward, and fumbling. Soon, however, they let their hesitation fall to the wayside and enjoyed the spinning and twirling.

"We had one at home," Sigri said when the dancers needed a break, flushed by excitement and exertion. "It belonged to my mother. My father didn't want me to touch it, so I could only practice when he was away. One day, Renya told on me, like the brat she could sometimes be. In anger, my father sold the instrument, ending my musical career."

The sixth and last day again belonged to Sigri. At dawn, she woke her friends. She considered letting them sleep a little longer. They looked so peaceful, nestled together like two woodchucks huddling deep in their burrow to outlast the world's coldness. But this was their last day, and Sigri had a full program lined up.

"Wake up," she called.

"It's dark," Jarne observed astutely, a ginormous yawn stretching his face.

"In here, it is," Sigri replied. "But outside, the sky is already getting lighter."

"Outside?" Mae groaned in disbelief. "It's freezing. Why?"

"Because it's my day, and there's lots to do. I suggest wearing warm clothes," Sigri said as she walked away.

Mae and Jarne stepped outside a few minutes later, dressed in several layers. Sigri seemed to have been up for hours, preparing. Stools and tables stood in a semicircle. The torches were lit, and steaming mugs of tea stood beside plates of cheese and dried fruits. In addition, Sigri had found dark wooden boards and chalky stones. She stood at the center, Queen Helgrid's staff in her hand, looking excited.

"Take your seats," Sigri said. "I'm going to teach you magic."

"I already know magic," Mae complained while Jarne piped in, "You'll teach me too?"

"Yes, both of you. It's magic either of you can learn, yet neither knows." Sigri let the mysterious statement hang in the air, ensuring she had her apprentices' full attention.

Mae narrowed her eyes, dreading what was to come. Jarne, on the other side, seemed clueless. His eyes were wide in anticipation. Sigri tilted her head, prolonging the moment of tense anticipation.

"Reading and writing," she finally said, spreading her arms like the master of a traveling mummers troupe presenting his star performer. Mae groaned, seeing her premonition fulfilled.

"You can do that?" Jarne asked, his excitement reaching new heights.

"Of course, you can't learn it all in one day. One needs to practice for many years. But I can teach you how to write your names, giving you the principles. I will show you in the dirt, and you can practice on your boards."

"I don't want to spoil the fun," Mae said, sounding far from amused. "But we don't have years to practice." There wasn't even another full day.

So far, the three friends had taken Sigri's advice to heart and had ignored the looming deadline, at least outwardly.

"True," Sigri said, not the slightest tone of disappointment in her voice. "Nobody can ever know how much time they will have. That shouldn't stop people from learning new things."

Mae was about to argue that she had a better-than-normal sense of her time left. It was less than twenty-four hours. But Sigri forestalled her, reading the argument on her face.

"It is my day," Sigri declared, "so I can choose. But there is more." Her expression became somber. "We have lost a friend—a sister on our journey. And our time together will come to an end soon." She took a deep breath and stood straight, her head held high. "When we go down to the bay, I want us to stop at a lovely creek. Four tall and straight birch trees stand there among fir and pines. I want us to carve our names into the trees. Renya's, too. That way, we won't be forgotten. The forests will remember us."

Sigri averted her eyes, needing to blink moisture away. Mae stood and rushed toward her sister.

"I'm sorry for doubting you, Sigri," she said, hugging the tall witch. "That is a beautiful idea. Thank you."

"Don't thank me yet!" Sigri half laughed, half cried. "You have much to learn, and I can be a stern teacher."

* * *

"TELL ME ABOUT your plans for the future," Mae asked, carving deep gouges into the tree. Her handiwork resembled only vaguely the letters Sigri had taught her earlier.

The three friends had started their trek down the mountain as soon as the sun reached its highest point. The day became mild, and the rocky trail caused the wanderers to sweat. Reaching the spot Sigri had chosen, Mae marveled at its beauty. Slanted sunbeams hit the white birch trees, making them glow. The stream gurgled, splashing over polished rocks. Not far off, a group of deer stood looking upon the intruders with apprehension, ready to flee. Mae touched their minds, soothing their anxiety. She wasn't here to hunt. This was their forest, and Mae would be gone soon.

"I dreamed of a normal life for so long," Sigri replied, a faraway look in her eyes. "I don't know how much reality can ever live up to the expectations."

She was already done carving her name. Turning to Mae, she added, "I wanted to start a family, pass on my knowledge and values, and see something grow." Her gaze grew in intensity. "We have focused so long on destruction: killing the duke, overthrowing the king, eliminating the curse. We've never built anything. These past weeks in Kristiansund, we were doing good, teaching, healing, and laughing. There must be more joy in our lives."

"So there's your plan," Jarne said. "Start a family and teach others."

"Perhaps, but that is only a part of it."

"What do you mean?" Mae asked.

"We have to learn, too. All of us have lived isolated lives. Do you know how to spin yarn, weave cloth, plow a field, or raise sheep? We have used our powers, and that has set us apart."

"You had no choice," Jarne said, "unless you wanted to hide forever."

"And you learned from the book," Mae added. "Maybe it washed ashore. You should look for it."

"I've asked the islanders to search. The book gave me glimpses into a world of possibilities. Still, the real magic is to find happiness in the simple things." Sigri stepped toward Mae, a sad little smile on her lips. "How are you doing?"

"Had you asked me to chop down the tree, I'd be long done. This? It's hard. I have the longest name."

"You'll be fine. I told you that we are skilled in destroying. Building something that lasts is much harder." She looked at Mae's work. Large and uneven letters so far spelled *METTE ANNGRE*.

"See! You're almost done," Sigri praised, "although you missed one *E*."

"I did? Where?"

"Not to worry." Sigri pointed. "The name remains readable; it's only a slight variation."

The friends needed twenty more minutes to complete the work, with Sigri helping Mae to finish the carving. Stepping back, the green witch regarded with pride what they'd achieved. From left to right, the four inscriptions read:

SIGRID RUNA - HEALER

RENYA LYND - FIGHTER

JARNE BIRGER - DREAMER

METTE ANNGRET - LOVER, LEADER, GOOD WITCH

Sigri turned toward Mae and Jarne. Taking their hands, she blinked rapidly, her face showing the strain of fighting emotions.

"I will leave you here." Sigri choked on the last word, her voice constricted. "I cannot stand goodbyes. I've said all I wanted. Thank you, both, for everything." She squeezed their hands harder. "I don't know where you will go. But I know that you will be together. Nothing in this world or any other world has the power to separate you." Her voice cracked, tears streaming down her cheeks. "Farewell, my friends, farewell."

The green witch turned and ran. Less than fifty strides away, she fell to her knees. Sigri's howls of pain pierced Mae's heart. Jarne started toward her, but Mae held him back.

"Don't. Let her be. She's right." Tears spilled over Mae's cheeks. "We'll only prolong the pain. We have our journey ahead, and Sigri has hers." Mae took Jarne by the hand and started toward the beach, where the boat waited to take the black witch on her last journey.

* * *

SIGRI WANDERED THROUGH the forest. She did not want to sleep. And even if she'd wanted, she wouldn't have been able to. Instead, she relished in all her senses, tasting the dew, smelling the night air, and listening to owls hooting. At some point, she came upon a moonlit meadow. Taking her shoes off, she delighted in the soft, wet moss under her bare feet. The witch sensed the animals watching her, mistrusting this strange intruder.

Soon, the sun would rise. Mae and Jarne would drink their potion, and Sigri had to launch the boat, making the separation from her friends permanent. How had they spent the night? Were they afraid? Of course they were. But they would have comforted each other. Had they made love under the stars? Sigri had ordered the islanders to provide blankets, firewood, and provisions—binding them to her will with threats and the promise of Queen Helgrid's riches.

It was time; Sigri had cried all the tears she would cry.

Making her way toward the ocean, her hand went to her side, feeling the reassuring shape of the flasks in her satchel. Her pace was steady, her jaw set, her head held high. The stars faded as the sky changed from black to indigo. One last time, she walked past the birch trees, her eyes unable to make out the engravings. Yet, she knew they were there and would still be there long after all traces of their time on this island had vanished.

Sigri chose a short detour, aiming for the rocky cliffs north of the arranged spot. Peering over the edge, her gaze swept over a lovely, half-moon-shaped bay of black sand. The full moon had almost set, its disk touching a ring of low clouds on the horizon. Holding hands, two figures lay side by side, illuminated by the faint glow of the fire's dying embers. To their right, a single-masted boat bobbed on the gentle waves, tethered to a large stone by a hemp rope. The eastern wind pushed against the ship, egging it on to leave these shores.

Sigri clambered down. Approaching Mae and Jarne, the healer spotted two unstoppered flasks lying in the sand. Good, they'd drunk her potion. It should last at least twelve hours, probably longer for Mae since she was smaller. Sigri had used a little white lie when talking about the potency of her potion. She wanted to alleviate Mae's concern about the distance the black witch would travel. The islanders had assured Sigri that the boat could float for eight hours before sinking. It could cover thirty leagues with the steady wind.

Sigri walked past her sleeping friends. She grabbed the rope and started hauling the boat ashore. This task took more effort than she had estimated, almost foiling her plans. Luckily, a short lull in the wind came to her rescue. The boat beached, and she checked its condition. As ordered, the islanders had drilled a hole into the hull and sealed it with a wooden plug. Satisfied with the vessel, she returned to her friends.

Sigri took her necklace off. Made from polished blue coral and shimmering pearls, Sigri had worn it since she was six years old, when her mother died. She had never taken it off until a few days ago, when she had added two links, allowing her to divide the necklace into two bracelets. She fastened one bracelet on Mae's wrist and one on Jarne's. The light was still faint, and she had difficulties seeing the tiny links as moisture pooled in her eyes again.

Wiping the tears away, she steeled herself. Sigri needed all her strength to drag Mae and Jarne across the beach. She laid them onto the blankets she'd draped over the wooden boards. Taking meticulous care, she cleaned and straightened their clothes and brushed their hair. Her entire body shaking, she kissed each on the forehead. Then she pulled the plug and hoisted the sail.

At once, the wind shoved the boat out to sea, accelerating the vessel until the rope pulled taut with a loud snap. The sudden movement pulled Sigri off her feet. Stunned, she got back up. Grabbing a hatchet to sever the rope, she looked out over the ocean, imagining the eternal resting place of the last black witch.

No time to waste. Sigri pulled the flasks from her satchel. She drained the first, numbing all sense of pain in her body. The second flask contained a sleeping potion. After drinking, she had about five minutes before she fell unconscious. The last flask, the tiniest of all three, the witch had carried from Heilladur. It contained a slow-acting poison. Once she drank, her heart would stop around the time the boat sank.

After gulping the content in one pull, she tossed the empty container into the sea.

Then came the dangerous part. Sigri concentrated, reaching into Mae's body, feeling her heart beating slow and steady. Her own heart raced, and her hands were sweaty. The healer's rational mind told her what she needed to do, and she had done it before. But this wasn't an unknown stranger, no hostile man who had taken Sigri captive. This was Mae, her good friend, her sister witch, her second sister. She needed to do it now.

With shaking hands but a focused mind, Sigri stopped Mae's heart.

Nothing happened. *Did it work? Has the curse taken Jarne?* Of course—he was closer. The curse would take him. What had she done?

Then the dark magic hit her, forcing Sigri to her knees. Her pain-numbing potion was useless. The curse attacked her soul, crushing her like an ant. Pain like she had never felt before, agony like nobody could imagine. Her body felt simultaneously smashed to a pulp and ripped apart. A fire burned her insides while ice froze her breath and muddled her brain. This was hell's retribution for all her evil deeds, and she deserved it. She had chosen to bear its burden to save her friends.

Mae!

The thought gave Sigri something to hold on to. Mae needed her. Mae was dead. Her heart had stopped beating. Sigri had murdered her friend. How could she? What was the point of it all? Why didn't the pain end? Why was Sigri's black heart still beating? To start Mae's again.

Sigri took the hatchet's handle between her teeth, biting hard on the polished wood. Summoning every ounce of her willpower, she reached into Mae's body. No time for subtlety. With a powerful tug, Sigri pulled on all of Mae's muscles. She felt the body jerk.

Could she detect a heartbeat? No.

Again, she pulled. Harder this time. And again, and again. She felt something tear in Mae's leg. She felt a finger bone snapping. Nothing, no heartbeat. Spitting out the hatchet, Sigri yelled in frustration.

"Renya, help me! I need you!"

She had only one more try in her. Concentrating all her essence, Sigri prepared to pull. But she didn't. Instead, she let the tension rise, the power pooling, her muscles straining, her mind burning. Still, she held back. Blood ran from her nose and ears. She couldn't breathe as her lungs were crushed, and her vision narrowed, black circles closing in. Seconds from passing out, Sigri released all her energy in a single burst. Shouting Mae's name in defiance, she pulled on her sister, willing her to live.

She had tried. There was nothing more she could do. Her body did not recover. Her brain cried for air, her limbs went numb, and her heart, racing like a hummingbird's wings, would explode any second. Sigri fumbled for the hatchet. One eye had gone blind; the other showed her only blurred shapes. Hacking at the rope, she missed nine times out of ten. Finally, a twang sounded, and the boat lurched. She was off. Lying back exhausted, she could feel the wetness of the water spilling into the boat.

Sigri had lost.

She'd lost her mother, her home, her sister, her dreams, and in the end, she lost Mae. One last time, she wanted to enter her mind to say sorry. Mae wouldn't feel it; she wasn't there anymore. Only an empty shell lay in the cave.

Thump, thump... thump, thump... thump, thump.

"By the mother of all, it worked. I've done it. I saved her!" Sigri laughed. In an outburst of boundless exhilaration, she shouted, "I'm coming, Renya."

And darkness took the last black witch, gently embracing her, soothing her pain, alleviating her doubts, and wiping the curse's foul taste from her lips. It comforted her broken soul on her final journey into the blue.

* * *

THE FULL MOON crept slowly over the horizon, bathing the world in a pale pattern of light and shadow. Two figures perched on the cliffs overlooking the Western Ocean. Wrapped in long hooded cloaks, they huddled motionless, almost indistinguishable from the numerous outcrops of volcanic rock that dominated the landscape. Only their eyes gave them away, sparkling in the reflected moonlight—one pair of pale blue and one pair of piercing green.

The sun had set hours ago, and the wind quieted as darkness fell. The gentle waves lapped onto the sandy beach, creating a rhythmic whisper soothing the night and calming the world. A seagull cried in the distance. Contemplating the meaning of life, the two figures watched the endless ocean as it stretched toward the horizon, meeting the field of stars that filled the night sky at the point nobody could ever reach. Yet the calm was an illusion. Shock and exhaustion clung to their bodies, while elation fought sadness in their minds.

"Are you cold?" Jarne asked.

"A little," Mae answered. Jarne placed his arm around her shoulder and pulled her tight.

"We can go below, if you like."

"In a moment. Let us sit here a little longer."

An hour earlier, Mae had woken stiff and disoriented. Her leg hurt, and so did her left hand. Blood thumped through her brain, creating a dull ache with every beat of her heart. It was dark, but there was a light. Blinking her eyes, a rocky ceiling came into focus, illuminated by the yellow glow of an oil lamp. She was in a cave or cavern, lying on her back. Was this hell? Once before, Mae had thought she had crossed into the underworld. Like that time, Mae felt cold. She shivered.

"You are awake," an excited voice said beside her, familiar and cherished.

"Jarne!" Mae snapped her head to the side, needing to see his face. He was there. Sitting on the floor, he leaned against the cave wall, an oil lamp by his side and a heavy book on his lap. He smiled.

"Good morning," he said. "Well, good evening might be more appropriate. Have you slept well? How are you feeling?"

"What... Where... Why?" Mae stammered before she almost shrieked, "What?"

"Lots of questions," he mused. "Let's start with the most important. We're still alive and still on the island, in a small cave close to the beach where we went to sleep."

Mae heard the words but couldn't make sense of anything. Her confusion was painted all over her face.

"How are you feeling?" Jarne asked again.

"Like a giant bear mauled me, chewed on my bones, and spit the remains into the dirt."

"Besides that."

"What do you mean 'besides that'? Isn't that enough?" Mae froze. There was something. Or, better to say, something was missing. "The curse!" she shouted, not believing her own senses. "It's gone! Help me up."

Jarne pulled her up, took her into his arms, and started to cry, explaining everything with a single word. "Sigri!"

After a long moment during which both had to hold on to someone, Jarne took Mae by her hand, and they stepped out onto the beach. The boat was gone, and the rope still tied to the stone floated on the waves. Mae pointed up the cliffs.

"It all makes sense," Jarne said, playing absentmindedly with the bracelet that had been half of Sigri's necklace. He'd helped Mae climb the ragged rocks. Finding some flat stones, they sat, dangling their feet over the edge. "Everything Sigri has done, everything she said. This must have been her plan since we set sail in Kristiansund."

"Longer than that. Sigri knew about my goal. I told her at the Witches' Castle that I wouldn't rest until the last black witch had vanished from this world. Since then, she must have thought about it."

"And she sacrificed herself for your dream."

"She did. But also for *her* dream. She wanted a family. Someone she could teach and love, and who would remember her. We are her family," Mae said, choking on the emotions.

Jarne took her hand, and both sat in silence, watching the endless sea and letting its peaceful sounds soothe their unsettled souls.

"Do you think there is another realm?" Jarne asked in a soft whisper. "Will she meet Renya again?"

"I don't know. I hope so," Mae confessed. "Regardless, the two are together in our hearts."

Mae smiled at Jarne, and he hugged her tighter.

"I'm sure something is out there," he said, his eyes trained on the horizon. "Some other place of warmth and love where the essence of people, their souls, live on."

"Then we should better make the most of the life we have here," Mae said with a chuckle.

"How's that?"

"Can you imagine how Renya would greet us if we squandered her sister's sacrifice?"

The End

My Inspirations

To my heroes of fantasy, who took me on eagle's wings into magical lands so vivid and rich that I often preferred them to the disheartening reality of our daily existence: You have shown me that courage and compassion are universal values, and that striving to be good requires character regardless of magical powers.

Thank you, J.K. Rowling and Brandon Sanderson.

To my favorite artists of wordplay who made me laugh and made me cry, who made me root for a crippled torturer, fear for an immoral assassin, and curse the naïveté of a peerless swordsman: Your dry humor made your stories a delight until you stabbed me in the heart with dark twists and oh-so-believable tragedy.

Thank you, Joe Abercrombie and Michael J. Sullivan.

To the incredible narrators of my most beloved audiobooks, who have brought to life heroes, villains, elves, dwarfs, men, and dragons, and who have made them more real and relatable than many other individuals I only know from video calls: You are, without any doubt, the most welcome voices in my head.

Thank you, Michael Kramer, Kate Reading, and Tim Gerard Reynolds.

To my family, who listened to my favorite stories on long car journeys, watched the extended versions of all my favorite movies with me, and heard me agonizing about the fate of imaginary characters: In doing so, you have allowed me to never grow up.

Thank you, Heike and Lennart.

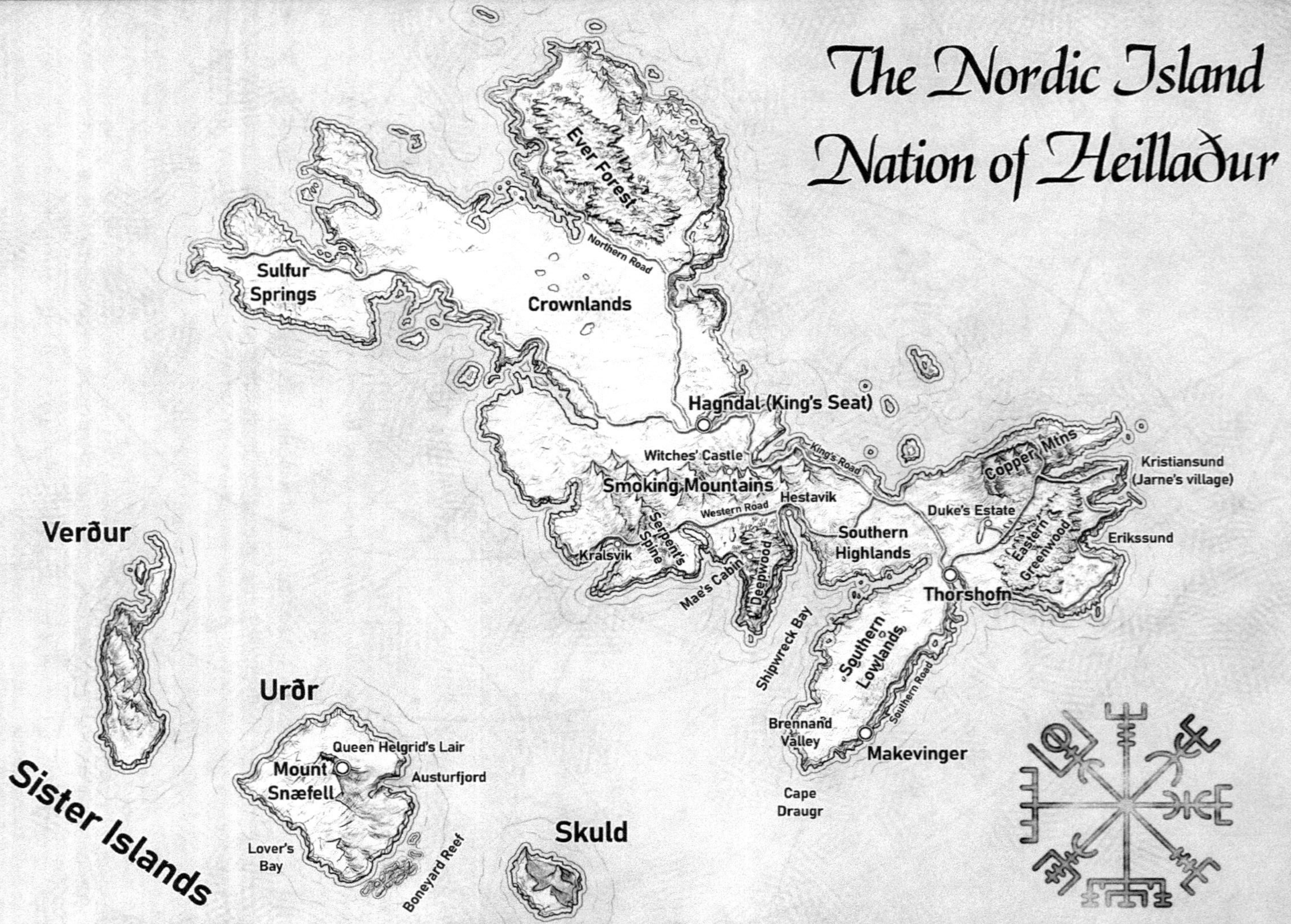

For a high resolution map see project-witchcraft.com/extras

The Southern Province
Hagndal (King's Seat)
Witches' Castle
Smoking Mountains
Serpent's Spine
Kralsvik
Mae's Cabin
Deepwood
Western Road
Hestavik
King's Road
Southern Highlands
Duke's Estate
Copper Mtns
Kristiansund
(Jarne's village)
Eastern Greenwood
Erikssund
Old Mine Road
Loch Misfurvatn
Thorshofn
Shipwreck Bay
Southern Lowlands
Southern Road
Brennand Valley
Makevinger
Cape Draugr

Martens International
BE CAREFUL WHAT YOU WITCH FOR
project-witchcraft.com